KINTH

TIMOTHY C. FINLEY

Fedd Books
P.O. Box 341973
Austin, TX 78734

www.thefeddagency.com

Published in association with The Fedd Agency, Inc., a literary agency.

ISBN: 978-1-957616-62-9
eISBN: 978-1-957616-63-6

LCCN: 2024902634

Printed in the United States of America

For Mom and Dad, who taught me words
and the worlds that exist within them. I love you.

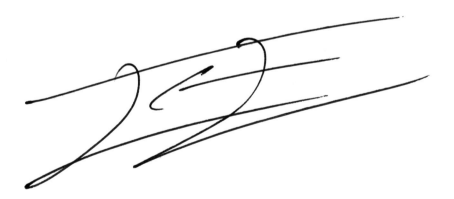

Prologue

Frederick was going to break some hospital equipment—he was almost sure of it.

He lay with his eyes closed as one of the several machines he was hooked up to beeped and beeped and beeped. If it weren't for the incessant noise, he would've been able to convince himself he was in bed at home, that he had simply overslept and his parents were having a lighthearted chat downstairs rather than whispering worriedly beside his hospital bed.

The gown he was wearing didn't make it any easier to deceive himself.

He had been awake for at least an hour, most likely more, feigning sleep while listening to his parents' muted conversation. They were careful not to wake him, but Frederick desperately wanted them to. Just to nudge him awake like they used to when he was a kid, ask how he was feeling and if he wanted a snack. Nothing about hospitals or mental health, just regular talk. He so wanted to have a normal conversation with someone, the kind that would help him feel a bit more human. A bit more normal.

This wasn't the first time that Frederick's mental health had landed him in the hospital, and he doubted it would be the last. His anxiety and depression were like an ever-constant, high-pitched ringing at a frequency only he could hear. Some days, the ringing faded enough that it almost felt like it wasn't there. It still was, of course, but he could at least pretend. Once his attention was drawn back to the anxiety, though, it became clear that it had never left, only faded into the background. Those were his best days, days when he almost felt like a normal person living a normal life, so long as he didn't think about it too much.

But those days were not common. Most of the time, the noise demanded to heard, demanded to be felt. The quiet ringing turned into a horrible, piercing whine that grew in volume until he felt it spread throughout his body and rattle his bones. On those days, there was nothing he could do but grit his teeth and do whatever it took to keep his head above water.

And then there were the bad days.

If the good days were a ringing, and the middling days a whine, the bad days were a roar. A thunderous cacophony that grew until it consumed everything that Frederick was. Every shaking breath, every frantic heartbeat—it was all fear and anxiety. The roaring would echo around the emptiness inside of him, compounding every second until the only thing left was a singular unshakable certainty that he was going to die.

Yesterday had been one of those days, and now he was in the hospital.

His parents were still having their muted conversation, and though they were only a couple feet away, Frederick still had to focus to make out what they were saying.

"Henry, what are we going to do?" Frederick's mother asked, her voice not defeated, rather defiant even in its worry.

"I don't know what we can do besides be there for our son," his father answered. It was startling to hear his voice so somber. The man rarely spoke without a smile or a mischievous lilt.

"We have to try something!" She was clearly straining to keep her voice at a whisper.

"We've tried everything. Besides, there's still Kinth."

"Don't you think we would've heard back by now?"

"Honestly, Emily, who knows with that place."

"I don't like betting our son's future on a place like that."

"I don't either. It's like if Area 51 decided they were going to dip their toes into the mental health field." Henry let out a heavy sigh. "But everyone says they get results. Outstanding ones. And that's what our son needs right now."

Frederick had hoped his parents would be tired enough to doze off. He wanted to put off the coming interaction for as long as possible. But it was clear they were far too worried to sleep, and the guilt of eavesdropping was getting to him as well. He made a show of stirring and slowly coming awake.

His parents stopped talking immediately, and his mother reached out to grab his hand.

"Oh, Freddy."

"Hey Mom." Frederick offered a half wince, half smile. "I'm so sorr—"

"You know, it would take quite a bit for me to be upset with you in this moment." Frederick's father cut him off. "But you apologizing for something that is not your fault might just send me over the edge."

There were so many layers to the look his father gave him in that moment. There was faux severity, with the all-too-familiar twinkle of mischief. But Frederick knew if he looked deeper, he would see something else—something he didn't know if he could bear to see.

Yet he had put them in this situation, and even though everything in him just wanted to act like nothing out of the ordinary was happening, he knew it would be wrong to shy away. To put his parents through such an ordeal and then turn away from the difficult things he made them feel. In that moment, he felt that would be unforgivable.

He made himself look.

He could see it in their eyes, and for the first time, he could see it clearly. His parents were breaking. Because of him. He looked into those stained-glass windows, the bright blues of his father and the warm greens of his mother. He had looked through these windows many a time. He had found so much in them over the years. Hope, excitement, pride, fear, anger and always love among many other things. But as he looked now, he saw something he had always feared he would see.

The windows were cracking. Small spiderweb cracks were branching across the once-perfect stained glass.

He had caused those fissures, and he knew it. He hadn't done it intentionally, and he knew they knew that., but he had caused them all the same. His parents' love for him wasn't diminishing in the slightest. Frederick knew that against all reason, they would continue loving him more and more with every passing day, but he was destroying them. His mind was a battlefield, and his parents were becoming causalities in the crossfire.

It wasn't on purpose, and perhaps it wasn't even his fault, but Frederick was certain his parents were slowly breaking down beneath the weight he inadvertently placed on their shoulders. He closed his eyes, unable to look any longer. Frederick made a promise to himself in that moment. He swore he would do whatever it took to relieve his parents of their burden. He would find a way to get better, or at least to take care of himself. There was no way he would let the glass shatter.

"Let's go home, Freddy."

Frederick's parents had squared everything away with the doctors so that he was able to check out immediately. There would be follow-ups and check-ins in the coming weeks, but the doctors had determined that Frederick was in no immediate danger.

The journey from the hospital room to the car was a bit harrowing. Frederick had been in bed for a full day and was still a bit shaky on his legs. His mother watched him take two or three wobbly steps before insisting he use the wheelchair the nurses had initially recommended. At first, Frederick refused. In the end, he ducked his head in embarrassment as his father wheeled him to the car. The man did little to turn away attention, whistling loudly as he strode through the hospital halls.

Frederick remembered very little of the drive home. His father steered their family car through the increasingly familiar streets. They both made one or two efforts to strike up conversation, but Frederick made it quite clear that he wasn't in a chatting mood. He knew they were just worried, that they wanted to be able to put on some pretense of normality, if only to prove to themselves that Frederick was, or at least would be, all right. Frederick would've loved to give that to them. There was nothing in the world he wanted more than to give his parents hope that he would be all right. But he didn't have it himself, and he was not a good actor.

As such, a silence filled the car, remaining until Frederick's father eased it into the driveway and put it in park. The three of them filed out and up the sidewalk to the front door of the house.

The door creaked as Frederick's father pushed it open. Frederick's mind had been racing the entire car ride home, desperately trying to find solutions, and he still had no idea what he was going to do next. His hands started to shake. The whine in his ears was growing once again. He couldn't just go back to the way things were. He wouldn't survive. How could he? How could anyone possibly survive something so insurmountable? He had sworn he would do whatever it took to survive, whatever it took to alleviate the burden he had become on his parents. He would take any path, no matter how hard; he would follow it to the end, no matter how painful. The more he thought about his next moves, though, the more he realized there was simply no path for him to take.

He followed his parents inside, barely able to keep himself from hyperventilating. He was vaguely aware of his mother's voice saying his name. He dragged his eyes to her, trying to fight the sheer panic and terror rising in his throat with every passing moment. She was holding a pile of mail, most of it now discarded, forgotten on the floor. All that remained was a single envelope, held in a vicelike grip.

Frederick knew what it was without having to ask. The roaring in his head softened, though it did not disappear. His mother's eyes were a mixture of hope and anxiety as she held out the letter. He took it and opened it with all the care he could muster, trying to force his hands to quiet so he could read it, but he simply could not remain still. His brain seemed unable to fully decipher the words on the page. In the end, he could only make out three words.

Frederick.

Kinth.

Accepted.

PART ONE

Chapter 1

Welcome to Kinth!

Frederick stared at the words on his computer screen in the dim light of early morning. He had spent the whole night reading through the entirety of Kinth's official website, doing everything he could to memorize every pixel of it. When choosing between preparedness and restfulness, the choice was not really a choice at all. It had almost become a nightly ritual for Frederick since receiving his acceptance letter.

He fought back a yawn, refusing to acknowledge that he had pushed himself too far.

"Not like I would've been able to sleep anyway," Frederick muttered to himself as he scrolled through the page for the hundredth time. His leg bounced up and down beneath his desk, and he had to concentrate to keep his hand from shaking on the trackpad of his laptop. Normally, he would've attributed the jitters to his anxiety, but there was something else coursing through him today.

We are very excited about the work we are doing here and would love to tell you more about it. Kinth was founded as a response to the Second Pandemic, a plague that swept through the young people of our world.

Frederick rolled his eyes. He had always hated the term "Second Pandemic," especially since it applied to him. It felt so dramatic, like the world was trying to make him sound valiant for being afraid of his own shadow. Frederick was part of a frighteningly large group of young people who had been diagnosed with Generalized Anxiety Disorder. Anxiety disorders had been on the rise for decades, but then they quadrupled over the course of a few years, and the reason was obvious.

Here at Kinth, we utilize the most brilliant minds our world has to offer as well as cutting-edge technology to help those who are most in need of assistance. The children of today face a most unique and daunting opponent. We, with the generous support of our many benefactors, vow to bring hope to those who too often live without it. There is a resoluteness in this generation that is often overlooked. They have survived one plague, and we believe they will survive this one too.

Frederick grimaced. The plague had sprung up with no warning. No one knew how it had started, and no one knew how the human race became immune in the end. Two hundred million people had died over the course of two years before that immunity came. That was more lives than had been lost in World War I, World War II, and the Bubonic plague combined. Millions of children were orphaned, and so many of those didn't have anyone left to take them in. It was a global crisis. Governments incentivized adoption to the point that it was foolish not to adopt at least one child.

These children made up what came to be called the "Second Pandemic." The plague had taken their families, their friends, their homes. The result was almost a third of an entire generation living with varying degrees of anxiety every day.

If you are interested in joining our list of benefactors click here.
If you are interested in applying for admission into Kinth click here.

Frederick stared at the link. He had followed that link, as had thousands and thousands of others. Kinth had a nearly perfect success rate with their in-patient program. Little was known about the methods they used, only that they yielded remarkable results. A success rate so high over the years that, even with the immense amount of funding they received, there was still too high of a demand for them to take on every potential patient. So they had developed an interview process. Prospective patients filled out an online application and waited to be contacted. Prayed to be contacted.

Frederick had been.

Now, all that stood between him and his ticket to a new life was an in-person interview at the world-famous Kinth Incorporated. An interview that was happening in just a few hours. Frederick stared down at his jittery limbs. He smiled at the excitement pulsing inside his body. He was finally going to get better.

Frederick jumped as the alarm on his phone began to blare. He had intended on trying to sleep, but the anticipation of the day to come had been far too much for him. He had given up quickly but had forgotten to turn off the eight alarms he had set the night before. After shutting off the screeching sound, he got ready as fast as he could.

He pounded down the stairs, following the smell of breakfast. Frederick's father stood over the stove, working to increase the height of a pancake tower without sending it toppling to the floor. He was lanky, much like a tree that had mastered the art of growing up but couldn't quite grasp the concept of growing out.

"Henry! If you waste all those pancakes, I'm going to make you sleep out in the garden for the next week," Frederick's mother scolded his father as she shuffled through a pile of mail at the kitchen table.

"Emily, my dear, I am creating a masterpiece. Please do not distract me." He carefully placed another pancake on the now recklessly tall stack.

"Morning," Frederick said, announcing his arrival as he strode to the refrigerator to pour himself a glass of juice.

"Morning, Freddy," his mother said as she looked up from the mail. "What kind of day are we working with?"

"Somewhere in the 3.2 range." Frederick and his parents had developed a 1-10 system to assess his anxiety. Reducing the often long and taxing conversation of his mental state to a single number was extremely helpful for Frederick. The mental energy it saved him paid significant dividends on a daily basis.

"Might be below a 3," Frederick continued, "if Dad wasn't about to carpet the floor with breakfast."

"My boy, I will carpet you with breakfast if you ever doubt me again," he responded without turning, though Frederick could hear the smile in his voice.

"3.2 is good! We can work with that!" There was relief in his mother's voice and even more in her eyes. Frederick couldn't blame her. He'd been nervous about today too. Today was everything: it quite literally determined the course of the rest of his life.

Frederick was five when the plague killed his family. He didn't remember much from that time. Mostly shapes and noises instead of anything concrete. A slew of therapists and counselors assured him that this was normal, a common defense mechanism for people in his situation. Frederick's first solid memory was arriving at Henry and Emily Rockseeker's house. Henry and Emily had tried to have children of their own for years with no success. They had treated Frederick like their own from the first day.

Henry finally finished his pancake monument and, through either dark magic or copious amounts of luck, transferred it to the kitchen table.

"Henry, how on earth are we supposed to eat all of these?" Emily let out with an exasperated sigh.

"My sweet, divine angel, whom I love with all I am, please do not ask such stupid questions. This was about art. Something as trivial as a meal could never interest me."

She ignored her husband, rolled her eyes, and placed several pancakes onto her plate.

"Eat quickly. We need to leave in twenty minutes."

"That'll put us there an hour before the interview," Frederick replied through a mouthful of breakfast.

"Yes, well, I think it's best not to take any chances." His mother shook her head. "Traffic can be so fickle on days like today."

"Saturday mornings?"

Frederick was forced to duck as a pancake flew by his head.

"Keep talking, honey," she said sweetly.

She was trying to hide it, but the worry was still clear in her eyes.

"Better listen to her." His father chuckled, but the worry was apparent in his eyes as well.

Frederick understood why they were so anxious. The interview today was his best chance of living a normal life. Or, at least, it was his best chance of living as normal a life as possible.

He and his parents continued to do their best impression of a normal day for the remaining twenty minutes before their departure. They talked about sports and weather. The pancake tower was torn down brick by syrupy brick until all that was left was the foundation. Overall, it was a fairly convincing attempt at normalcy.

After the twenty minutes were up, Frederick's mother grabbed the keys and tossed them in his direction.

"Time to go."

Frederick gave her a quizzical look. She never let him drive himself to appointments, saying that the stress while driving caused panic attacks. And even though she claimed to be no expert in such things, she thought it best not to risk being behind the wheel if it were to happen.

What on earth makes this any different? Frederick thought. After all, this was bigger than some stupid session with a therapist. This was everything—his entire future.

"You can pick the music, but if you play anything by some guy wearing eyeliner and singing about hating his parents, you are walking home."

"You never let me drive," Frederick replied. "Why are you letting me drive?"

"Well, we figure if you're going off to Kinth, you'll need to practice driving yourself around," his father interjected. "Also, we thought you might appreciate the distraction."

"Henry," Emily sighed, "distractions are typically more effective when the person is unaware they are being distracted. Also, perhaps we shouldn't be encouraging distracted driving to our son?"

"Driving as a distraction, my dove, not distracted driving," he mumbled as he walked out the front door. Frederick smiled to himself, tossed the keys in the air, and caught them without looking.

A distraction sounded great.

"The mailbox had it coming, standing there arrogantly, so close to the driveway. It's not your fault, Freddy."

Frederick stood among the shattered remains of what had been his family's mailbox. His father insisted he had been meaning to replace the mailbox for months anyway. Though, after they cleared the street of the scraps of wood, Henry suggested that maybe he should drive the rest of the way.

Well, I almost made it out of the driveway without ruining everything.

Frederick wanted to be angry that his father was taking the keys, but his hands wouldn't stop shaking, and his breath remained a step out of reach. He nodded and climbed into the back seat. His mother offered him the aux cord to play his music, but he shook his head and placed his headphones over his ears instead. He could feel his number slowly climbing—3.2 became 3.6 became 5.2. His heart was beginning to pound so hard, it felt like his rib cage was rattling inside his chest. Sweat dripped from his hands like they were a broken faucet. He needed to shut everything out and calm down before they got to the interview.

He closed his eyes and tried to focus solely on his music. He felt his pulse start to regulate as he took several deep breaths. Frederick kept his eyes closed until he felt his father put the SUV in park and turn off the engine. Then he opened them and looked out the window.

Before him stood the Welcome Center of Kinth Incorporated—a three-story building with very little to offer aesthetically. It was a squat gray structure without any noteworthy details. Frederick was amazed at how ordinary it appeared. It looked more like a place that sold paperclips than a solution to a global crisis.

"Hm," Frederick's father grunted.

"Henry!" his mother hissed.

"Well, it's not exactly an architectural marvel, is it?"

A glare was the only response Henry received, and he raised both hands to shoulder level in surrender. Emily released her husband from her glare and smiled at Frederick.

"Ready?"

Frederick followed his parents up the sidewalk and through the front doors of the building. They found themselves in a waiting room that matched the exterior in blandness; off-white walls filled with prints of generic landscapes surrounded them. Chairs lined the walls with small tables dispersed intermittently, piled high with dated magazines. Against the far wall, a window was cut out, with a receptionist on the other side.

He was on the phone and seemed deep in conversation, not acknowledging them at first. The small man bore an uncanny resemblance to a cartoon mouse.

This image was magnified in Frederick's mind by the comically large pair of glasses balancing on the man's comically small nose. As they walked toward him, the mouse-man glanced their way and quickly ended his phone call.

"Hello there," he said with a smile, "how may I be of assistance?"

Frederick was startled by the deep tenor of the man's voice. All images of squeaking rodents were banished from his mind.

"Hello," Emily replied, "our son has an interview for admission."

"Ah, yes! You must be Fred! Welcome to Kinth."

Frederick winced at the abbreviated version of his name. He could stand Freddy, but Fred was a nonstarter.

"Actually, he prefers Frederick," his mother rushed to say.

"I'm so sorry! I didn't mean to offend!"

"No worries. It's really okay. I don't really care that much," Frederick said, feeling his face get hot. He hated being called Fred, but he *loathed* attention being drawn to that fact.

"How did you know it was him?" Henry asked suddenly.

"Pardon?" the receptionist replied.

"You didn't have to look him up, and we're an hour early. Surely there are other interviews today." Collectively, they glanced around at the empty chairs and idle magazines. Frederick very much doubted his father's assumption.

"Nope," the receptionist said cheerfully, "Frederick is our only interview for the day."

Frederick felt his heart rate spike. The only interview for the entire day? How was that possible? Thousands of people applied for admission—surely they had more than one interview per day.

"Slow day?" Frederick asked, embarrassed at the pitch at which his voice came out. He had assumed there would be dozens of other applicants here. Admittedly, the thought of sitting in a room with thirty other people, waiting for his turn to be psychologically picked apart to see if he got to live a normal life, was daunting. However, that was much better than being the only one psychologically picked apart.

"Ha!" The receptionist let out a bark of a laugh. "Aren't they all?"

Frederick and his parents shared a confused glance but didn't pursue the topic further.

The man slid a clipboard under the glass.

"Here you go, Frederick. If you could fill out these forms for me, then you should be good to go. It's all pretty standard stuff."

Emily reached for the paperwork. "I got it, Freddy. You just sit down and relax."

"Actually," the receptionist cleared his throat uncomfortably, "I need Frederick to fill out the forms himself. It's a legal issue, I'm afraid."

"No worries," Frederick said as he snatched the clipboard from the desk and sat in the closest chair. He made sure his back was to a wall so his parents couldn't hover over him.

Once he was settled, he began filling out the first of several pages. Sure enough, he found that it was all fairly standard. Name, address, social security number, emergency contacts, and so on. Frederick did his best to write legibly as he worked quickly through the first page. It looked like the application was about ten pages, but at this pace, he would be done in no time. Frederick flipped to the second page.

Do you belong?

Frederick stared at the question, certain he had misread it. How on earth was this anything resembling normal paperwor—

No

Frederick blinked in surprise at the single word he had scrawled on the page. He honestly hadn't meant to write anything. He was still processing the question and hadn't given any thought to what it might actually be asking. Belong where? Here? His house? Frederick shook his head to try and clear some of the clutter.

The truth was, Frederick had never really felt like he belonged. He had never talked to his parents about it—he hadn't wanted to hurt their feelings. They had done everything in their power to make him feel at home, to make him feel like a part of the family. And he did. He genuinely felt like part of their family, but he never felt like he was home. He felt like he had left for college, and while he was away his parents had moved out of his childhood home. And now, whenever he was there, he felt like he was only visiting. When he walked through the hallways of his house, he didn't feel any connection to it. It was just a building that happened to contain all his belongings. A storage facility. It was all familiar, but it wasn't home. He wasn't even sure if he knew what feeling he was missing out on. He often worried that he would never feel it, or if he did, he wouldn't be able to identify it.

Frederick realized with a start that he had been staring at the same page for several minutes without writing anything further. He blinked and looked up to see both of his parents giving him a look that stood somewhere between confusion and concern.

He smiled at them in what he hoped was a reassuring way, then turned to the next page.

Are you worthy?

I hope so.

This time, Frederick had written his response before he was even able to marvel at the oddness of the question. Once again, he felt the words eating away at the back of his mind. He had often wondered if he was worthy. Worthy of his family. Worthy of happiness. Worthy of a chance to get better. He wanted to believe that he was, but he could just be so *useless*. How could someone who spent weeks unable to get out of bed be worthy of anything?

Frederick could feel himself about to spiral, and he doubted his mother would let another five-minute blank stare go by without intervening, so he shoved the thought from his mind and turned to the next page.

What do you fear most?

He paused before writing down his answer this time. Frederick didn't need to think about this question. Every day of his life was spent thinking about it. Every moment. He wished he could ignore the question for one second. One. Damn. Second.

Frederick closed his eyes and tried to paste a thoughtful look on his face to keep his parents from realizing that he was freaking out. He ground his teeth together and took several deep breaths, praying that somehow they wouldn't notice.

"The only way out is through," Frederick whispered to himself.

It was a phrase his father loved to repeat anytime Frederick tried to give up on something. He opened his eyes once more and scribbled his answer.

That I'll be alone.

It wasn't a unique fear, and Frederick was aware of that. He was convinced that everyone feared it on some level—that in the end, when everything was said and done, there would be no one else there. But he also knew he had more reasons to think that than anyone else. He had no friends, no job, no future. He had his parents, but they wouldn't be around forever, and when they were gone, who would be left?

Just him.

If he didn't get into Kinth, he would never get better, never meet new people, never make new friends, never fall in love. Although, honestly, he didn't need all that.

As long as he wasn't alone at the end.

Frederick completed the paperwork in a sort of haze. The rest of the questions were lacking in oddity; in fact, they were practically oozing with normalcy, transitioning back to inquiries about allergies and family medical histories.

"Perfect! Thank you so much!" The receptionist reached out and took the clipboard from Frederick when he approached. He flipped through it to make sure Frederick hadn't missed anything. Then he removed the pages, placed them in a large envelope, and dropped that envelope into a slit in the wall behind him.

Frederick's parents walked up to the desk beside him, his father giving him a reassuring pat on the back and his mother flashing a fond smile. Her smiles were becoming less and less convincing. They seemed to be growing more frail as the worry fed off them. That growing weakness had been part of the reason Frederick had fought so hard to get here, to this interview. He could see his parents beginning to struggle under the weight of him. He would never forgive himself if they broke beneath that weight. He knew they didn't blame him for any of it, but he almost wished they would. Maybe if they all acknowledged the burden he placed on all three of them, they could be better equipped to deal with it. They would never let him frame it like that, though, so there was no reason for him to try to.

"Just one more thing before I send you off, Frederick," the receptionist chirped at him. The man produced a thick pair of goggles from behind his desk. They were large and bulky and looked very similar to the VR headsets that had been all the rage lately.

"Just throw those on for me," he said, sliding the goggles across the desk. "This is just a simple eye test. No worries if your eyes aren't stellar. This isn't taken into account when reviewing applications. We just like to get a general baseline for each applicant. It's very similar to what you do when you get your driver's license."

Frederick slipped the goggles over his head. They fit snugly, and he had to fight down a slight twinge of claustrophobia as he put them on. Cautiously, he moved the anxiety to the back of his mind to simmer, trying to focus on what the receptionist was saying.

"Just tell me when you can see the blinking lights and from which side you see them. Ready?

"Yep!" Frederick said, unable to match the man's cheerful tone.

He stared into the blackness of the goggles until blinking lights filled his vision.

"Now."

"Perfect. And where do you see them?"

"Both sides."

"Fantastic!" Frederick could hear the man scribbling on some paper. "Just one more thing. Please keep your eyes as wide open as possible."

Frederick heard a click. A bright red light started from one side of his vision, working its way across and then back to the starting point.

"Are you scanning me?" Frederick asked incredulously.

"Something like that," the man laughed in reply. "Just checking to make sure everything is in tip-top shape! You can remove the goggles now."

Frederick removed them and handed them carefully back to the receptionist, who gave them a quick glance before placing them with equal care into what looked like a safety deposit box.

"Well, Frederick, that should do it. If I could just get you to step through that door."

The receptionist gestured to a door to Frederick's right. He hadn't noticed the door until the man pointed directly at it. It was painted the same off-white as the walls, and there seemed to be no doorknob. Frederick shared one more confused look with his parents and started toward the door. They followed closely behind—until the receptionist called after them.

"Excuse me! I'm so sorry, but I'm afraid only applicants are allowed through that door. I will need both of you to remain here."

Frederick could sense his parents tense up behind him.

"I'll be fine," he said to them without turning around. He was worried that if they saw the color of his face, they would know he was most certainly not fine. He listened as they stood for a moment and then slowly moved to the two chairs closest to them.

"Good luck, hun," his mother called. Frederick raised his hand in acknowledgment and walked toward the door. As he approached, it eased open.

"Well that was a little overdramatic," he heard his father mutter. There was a light smack as Emily slapped his arm. Frederick smiled and walked through the door.

Chapter 2

Contrary to what Frederick had anticipated, there was no one waiting on the other side of the door. Instead, he was met with a view of a long, narrow hallway. There were no visible doors on either side of the corridor. In fact, there seemed to be nothing in the hallway at all. Just the off-white walls and ceiling, with the occasional LED light fixture to provide the harsh lighting.

Was he just supposed to walk until he found someone?

Was he supposed to wait here?

Surely it would've been easy to provide *some* instruction before sending him through the door. Frederick decided to wait for a single minute, and if no one had come to collect him, he would follow the hallway to wherever it led.

He counted to sixty, stretching the seconds.

Nothing.

Well, perhaps he should wait another minute.

He counted to sixty again. And again. And again.

After the tenth time, Frederick decided no one was coming. He felt foolish.

What if this was some kind of test? What would it even be testing? He could think of a few things—willingness to take initiative for example. Whatever the test, though, he assumed standing in place and counting to six hundred would not earn him a passing grade. He started down the hall briskly, trying to make up for the time he had wasted. As he walked, he began to think of excuses for why he had stayed in place for so long.

"I could've sworn the receptionist told me to wait until someone came to get me," Frederick mumbled to himself, then shook his head. No, that wouldn't do.

"Sorry I took so long to get here. I had to use the restroom." Frederick rubbed his eyes as he walked. "Where on earth would you have gone to the bathroom, you oaf? Did you pee on the wall? There hasn't been so much as a closet, much less a bathroom."

He shook his head at himself and rolled his eyes. Best to just hope they didn't ask where he had been. Perhaps he could pretend it hadn't happened. Maybe the receptionist hadn't told anyone he had arrived. He had been early, after all—maybe waiting was for the best. This would put his arrival closer to his interview time anyway. Feeling slightly better but still rather foolish, Frederick continued down the hall.

How long is this thing?

Frederick checked his phone and, with a start, realized he had been walking down this hall at a steady pace for ten minutes. A feeling of unease washed over him as he picked up his pace. Surely he was getting close.

After a couple more minutes at his brisk pace, the hallway abruptly came to a halt. At first, it looked as if it simply ended, and Frederick was worried he would have to walk back to the waiting room and explain how he had been gone for almost thirty minutes without finding where he was supposed to go. However, as he got closer, he noticed two doors, one on the left side of the hallway and one on the right.

They were similar to the door in the waiting room, the exact same color as the walls, and also with no visible doorknobs. They were only discernible by the faintest of outlines. Frederick closed his eyes and felt his teeth grinding together. He tried to control his breathing but had little success. His number was rising, and he felt helpless to stop it.

"What kind of place is this?" he muttered through clenched teeth. "And why the *hell* didn't they tell me where to go?"

He ran his hands through his hair, and it took everything in him to not pull out a clump. On a whim, he chose the left door and threw his shoulder into it. He saw no way to open it—hopefully, brute force would do the trick. He also knew that if he spent any time trying to decide which door to go through, he would likely have a full-blown panic attack. He wasn't in a state to do any additional wondering.

The only way out was through. Though he was beginning to doubt that there was a way out at all.

The door gave way embarrassingly easily. Frederick cursed as his momentum carried him through and to the floor on the other side. His cheeks flushed as he scrambled to his feet. He groaned as he found himself in a large, poorly lit room. It seemed to be some kind of storage area; it smelled like a warehouse that had been left to its own devices. The scent of moldy boxes and dusty floors assaulted his nose. Towers of crates rose toward the ceiling, and there were several pallets on the floor covered with large tarps. Frederick looked at the nearest pallet and saw what appeared to be canned food and some other nonperishable items poking out from underneath the tarp. Another pallet held several cases of bottled water.

Odd.

Kinth was supposed to be the best of the best. He hadn't expected them to survive off water and Chef Boyardee. Frederick pushed the thought to the back of his mind and scanned the room to find any indicator of where he was supposed to go. There seemed to be no other doors in this room besides the one he had come through. Looking back at it now, he found it swinging idly on its hinges.

Employees Only

Keep Out

Frederick gasped. The words were written in large red letters across the front of the door. That hadn't been there before, had it? No, it hadn't. He was sure of it. There was simply no way that he had spent all that time in that off-white hallway and hadn't noticed giant red letters on the first door he encountered. Regardless, Frederick was clearly somewhere he shouldn't be. He scrambled toward the door until a sound froze him in his tracks.

It was a low, gravelly noise, like a mixture of a dog's growl and a large stone being dragged across cement. It seemed to come from under a tarp about twenty feet to his right. The tarp was covering a box or something similar in shape. It stood in a particularly shadowy part of the room, and Frederick struggled to discern its nature. He knew he should run. He shouldn't be here, and that noise coming from under the tarp sounded like nothing he had ever heard. It felt distinctly alien, and yet . . .

Frederick was at the source of the noise before he even realized he had started walking toward it. Despite himself, he reached for the tarp and gripped it firmly. He was terrified, but he had to know. Where had he heard that sound? He steeled himself and ripped the tarp free. What he found beneath was not a box but a cage. At first, Frederick thought it was empty. But then, from the back of the cage, he saw two perfect blood-red circles turn toward him.

Frederick yelped and stumbled back through the door, slamming it shut behind him.

He sat gasping for air just outside. For several minutes, he tried desperately to calm his breathing.

"That didn't just happen," he whispered to himself. "There's no way."

Frederick had plenty of issues, but hallucinations had never been one. He wasn't sure what frightened him more—the image of those eyes staring from the shadows or the prospect of his first hallucinations starting right before the most important moment of his life. The interview he was going to be late for despite arriving an hour early.

In a panic, Frederick leapt to his feet and turned to the other door. He took several deep breaths in a frantic attempt to calm himself. He wasn't hallucinating. He couldn't be. The whole day had slowly been spiraling out of control. Ever since he backed into the mailbox, his anxiety had been steadily climbing. Surely, it had just gotten bad enough that he convinced himself he saw something that wasn't there.

"It's like when you're sleeping but aren't all the way asleep yet, and you see a coat hung on a door and think it's a person." Frederick spoke aloud to no one in general, an effort to bring himself back to reality. "I'm not hallucinating—I'm just stressed. It's a dark room with a lot of weird shadows. It would've been stranger if I didn't think I saw anything,"

His words fell flat onto the floor of the hallway. He stared down at where they lay, barely controlling his breathing. Then, he took one more slow breath and squared his shoulders. He would worry about that later. For now, he needed—

Interviews

He stopped short and stared at the large red letters printed neatly in the center of the door. Right at eye level, plain as day. How could he have missed that? And of course, the answer was simple. He couldn't have.

"What the actual hell," Frederick whispered, gently touching each of the letters. He half expected the paint to still be wet. But no, if anything, the letters had been there long enough that they had started to fade.

Frederick tried to clear his mind. There had to be an explanation for how he didn't see it, but whatever it was, he couldn't focus on it or he would have a full-on panic attack. He closed his eyes tight, exhaled through his nose, and let his mind go as blank as he could. Then he squared his shoulders and pushed through the door.

Frederick found himself in a hallway that was nearly identical to the one he had just left. He felt like a rodent in an experiment, trying different doors in hopes of finding cheese, all to no avail. He tried to force the thought of mice wandering mazes from his head as he set off down the hall. Thankfully, he didn't have to walk far before it turned ninety degrees to the right. A few more yards and he was met by another right-hand turn. It wasn't much, but he was grateful for some variety. After thirty more feet or so, the hallway branched off. He could either turn left or continue straight. The odd thing was the arrow on the wall directing him to take the left turn. After all this time, he was finally receiving direction? It made no sense, but his heart was pounding, and he was in no state to question such things. So, without further thought, he followed the arrow.

"Holy crap, it has a doorknob."

Frederick marveled at the door before him. A totally normal wooden door. He felt like he had just woken up from some bizarre dream. Finally, something he could wrap his head around. The relief was so potent, he wanted to cry. He took a moment to collect himself before opening it.

Inside was a spacious office, almost exactly what he pictured an English professor's office would look like. The walls were lined with bookshelves that reached the ceiling. Frederick could tell by the spines of the books that each was well used and not merely for decoration. In the corner, a large globe stood next to an overstuffed reading chair. Beside the chair was a small table with a bottle of scotch placed in its center, so precisely it seemed to have been done with care. In the middle of the room was a large mahogany desk. On the side nearest Frederick, two chairs angled slightly toward one another. Behind the desk sat a large leather chair.

To his horror, Frederick realized that all three chairs were occupied. And, to further his dismay, the occupants were all staring at him with pointedly annoyed expressions.

"Excuse me, young man," the man behind the desk addressed him, "typically one knocks before entering a room."

He was an older man, early sixties perhaps. His hair was dark but laced with gray. He had a large beard, and a pair of spectacles balanced lightly on his nose. A lab coat covered the sweater he wore, and there was a colorful bow tie around his neck. He may have cut a comical character if not for the intensity of his stare.

"Can I help you?"

Frederick struggled to find a response. His head was spinning, and his mouth had gone completely dry.

"Interview?" Frederick had intended for it to be an entire sentence, but he had to settle for the single word.

"Ah, I see." The man checked his watch. "I thought you had decided not to show up." He looked away from Frederick and addressed the two men sitting across from him. "We can circle back to this. Grab lunch, and we'll finish up. This shouldn't take long."

The two men stood and left without so much as glancing back at Frederick.

"Please," the man said as he gestured to one of the now-vacant chairs. Frederick hastily took his seat, and the man behind the desk studied him intently.

"I must say, Frederick, I am disappointed. I was very impressed by your application, but your behavior today is hardly encouraging. I do not tolerate tardiness. I find it very disrespectful."

Frederick tried to speak, but it felt like his mouth was filled with sand. He was sweating uncontrollably, and he couldn't seem to catch his breath.

"S-sorry—I, uh, couldn't find where I was supposed to go, and then I saw this door and didn't realize it was your office. I'm really sorry, Mister—uh, Mister . . ."

"Gray. And it's *Doctor* if you don't mind. Frederick, I don't appreciate excuses. Here at Kinth, we find it is essential to take responsibility for one's actions. I expected more from you." Dr. Gray adjusted his glasses.

Frederick could feel himself losing control. He tried desperately to calm himself, but his number was getting higher and higher. Every word from Dr. Gray's mouth made it rise even faster.

"So tell me about the nightmares. How often do you have them? Is it always the same dream, or are there others besides the shadowy monster?"

Frederick's mouth hung open, and his eyes went wide.

"How did you— I never told anyone—"

Frederick was truly panicking now. The floodgates had opened, and he was drowning. He gasped for breath and raised a shaking hand to his forehead.

"Please, Frederick. Answer the questions." Dr. Gray took his glasses off and rubbed his eyes.

He sounded exasperated, as if Frederick should've expected that he would know of his recurring nightmares. The ones that he had pretended not to have his entire life. The ones that he had almost convinced himself had finally stopped. How many therapists had he fed false nightmares? At first, he had tried denying that he had nightmares at all, but children only wake up screaming for so many reasons. How on earth had Dr. Gray known about those nightmares? It simply wasn't possible.

"I . . ." Frederick trailed off, unable to find any words. He looked up at Dr. Gray.

The doctor stared back intensely, as if trying to look directly into Frederick's brain. He said something, but Frederick was so distracted by the burning stare that his brain couldn't decipher the words.

"W-what?" Frederick stuttered.

"I said, perhaps you are not Kinth material after all. I think we are done here."

Frederick's vision started to blur. He was blowing it. Everything he'd worked for, everything his parents had sacrificed for, he was wasting all of it. He had just launched his only hope of being a normal person out the window. He hadn't been able to answer a single question. Not one question! And it was already over.

Dr. Gray was saying something to him now, but there was a roaring in his ears, and he couldn't have heard the doctor even if he had been screaming through a bullhorn. Frederick closed his eyes and tried desperately to breathe. He could feel himself losing consciousness as the air still refused to enter his lungs.

Then it was over.

His lungs opened up, and air rushed in. He gasped for it greedily, hauling in every bit of oxygen he possibly could. Opening his eyes, he saw that Dr. Gray was staring at him with the smallest smile tugging at the corner of his mouth. There was a wild glint in his eye. He looked . . . excited? No, that wasn't quite right.

He looked *hungry*.

Frederick shivered and realized he was freezing. Glancing at the ceiling, he saw that he was sitting directly under a vent that was blasting cold air. He looked back at Dr. Gray, who set down a small remote.

"Sorry about that," the doctor said casually. "It seemed a little warm in here to me."

"It's fine," Frederick responded, astonished at how fine he really did feel. In fact, he felt much better than fine. The roaring in his ears was gone. His vision had cleared. He found he could read the fine print on the spines of the books in the far corner of the room. He could've sworn he could even smell the scotch where it sat on that table in the corner. He forced his confusion to the back of his mind.

Dr. Gray stood and walked over to the bottle, pouring himself a glass and chuckling. His frustration and disappointment had vanished.

"Please, Dr. Gray, at least let me finish the interview. This means everything to me, and if I don't get to at least have the interview, I'll never forgive myself."

"My boy," said the doctor, the glint in his eyes even clearer now, "we already finished the interview. Welcome to Kinth."

Chapter 3

"What?" Frederick tried to comprehend exactly what the doctor had just said to him.

"I said, welcome to Kinth." Dr. Gray was smiling at him now. The hungry glint in his eyes seemed to have subsided, but Frederick felt that it was lurking just beneath the surface.

"But you just said I wasn't Kinth material."

"Ha!" Dr. Gray barked. "That was almost an entire minute ago, Frederick. Do try to keep up."

Apparently, he meant it both conversationally and literally because he stood and walked out the same door he had sent the other men through.

Frederick did his best to control his excitement and stay present in the conversation. *I did it! I got in! I didn't disappoint my parents. I didn't fail. I'm going to live a normal life. This is going to take some doing to get there, but it's happening.* None of it had made any sense, but Frederick didn't care about that at the moment. Perhaps the key was to lean into not understanding, if only for the time being.

Frederick followed Dr. Gray into a hallway that was identical to the ones he had taken to get to the doctor's office. Dr. Gray walked briskly; clearly, he was the kind of man who tried to squeeze as many things as possible into every second of every day. This was the walk of a man who had purpose, and if you couldn't keep up with him, you were not worth his time. He was a tall, solid man and cut an intimidating figure. Frederick had to do something between a walk and a jog just to keep pace with the large man.

"So, uh, what happens now?" Frederick asked timidly.

"Now the real test begins. We were waiting for our twentieth"—Dr. Gray clapped him on the shoulder—"and now we've got him."

"Twentieth?" Frederick could tell that Dr. Gray thought he had helped clear things up, but he had done nothing of the sort.

"Yes, yes, yes." Dr. Gray's tone was somewhere between excited and annoyed, like a child on Christmas morning being forced to wait to open presents. "Of the tens of thousands of applications we receive online, about three hundred applicants are given an in-person interview. Of those three hundred, we select twenty to undergo further testing. Of those twenty, ten are admitted into our program."

Frederick froze.

"Further testing? But you said I was in. There's more?"

"Of course! Frederick . . ." Dr. Gray stopped and looked back at him. "We are the only place of our kind in existence. Our program has a flawless record. Did you really think a single online application and one ten-minute interview would be enough to determine who belongs?"

Frederick felt anxiety wash over him once more and had to fight to keep from curling into a ball on the floor.

Testing? And the testing would eliminate half the applicants? Half! Not only would he have to beat out ten other people, he would have to beat out ten other people who had performed so well, they had been in the top twenty out of three hundred out of over ten thousand applicants.

He reminded himself he had also done enough to be one of those twenty, but he was willing to write that off as a fluke. He hadn't done anything except get lost, wander in areas he wasn't supposed to be, and nearly have a panic attack.

Dr. Gray started down the hallway once more, motioning for Frederick to follow.

"Unfortunately, I do not have the time to walk you through the entire testing process," Dr. Gray said as he checked his watch and then cursed softly to himself, "and it seems I don't have time to discuss your brief, shall we call it, 'detour' on the way to my office."

He gave Frederick a quick glance, and the hunger rose to the surface of his eyes once again. Frederick felt his face flush. Of course he would know about that. One of the biggest companies in the world, and he assumed they wouldn't have security cameras? Embarrassment aside, he couldn't hide the disappointment on his face that Dr. Gray couldn't tell him more about what he saw. What was that room? Was there something in that room, or was it a hallucination? Why did he get so confused?

"Don't worry, Frederick, we will discuss that later. Arthur? Would you mind showing Frederick to his room?"

Frederick breathed a small sigh of relief, trying to retain as much as he could about the interaction to ask Dr. Gray about later. He was so preoccupied with the conversation, he hadn't noticed that they'd made their way back to the waiting room.

How was that possible? It had taken him almost an hour to get to the office. Even with his detours on the way there, it should've taken longer than five minutes to return. They also had walked in a totally different direction. This was clearly the same room, though—the only difference being that his parents were no longer present.

The mouselike receptionist Frederick had met earlier stood from behind his desk.

"Yes, sir." He beamed at Frederick, "Good to see you again, Freddy! I'm thrilled to hear you'll be staying with us a little while longer! Please, right this way."

He gestured to the same door Frederick had initially gone through.

"Where are my parents?" He walked to the front door and stared into the now-empty parking lot. His parents' car was gone.

"Ah, yes, I'm so sorry," the receptionist answered. "Once you were admitted for further testing, I had to ask them to leave. You'll see them next week once the testing has concluded." He gestured once more to the door. "I'm sure you have plenty more questions for me, Frederick, and I promise to answer them when I can. However, I must insist we walk as we talk. Our schedule grows tighter by the second."

Frederick turned to look at Dr. Gray and was startled to find no sign of the man. The receptionist, whose name was apparently Arthur, sighed and reached under his glasses to rub his eyes.

"Sorry about that, Frederick—he's developed a dramatic side as of late. I'm not sure he realizes quite how annoying it is. Not to mention rude."

"It's fine," Frederick said, staring at the space that had previously been occupied by the doctor. "Guess he's pretty light on his feet. I didn't hear a thing."

"Most people don't." Arthur snorted, then awkwardly cleared his throat. Then he walked through the door, gesturing again for Frederick to follow.

"Where are we?"

Frederick was totally and utterly confused. The hallway he now stood in bore no resemblance to the one he had encountered his last time through the door. Gone were the off-white walls, LED light fixtures, and linoleum floors. In their place, he found a floor covered in plush carpet. The walls were painted a soothing forest green, and there were paintings dispersed every dozen steps or so. Instead of the harsh LED lighting, sconces hung above each painting, illuminating them and providing a warm light to the entire hall.

Frederick stared around in disbelief. Arthur gave him a slightly confused look.

"What do you mean?"

He felt his face grow hot. How embarrassing. Of course they had just gone through a different door—he was flustered from the interview, and the short walk back had confused him.

"Oh, uh, sorry. I just thought we had gone through the same door I went through earlier. I didn't realize it was a different door. Sorry, I just got a little turned around."

The look of confusion on Arthur's face deepened, flirting with full-on concern.

"Frederick, that was the same door. You don't recognize this?"

Frederick searched the man's face for any clue that he was playing some kind of joke. Surely you wouldn't prank someone in the middle of an application process they had been chosen for because their anxiety levels often rose to heights that made it nearly impossible to function. Arthur didn't strike Frederick as the cruel type, and there was no other word for playing a joke at this moment.

Well, it's official. I've totally lost it. Frederick did his best to plaster a smile to his face. "Oh yeah, of course, I just meant it feels so much different this time around."

He cringed at how flat that explanation fell. Arthur cocked an eyebrow but didn't pursue it any further. He turned wordlessly and continued down the unfamiliar hallway.

They strode along, accompanied by a fairly steady stream of chatter from Arthur. He was a much smaller man than Dr. Gray, so Frederick didn't have to do his half walk, half jog to keep up. The man seemed to be brimming with energy. Not an anxious energy, just a clear desire to be moving at all times. His hands were constantly moving, removing coins from his pocket, flipping them, and returning them to his pockets. He straightened paintings as they passed, talking all the while.

"So did the doctor describe the testing process to you?"

"He told me that there were twenty of us and only ten would be accepted, but he didn't say anything beyond that. He said you would fill in the details since he didn't have time."

Arthur rolled his eyes and rolled a coin across the back of his hand.

"That man, always skipping out on the legwork. Well, it's fairly simple: There will be four tests conducted over the next week. You will have one test a day starting the day after tomorrow."

He turned to look at Frederick, giving him a comforting smile.

"We thought a full day to settle in would be helpful. And you can also get to know your fellow applicants!"

"What kind of tests will they be?" Frederick's fingers began pounding a rhythm into the side of his leg. The whole idea made him nervous. It also unsettled him that receiving a place meant someone else would be going home. He hadn't met any of them, but if they were here, it was likely that they were just as desperate as he was.

"Nothing too wild. There will be two psychological tests. Those will be the first and fourth tests."

Arthur seemed to notice Frederick tense up.

"It's nothing too strenuous. Just a basic test of your mental state. It's more an IQ test than anything else. Nothing to worry about." He gave Frederick a comforting smile and straightened a painting without breaking stride.

"The other two tests will be physical. Those will be the second and third tests."

Frederick furrowed his brow. He could think of no reason a program like this one would have any kind of physical fitness requirement.

"I know what you're thinking," Arthur continued. "'Why on earth is there a physical test?' And that's a fair question. Our methods here are extremely effective. At the same time, they can be rather taxing on certain individuals, so we are simply trying to ensure any applicants who are admitted can handle anything we throw at them."

Arthur flipped a coin over his shoulder, and Frederick caught it without thinking.

"Looks like you will be fine," Arthur chuckled, turning to Frederick and giving him a wink. "Each test is scored based off of time needed to complete. We will then look at the twenty sets of scores, and the ten applicants with the most impressive scores will be admitted."

And the other ten will be left to fend for themselves, Frederick thought.

He was having trouble coming to terms with the fact that his entire future and any hope of recovery and growth now depended on what were, as far as he could tell, a couple ACT-style tests and a glorified PE class. He tried his best to maintain a calm appearance as he walked. Internally, he was doing everything he could to talk himself down. He wasn't particularly confident in either his physical attributes or his mental abilities, but he felt he could at least hold his own in each category. He was well read, generally intelligent, and fairly active. As long as he kept his head, he figured he would have a shot. Everyone else would probably be just as much a nervous wreck as he was—he wouldn't finish with the top score, but he thought he had a reasonable chance at tenth.

Frederick felt himself begin to relax, of all things. This was certainly not the response he expected from himself. It just felt so good to have a little bit of clarity. Between all the wandering through endless hallways, disappearing doctors, and potential hallucinations, he was content to simply have a clear path before him.

Unfortunately, thinking of what he did or didn't see in that storeroom again quickly banished any semblance of ease from his mind. What was that under the tarp? He had told himself it must've just been a shadow and a roaring in his ears when he was trying to find the interview room, but now that things had calmed down and he wasn't alone anymore, Frederick wasn't so sure. Was it just a shadow, or was he really seeing things that weren't there? Frederick wasn't sure if he was more afraid of whatever monster was lurking in the back rooms of Kinth or the idea that he might have to deal with hallucinations on top of everything else. He could still feel those red orbs staring into his soul and hear the otherworldly growling sound vibrating in his head, and it sent his heart beating wildly into the back of his chest. Frederick shook his head and pushed the image from his mind with some considerable effort. If he was going to keep his head on his shoulders, he was going to have to block that out.

Arthur continued down the hallway, chatting away constantly. None of it seemed to be very relevant, and Frederick found his mind wandering as he followed the small man. After several minutes, Arthur stopped abruptly, and Frederick nearly ran over him.

"This is where you'll be staying." Arthur gestured to the room they had just entered. It looked like the kind of large common space one might find in a dorm. There were couches in front of TVs, a few large, circular tables, and shelves piled high with games and books. There was even an old ping-pong table in the corner of the room. Five doors around the edge appeared to lead to bedrooms. It looked like about half of the applicants were in the common area.

A small group sat around one of the tables, playing a card game Frederick didn't recognize. One of them noticed him—a stocky boy who looked to be about Frederick's age. He nudged the others and nodded toward him.

"Hey, Arthur," the stocky boy called, "is that Twenty?"

"This is indeed applicant number twenty," Arthur called back. His response was met with a small cheer from some of the applicants in the room.

"It's about time! I thought I was gonna die here," a girl sitting next to the stocky boy yelled. "I don't think my heart could've handled another game of cards."

"We could still play poker if you weren't such a bad liar, Thirteen," the stocky boy said as he stood from the table. He extended his hand to Frederick as he greeted him. "Hi there, I'm Seven. It's nice to meet you, even if I wasted half of my young adult life waiting for your skinny butt."

Frederick raised an eyebrow as he shook the boy's hand.

"We all go by our applicant number. I was the seventh one here, so I am Seven. Which makes you . . ." He raised his eyebrows, waiting for Frederick to finish his sentence.

"Twenty."

"He's a daggum genius." Seven threw his arm around Frederick's shoulder, then spoke in a confidential tone. "We figured since half of us are going home, it's best not to use first names and get too attached, you see?"

Seven didn't strike Frederick as the kind of person who needed Kinth. He spoke and walked with a certain kind of swagger—a high level of self-confidence that felt out of place. But, as Frederick looked around the room, he realized they all had a certain air about them. He had expected to see darting eyes, hunched shoulders, nervous hands. Instead, nearly everyone sat with their shoulders back, chins high, and a confident glint in their eyes. There were some who had doubt lurking there, but even they shot him defiant glares and looked him up and down, clearly sizing him up.

"This way, Frederick." Arthur gently led him toward one of the closed doors. I'll show you to your room."

The room was nothing remarkable. There were five of them, with four applicants to each room, all sparsely furnished. A bed in each corner, accompanied by a nightstand with a small lamp perched atop. Three of the beds had numbers carved into the headboards.

7, 13, 19.

"Well I'll leave you to get settled in and let you get acquainted with your fellow applicants. Dinner is at six. It will be served in the common area. Please feel free to take advantage of any of our leisure activities." Arthur smiled warmly at Frederick and walked out of the room.

The space Arthur left in the open doorway was quickly filled by the boy called Seven, the girl called Thirteen, and another girl who Frederick assumed was Nineteen. Seven tossed something to Frederick, who caught the object awkwardly. He looked down and saw it was a small pocket knife. He gave Seven a confused look—this didn't seem like the kind of thing they would be allowed to have.

"Here ya go, Twenty. Time to mark your territory." He nodded to the bed without a number carved into it. "Feel free to let your artistic urges guide you. As you can see, mine ran wild."

Frederick looked at the stocky boy's bed and saw a crude stick figure carved above the number with arms raised triumphantly. Frederick had a feeling that this guy would take some getting used to. Frederick flipped open the knife and carved a rough approximation of the number 20 into the headboard as quickly as he could, then tossed the knife back to Seven.

"Ah, yes." Seven nodded approvingly. "I respect the minimalist approach. Very clean."

He nodded to the girls standing beside him.

"Blonde one is Thirteen; brunette is Nineteen. We are your roommates."

Both girls walked up to Frederick and shook his hand. Thirteen was of average height and athletic build. Her face was dusted with freckles, and her blue eyes were cunning. She seemed to be trying to take in a thousand pieces of information at once. In general, she had an intense but friendly air about her.

Nineteen was significantly smaller than the other three occupants of the room. She was a wisp of a girl with short brown hair. She was clearly more timid than Thirteen, and Frederick barely felt her hand as he shook it. He got the distinct feeling that if he made any sudden movements or loud noises, she might dart off.

"Consider yourself lucky, Twenty," Seven said, just a little too loud. "You'll only be around us for a week. I've had to put up with Thirteen's snoring for four months."

"Oh shut your trap, Seven," Thirteen snapped. "You're the one that snores.

Not to mention you have the most terrors. I haven't been able to sleep more than an hour since I got here without you screaming for your mom."

"Oh foolish, foolish Thirteen," Seven clucked disapprovingly, "this is why you are so terrible at poker. Your bluffs are simply too easy to call. You realize I have a literal scoreboard, right?"

Seven pulled a small notebook out of his back pocket and brandished it. He opened it, and on the front page, there were nineteen boxes, each with varying tallies.

"As you can see here, you have the exact same number of terrors as I do, and I've been here four months longer than you." He pointed at each of their respective boxes, and Thirteen rolled her eyes but offered no rebuttal. From what Frederick could see, most of the applicants had several checkmarks by their names. There were only four or five with fewer than five checkmarks, and none had zero.

"You keep track of everyone's night terrors?" The idea made Frederick more than a little nervous. He wasn't especially prone to night terrors, but he was no stranger to them either.

"That I do, Two-Oh." Seven threw his arm around Frederick's shoulder once more. "I'm especially intrigued to see how many the long-awaited Twenty can rack up in one week's time."

The stocky boy began to lead Frederick out of the room into the common area once more.

"Let's meet the rest of the happy fam, shall we?"

Seven led him around and introduced him to several of the applicants. They showed varying degrees of interest and hostility. Frederick had suspected the introductions would be awkward, and he was correct. It was not a room that brimmed with social competence. There were a few who seemed genuinely interested in him, but most of them avoided eye contact, mumbled a hello, and returned to whatever they had been doing to pass the time.

The last group of introductions Seven made was to the table he and Thirteen had been sitting at when Frederick had entered the room with Arthur. Seven, Thirteen and Nineteen sat down, and Seven gestured for Frederick to do the same. The only other person sitting at the table was a boy with short, perfectly sculpted blond hair.

"This is One," Seven said, nodding to the boy, who was sitting directly across the table from Frederick.

"Nice to meet you." One stood and reached across the table to shake Frederick's hand. He was taller than Frederick had expected, six-four at least. His smile revealed teeth that were agonizingly straight. "We've been waiting for you, Twenty. You sure took your time getting here." He had a vaguely Southern accent, like he had been born in the South but raised elsewhere.

"So did you get the full treatment?" he asked as he sat back down and began expertly shuffling a deck of cards.

"Oh I didn't get any treatment," Frederick responded. "I just had the interview, and then Arthur brought me straight here."

One laughed and began dealing the cards, making no indication as to what game they were playing.

"Everyone gets the treatment, Twenty." He finished dealing and glanced at his cards before scowling. "I doubt he made an exception with you. You do seem special, but I highly doubt you are *that* special."

Seven looked at his cards and rolled his eyes, throwing them away in disgust.

"How long did it take you to get to the office? Nineteen here holds the record. Only took her twenty minutes, or so she says." Seven raised his eyebrows at the small girl, who flushed and hid behind her cards before throwing a few chips into the center of the table, evidently placing a bet.

"You all had trouble getting to the office too?" Frederick was flooded with relief that his ordeal hadn't been entirely unique. He smiled and looked at his own cards, entirely unsure what the point of the game was and thus the quality of his hand.

Thirteen snorted and tossed chips into the center of the table, matching Nineteen's previous bet.

"Trouble is certainly one way of putting it. It took me almost an hour to get to the damn storage room," she said, apparently disgusted with herself.

"Better than me," Seven mumbled. "That's how long I spent in the hallway after I got out of there."

Frederick tried to wrap his mind around everything he was hearing. They had all gone into that storage room? Had they all seen that . . . thing? The question paced across his lips, but he found he couldn't ask it, not yet. If they had been to the storage room but hadn't seen anything, then he would be right back to where he had been before. His relief would be gone as quickly as it had appeared. He knew it defied all reason, but he pushed the thought away, unwilling to risk feeling that way again.

"You calling or folding, Two-oh?" Seven elbowed him.

Frederick blinked, his attention returning to the game. His eyes darted from his cards to the chips and card still on the table. He looked for anything that would give him any indication as to what the game was, but there were no such indicators to be found.

"What are we playing?" Frederick looked at his cards once more, hoping to perhaps see the name of the game written on them or at the very least some vague instructions.

"Cards. Isn't it obvious?"

Frederick cursed himself—he had never heard of a game called cards. He was just starting to make friends, and now he was going to make a fool of himself for not knowing how to play a simple game.

"Oh, uh, I don't know how to play." Then he added lamely, "Sorry."

"Well, none of us know either." Seven rolled his eyes. "Doesn't stop us."

Frederick frowned once again and chewed on the inside of his lip a bit as he looked at the anticipation in the eyes of the others around the table. He cleared his throat, scratched his head, and grabbed a few of the chips that lay in front of him. Wincing at the pang of uncertainty he felt, he held out the chips and gave them an unsteady toss into the middle of the table. One nodded and began laying cards face up on the table, seemingly at random. Frederick breathed a small sigh of relief.

"All right, let's see 'em." Those still in the hand laid their cards down faceup on the table, and Frederick followed suit.

"Dammit!" Seven and Thirteen yelled in unison, causing Frederick to jump. Nineteen smiled sheepishly and began to drag the chips in the middle toward her pile.

"How does she always win?" Seven continued, tossing his cards high in the air in frustration.

Frederick watched in confusion and amusement. From what he could tell, no one even glanced at the other players' cards. They truly were just playing "cards" and nothing more. No rules to speak of, simply "cards." Frederick smiled, stifling a laugh at the absurdity. He couldn't decide if he found this to be the dumbest or best "game" ever.

"You can only play the same four card games so many times," One said to him, clearly noting Frederick's bewilderment. "So tell us more about your interview. Did the good doctor use the fake meeting technique?" One began gathering the cards and shuffling them once more.

"I, uh, I guess I'm not sure. There were a couple guys in lab coats talking to him when I got there." Frederick's mind was reeling. This wasn't what he'd expected from Kinth at all. Ever since he'd arrived, he felt like he was a guinea pig in a strange experiment, but he kept telling himself that he had to be wrong. The more he heard from the others with him, though, the more that sinking feeling returned.

Seven rolled his eyes, and the others nodded knowingly.

"Let me guess, he gave you the whole 'I expected more from you' spiel."

Frederick gave a slow nod and shifted uncomfortably in his chair.

"So . . . all of you . . ." He trailed off before finishing his question.

"Yep," One said a bit too cheerily as he dealt the cards once again. "Everybody had a little bit of variance, but overall, it's basically the same. Sent through the door, wait for God knows how long for someone to come collect you, start off down the never-ending hallway. A little over half of us chose the left door. Spent some time in the storage room." One paused here. That smile waned ever so slightly. Clearly, there was something here he didn't mention. Frederick got the feeling from the tension he sensed from the others that they had all experienced something in the storage room. Something that had shaken them to the point that after all these months together, they still hadn't talked about it. And he had a decent guess what it was.

One cleared his throat, and his smile returned to full luminescence.

"Then we made our way to the office and met the doc. He's always in the middle of something. For most of us, it's a meeting; for some people, he's in the middle of an important document. Hell, he was halfway through a painting when Twelve stumbled into his office."

"Don't think that one was quite as effective as he hoped," Thirteen said as she studied her cards. "He hasn't used it since."

"Effective?" Frederick asked. "Effective in what?"

"Isn't it obvious?" Thirteen said lightly. "Making us break."

Frederick's eyes went wide as it all clicked into place.

"There it is." Seven chuckled softly and rearranged his cards. "He's finally getting it."

"You mean they were trying to mess with my head?"

"Yep."

"The never-ending hallway?"

"Indeed."

"The storage room?"

"The 'Keep Out' sign that came out of nowhere?"

"Yeeeeep."

"The off—"

"Do we really have to go through all of it, Two-Oh?" Seven interrupted him. "Yes, every bit of it was orchestrated so you would freak the hell out in his office."

"But why?" Frederick looked at each of them, trying to demand an answer with his eyes. But they had all grown quiet, their focus now glued to their cards. He looked down at his own cards, though they unsurprisingly had no answers to offer.

"We think he was testing something about us, how we would respond," Nineteen said. Frederick jumped at the sound of her voice, even though it was barely above a whisper. "We think it had something to do with the AC. That's when we all calmed down."

Frederick had to admit it made some sense. He had calmed down when the air had turned on as well, but . . .

"That makes no sense," he said, shaking his head furiously, a futile attempt to clear its contents. "What, did we just overheat? My panic attack was caused by being a little too warm?"

"We have no idea," One said, gently setting down his cards then looking Frederick directly in the eye. Frederick was astonished at how hard and determined the boy's eyes were.

"But we are going to find out."

The others all nodded in agreement. Frederick saw the same determination in their eyes that he saw in One's. It seemed Kinth wasn't just some haven for young people trying to rebuild their lives. Frederick would have been more disappointed, but the determination and excitement from the others bolstered him. Maybe Kinth was something far darker than he ever could have imagined, or maybe it was just a program with sketchy methods. Either way, he was tired of feeling confused, lost, and tricked. He was ready to figure out what was going on.

"How do I help?" Frederick asked, wondering if they could now see it in his eyes as well. "What do we do?"

"We pass," Thirteen whispered. "The only way to get more information is to hang around. And now that you're here . . ." She paused. "Well, now that you're here, there's only one way to do that."

"What about the others?" Frederick asked.

One shook his head in annoyance. "They won't talk to us about it. We know they all had similar experiences, but they won't give us any more details. It's like they don't want to accept that Kinth is anything other than a one-way ticket to a better life." He let out a frustrated sigh and ran his hand through his hair. "I think they're scared of getting kicked out. I guess we can't blame them for that." He said the last part mostly to himself. After that, they sat in silence for an uncomfortable period of time. Then, slowly, Frederick set his cards faceup on the table.

"Are you kidding me?" Seven yelled at One. "You let the new guy win?"

Chapter 4

Frederick woke up to screaming. It was a horrible, guttural sound, like an animal whose leg had been caught in a trap. He bolted upright and scanned the room in a panic, trying to locate the source of the terrible noise. In the dim light of his room, he could see the faces of his roommates, all staring directly at him.

Frederick's eyes widened with horror as he realized that the awful noise was tearing from his own throat. His screams cut off, and he raised a shaking hand to his mouth. His chest was pounding, and he raised his other hand to his heart in a futile attempt to slow its panicked rhythm.

Seven stepped carefully out of bed and walked over slowly. He approached Frederick like the injured animal he had sounded like mere seconds before.

"Hey Two-Oh," he said in a soft voice, "you okay, buddy? You back with us? It was just a terror, nothing to worry about."

"I . . . I don't—" Frederick's brain knew he was no longer in danger, but his body hadn't come to the same realization. He felt like his veins had been pumped full of adrenaline. His eyes darted around the room, and he couldn't get his breathing under control despite his best efforts.

Seven was within an arm's length now, and he tentatively placed a hand on Frederick's shoulder. Frederick flinched at the boy's touch but didn't pull away.

He felt his heart settle back into its usual rhythm.

"I'm fine," Frederick managed to whisper between deep breaths. He put his face in his hands and released a long breath between his fingers. This wasn't Frederick's first nightmare, obviously; it wasn't even his first night terror. He had been waking up screaming for as long as he could remember. But this—this was something different.

"I'm sorry," Frederick said from behind his hands. "I didn't mean to wake you."

"Ha!" Seven barked out a short laugh, his tone much lighter now that he saw Frederick was recovering. "Well I'm not sure what you were trying to do, then. You could've woken a coma patient. I gotta say, you got some impressive pipes, bud."

Seven clapped him on the shoulder and walked back toward his bed.

"It's okay, Twenty," Thirteen called from across the room. "Everyone has a terror on their first night, or at least we all did. From what we can tell, all the others did too. You have nothing to apologize for."

"So you knew this would happen?" asked Frederick. He couldn't help but feel slightly betrayed. Why had they let him go into this blind? Surely it would've been better if he had known beforehand.

"Yeah, sorry," she replied awkwardly, averting her eyes and running her hands through her hair in a nervous gesture. "We wanted to tell you, but Dr. Gray told us not to warn anybody about it."

"And it's not like knowing a nightmare is coming makes it any less awful." Thirteen said. "Just ruins the night before too."

"You don't have to worry about going back to sleep, though!" Seven offered, a little too enthusiastically. "No one ever has a second one, as far as we can tell. Not on the first night. You'll sleep like a baby."

"I'm not sure I'll be able to even if I 100 percent believe you," Frederick said softly. "I have a feeling I'll see them as soon as I close my eyes."

The image was branded into his memory, and he felt the scar would not soon leave him. It wasn't even the first time he'd had this particular dream, but the dream had never felt so . . . close.

It was a simple dream: He stood alone in the middle of a pitch-black room. He could sense something else in the room with him, though it made no sound. He stood there for ages until suddenly, he heard a low growl that built into a horrible thrumming screech. When he looked toward the source of the noise, slowly, ever so slowly, they would turn to look at him. Two horrible, glowing, blood-red—

"Eyes," Nineteen whispered, more to herself than anyone else. She was sitting on her bed, hugging her knees, staring horrified into the air in front of her.

"Shhhh," Seven and Thirteen hissed at her in perfect unison.

The smaller girl buried her head in her knees and began to cry. Thirteen got into bed with her and rubbed her back while making soothing noises.

"You saw them too?" Frederick asked, his pulse once again rising. "Did you all see them?"

"We don't know what you're talking about," Seven responded, though he wouldn't meet Frederick's eyes.

"What do you see, then?" Frederick prodded. "In your terrors, what do—"

"Twenty!" Thirteen said, sharply cutting him off. "Drop. It." Her voice was firm and threatening. He met her eyes, and she nodded toward Nineteen, who was still weeping softly in her arms.

"Sorry," Frederick said, feeling his face grow hot with embarrassment. How could he be so inconsiderate? Pushing the subject when it was clearly distressing Nineteen.

"Just go back to sleep, all of you," Thirteen said from her place in Nineteen's bed. "God knows we need the rest."

She gently guided Nineteen into a sleeping position, and the smaller girl gradually stopped crying. Thirteen and Seven both returned to their beds and slipped under the covers without further comment. Frederick lay back down and rolled over so he was facing the wall. He couldn't stand to stare out into the darkness of the room. He wouldn't risk his mind conjuring images of burning eyes.

Seven was right. Frederick did sleep heavily the rest of the night. He had been so exhausted from the terror that he had passed out almost immediately, and his sleep was both sound and uneventful.

In the morning, Frederick sat up and saw that he was the last of his roommates to wake. The other three beds were vacant, and there was no sign of their occupants. Frederick stretched and rubbed the sleep from his eyes, then noticed that a clean pair of clothes had been placed on his nightstand, along with some toiletries. He scooped it all up and made his way to the bathrooms. There was a door in the corner of the bedroom that Frederick had assumed was a closet at first glance. Seven had shown him the night before that it was actually a small hallway containing four individual bathrooms. Frederick found it remarkably odd that they squeezed four applicants into one room but gave each their own bathroom. The bathrooms were surprisingly large as well, significantly larger than Frederick's own at home.

He showered quickly and brushed his teeth. The familiar routine, though performed in a wildly unfamiliar environment, had a calming effect on Frederick. He felt the ball of tension in him begin to loosen. He did a brief self-assessment and was shocked to find that his number for the day was only a 4. It should've been at least double that considering everything that had transpired.

He was in an unfamiliar place with unfamiliar people and would soon be tested to see if he would even get to stay in this place that was his best hope of being a normal person. He had experienced a horrible night terror the night before and woken up screaming.

And yet he felt hope, true hope for the first time in so long. He had been hopeful that he would be admitted to this place in the same way someone wished they would win the lottery. But now he was close, and it all felt so real, like he could almost reach out and touch it.

Frederick finished getting ready and rushed to get dressed. He was surprised to find how well the clothes fit him. A pair of incredibly comfortable, though admittedly not very fashionable, sweatpants and a simple gray T-shirt. The shirt had the Kinth logo—an open door leading to a star-filled sky—stamped on the breast pocket. Frederick had seen the logo a thousand times. But seeing it here, inside Kinth itself, awoke something inside of him.

Frederick made his way out to the common area, where he found all the other applicants sitting at various tables eating breakfast. He scanned the room and spotted Seven waving him over to a table where Nineteen, Thirteen, and One were all sitting. There was an empty seat and a full plate sitting next to him, so Frederick made his way over and sat down.

"Eat quick," Seven said through a mouthful of sausage. "They're giving us some kind of test overview in fifteen minutes."

"They're taking us to the conference room!" Nineteen said excitedly.

"What's special about the conference room?" Frederick asked.

"Almost definitely nothing," Thirteen responded with a grin, "but it'll be the first time they've let us out of this damn common room!"

"What?" Frederick paused with a waffle halfway up to his mouth. "You haven't left this room? Since you got here?"

"Nope," One replied cheerily. "They said we would be 'confined to our quarters until a twentieth applicant was found to prevent any of the current applicants gaining an unfair advantage.' Why do you think we were so excited to see you?"

"You may be pretty, Two-Oh, but you ain't that pretty." Seven guffawed and slapped Frederick on the back. Frederick glanced around the room and noticed that not everyone's mood quite matched that of his compatriots. There was a palpable nervous energy. Frederick couldn't blame those whose legs bounced anxiously or whose hands wouldn't stop shaking. They all knew that the room would be significantly less crowded by this time next week.

The excited chatter and nervous energy were rudely disrupted when Arthur burst through the door, striding into the common room.

"Applicants, please follow me to the conference room so we may begin a brief briefing," Arthur said, then paused to allow his audience to appreciate fully what he clearly thought to be clever wordplay before continuing, "regarding this week's testing."

The twenty applicants responded with a cacophony of chairs scraping as they all stood in a hurry. Arthur smiled and turned on his heel, walking right back out the door. Frederick and the other applicants rushed out after him.

The walk to the conference room was a short one. As it turned out, "conference room" was a bit of a misnomer. Arthur led them through a pair of double doors that opened into a small, amphitheater-type space. There was a small stage with four rows of seats arranged in an ascending semicircle. It looked more like where someone would put on a play than host a conference.

"Please, take a seat. Dr. Gray will be with you shortly," Arthur said, smiling at them before taking a seat himself.

There was no shortage of room as the applicants filed into the rows. The applicants divided up into the small clans that had formed over the last several weeks and months in the common room.

Frederick sat between One and Seven near the center of the fourth row, which also happened to be the back row. The room was soon filled with muted conversation and the nervous shuffling of feet one would expect in such circumstances. They sat waiting for the doctor for five minutes.

Then five more.

Then five more.

After twenty minutes, Frederick couldn't help but think back to his time spent waiting in the hallway before making his way to Dr. Gray's office. Was this another attempt to keep them off balance?

There was a clock on the wall by the door they had entered through, and for that first twenty minutes or so, he did his best not to check it.

After thirty minutes, he couldn't help but glance at it.

Another ten minutes, and he couldn't look at anything else.

Frederick watched as the hands of the clock made their way lazily around the face. The anticipation continued to build. The muffled conversations in the room were slowly consumed by the anticipation of the occupants.

It was almost exactly an hour before the doors slammed open and Dr. Gray walked onto the stage and to the podium in its center. The doctor was reading from a clipboard, which he held in one hand while running the other through his wild tangle of hair. He placed the clipboard on the podium and began mumbling to himself, apparently totally unaware that he was not alone in the room. After about thirty seconds of this, Arthur loudly cleared his throat.

Dr. Gray's head shot up, and he seemed visibly startled as he saw the occupied seats surrounding him.

"Good lord! Why on earth are you all here already? And why were you all just staring at me? Give me some warning next time for pity's sake!"

Arthur scuttled up onto the stage and had a frantic, whispered conversation with Dr. Gray. The older man looked extremely confused and then not a little bit embarrassed. He cleared his throat and turned away from Arthur to address them.

"It has come to my attention that you all have been waiting here for quite some time. Please forgive my tardiness. Shall we begin?"

"Is this guy for real?" Seven leaned over, whispering to Frederick and One. "He had no idea when he was supposed to be here. We've been waiting months for this, and he can't even be bothered to check his schedule?"

"Well," One whispered back, "we always knew he was a bit eccentric. His head is always somewhere else. Probably what's made him so successful."

Thirteen shushed them harshly, and they turned their attention to the stage.

"Well, I must say I am very excited to have you all here," the doctor began. "You all should be very proud to have made it as far as you have. It is no small thing you have done." He paused and started clapping. Arthur joined enthusiastically, and the applicants half-heartedly followed suit.

"Now, I'm sure you all are tired of waiting, except perhaps our most recent addition," he said as he squinted into the crowd and gestured vaguely to Frederick, who shrank in his seat. "So what comes next? That is the question on everyone's collective mind, I imagine. Now, I know you are aware there will be four tests. Two that will test your mental prowess, and two that will test your physical ability. I'm afraid I won't be telling you any of the specifics, because the test loses a significant amount of its effectiveness if you are permitted to prepare. I will, however, give you some general details to guide you." Here, the doctor paused and took an uncomfortably long drink from a water bottle he produced from somewhere behind the podium.

"The second and third tests will be of the physical variety. Now, don't lose heart if you are not the most physically gifted person here. We are testing your physical ability, yes, but this isn't simply who can lift more weight or who can run faster. Although, those things will not hurt your chances, so I encourage you to give it your all."

He cleared his throat again. "The first and fourth tests will be of the mental variety. Scores will be posted in the common room within thirty minutes of each test. We will be posting all scores publicly, so you will know where you stand at all times."

Frederick felt a spike of anxiety at that. The prospect of failing was daunting enough. Failing and having those scores posted for everyone else to see would be truly horrible.

"Any questions so far?" The doctor scanned the audience. "No? Good. It pains me that I have to say this, but any cheating will result in immediate removal from the premises. Also, in case that isn't enough to dissuade you, each applicant will be given a totally unique test, so even attempting to cheat is pointless."

Seven let out an exasperated sigh at this, and Thirteen elbowed him in the ribs.

"What? I don't need to cheat. I just like the challenge," he mumbled, massaging his ribs.

"Once a mental test has begun," Dr. Gray continued, "you are forbidden to speak until its completion. This means no questions, no lighthearted banter, no asking permission to use the restroom. If you do so much as say 'bless you,' you will immediately be considered done and will turn in your test as is. Is that understood?" He looked sharply into the crowd and was met with a collective murmuring of assent.

This stipulation was odd to Frederick. It seemed harsh to refuse the right to ask clarifications during the test when they were being given so little information before it. He glanced at One and saw a frustrated look flicker across on his face. The other boy was clearly having the same thought.

"Phenomenal," the doctor said. "Well, I think that just about covers it. Arthur, do you have anything to add?"

"Just good luck and give it your all!" the small man shouted, offering two over-enthusiastic thumbs up.

"Well, if that's everything," Dr. Gray said, picking up the clipboard and rifling through the documents before looking out at the applicants once again. Frederick was taken aback to see the wild hunger in his eyes once more. It was the same look he had given Frederick in his office. They had ceased being people to the doctor. They were things he would go any length to obtain.

"Let us begin."

Chapter 5

"What, like right now?" Thirteen called out incredulously.

"Yes, my dear," Dr. Gray answered with a grin that bordered on maniacal. "The first test will begin immediately. Arthur will show you to the testing room. The no-talking policy begins now."

Frederick glanced over at Seven, who sat with his mouth half-open, an objection dying on his lips. Frederick turned to look at One. He was shocked to see the blond boy smiling to himself. He had been expecting this.

Of course they would start immediately. Why would they be given a full day to mentally prepare?

Frederick chided himself for not having One's foresight. Though, that was probably harsh. One had been here longer than any of them. He would obviously know how Kinth worked better than the rest. Judging by their faces, no one else had anticipated it, so Frederick decided to go a bit easy on himself. Still, he felt beads of sweat form on his head and glide down his face. He wasn't at all prepared for this. He had been counting on the extra day to gather himself emotionally, and that time had been ripped away from him.

Arthur walked wordlessly out the door, and the applicants stood to follow him. Frederick shoved his hands into his pockets in an effort to stop them from shaking. He glanced around and saw his own anxiety mirrored in several of the faces of those around him, Nineteen perhaps most of all. There were a few, especially One, whose faces bore a wild kind of excitement. The look wasn't unlike the one Frederick had now seen multiple times on Dr. Gray. Lastly, there was a group who carried a grim determination. They were not happy about this. In fact, they looked downright pissed. But it was happening, and they'd be damned if they weren't going to meet it head-on. Seven and Thirteen fell into this group.

Frederick's legs felt uncertain beneath him as he plodded out of the room. He removed his hands from his pockets to wipe sweat from his brow and decided it would be best to leave them out. The others might see him shaking, but he would need his hands to break the fall if his legs gave out on him.

Fortunately, Frederick's legs did not give out on him during the short walk from the conference room to their destination. It was a room marked *Testing* in the same red print he had seen in the hallway on his first day. Inside was an area that resembled a high school classroom, complete with desks and a chalkboard. As he stepped through the door, Frederick was struck by how much colder the room was than the hallway. He had thought his excess sweat had been a result of anxiety, but now he was nearly certain that the hallway had been significantly warmer. The cool air cleared his mind ever so slightly as he scanned the room. There were six rows of chairs and desks that went five deep. On each desk, a small stack of papers lay stapled together.

Weird. Why have the extra chairs when you knew from the beginning there would be twenty applicants? Frederick thought to himself.

"Please, take your seats," Arthur instructed them as he sat down behind the desk at the front of the room. "Each desk contains a number—find your number and sit at the assigned desk."

Seven groaned in annoyance and stood up from the chair he had already selected. Frederick flinched as Arthur glared at the boy. While loud groaning hadn't been explicitly outlawed, Frederick suspected Seven was pushing it.

Frederick found his desk in the fifth chair of the very back row. Curiously, the desk to his right was vacant, and upon closer inspection, Frederick saw that it didn't even have a chair. This meant Frederick was sitting closer to the exit than any other applicant.

This will make any embarrassing exits more subtle, I suppose.

"Begin."

Frederick's thoughts were rudely interrupted by the simple command from Arthur.

He hurriedly sat down and inspected the first page of the test.

Applicant #20

Please fill out the following pages to completion to the best of your ability. When you have completed the test, please present it to Arthur and proceed through the door behind him.

Frederick paused and looked behind Arthur, and sure enough, there was a door there. It was just to the left of the chalkboard, the same color as the wall, very similar to the door in the waiting room. Frederick was unsure why they made the door so incredibly difficult to see if they were just going to tell them where it was.

You will not only be graded on the accuracy of your answers but also the speed with which you provide them. Please do not impede other applicants in any way. Doing so will result in immediate expulsion.

Frederick wasted no time turning the page as he heard other applicants hurrying to begin the test as well.

Please circle either True or False

   13 is a prime number

      True

   The word "Racecar" Is an example of an anagram

      False

   Mercury is the closest planet to the sun

      True

Frederick was taken aback by the ease of the test thus far. The next two pages were full of similar questions. He scanned them once more, certain he was missing something. But no, he wasn't. He answered all of the questions and was certain beyond any doubt they were correct. He flipped quickly to the final page.

   You belong here

      True

Well that's new, Frederick thought. He blinked in confusion, then shook his head. He couldn't afford to contemplate the oddity of the question nor the certainty with which he placed his answer. They had danced this dance before, and pondering it would only have an adverse effect on him. He stood and rushed to the front, where he wordlessly handed Arthur his test. Arthur took the test and began flipping through the pages, presumably checking to make sure that Frederick had completed it.

As he waited, Frederick scanned the room, searching for his friends. He saw One and Thirteen sitting next to each other toward the back. They both looked to be nearing the ends of their tests and wouldn't be far behind him. Seven was in the second row, his face screwed up in concentration. He seemed to be moving slower than the other two but had at least made it past the first page.

Nineteen was sitting in the middle of the front row, just a few feet away from him. She appeared to be finished already, although she hadn't turned in her test yet. She sat with her hands clutching the desk in what appeared to be an attempt to keep them from shaking.

She doesn't want to be the first person to turn in her test, Frederick realized.

Sure enough, as Arthur returned his test to him, the small girl stood sheepishly from her seat and approached the desk. As she did so, Frederick noticed that she had been given a stool instead of a chair to sit in.

Weird.

As she approached the desk, Frederick tried to make eye contact with her to give her a reassuring smile. She looked like she could use one. But Nineteen's eyes seemed to be glued to her shoes, so he could offer no encouragement. He turned back to Arthur, and the mousy man smiled at him, nodding encouragingly to the closed door by the chalkboard. Frederick walked briskly to it and pushed through.

As he stepped through the door, Frederick immediately began to shiver. The classroom had been cold, but the room he now found himself in was downright freezing. The space was empty and large. On the far wall, there were twenty doorways, each with a large red number painted above it. Frederick groaned quietly to himself.

Of course there was more.

There was always more with these people. The test had been far too brief and far too easy to tell them anything. He should've known. The lack of time to prepare was really starting to catch up with him. But there was no time to dwell on such things. Frederick squared his shoulders and jogged to the door with the number 20 painted over it and stepped through.

This room was significantly smaller than the last but equally cold. It was about the size of an exam room at a doctor's office and had a similar aesthetic. Sterile walls surrounded Frederick, and harsh LED lights illuminated his surroundings. The room was empty except for a door on the far wall. In the wall next to the door was a small screen about the size of a tablet with a small plaque above the screen. Frederick approached the plaque and squinted to read the tiny writing.

Please proceed through the rooms as quickly as you can. If you get stuck, please wait for the timer to hit 0:00, and at that point, the door will open.
You may talk again.
Good luck.

There was no other writing on the plaque that Frederick could make out. He looked at the small screen on the wall and found that there was indeed a small timer in the top right corner of the screen. It was set at ten minutes and counting down.

"Interesting," Frederick whispered to himself. "So it's as much about speed as getting the right answer. If you get the question wrong, you are punished by losing time."

In the middle of the screen was a single question with a small digital keyboard to type the answer.

What number comes next in this sequence?
1,1,2,2,4,8,12,96,___

Frederick typed *108* into the keypad with no hesitation. It had clicked as soon as he read through it. A sequence where you alternate adding and multiplying the two previous numbers: 1+1=2, 1X2=2, 2+2=4, 2X4=8, 4+8=12, and 8X12=96, so 12+96=108.

Frederick blinked as the door opened. He was terrible with numbers—always had been. He had struggled with math his entire life. No number of tutors had been able to help him grasp the subject. This question would not have been overly taxing to the average person, but for Frederick, it should've been much more difficult. The fact that he had been able to multiply 8 and 12 in his head so quickly, let alone figure out the entire sequence, astonished him. He shook his head, pushing his confusion to the back of his mind, then stepped through the now open doorway.

Inside the new room were three doorways. Above the doorways was another clock counting down from 10:00. Besides the doorways, the space was the same size as the last one and empty as well except for a lectern in the middle of the room. On the lectern was a neatly typed piece of paper. Frederick's shoes squeaked as he walked across the linoleum floor to read what was on the page.

Before you, there are three doors. If you go through the correct door, you will advance to the next room. There is one door that will add an additional delay of ten minutes. Finally, one door will lead you outside. If you go through this door, you will no longer be welcome at Kinth and will be transported home immediately. Please, choose wisely. At Kinth, we want to change the way you think. To advance, choose the door most recent. To delay is a pain many applicants have felt. Fear not the door to exit, for that door has no girth.

Frederick reread the instructions and glanced up at the doors. Surely they weren't serious. Expulsion because you got a question wrong? In the first test? That seemed closer to lunacy than strictness. Why punish the applicants so harshly for missing this question when the penalty for missing the last one was almost nothing by comparison? Beyond even that, he could simply wait ten minutes for the clock to reach zero, and the correct door would swing open.

They want us to doubt ourselves. They want us to hesitate, to just wait the ten minutes for the door to open. This is a test of resolve.

Frederick ground his teeth in frustration. It wasn't supposed to be like this. He'd never expected there to be so many mind games. Frankly, he was getting sick of feeling like an experiment. He stared at the doors for several long seconds before it clicked. He knew the answer. Frederick set his jaw and walked confidently to the center door. Unlike in the previous room, these doors seemed fairly standard,. He grasped the handle firmly, twisted it, and pushed through.

The room Frederick stepped into, if you could even call it that, was miniscule compared to the previous ones. The ceiling was so low that his hair brushed it as he walked, and he could lay his palms flat on opposite walls with no difficulty. There was a small flicker of claustrophobia somewhere in Frederick's stomach, but it quickly passed. In front of him was a small door with another screen in its center. It had the same ten-minute timer counting down in the top right corner. As he squinted at the screen, he saw that there were instructions flashing at him.

Memorize the Following Sequence

Underneath was another countdown, this one from five seconds. As the number reached zero, the screen filled with a picture. It was a photo of several common household items lined up. It looked like there were thirteen items. Each had a random number above it. The numbers were in a variety of colors. The image stayed on the screen for about ten seconds, and Frederick studied it intently, committing as much to memory as he could in the short timeframe. The image disappeared and was replaced by more instructions.

Repeat the colors of the numbers in reverse order. Start with the 13th number and finish with the 1st.

Below the instructions were several squares representing each of the possible colors. Frederick looked up at the ceiling to think and was briefly distracted once again by how close it was, so he closed his eyes instead. After a few short moments he opened his eyes and punched his answer in: *Green, Green, Black, Orange, Red, White, Orange, Purple, Blue, Brown, Red, Green, Blue.*

The door slid open quietly, and Frederick stepped through. He was stunned at how easy it had been for him. If you'd asked him to do that on most days, he would've laughed at you. But something about today was different. It was all on the line. This would determine the rest of his life. He couldn't be the person he usually was—he had to be more.

Frederick stepped into a narrow hallway. It had a tile floor and bare, off-white walls. He strode quickly down the hallway, which curved gently to his right before eventually straightening out. He got the impression that the path he had just taken vaguely resembled a horseshoe.

At the end of the hall was another normal door. There was no screen on the door or on the wall. Instead, there was simply a piece of paper taped up beside the door. The only other thing in the hall was a small scoreboard like the kind high schools would use to keep score in volleyball. It had two sets of numbers, one through nine, that could be flipped through to make any number up to ninety-nine. Frederick approached the paper and read the simple question.

How many chairs were in the testing room?

Frederick turned to the small score-keeping device. He paused only briefly before flipping through the numbers to get to his answer: *29.*

He tried the door and found that it opened with ease.

Frederick was shocked as he stepped through the door and into the common room. The room was empty except for Arthur sitting reading a magazine with his legs propped up on a table. He jumped as Frederick stepped into the room.

"Dear heavens, I wasn't expecting anyone so soo—" he began to say, but he was interrupted as One stepped through a door several down to Frederick's left.

Frederick hadn't seen it before One stepped through.

"Two of you finished already—" Arthur was once again interrupted as Nineteen stepped through another hidden door, this one directly to Frederick's left. Arthur was clearly having trouble collecting himself. He was trying to say something to them but could only stammer instead. He paused, took a deep breath to compose himself, then plastered his familiar, over-enthusiastic smile on his face.

"Well done! I'm very impressed; these are some of the best times I have ever seen!" Arthur exclaimed. He adjusted his glasses and muttered to himself, "Well actually *the* best I've ever seen. And *three* of them." He shook his head and began glancing over each of their heads, writing something down on a clipboard that sat in front of him. Frederick glanced above the door and saw that there were digital clocks above their doors indicating their time.

It had taken him seven minutes and thirty-five seconds to finish. He could've sworn it had been longer than that. It had taken One seven minutes and thirty-eight seconds, and for Nineteen, it was seven minutes and forty-one seconds.

One walked over to him, his smile looking a bit more mischievous than usual.

"I knew Nineteen was gonna give me a run for my money, but it looks like I should've been just as worried about you," One said. "You really live out the whole 'last shall be first' mentality, eh, Twenty?"

Nineteen joined them quietly, a small smile of her own emerging.

"Congrats, Twenty," she said with a broad smile. "First place is a big deal."

"Thanks, but you would've beaten me if you'd turned in your test sooner," Frederick replied, now smiling as well. Nineteen blushed and turned away, looking thoroughly embarrassed if not slightly pleased with herself.

"Please, make yourselves comfortable!" Arthur called from behind his clipboard. "I imagine no one else will be finishing for quite some—"

Another of the hidden doors on the wall swung open, and Thirteen stepped through. Her face, which had been smug as she stepped through the door, fell as she saw the others standing together.

"Are you kidding me? All three of you? I don't know how I could've gone any faster," she said as she stomped over to them in frustration. "At least I beat that oaf Seven," she mumbled to herself, dodging One's attempted congratulatory slap on the back.

Arthur stared slack-jawed for a moment at the four applicants, who were now laughing and joking with one another. Then he joined them in laughter, though his was much softer. Shaking his head, he recorded Thirteen's score and picked up his magazine again.

One, Thirteen, Nineteen, and Frederick sat around one of the several tables, casually playing cards as they waited to see who would be next through the door. After fifteen or so minutes, applicants began trickling in. Seven stepped through his door a full thirty minutes after Frederick had. The stocky boy was red in the face and seemed to be absolutely fuming. He made his way over to their table and sat down with a frustrated thud, and One began to deal him in.

"How long have you all been done?" he mumbled, catching playing cards as they slid toward him across the table. The other four applicants glanced at one another nervously, not wanting to kick the boy while he was down.

"Not too long," One said casually. "Just twenty or thirty minutes."

"Not too long?" Seven shouted. "That's an eternity!"

He dropped his cards in frustration and ran his hands through his hair nervously.

"I'm screwed," he said, glancing around the room, trying to ascertain how many had finished before him.

"You finished fifteenth," Thirteen said, then hastened to add, "but you still have three more tests to make up ground. Don't start whining until things are looking really bleak."

Seven actually perked up at that. "Yeah, you're right. I'll just have to finish first on the next three tests." His tone was devoid of any sarcasm. Frederick smiled and looked down at his cards. Seven really, truly believed he would find a way.

"Speaking of," the boy continued, "who finished first? Was it one of you?"

One threw a few chips into the middle of the table and nodded at Frederick.

"The newbie got me by a few seconds—Nineteen and Thirteen weren't far behind."

Seven let out a low whistle and raised his eyebrows at Frederick.

"I'm impressed, Two-Oh. We all assumed One would finish first," Seven said. He broke into a large smile. "Thank goodness somebody beat that pretentious know-it-all, eh?" One laughed in response and laid down his cards, shrugging as he pulled the chips in the middle of the table toward him.

"So what gave you the most trouble, Seven?" Thirteen poked at him.

"That ridiculous door question," he responded, his scowl returning. "I must've read it a hundred times. I tried going back through the door I came in. You know all that 'door most recent' stuff. It wouldn't budge though. After about five minutes, I just guessed. Got that damn additional ten-minute delay."

The rest of the table paused and turned to look at Seven, mouths agape.

"You *what*?" Thirteen almost yelled at him.

"I guessed?" Seven said, seeming confused at her sudden outburst.

"He's an idiot," Thirteen said with her eyes wide. She looked at the others for confirmation and found it. "You absolute buffoon. You realize you had a 33 percent chance of getting kicked out, right?"

"Why didn't you just wait five more minutes for the door to open?" Frederick asked in disbelief.

"That's not my style, Two-Oh. You should know that by now," Seven scoffed back at him. "I don't give up that easily. Besides, I'm a gambler at heart!" He dropped a handful of chips on the table in an attempt to drive his point home. "You guys figured it out, though? What was the answer?"

"The center door," Nineteen said quietly, looking uncomfortable as all eyes turned to her. She hurried to finish her explanation. "It was an anagram puzzle—the first clue was in the line, 'at Kinth we want to change the way you think.' If you rearrange the letters in Kinth you get the word think. Once you were looking for anagrams, it was pretty easy. 'To advance, choose the door most recent.' If you rearrange the word 'recent,' you get 'center.' 'To delay is a pain many applicants have felt.' Rearrange 'felt' and you get 'left.' 'Fear not the door to the exit, for it has no girth.' Rearrange girth and you get 'right.' So left was the delay, center was the door that took you to the next room, and right was the exit."

Seven whistled low again.

"Glad I didn't pick right, I guess," he said, then looked up sharply. "What about the chairs question? I paid close attention to the room. I thought they might try to pull something like that. There were six rows with five chairs each. That's thirty. Then there was one chair missing, the desk next to Twenty. So that's twenty-nine. Then Arthur had a chair behind the desk, so that's back up to thirty. What am I missing?"

"Nineteen had a stool, not a chair," One said and shrugged at him. "That makes twenty-nine."

"Are you serious?" Seven said in disbelief. "If that's not the dumbest . . ."

He trailed off in a collection of profanities that could only be described as artistic.

The group sat pretending to play cards as they waited for the rest of the applicants to finish. They chatted idly, but there was an intensity hidden behind the casual words. They all wanted to know what kind of lead they would be protecting. Frederick hated thinking of it in terms of a competition, but it was so hard to think of it in any other way. There were a finite number of spots, and that meant that one person getting a spot sent someone else home. He looked around the table at his newly acquired friends. He wasn't sure how he would handle making it in if any of them didn't. They had been here so much longer than he had, and surely they needed Kinth just as badly as he did. As they sat around the table, joking with one another, he could feel the longing from them that he felt in himself. A longing to stay, to belong, to do more than simply survive. It lurked just beneath the surface. He could hear it in their voices when they laughed. He could see it in their eyes when they smiled. Yes, they needed this just as much as he did. And who was he to take that from them?

Frederick was jerked from his thoughts as Arthur received a phone call. The entire room went silent, all eyes turning to the receptionist.

"Hello? Yes. Yes. Certainly. Yes, sir. I'll tell them," Arthur spoke into the phone before hanging up and turning to address the room. He looked as if he was going to yell for them to quiet down but then realized that every single person in the room was dead silent and already staring at him.

"Well done on your first test! We had some extremely impressive scores this time around. Those of you who did not perform as well as you hoped, don't fret! You have plenty of testing left to make up for any poor showings." Arthur's patented smile of encouragement emerged as he spoke, and Frederick couldn't help but feel optimistic for Seven. How could someone see that smile and not know with absolute certainty that everything would work out in the end?

"As you may have noticed, we are missing a couple of applicants."

Frederick glanced around quickly. He had been so engrossed in his own thoughts that he hadn't noticed. He did a quick headcount, and sure enough, there were only eighteen applicants in the room.

"Two and Eleven," One whispered to Frederick with a look of disbelief. "I can't believe they're already gone. I never particularly liked them, but I've been around Two for so long. All that time, and he couldn't even make it past the first test."

One shook his head and turned back to look at Arthur. Frederick glanced at Seven and saw he had turned slightly green. The reality of how big his gamble with the doors had been was finally hitting him.

"Obviously," Arthur said loudly in an attempt to quiet the whispers that had rippled across the room, "this shows you that the threat of expulsion in tests is not an empty one. Please do not take any of it lightly." He looked around the room, and Frederick could've sworn he made eye contact with Seven before continuing.

"That being said, I am so proud of you all and of the grit you have shown today. This is truly one of the most impressive groups of applicants I have ever had the opportunity of encountering."

The man adjusted his glasses, and Frederick almost thought he had wiped a tear or two from his eyes. He cleared his throat and addressed them once more.

"Dr. Gray would like to pass on his congratulations, and he encourages you all to spend the rest of the day relaxing and resting. The first physical test will begin tomorrow at 6 a.m. sharp. We will meet here in the common room at 5:45. Any form of tardiness will be severely punished. Based on what I've seen from other groups of applicants, the punishment for tardiness is not a death sentence, but it might as well be. It is reflected strongly in your scores and should not be taken lightly." Arthur paused and cleared his throat uncomfortably. "Also, I would not recommend eating before, as the test has been described as . . . rigorous."

A series of nervous murmurs made their way throughout the room at this statement.

"He expects me to go without breakfast?" Seven asked, dumbfounded. "I haven't gone without breakfast in years! Maybe I should've chosen the right door." He mumbled the last part to himself, and Frederick found himself smiling at the stocky boy. He would find a way for all of them to pass, no matter what it took.

He turned to see One looking directly at him. It seemed the blond boy had noticed the look Frederick had given Seven, had seen the determination in his eyes. One's eyes burned with the same determination. The nod he gave Frederick was almost imperceptible, but it was there. Frederick nodded back. They were in agreement, then. Seven would be passing. They all would.

The rest of the day passed uneventfully. The emotional exhaustion of testing a day earlier than they had planned was clearly weighing on the applicants. They spent the time in relative silence, counting the minutes until it was time for them to sleep.

Frederick stood and released a long yawn, even though it was barely nine o'clock.

"I'm going to sleep. This waiting is driving me crazy," Frederick said.

"Imagine doing it for weeks," Seven said as he rolled his eyes.

"You wanna compare times, Seven?" One asked, raising an eyebrow.

"Yeah, yeah, yeah. We get it. You were born and raised in this place and have never seen the sky or actually touched grass."

One rolled his eyes and walked toward his room. "See you all in the morning."

Chapter 6

Frederick was torn from sleep by a hand clamping firmly over his mouth. Instinctually, he shouted and thrashed in his bed. The owner of the hand, who had successfully muffled his shout, pressed down on him in an effort to still him.

"Twenty, it's okay. It's One."

Sure enough, the tall blond boy loomed over him in the darkness. Frederick managed to calm himself with no small amount of effort. Once One saw that Frederick had regained his composure, he slowly removed his hand from Frederick's mouth.

"Why?" gasped Frederick. He felt stupid at his inability to produce more than this single word, but his heart was still pounding wildly. He was so caught off guard that his brain couldn't manage any more than the one syllable.

"I need your help," One whispered. "Try not to wake the others. I'll explain outside."

One left without checking to see if Frederick was following. He began debating internally what he should do. He needed his rest for the test in the morning, but surely One wouldn't have snuck into his room in the dead of night unless it was something important, dire even. Frederick was slipping his sneakers on and tiptoeing toward the door before he even realized he had made up his mind. Taking care, he treaded past his sleeping friends, making sure not to trip over the small pile of clothes Thirteen had thrown at the foot of her bed.

Frederick emerged into the common area and gently closed the door behind him.

One sat at a nearby table, absentmindedly shuffling a deck of cards. He took a break to pull a chair out for Frederick. Frederick debated returning to his room. Clearly, this was no emergency. Still, his curiosity was much too powerful for him to truly consider returning before hearing what the other boy had to say.

He sat in the chair wordlessly, waiting for One to start the conversation.

The blond boy sat in silence for a full minute, and the only sound in the room was the shuffling cards. Finally, One set the deck down on the table and eyed Frederick, almost as if sizing him up.

"What do you think?" One asked.

Frederick furrowed his brow. "About what?"

"This place. Kinth," One answered simply, his eyes still dissecting Frederick.

"I mean, I don't know." The words came out slowly. "It's obviously not what I expected, but it was never going to be. I've been to so many different places that were supposed to fix me, and none of them did—none of them even helped a little bit. So I guess I expected this place to be different from all the others. I mean, everyone said it would be. I just had no idea what exactly that would mean. "

One quietly waited for Frederick to continue.

"It's weird. But that's okay if it works," Frederick concluded somewhat lamely.

One stared at him, still silent.

"What's this all about?" Frederick asked. "Why did you wake me up?"

"I have two things for you, Twenty." One leaned forward. "An observation and a proposition. If you're willing to hear them both."

Frederick nodded slowly.

"Observation first, then." One stood and began pacing. "I never expected this place to be normal. Like you said, it was never going to be what we expected, whatever that may be. For them to get results that were so different from everyone else's, their methods would have to be different too. Still, I thought there would be some kind of rhyme or reason for what we were doing. But it's just a series of curveballs."

One stopped pacing and looked Frederick directly in the eyes. "I think there's more going on here. Or at least, this isn't just some high-level program to help us move on from anxiety." He let the words hang in the air.

"More?" Frederick asked. "Like . . ."

"Oh, I have absolutely no idea." One shrugged. "I doubt it's anything too dastardly. Most likely, they're feeding us a bunch of half-truths and keeping all the juicy bits of info to themselves."

"You think they're lying to us?'

"Not exactly," One said. "But do you really think the most renowned and mysterious corporation in the world is telling us, a bunch of hyper-anxious teenagers, everything?" He raised his eyebrows skeptically.

"I guess not," Frederick conceded.

"And I'm not sure that I agree with their decision to withhold information from us. "Which brings me to the proposition." One said, arching a conspiratorial eyebrow.

"You want to find out," Frederick said.

"Yes." One smiled. "And I want your help."

Frederick ran his hands through his hair.

"Why me?"

"Because you noticed it too." One sat down and began shuffling the cards again. "I mean, everyone has noticed that this place is less than traditional shall we say. But I can tell you see that something bigger is going on here. And you're dying to know what it is."

Frederick turned One's words over in his head, letting them sink in fully. He had noticed the oddness of Kinth, of course. It was always occupying some space in his mind. Ever since he had set foot in the place, he had been thinking about it on some level.

He was surprised to find that One was right—it was eating him up from the inside. What had started as a flicker of curiosity had grown into a raging inferno of needing to know the truth without Frederick even realizing. That giant question mark was hanging over every single thing that happened in the building. If he really wanted to trust this place to help him recover enough to have any sort of real life after this, Frederick had to find answers, or it would drive him insane.

Well, more insane than he already was.

"What do you want to do about it?" he asked.

One's smile broadened.

"That brings us to the second proposition."

"You didn't mention a second proposition," Frederick said.

"Wanted to make sure you were on board with the first." He set the cards aside and leaned in toward Frederick, lowering his voice to barely a whisper. "I want to find out what's going on. Now."

"Like now, now?" Frederick asked in disbelief.

"Well, we can't exactly do it during the day. They didn't give us a hall pass. Not to mention we have the tests during the day. This is our only chance. Together, we can find out what's going on here. We sneak out for an hour, find out what we can, sneak back in before anyone knows we're gone."

Frederick chewed on his lip, considering the proposal.

"What if they catch us?"

"They won't," One said simply.

He realized with surprise that he believed One completely. There was no part of him that doubted what the other boy had just told him.

"Twenty, I know this makes you nervous—and it should," One continued. "But this is important, right? Can you live the rest of your life not knowing what they are really up to here? What if we don't make the cut? What if we are left behind and we never know what is really going on here? Would you really be able to go home and sleep soundly without knowing what they're really doing here?"

"No," Frederick said, and he meant it. "But . . ." He trailed off, unsure of what he had been going to say.

"Look," One's voice softened, "I know it's risky. But honestly, I think they really want to help us here. I just think that's not the only thing they want. And it's not enough for me to just turn my head the other way and pretend nothing else is going on. I'm gonna take their tests, and I'm going to try to stay here, but I'm going to do it on my terms. I refuse to just be a number to them, to just slip into the background and do as I'm told."

One looked at Frederick and raised his eyebrows expectantly. Frederick had nothing to offer in way of response. He knew it probably wasn't a good idea. He knew it was a risk that likely wasn't worth taking. But he also knew that he couldn't just carry on like nothing else was going on. A part of him screamed to find out what was happening. He felt as if something had woken up inside him, a new side, or perhaps one that had simply lain dormant for many years. Whatever it was, he knew it wouldn't be satisfied unless he did all he could to discover the truth of Kinth and the truth about himself.

Frederick met One's eyes and nodded firmly.

"Good, then it's settled." One stood from the table and stretched. "The three of us will leave right away."

"The three of us?" Frederick's eyebrows furrowed in confusion.

"Um, I'm not sure I should come," Nineteen said quietly from behind Frederick. Frederick jumped and turned around. Nineteen stood just outside the door to their room. She gave him an awkward wave, which he returned.

"No Seven or Thirteen?" Frederick asked.

"As if they would ever wake up before noon unless they had absolutely no choice." One snorted. "And of course you should come, Nineteen. You're smart, and we need that. Not to mention, you managed to sneak up on our dear Twenty here without any problem. This sounds right up your alley."

Nineteen stood timidly, still only a step or two from the door to their room.

"Is it a good idea?" Nineteen whispered. "If they're hiding things, if they aren't who they say they are, do we even want to know?"

"I would want to know regardless, but I can't answer that for you," One answered. "What I will say is that I don't think they are the bad guys or anything like that—they just don't trust us enough to let us in on the truth, so we take matters into our own hands. And if they do end up being evil comic book villains, isn't it better we find out now?"

One shrugged nonchalantly. "It's simple math, Nineteen." He turned and walked toward the exit. "What's bigger? Your desire to stay out of trouble or your curiosity?"

Nineteen chewed on her lip for a few more seconds, then took a determined though still slightly shaky breath and moved to follow One.

Frederick stood and joined her, quietly following One out into the hall.

The door clicked shut behind them. Frederick was a bit surprised that it had been left unlocked, though locking it could certainly be a fire hazard. It seemed risky to leave so many teenagers with the option to roam a multibillion-dollar facility unsupervised.

"They probably assume the crippling anxiety is enough to keep most of us from wandering," One whispered.

"What?" The statement caught Frederick totally unawares.

"You were wondering why they would leave us with essentially full access to this place," One answered. "They probably assume no one has any desire, or maybe even capacity, to explore."

One moved smoothly down the hall. There was an ease and confidence that oozed from his gait. Frederick cringed at the thought of how he must look in contrast. He was doing everything he could to keep from jumping at every shadow he saw.

"Where are we going?" Nineteen asked from beside Frederick. She moved with the same anxiety that Frederick felt.

"I have no idea," One said. "We aren't looking for anything in particular, and I have no idea where anything is here anyway. So unless either of you have a better idea, I plan on wandering until we find something interesting."

He turned back to look at them with eyebrows raised.

"Works for me," Frederick said, trying to summon a confidence he didn't feel.

Nineteen grimaced, and Frederick could tell she was loath to continue without a more concrete plan. However, he could also see that she knew this was the closest thing to a plan they were going to get.

"Good," One said and nodded firmly. "Stay on your toes."

They wandered the winding halls for several minutes. There was little change in scenery as they walked. Nothing decorated the walls, and there were very few doors. The occasional one they did pass never led to anything more than a storage closet. The white walls and white floors all began to blend together under the LED lighting. Frederick had to fight off the wave of disorientation brought on by it all.

"I can't tell if we've walked ten yards or ten miles," he said, almost to himself.

"It is almost impossible to gauge how far we've gone, isn't it?" One said, his voice seeming more intrigued than annoyed. "I wonder why they did it this way."

"The same reason all hotels paint their hallways that same color of green," Nineteen said. "Well, I guess the opposite reason. It's like instead of trying to calm people down, they're trying to unsettle them." Her words followed them down the drab halls.

Further discussion of the topic was cut off as they rounded a corner. One almost tackled Frederick and Nineteen in an effort to push them back around the corner. In the brief moment before he was forced back, Frederick caught sight of two figures in lab coats walking away from them down the hallway. One flattened himself against the wall, peering carefully around the corner. Frederick felt his heart thunder in his chest. His blood was pumping furiously, and he felt like every cell was on high alert.

Several seconds passed before One relaxed and stepped away from the wall. He turned and gave Frederick and Nineteen a rueful grin.

"Well, that could've gone worse."

"Where did they come from?" Nineteen hissed, her eyes darting fearfully. "Surely they haven't just been walking ahead of us this whole time."

As Frederick looked at her, he was reminded of a baby deer. She looked skittish, so much so that Frederick wondered if it had been best to bring her along after all.

"I think they came from a room up ahead," One said, making his way toward it.

Sure enough, there was a door on the left side of the hallway. It was the first non-closet door they had encountered to that point. It bore no markings but had a small window that allowed them to peer inside.

The room was spacious and filled from wall to wall with plants. There were lights and water apparatuses hanging over the many plants, which varied greatly in species. There were shrubs, flowers, grasses, weeds, and even a few saplings. Frederick scanned the room for more coat-clad figures but saw none.

"What on earth do they need a greenhouse for?" Nineteen whispered.

"Only one way to find out," One whispered and pushed the door open.

"What are you doing?" The panic was clear in Nineteen's voice.

"What we came to do," One asked in genuine confusion. "What's the point of this if we aren't going to actually check out anything we find?"

One walked through the door, and Frederick felt himself following close behind. Nineteen hesitated for a moment in the open doorway before stepping timidly into the room.

They each wandered in a different direction, not speaking to one another. Frederick studied every plant closely, looking for anything he might recognize. He wasn't a botanist by any stretch of the imagination, but he wasn't a total stranger to plant life. He tried to focus, but the beauty of the plants was distracting. They grew in vibrant colors and distinct shapes, some of which Frederick had never seen before.

"Do you guys know much about plants?" Frederick whispered hoarsely.

"Not really," One said.

"I know a bit," Nineteen said, not looking away from the plants.

"I don't recognize any of these, do you?" Frederick asked.

Both his friends shook their heads.

"They're gorgeous, whatever they are," Nineteen said softly, reaching out to inspect one of the saplings.

All three applicants froze. A muffled buzz of conversation made its way through the door, growing steadily louder.

"They're coming back!" Frederick whispered.

One moved without hesitating, grabbing Frederick and Nineteen by the arm and dragging them into a closet at the back of the room. The door clicked shut just as the one to the room swung open. Frederick could just see out of the closet through the small crack near the hinges. His perspective was severely limited, but he was able to observe the entrance as well as a small portion of the room.

Their assumption that it was the same two figures they had seen earlier had been incorrect. Three middle-aged men wearing lab coats and carrying clipboards walked through the door, conversing.

"Promising group, I'd say," said the tallest of them. He had a carefully sculpted beard, trimmed close to his face, and his voice carried a hint of a British accent.

"It's far too early to tell," said the shortest man. He was built much like a fire hydrant, short and thick, with only wisps of hair futilely trying to cover the top of his head. "We haven't even really got into the testing yet."

"Oh, don't be such a killjoy, Matthews," said the final man. He was of average height and build with almost no distinguishing features. He had the kind of face people would forget as soon as it left their field of view. "Let us be a bit optimistic."

"What is there to be optimistic about?" The short man, Matthews presumably, sneered. "You all said the same thing about the last batch, and how long has it been since we heard from them?"

Frederick exchanged a worried glance with Nineteen. He tried to catch One's gaze as well, but the other boy was fixated on the trio.

"Matthews!" the Brit snapped. "You know we aren't supposed to talk about that. Even if we were, that's in poor taste, and you know it."

The short man grumbled, and all three began moving throughout the room in silence, observing the various flora and making notations on their clipboards. Soon, they were out of Frederick's field of vision. He strained to catch sight of them once more but with no success.

The sounds of the three men moving slowly throughout the room consumed Frederick's senses. The inability to see them was infuriating. He knew they were simply moving about with their clipboards, but the fact he couldn't see it with his own two eyes was maddening. Frederick closed his eyes tightly and tried to focus only on his hearing. He strained his ears to try and pinpoint the exact location of all three men.

Frederick's stomach dropped. One of the men—he had no idea which one—was moving steadily toward them. The light footsteps and gentle scratching of a pencil were inching closer and closer to their hiding place.

Frederick struggled to steady his pounding heart. It was a relatively small room, so of course, they would eventually wander close to the closet. Still, he had to fight against panic as the man continued to draw nearer the door.

"We done here?"

Frederick almost jumped out of his skin. The voice had come not three feet from them on the other side of the door. It was the man they had called Matthews. Frederick jumped again as there was a loud crash followed by a flurry of cursing.

"What have you done now, Matthews?" said the forgettable man.

"I haven't done anything! Some idiot left a flower pot in a spot where it was bound to get knocked over!"

"I watched you put that there yesterday," the Brit said in an annoyed voice. "I even told you it would fall if you left it."

Matthews made no reply to this.

"Just clean it up, and let's go," said the forgettable man. "I'm not trying to be here all night."

Nineteen pulled frantically at Frederick's sleeve. He glanced down at her in confusion. The small girl's eyes were wide with fright, and she was pointing frantically at a broom in the corner of the closet. Frederick felt himself fill with the same fright he saw in Nineteen's eyes. He tried to get One's attention, but the boy was tense, coiled like a spring.

"I don't get paid to be a damn janitor," Matthews mumbled. "Someone else will take care of it. That specimen was useless anyway."

The distinct sound of Matthews trudging away followed the words. His companions made no effort to convince him otherwise, apparently used to the small man's behavior.

All three men entered Frederick's vision again as they made their way out the door. They strode with purpose and disappeared quickly, their heads buried in their work. Frederick and his companions sat in silence for a full minute, barely daring to breathe. Finally, One exhaled and smiled as he stepped out from the closet.

"Well, that was stressful," he said lightly.

Frederick's heart was just beginning to beat at its usual pace as he emerged.

"I did not enjoy that," Nineteen said softly. Her hands shook, and her eyes were glued to the ground.

"It was certainly closer than I would've preferred," One offered, then bent to inspect the shattered pot on the ground. "You almost did us in, little buddy."

Frederick moved over and carefully picked up the fallen plant.

It was a small flower that burned a brilliant shade of red, so much so that Frederick half expected it to burn him as he retrieved it from the shards of pottery and clumps of dirt. Without thinking, he raised it to his nose and breathed in deeply.

Something unlocked in his mind, a faint memory so dim it was more general colors and shapes than anything specific. He was moving through a sea of red and was assaulted from all directions by a smell. It wasn't a bad scent—far from it. It was light and pleasant, yet earthy and distinct. It was the kind of smell that wasn't remarkable in and of itself, but it carried a weight of memories that gave it significance. Frederick breathed in again, trying to unlock the memory fully. He grasped at it desperately to no avail. It slipped through his fingers like wisps of smoke. His entire life, he had felt that he was searching for a missing part of himself, some small thing that would make all the pieces fall into place. This flower wasn't it by any means, but it was the closest thing he had ever come to finding that missing piece. He couldn't explain it, but he was certain that if he could understand the tiny plant, he would finally have all the answers about himself that he'd searched so long for.

Frederick was taken aback by the overwhelming emotions brought on by the tiny plant. He shook his head violently in an effort to clear it.

"You okay, Twenty?" Nineteen asked, kneeling beside him.

He merely held the flower up to her in response. She took it cautiously, giving Frederick a confused look. He offered a small nod of encouragement, and she eased the flower up to her nose. She closed her eyes in the same way Frederick had.

"You remember too, don't you?"

Nineteen nodded without opening her eyes. A soft smile crept across her face.

"Remember what?" One asked quietly.

"I have no idea. But I remember it. Or I remember that I had a memory of something once," Nineteen said and handed the flower to One.

He brought it to his nose and breathed deep, holding the breath in for a prolonged moment. Then he smiled and breathed again and again. "It's beautiful."

Frederick knew he wasn't just talking about the flower.

One handed the flower back to Frederick ,who held it uncertainly, knowing he should return it to the ground but at the same time finding himself unable to do so.

"They are just gonna throw it away anyway," One said with a mischievous grin.

"You don't think they'll notice?" Frederick asked uneasily.

"No way. That jerk who knocked it over probably won't tell anyone what happened. Whoever cleans it up will assume it was just a pot of dirt."

Frederick twisted the stem of the flower between his fingers thoughtfully.

"We both know you're gonna take it," One said. "Let's not waste any more time." The blond boy began to move toward a door in the back of the room that Frederick hadn't seen before. It looked more like a door to another room than another closet.

Frederick glanced at Nineteen, who shrugged.

"Don't look at me," she said with faux indifference. Frederick could tell from her body language that she was hoping he would take it. Her eyes kept darting back to it, not longingly necessarily, but it was something not far from that.

Frederick made up his mind, tucking the flower carefully into his pocket and making sure it wouldn't be crushed as he did so.

Both Frederick and Nineteen hurried to catch up to One, who was already pushing through the door into the next room. It was about the same size as the room they had just left, but that was where the similarities ended. The room was packed tight with desks that were, thankfully, vacant. Each desk seemed to be drowning under stacks of files and loose papers. Frederick could almost hear the desks groaning beneath the weight of all the paper. The walls were lined with bookshelves that were stuffed with books, files, and binders. Everything in the room had an essence of bursting seams. It felt as though one wrong step would cause the whole of it to come crashing down.

One walked up to the nearest desk and peered at the papers. "Holy crap, guys!" he exclaimed.

"What?" Frederick and Nineteen asked in unison as they hurried to his side to see what One had found.

"Receipts," he said flatly, tossing the paper he had been holding back onto the desk. "I believe we have found the accounting department. Not quite as interesting as the greenhouse."

Nineteen walked over to the wall and inspected the nearest bookshelf. She walked the length of the room, letting her hand run across the spines of books and the backs of folders.

"The thing is, there's probably a wealth of knowledge in here. It's just far too disorganized for us to find anything useful."

"We'd have to get wildly lucky to find anything we were looking for," Frederick said as he walked over to another desk and shifted some loose papers around, making sure to leave them back exactly as they had been.

"Well we aren't looking for anything specifically, so anything we find is what we are looking for," One said brightly, grabbing a handful of papers and plopping down into one of the desk chairs. Frederick was afraid the boy would prop his feet up on the desk and cause a miniature avalanche.

They worked in silence, combing through the papers in an attempt to find anything remotely interesting. Frederick moved to a desk close to the back of the room. It sat just a few feet away from a door much like the one they had entered through. He had assumed there would be several entrances to this room, and he appeared to be correct. However, the only entrance to the accounting department being from a greenhouse wouldn't be the strangest thing about Kinth.

Frederick sat down in the chair by the desk and searched, with little hope of finding anything. Most of what he did find was so incredibly dull, he almost couldn't comprehend what it said. Pay stubs, business expenses, time-off requests, and maintenance bills all blended together. Soon, Frederick was barely registering what he was looking at. He went through the motions, trusting his brain to alert him of anything that seemed relevant. As he shuffled mindlessly, something began tugging at the corner of his mind. The hair on the nape of his neck stood straight up, and he felt his senses snap back into focus.

Something was wrong.

A feeling of dread was consuming his body inch by inch. He stood, knees slightly bent, ready to leap into action if need be.

"Twenty, what—"

Frederick held up a hand, cutting off Nineteen's question before she could finish delivering it.

The feeling tugging at Frederick's mind became clearer and clearer. It was a feeling of intensity that he had felt before. Similar to the sensation the flower had given him and every bit as terrible as the flower had been wonderful. Frederick clenched his teeth as he realized it was coming from behind the door nearest to him.

He looked at Nineteen and One and motioned for them both to stay where they were.

Every internal voice Frederick had was screaming at him to run away as fast as he possibly could. To run home to his parents, curl up in bed, and never think about Kinth or whatever lay behind the door ever again.

And yet he took a step toward the door. And another. And another.

Something else inside Frederick pushed him forward. It didn't have a voice. It didn't need a voice. Frederick needed to know what was on the other side of the door. He reached out and grasped the knob firmly, twisting it slowly.

It was locked.

He tried again and again. Each attempt became more frantic as he attempted to force his way into the room. He was vaguely aware of Nineteen whispering hoarsely at him, but he ignored her. All that mattered was that he get into the room and face whatever was inside.

Frederick took several steps back away from the door, preparing to throw himself into it. He knew that he could generate enough force to break the door open; the way his blood was coursing through his veins, he suspected he might be able to shatter it. His legs tensed, and he set his jaw. Just as he was about to throw himself forward, a small hand caught his arm.

"Twenty!" There was genuine fear in Nineteen's voice. "What are you doing? What's going on?"

Frederick looked down at Nineteen and blinked. Her eyes were brimming with concern and confusion.

"What's going on?" she repeated.

"The door," Frederick said. "Can't you feel it?"

Nineteen looked at the door warily. "I feel something," she said. "Something bad. I can't tell what it is, but it's nothing that makes me want to open the door."

"I have to know," Frederick said, more to himself than to her.

Even as he said it, Frederick felt something fighting against the instinct that had taken over. This was something more complicated than simply fight-or-flight. More complicated than curiosity and the need to understand. It was something he couldn't put to words, and doubted he ever would. All he knew in that moment was that it was giving him pause. The desire, or rather need, to get through the door was still present. It just wasn't the only thing present anymore.

Nineteen pulled gently on his arm.

"I think we should go."

Frederick blinked a few times, then nodded at her words. He allowed himself to be steered toward the door through which they had previously entered.

Frederick caught a glimpse of One as Nineteen led him away. He was still sitting in the same chair where he had been before, still in the same relaxed position. Though, Frederick was certain he was no longer as relaxed as he had first appeared. Even at a glance, Frederick could see One's muscles poised and ready to spring into action should it be necessary. His face bore a disinterested façade. He looked as if he might yawn mightily at any moment.

But his eyes gave him away.

Frederick saw in his friend's eyes the same thing he had felt burning inside of him. No amount of acting could've hidden that. And he saw something else in One as well. Not combatting the other thing he had seen but existing together with it. It was difficult for Frederick to articulate exactly what it was—all he knew was that it was directed at him.

Nineteen led Frederick through the door and back into the greenhouse room. He barely registered the passing plants as they hurried back out into the hallway, and Frederick was just barely aware of One following behind them.

With each step they took away, Frederick felt his head clear a little bit more.

"Are you okay?" Nineteen's voice was filled with concern.

"I'm fine, Nineteen," Frederick said as he gave her what he hoped was a reassuring smile. "Sorry about that. And also, thanks."

She gave the smallest of nods in acknowledgement, her eyes still studying him.

One caught up to them quickly, his long strides closing the gap with little effort.

"Well I think that's enough exploring for tonight, don't you?" One remarked. Frederick couldn't help but smile at his casual tone.

They returned to the common room without further incident. Frederick had been almost certain that they were going to encounter some kind of security on their return. He half expected sirens to begin blaring and for a SWAT team to crash from the ceiling.

No sirens came.

They sat at one of the round tables in the common room, One shuffling a deck of cards and dealing it mindlessly. They had all silently agreed that some unwinding was in order before any of them tried to sleep. They didn't talk as they "played." In fact, there was even less structure to the faux poker than usual. It soon dissolved into a cycle of One shuffling the cards and dealing them out, then Nineteen and Frederick collecting their hands and arranging them carefully. Someone would lay their cards down and then everyone would return the cards to One, who would repeat the process. They had no desire to even give the pretense of playing a game. It was enough to have something to do with their hands as they turned the events of the night over and over in their minds.

Finally, it was Nineteen who broke the silence.

"Twenty," she said without looking up from her cards. "Can I see it again?"

Frederick didn't have to ask what she meant. He had been absentmindedly spinning the stem of the flower between his fingers beneath the table.

"Sure." He handed the flower to her, and she took it with delicate hands. The transaction was done with the level of care someone would use when handling an incredibly precious and fragile piece of art.

Nineteen turned the flower over in her hands, inspecting every inch of the plant. Frederick wasn't sure what she was looking for, and he doubted she had any idea either. Maybe she wasn't looking for anything at all, just waiting for the small thing to communicate with her in some osmosis-adjacent fashion.

One collected the cards and shuffled them repeatedly, no longer dealing them out.

"Have you all ever seen anything like that before?" he asked.

"I've seen flowers similar, I guess, but nothing exactly like this," Nineteen answered without looking away from the flower. "I'm not an expert by any means, but it's new to me."

"I don't know anything about anything," Frederick said, "but there's obviously something different about it."

"Agreed," One said thoughtfully. "Maybe we should ask Seven and Thirteen what they think."

"Couldn't hurt." Nineteen shrugged as she handed the flower back to Frederick. Even as she passed it off, her eyes lingered on it for a fraction of a second. Frederick took the flower and tucked it away.

A comfortable silence grew in the space between the three applicants. Each stared at nothing in particular, all seemingly deep in thought.

"I feel like I'm trying to put together a puzzle," said Frederick, surprising even himself as he broke the silence. "But I've never seen the picture on the box, so I have no idea what it's supposed to look like."

"And all the pieces are an identical color." One nodded.

Nineteen sighed. "And someone took all the edge pieces."

The three of them smiled ruefully at each other. Frederick felt frustration bubbling inside of him, but it was no match for the excitement that burned inside his chest. A gauntlet had been thrown down, and he was keen to pick it up.

"We have to go back," One said, his smile waning slightly. "We have to go back, and we have to take Thirteen and Seven." He paused for a beat to study Frederick and Nineteen's faces. "You know that, right?"

Frederick nodded. There hadn't even been a question in his mind. He had to know more. For the first time in his life, he felt like he was getting real answers, like he was taking tangible steps forward.

Nineteen looked markedly less certain. The small girl squirmed in her seat. "I want to know," she began slowly. "Really, I do. I'm just not sure I have to know. Does that make sense?" She shook her head in frustration. "I don't know! There's this thing in my brain. This itch I know will never go away if I don't figure out what is going on here. I just can't—" Her mouth worked silently, trying to form the right words. Frederick saw tears start to well up in her eyes. "I just can't go back to how it was before. I don't know how it was for you before this, but if you are here, I can imagine it was pretty bad. I came here to get better, or as close to better as I could find."

One placed a comforting hand on Nineteen's shoulder and leaned in close.

"It won't ever be like it was before." His voice was comforting but firm. "Not for you, not for me, not for any of us. I promise you that. We've got each other now, and we are going to get answers. We will be so much more than we ever were before."

Nineteen dragged her tear-filled eyes up to One's and gave him a small nod and smile.

"So it's decided," One said. "We go again as soon as we can, and we take Seven and Thirteen with us."

He paused as if giving them one last chance to object. When they didn't, he nodded, seeming pleased that the matter was closed.

"Well, we should probably call it a night," One said as he stood from the table and stretched. "If we hit the hay now, we can still get a few more hours of sleep before the next test. I imagine we will need it. I know I probably don't need to say this, but don't talk to anyone about this. Not even Seven and Thirteen. We'll tell them tomorrow night before we leave."

Frederick and Nineteen nodded solemnly.

They said their goodnights and made their way back to their respective rooms. Frederick and Nineteen returned to their beds, in no real danger of disturbing either Thirteen or Seven. Frederick removed the flower from his pocket and placed it carefully in the trunk at the foot of his bed. He covered it lightly so that someone would have to do more than simply open his trunk to find it. He doubted anyone would be rooting around in his things, but it didn't feel like the kind of thing to leave up to chance. He shut the lid to the trunk and crawled into bed, pulling the covers up to his chin.

It took Frederick several minutes to quiet the thoughts bouncing around his head. Once he did, he quickly fell asleep.

Chapter 7

Frederick awoke to his alarm at exactly 5 a.m. He rolled out of bed and made his way to the shower, turning the water as cold as it could possibly go. He shivered as the icy flow shocked his body fully awake, bringing everything into sharp focus. He needed to start planning.

He was bombarded by thoughts from the night before. There was a part of him, not a small part, that needed to know what was behind the door. But he couldn't worry about that now. That was important, but there was something that trumped it.

Frederick needed to find a way to help the others succeed. One would also be planning something, but they were both too smart to try planning together. They couldn't risk getting themselves and the rest of their friends kicked out. It took a considerable amount of effort for Frederick to force his thoughts away from the events of the previous night. There would be time for his curiosity later, but for now, he needed to focus on helping his friends.

However, no matter how hard he tried, Frederick couldn't totally silence the musings.

Several minutes of thought yielded no obvious course of action. He thumped his head softly against the shower wall as he tried to think of something, anything, that could help his friends. The problem was the total mystery shrouding the tests. If he knew the general format of the test, perhaps he could prepare, but he didn't have the faintest idea. Even if he did, he worried he would be of no help anyway. Frederick wasn't unathletic; in fact, he considered himself to be above average athletically. But, if the test was really as vigorous as Arthur said, he would need to focus all his energy on keeping his own head above water.

Frederick sighed and turned off the shower. There was nothing for it—he would just have to improvise.

After dressing, he walked back to his room. He found his stride to be uncharacteristically confident—a product of him riding the high of knowing there was nothing more to do. He was unprepared, and all he could do was wait.

As he walked into his room, he glanced at the clock on his nightstand, which read 5:40. Five minutes until Arthur would be gathering them for the next test. He had cut it significantly closer than he'd meant to, but it shouldn't be a problem. He saw that the rest of his roommates had already gotten ready and headed to the common room.

I should probably join the—

Frederick's train of thought was rudely interrupted by a loud snore coming from Seven's bed. He blinked in disbelief at the rumbling mound buried beneath the blankets.

"Seven!" he shouted at the unconscious boy, who mumbled something and rolled over, trying to remain in his slumber. "Seven! Wake up! We have to be ready in five minutes!"

"What if I just slept through this one?" a voice called from underneath the bedding. "I already failed one test. What's the harm in failing another?"

At that moment, Thirteen stormed into the room.

"Seven, what the actual *hell* are you doing? If you fail this test, you are gone! Do you not get that?" the irate girl yelled as she shoved him out of bed. He was so tangled in the blankets, he was unable to break his fall and landed directly on his head. Frederick winced at the force of the impact.

"Fine, fine, I'm up, I'm up," Seven mumbled from his place on the floor. He stood up, rubbing the small bump that was forming on his forehead. "Seems like assault was maybe a little bit overboard, eh Jinx?"

"If you call that assault, you'll be horrified by what I'll do to you if you aren't in the common room in thirty seconds." Thirteen walked toward the door, then paused and stomped back up to the boy. "And I told you to *never* call me that."

"Jinx?" Frederick asked as he and Seven followed Thirteen out the door.

"Yeah, you know, unlucky number thirteen. Jinx. I think it's pretty clever, but she can't stand it. I make sure to only use it when she's especially pissed off." The boy gave Frederick a sly smile as they walked into the common room.

The clock on the wall read 5:44 as Frederick and Seven joined the others. Arthur stood near the door wearing a sweatsuit that matched that of the applicants. He had also replaced his glasses with a slightly comical pair of goggles. He was doing some light stretching while jogging in place.

"Looks like ol' Arthur will be joining us today," One said. His words had a lighthearted air to them, but there was concern lurking on his face.

"Looks like it," Frederick said. "He never really struck me as the athletic type."

"You'd be surprised." One said with a grim look.

"Please follow me!" Arthur exclaimed. "I'll lead you to the testing area. Don't lag behind, as we don't have much time. I'll give you all more instructions once we arrive."

The clock turned to 5:45, and Arthur darted out of the room at a full sprint.

Unfortunately for Frederick and his friends, they were standing toward the back of the group that had gathered around the man. They reacted swiftly, however, pushing past some of the other applicants who had been caught off guard by the sudden exit. The five of them barreled down the hall and soon made their way in front of the other applicants, One leading the pack. They were forced to run at a dead sprint just to see which turns Arthur was taking. There were several times that Frederick only caught a glimpse of the small man before he disappeared around a corner.

Frederick smiled as he sprinted down the hallway. He relished the cool air in his face and the slight burning in his legs. He could hear the other applicants' footsteps pounding down the halls behind him. They had apparently snapped out of their stupor fairly quickly. He chanced a backward glance and saw a few of them a short distance behind. They were doing their best to keep up, but the delay had been costly. He doubted they could see Arthur at all. Frederick's eyes went wide as a plan began forming in his mind. He had to keep himself from laughing. Maybe he had found a way to help his friends after all.

He summoned every ounce of energy he had and picked up his pace until he was neck and neck with One.

"I've got an idea," he panted, keeping his voice as low as he could.

"Oh yeah? Well I'm sure it's brilliant, but I'm not sure this is the best time for a brainstorming session," One said, his voice remarkably even for someone who was in the middle of a sustained sprint.

"The other applicants can't see Arthur. They're only following us. If we time it right, I could make sure they see me make a wrong turn. They follow me down the wrong hall, and that gives the rest of you a head start on the next test."

One's eyes flashed, and he grinned wildly at Frederick. "Not bad. I didn't think you had it in you. I only have one change to make."

"What is it?" Frederick asked.

"It should be me." One cut off Frederick's objection. "I'm faster than you, trust me. I can lead them the wrong way, then double back. Plus, the other applicants are more likely to follow me. I have a bit of a reputation."

Frederick opened his mouth and tried to object again, but One cut him off with a sharp glare.

"This isn't a discussion, Twenty. We are doing this my way."

Frederick saw there was no point in arguing with him and simply nodded.

"Good. Try and leave some breadcrumbs for me along the way, eh?" Frederick nodded again, and One slowed until he was at the back of their small group. He waited for there to be a short stretch of hallway between turns. As Arthur turned left, Frederick followed, and he chanced another glance over his shoulder right before they made the next turn, catching a glimpse of One running the other direction. He was unable to see what the other applicants did as he was forced to dart down another hallway after Arthur. He turned his focus fully to his breathing and keeping pace with the receptionist, although Frederick felt that "receptionist" didn't quite encompass the full spectrum of duties that Arthur provided.

As Frederick continued to follow Arthur, he did his best to scuff his shoes into the ground in the direction they were going. The soles left a faint mark on the otherwise perfectly white floors. He nearly tripped the first two times he tried it, but had no problems after the third attempt. After five or six more turns, Arthur led them into a large waiting room very similar to the one Frederick had first met the man in. He slowed to a walk and turned to look at them. His eyes went wide as he took in the applicants staring back at him.

"Oh my! Only four of you? Where is everyone else?" Arthur questioned the small group.

Frederick smiled in spite of himself. There was no sign of One or the other applicants. Their plan seemed to have gone off without a hitch.

"Only the five of us, boss," a high-pitched voice called from Frederick's elbow. Frederick jumped and looked down to see a tiny boy standing next to him, breathing heavily. Frederick recognized him as Eight. He seemed to be by far the youngest of the applicants, though Seven had mentioned that he wasn't as young as he looked. He clearly had not hit his growth spurt yet, and as Frederick studied the sly look on his face, he felt the overwhelming urge to make sure his wallet hadn't been swiped. Frederick had no wallet at the moment, of course, but the sentiment remained.

"You almost had me there with that trick, boss," Eight whispered to Frederick, awkwardly holding his arm up above his head to elbow him in the ribs. "Mighta got me if I hadn't suspected you all would try to pull some garbage like that. I love the thought, though. Really good stuff." He smiled and elbowed him once more.

Frederick's eyes shot to Arthur to make sure he hadn't heard what the boy had said. Fortunately, he seemed to be focused on the hall from which they had come. He stood with a stopwatch and clipboard in hand.

"Maybe we don't talk about it quite so loud," Frederick muttered to him.

"You got it, boss."

The boy winked and tried to elbow Frederick a third time. Frederick deftly dodged the attempt and turned his attention to the entrance of the room, praying One would be able to follow his makeshift breadcrumbs.

It was a solid five minutes before One came sprinting down the hall. He was grinning like a madman and seemed to be on the verge of bursting into laughter. Not far behind him were the rest of the applicants.

"Sorry I'm late, Arthur. I took a slight detour."

The man didn't acknowledge the comment, as he was too busy hastily recording times as the last of the applicants jogged into the room. Frederick smiled to himself, realizing this was part of the test. It appeared the gamble had paid off. The other applicants who arrived after One were all panting heavily, and more than a few were glaring daggers into One's back. They seemed to have figured out that the detour wasn't unintentional.

"Glad to see you all made it alright," One said as he walked over to join them, seemingly oblivious to the anger directed toward him. "Thanks for the directions, Twenty. They were a lifesaver." He nodded at Frederick. "I should've known there would be no losing you." he nodded at Eight, who responded only with a wide grin.

"You planned that?" Thirteen whispered at One, her eyes wide with anger.

"Wasn't my idea." One smiled back and nodded at Frederick.

"Are you serious?" Thirteen asked, her ire now turned on him.

"That's brilliant!" Seven said quietly, grinning widely now as well.

"Brilliant? It's irresponsible! What if they say you cheated?"

"Well, they probably can't prove anything. All he did was turn down a hallway. He didn't make anyone follow him," Nineteen whispered, not meeting Thirteen's icy glare.

"See?" One said, putting an affectionate arm around the blushing Nineteen. "Nothing to worry about. Just focus on the task at hand."

Arthur cleared his throat loudly and addressed the room.

"Now that you all have arrived, I will explain the next part of the test." He gestured to a door in the wall behind him. "Through this door is a large testing area. As soon as I open the door, a five-minute timer will start. You may spend those five minutes however you desire. Once the time has elapsed, I will be entering the room with a few assistants. Your goal is to avoid being touched by me or any of the assistants. As soon as you are touched, your time will be recorded and you will be escorted to a viewing area outside the testing area. Obviously, the longer you avoid being touched, the better your score will be.

"Once we begin, a thirty-minute timer will start. Your score will be the total time left on the clock when you are caught. For example, if you elude us for twenty-eight minutes your score will be 2:00. If you manage to elude us for the full thirty minutes, you will receive a perfect score of 0:00. For those of you who delayed in getting here, the time that elapsed between my arrival to this room and yours will be added to your final score."

Arthur raised a hand to quiet the objections that arose from those who had been late.

"I am sorry, but I warned you that tardiness would not be tolerated."

One flashed Frederick a brilliant smile. Their plan had not only worked, it had been even more effective than they had hoped.

"This goes without saying, but any physical altercations with any of the assistants or other applicants will absolutely not be tolerated. This means no shoving, tripping, biting, etc. Now, if there are no more questions . . ."

Arthur paused for just a moment, then opened the door.

As the door clicked shut behind them, a large digital clock above the door frame blinked on, displaying *5:00* briefly before beginning to count down. Frederick turned to survey the room before him and had to stifle a gasp. He now stood on the edge of a clearing. Directly in front of them was an open grassy area, flanked by a pair of small tree groves, each beginning about twenty feet away. He gaped at the branches swaying gently in the breeze.

"What the . . ." Seven trailed off as he took in the foliage that now surrounded them.

"It's artificial turf," said Thirteen while kneeling to inspect the grass. "I bet the trees are fake too."

Frederick hurried over to study one of them, and sure enough, it was synthetic. It was remarkable how much they looked and felt like real trees, though. He ran his fingers over the rough bark and winced as a splinter lodged itself in his finger. He couldn't identify what exactly it was about the trees that gave away their true nature, they just felt . . .off. Something about how the leaves moved on the wind, how the light reflected off the bark, it all felt wrong. It was an extremely unsettling sensation.

As he inspected the entire area more closely, he realized they were still indoors. He could make out a wall on the far side of the clearing, and when he looked up, he could spot the ceiling with beams crisscrossing where blue sky should've been. It appeared they had also rigged the lighting in a way that imitated sunlight remarkably well. Overall, it was a very surreal experience.

"No time for botany, I'm afraid," One called to them. He nodded at the clock above the door, which had just ticked below four minutes. The other applicants got the same idea, sprinting into the trees on either side of the clearing.

"What's the plan, One?" Seven stalked over to them. He was smiling broadly. "I'm ready for some redemption."

"We don't have time for anything resembling a real plan," One answered, rubbing his chin. "Seems like we should pair off. Best not to all be together if we can avoid it. I'd like to spread our eggs into as many baskets as we can. Nineteen and Thirteen, you hide in the trees to the left as best you can. Seven and Twenty, you take the trees on the right. Try to find places that keep you hidden but that you can easily run from if you need. They are gonna know every nook and cranny of this place. The worst thing you can do is back yourself into a corner."

"What about you?" Thirteen demanded.

One's eyes grew wild once more, and he flashed a knowing smile at them. Frederick could feel the excited energy emanating from him. He began to bounce back and forth on his toes like a boxer before a title fight.

"I think I'll do a little bit of roaming."

Frederick didn't have time to fully process the implications of the statement before Seven grabbed his arm and dragged him toward the trees. Before long, they were both sprinting through the overgrowth, jumping over logs and ducking under branches. They ran until they hit a wall.

By Frederick's best estimate, they were about fifty yards from the door they had entered through. Assuming the room was roughly symmetrical, it was about the size of a football field. They doubled back, trying to find a central spot in which to hide. They passed several other applicants, who had found hiding spots of varying effectiveness. At one point, Frederick was about to squeeze into a small space between a boulder and a tree, but was shooed away by an applicant who already occupied the spot.

Their search became frantic as their internal clocks alerted them that their five minutes was almost up. Seven pointed silently to a tree with a low-hanging branch. The leaves were thick, and you could only see up into the tree if you got up next to the trunk and looked straight up.

Frederick shook his head and whispered, "It's not bad, but if they see us, we're screwed. What happened to not backing ourselves into a corner?"

"We aren't exactly drowning in options, are we Two-Oh?" Seven hissed back. "And look, there's a branch from another tree that reaches over. If they find us, we could cross over . . . maybe." Seven's tone didn't instill confidence in Frederick, but they were out of options. So he swallowed any further objections, nodded, and scrambled up the tree as fast as he could.

They climbed as high as they dared, stopping when the branches began to creak under their weight. Frederick was surprised to find that he actually had a decent view from his vantage point. He could see the door they'd entered through and almost the entire clearing through a small break in the leaves. Frederick nearly toppled from his perch as a loud horn blared, presumably indicating a start to the proceedings. The door slid open, and Frederick saw Arthur and four other figures step through. Arthur's assistants were unfamiliar to Frederick, though they cut intimidating figures. Each one was tall, athletic, and extremely muscular. Arthur looked especially small standing next to them.

"Hey there, Arthur."

All five figures froze, and Frederick's breath caught in his throat as a voice cut through what had been an almost perfect silence.

One strolled lazily out into the middle of the clearing, hands in his pockets. He had been standing in the only place in the clearing Frederick hadn't been able to see.

"Hello, One!" Arthur called cheerily, though his posture indicated he was confused by this display. "Did I not explain the objective of this test clearly?"

"No, you did a great job!" One responded, matching the man's cheery tone. "I'm just not really one for hiding. I prefer tag to hide-and-seek."

"Fair enough," the man chuckled from behind his goggles. "Perhaps you should attend to One, Andre? Give us a call if you need any assistance."

The largest of the assistants stalked toward One as Arthur and the rest of his assistants bolted into the trees. Frederick's breath caught in his throat as One's pursuer closed the gap between the two of them until he was just a few feet away. He paused for just a moment, perhaps expecting the boy before him to run. One yawned and cracked his neck. Frederick knew there was no world in which One would be running now. The massive assistant seemed to reach the same conclusion. He crouched and lunged forward, arms stretched wide as if to embrace One.

Frederick sat slack-jawed as he watched One effortlessly avoid his pursuer. He moved lightly on his feet, hands still in his pockets. He ducked beneath arms and spun away from grasping hands. The boy and man danced their way slowly to the one part of the clearing Frederick couldn't make out. He strained, craning his neck in an effort to catch a glimpse of them once more.

Seven hissed at him and gestured wildly. Frederick remembered himself and pressed his body tightly to the trunk. He placed a loose hand over his mouth in an attempt to dampen the sound of his breath. Seven sat a few feet below him on the opposite side of the trunk, employing a similar method to quiet his breathing. Everything was far quieter than Frederick had imagined it would be. He'd thought there would be sounds of people tearing through underbrush and of Arthur and his assistants calling out to each other. He heard none of these things, only the occasional cry of frustration as an applicant was found.

By Frederick's best guess, they had been sitting in the tree for nearly fifteen minutes when Arthur darted silently beneath them. Frederick felt his heart rate spike. His heart pounded with such vigor that Frederick was certain it would give him away. He tried to do his best to calm down and slow it.

Obviously there is no way Arthur can hear my heart beating from thirty feet away, Frederick thought to himself, *but sti—*

"Hello boys," Arthur called jovially from the bottom branch of their tree. He had apparently circled around behind them, using the cover the leaves provided against the tree's occupants.

"Go!" Seven barked. He swung from his position and bolted for the branch that connected their tree to the one next to them. He made it successfully across, and Frederick hurried to do the same. The branches groaned beneath his weight as he scurried.

"Not bad, gentlemen! It's always risky to choose a tree. This is an ingenious way to avoid being cornered!" Arthur shouted as he began climbing toward them, having lost none of his cheer.

"Nothing for it. Get to the ground. We gotta run for it!" Seven shouted.

Both boys half climbed, half fell out of the tree as they sacrificed grace for speed. They landed heavily on the ground. Seven hauled Frederick to his feet and tore through the trees. The boys ran with all their might, grunting as branches did all they could to slow them.

Frederick chanced a glance over his shoulder and spotted Arthur sprinting through the trees behind them. He was gaining ground.

"We gotta split up!" Frederick shouted as he leapt over a log, barely breaking his stride.

"Good luck!" Seven yelled as he changed direction.

Frederick didn't risk a response. He would need every bit of air he could salvage. Turning sharply, he bolted in the opposite direction from Seven. He didn't dare another look over his shoulder. A simple misstep at this point would mean game over. He could sense Arthur behind him anyway. Frederick breathed a sigh of relief—this meant Seven would get at least a little bit more time as long as he could avoid the other chasers. Frederick felt a smile spreading across his lips. His heart was pounding from exertion, as well as the anxiety that being chased brought.

He shouldn't have been enjoying this so much.

His legs found a gear he hadn't known they had. They fired like twin pistons as he dashed through the trees, relishing the wind on his face and the slight burn of air tearing in and out of his lungs. He felt so incredibly *alive.*

If Arthur could catch him when he was like this, then so be it. But of course, he couldn't. No one could. He had hit his stride fully now, and his feet pounded a perfect rhythm into the earth.

Then an assistant stepped out from behind a tree ten feet in front of him.

Frederick yelped in surprise and reacted almost instantly, grabbing onto the trunk of a smaller tree to his left. He used the tree to shift his momentum ninety degrees, narrowly avoiding the assistant while retaining his speed. Frederick winced in pain as the rough bark tore at his palm. His maneuver had been effective in keeping himself from running directly into the arms of the assistant, but it had allowed Arthur to gain a precious few steps. He strained to regain the earlier separation, and soon, the gap between them was growing. He felt a spike of excitement at that.

He was getting away.

Smack.

Frederick skidded to a halt and stared in stunned silence at yet another assistant, who had been hiding behind a tree he had sprinted past. Frederick's chest stung from the slap the man had delivered to his chest.

"Applicant Number Twenty caught," the man said into an earpiece before sprinting off toward the clearing.

"Get to the viewing area!" Arthur called back at Frederick as he sprinted after the man. "I imagine you will want to see this."

Frederick was fuming as he made his way back to the entrance, but a small part of himself was still pleased with his performance. It had taken three of them to catch him, and he had bought Seven some time. The clock above the door had just ticked above twenty-five minutes, so his score would be just north of 5:00. At worst, that would put him in a tie with anyone who had been penalized but lasted the full half hour.

He stepped through the door, where he was met by a Kinth employee who led him up a staircase to the viewing area. It was a spacious room that resembled box seats in a stadium. A large glass pane separated the room from the testing area. It must've been one-way glass for them not to have spotted any light from inside the testing area.

Frederick's frustration melted away almost immediately as he saw the number of applicants already in the viewing area. He counted fifteen including himself, meaning there were only three remaining. He checked for his friends and saw Thirteen and Nineteen with their faces pressed against the glass on the far side of the room. Frederick's heart soared as he looked around the room and realized that two of the missing applicants were One and Seven. He hurried over and pressed his face against the glass as well.

One stood defiantly in the middle of the clearing, a look of complete confidence carved into his features. He was smiling broadly at the five pursuers who now surrounded him. They moved toward him with caution, closing the gaps between them and removing the possibility of escape.

"He's been there the whole time," Thirteen said in an awed voice without taking her eyes off the boy in the clearing. "While we were all hiding, he was just dodging around in the clearing. It started with one assistant, and then two, and then the other three joined." She shook her head in amazement.

"Have you seen Seven?" Frederick asked.

Thirteen and Nineteen both shook their heads. Frederick's smile widened. The assistants were all so focused on One that Seven was almost guaranteed a perfect score.

One said something to Arthur that Frederick couldn't hear through the glass. Arthur laughed and lunged at the blond boy. One stepped backward and turned to the side, narrowly avoiding the man's grasping hands. He rushed toward the nearest assistant, and the sudden charge caught the man off guard. One slid between the man's legs before he could recover.

This took him outside the circle the pursuers had created, and he ran for the cover of trees. Frederick shouted in excitement despite himself. If One could get to the trees, he would easily be able to avoid the pursuers for the few remaining minutes. The man One had slid under reacted quickly, though, turning to chase him toward the trees. One was moving at a slower pace than Frederick would've expected.

"He's getting tired," Nineteen whispered, sounding nervous.

The man was closing the distance between himself and One. It looked as if he would reach One mere steps before the tree line. One ran forward, the look of confidence still prominent on his face. There was something else in that look, something that Frederick couldn't quite place. The gap between applicant and pursuer was less than a foot now. The man reached for One right as they approached the trees. One produced a burst of speed and sprinted not between the trees but *up* one of the solid trunks. He took three steps up the trunk before pushing off, lazily flipping through the air and landing lightly on his feet. The assistant tried to skid to a halt but still hit the tree with a solid *thunk*. He crumpled to the ground, clutching his face in pain. One waved an apology and began sprinting across the clearing once more.

"Or not," Nineteen said in awe.

"That idiot," Thirteen whispered as she tried to smother a smile. "He could've gotten away. He's just showing off now."

"I don't think he's showing off," Nineteen said thoughtfully. "I think . . . well, I think he's making a point."

Frederick watched as One moved effortlessly between Arthur and his assistants. He sprinted circles around them, watching them slide by as he stopped on a dime before darting forward again. He countered everything his pursuers tried, always just inches out of reach. But the more Frederick observed, the more he realized that those inches might as well have been miles. The men were more likely to reach out and grasp the sun than to graze the blond boy dancing between them. Frederick looked around and saw astonishment on the faces of the other applicants who had gathered around to watch. He could see that some of them had reached the same conclusion he had. Some of their faces showed despair, and he couldn't blame them. He felt it deep in his stomach. Somewhere he didn't want to acknowledge.

He's a totally different level; you can never be that.

He suspected they were hearing those same words whispered to them.

If Frederick had been one of them, he might've given up right then and there. But One was on his side; this freak of a human was in his corner. Frederick realized that this must have been exactly what One wanted. To deflate all the other applicants and to reassure his friends. Why else would he do it like this? So flashy and on display for them all. It was the only thing that made sense.

Frederick could see the clock above the door from his vantage point in the viewing room. He felt his pulse quicken as it counted ever so slowly toward 0:00. Collectively, the room held its breath as the seconds ticked by. With ten seconds, Arthur and his companions threw themselves at One in one final desperate attempt to best him. One avoided this attempt just as easily as he had avoided the others. He turned on his heels and paused before rolling backward. All five men flew past him, falling heavily to the ground. One came to his feet with three seconds left. He brushed himself off, walking casually to the door as the clock finally reached 0:00. Frederick and his friends erupted in cheers. Thirteen banged on the glass, and One waved cheerfully in their general direction.

Moments later, Seven burst from the trees.

He ran at One with his arms held high, leaping up and down like a soccer player celebrating an especially wonderous goal. One held his hand out for a high five. Seven had different ideas, however, tackling One to the ground and pounding his chest in celebration.

Another figure burst from the trees. A small boy who wore a smile that could've illuminated the darkest room.

Eight did a cartwheel as he ran, closely followed by a somersault. He jumped in circles, his hands also raised above his head. He ran to One and Seven, making some rude gestures at Arthur and his assistants as he passed them. Eight jumped on Seven's back in an attempt to complete the dog pile. Seven stood easily while Eight remained clinging to his back, beaming at the other two boys.

Frederick, Thirteen, and Nineteen tore themselves away from the window and rushed down the stairs to congratulate their friends.

"What even *are* you?" Seven exclaimed as they approached. He wore a smile that took up his entire face, barely leaving room for his eyes and nose.

"That was some *Matrix* stuff man! You flipped *over* a guy! Like over, over! Like you were in front of him and then you were above him and then you were behind him!"

"Yeah, Seven, I was there," One replied with a laugh.

Eight was staring up at One with a look of awe. "I think I'm gonna stick with you going forward, boss," the tiny boy whispered reverently.

One smiled and tousled Eight's hair playfully. "You seem like the kind I'd want to keep close," One said, "although maybe not too close. Don't think I don't know you're the one who keeps stealing my toothbrush."

Eight's face lit up mischievously. "Won't be stealing it anymore there, boss," he chirped. "Nah, can't do that now. I owe you. They were about to find me before Arthur called that last one over to help catch you. Don't think I had a snowball's chance if you didn't distract all of them."

Frederick smiled at the barrage of words and the way Eight bounced on his feet as he talked. The energy inside him seemed nearly bottomless.

Frederick opened his mouth to congratulate all three of them but was cut off as Arthur walked up to their group. He had changed into his glasses, the goggles he had been wearing now held loosely in his right hand.

"That was brilliant, One! Truly brilliant! I haven't had that much fun in years." Arthur produced a grin that somehow rivaled Seven's in size, something Frederick would've sworn was impossible had he not been staring directly at it.

"You really got us good. I haven't seen anything quite like that. And may I just say I *adore* your flair for the dramatic!" The receptionist turned to Seven and Eight. "And you two! Well done as well! Lasting the entire half hour is no small feat. Very impressive, very impressive indeed!"

"Hey, thanks, boss! I've always liked a good ol' game of hide-and-seek," Eight said brightly. Frederick was astonished to see that the boy was somehow now wearing the goggles that had been in Arthur's hand just a moment earlier. How he had managed such a thing without Arthur noticing was beyond Frederick. The receptionist did a double take before laughing uproariously and snatching the goggles back from the smiling boy. It took Arthur almost a full minute to collect himself. Finally, his laughter subsided. He coughed and wiped tears of mirth from his eyes.

"Back upstairs, now, with all of you." His voice sounded like there was still a very real possibility he would break into laughter again at any moment. They quickly obeyed, hiding smiles themselves.

The mood in the viewing area was markedly different. Whispers rippled across the room as Frederick entered with his friends. The other applicants scowled at One, clearly displeased by his spectacle. Frederick was surprised to find them glaring at him as well.

"Why do I get the feeling I'm not very well-liked in this room?" Frederick said out of the side of his mouth to Thirteen.

"Ha! I can't imagine why," she scoffed at him. "You only finished first in the first test, then fourth in the second test, and played a crucial role in almost all of them getting a penalty in the second test."

"But they don't know I had anything to do with that!" Frederick whispered back.

Thirteen raised her eyebrows at him, looking skeptical. He glanced around the room once more and concluded that they certainly did know. They weren't dumb—they had seen him with One. Even if they didn't know One's distraction in the hall was Frederick's idea, they knew it benefited him. That was more than enough for them to resent him.

"Well done to everyone." Arthur interrupted Frederick's thoughts as he addressed the whole room. "You are now halfway through the testing process! I'm very impressed with all of your performances thus far. Obviously, there have been some performances that have been especially impressive and some that have been . . . less so. Still! There is much testing yet to come! I have seen several applicants grow cocky and ruin their chances with the third and fourth tests. I encourage you all to be vigilant. Give your all until the conclusion of the final test!" Arthur turned on his heel and walked out the door as he called to them, "Now, if you would please follow me back to the common room. You all need your rest."

The applicants followed Arthur out of the room and back down the halls to the common room. As they walked, Frederick and One were jostled several times by other applicants. Frederick would've thought nothing of it if it hadn't happened six different times. He sighed wearily and exchanged a chagrined look with his friend.

The applicants entered the common room, and Arthur gestured for them to sit down. Once the clattering of chairs quieted, the man walked over to a television on the wall and switched it on. The screen flicked on to reveal a scoreboard.

"Here you will see your current standings," Arthur said, pointing to the TV. "I will be leaving this up for the remainder of the testing period. We think it most fair for every applicant to know precisely where they stand at any given moment. Applicants are listed in order of least time accrued to most time accrued. The lower your total time is, the better you have performed, obviously. "

Murmurs filled the room as the applicants collectively leaned forward and searched for their names. Frederick was shocked to find his name at the top of the list. He had forgotten that One had been slapped with a ten-minute penalty. They had functionally tied on the second test, and Frederick had narrowly beaten him on the first test. To Frederick's delight, he found that all of his friends were currently in the top ten scores. Seven had vaulted up the scoreboard thanks to his performance in the second test combined with One's stalling tactic.

"Not bad for the new guy!" Seven said loudly, throwing his arm around Frederick and ruffling his hair. Frederick slipped out of his grasp and tried to make himself as small as possible. He was pleased to be doing so well, of course, but more attention was not what he needed at the moment.

"Your testing will continue tomorrow evening," Arthur said, clearly annoyed at Seven's outburst, "so please take this evening and the day tomorrow to rest up for your second physical test."

Frederick and his friends spent the rest of the evening lounging and playing cards. Frederick found it slightly difficult to truly relax with all the dirty looks they were receiving. Thirteen and Seven, however, were loving the attention. They smiled and blew kisses at those glaring at them.

"Don't taunt them," Nineteen whispered urgently. She seemed to be trying to hide behind her playing cards, not wanting to be a part of the exchanges.

"If they're gonna hate us just because we're kicking their collective butt, I'm not gonna hold back," Seven said through an exaggerated smile, and Thirteen nodded in agreement.

Nineteen turned to One, looking for some kind of support, but the boy was clearly struggling to hold back laughter. Frederick felt a smile tug at the corners of his mouth as well.

"I wouldn't worry about it, Nineteen," Thirteen said loudly. "They won't be here to bother us much longer anyway."

The eyes only grew more resentful as the group retreated to their rooms to get ready for bed.

"Well, that's enough for me. Seems like we should all head to bed, eh?" One said as he stood from the table. "Who knows what tomorrow has in store."

Frederick almost missed the subtle wink One sent his way. He glanced at Nineteen, who gave him the smallest of nods.

Tomorrow, they would have answers.

Chapter 8

Frederick lay in bed fully dressed, waiting patiently for his door to open. He and One hadn't had an opportunity to speak in private. Their stunt in the second test had drawn attention—lots of attention. It seemed that wherever Frederick and One moved, eyes followed them, so they had eventually given up. One had whispered a single word to Frederick.

"Tonight."

So Frederick waited.

It took One longer to come than he had expected. Almost a full hour passed before the hinges squeaked softly and the bedroom door slid open. One slipped into the room and shut it behind him. Frederick rose quietly and walked over to meet him as Nineteen did the same.

"Sorry I wasn't here sooner," One said in a low tone. "I had to wait for my roommates to fall asleep. I didn't want to have to try to explain everything anyway. Even if I could have, I can't imagine it would've done us any good. I can't say I trust any of them."

"Seems smart. Maybe we can trust Eight eventually, but it's still a bit too soon," Frederick said.

"Agreed." One nodded, then turned to survey the two snoring forms in the room. "I don't suppose either of you want to volunteer to wake up Thing 1 and Thing 2?"

Frederick and Nineteen shook their heads. One sighed and made his way over to Thirteen's bed. He grabbed her shoulder and gave her a soft shake.

"Thirteen, it's One. Wake up."

The lump beneath the sheets continued snoring, oblivious. He shook her harder and called her name a bit louder. Still nothing.

One closed his eyes in frustration, then looked over to Frederick and Nineteen.

"I think they're both technically dead while they are sleeping."

Nineteen took a deep breath and walked over, motioning for One to step aside. He did so, performing a mock bow as he moved out of the way. She crouched beside Thirteen's bed and said in a quiet but firm voice, "Thirteen! They're almost out of breakfast!"

Thirteen's eyes shot open, and she bolted upright.

"Over my dead body," she mumbled, and stumbled out of bed, nearly tripping over the tangle of sheets and blanket. She blinked and squinted against the darkness. "The hell are you doing here, One?"

"Not serving you breakfast," he said through a smile.

Thirteen turned to Nineteen with betrayal written plainly across her face. "Tell me you didn't lie about there being breakfast."

Nineteen smiled apologetically, causing Thirteen to shake her head in disgust. "You better have a good reason for both waking me up in the middle of the night and lying about the most important meal of the day."

"We do," One promised. "We'll explain everything once we wake up Seven."

Thirteen rolled her eyes and walked over to the snoring boy. Without breaking stride, she slapped him firmly on the side of the head. He bolted upright, clutching the side of his head in pain.

"What the—" he stammered in confusion. "Why the hell did you hit me?"

"There was a spider on your head. It's gone now." Thirteen yawned.

Seven leaped out of bed and began batting at his clothes as if the spider were still crawling on him.

"I said it was gone, Blockhead. No need to blow a fuse."

"Don't tell me wha—" Seven cut himself off and stared at One in confusion. "What are you doing in our room in the middle of the night?"

"I was chasing the spider," One said with a straight face. "But while I'm here, Nineteen, Twenty, and I have some things to share with you."

"So you snuck out," Seven said slowly.

"Without us," Thirteen interjected.

"And found a greenhouse," Seven continued, "almost got caught by some scientists, stole a flower, found the accounting office and a door that gave off weird vibes."

"Yep, that just about covers it," One said lightly.

Seven nodded as if he had received a bit of news he had been expecting. "It's good for me to have official confirmation that you all are completely and totally out of your minds."

"So nice to not have to wonder anymore," Thirteen agreed.

"You'll see," One said simply.

"I'm going back to bed," Thirteen said with another yawn. "I'm sure it's all very interesting, but I don't see how it helps us. Not to mention, we have another test tomorrow, and I'd like to keep my streak of not sucking as long as possible." She turned to Seven. "You don't have a streak to worry about, so I think you should go with them."

Seven threw a pillow at Thirteen without looking at her. "Yeah, I think I'm good here. Next time, don't wake me up for your midnight insanity trips, okay?"

He crawled back beneath the covers and curled into a ball. Thirteen moved toward her bed, clearly intent on doing the same.

"Wait!" Nineteen whispered with an intensity Frederick wasn't expecting. The small girl turned to Frederick. "Where is it?"

He pointed wordlessly to the trunk at the foot of his bed. Nineteen hurried over to it, threw open the lid, and carefully removed the flower from its hiding place within. She cupped it in her hands and carried it almost reverently to Thirteen. She held it out, waiting for the other girl to take the offering.

Thirteen stared at the flower, her brow furrowed in uncertainty and confusion. Frederick glanced over his shoulder and saw Seven peeking out from his blankets, closely watching the interaction.

"It's very pretty, Nineteen," Thirteen said. Frederick saw something flicker in Thirteen's eyes as she spoke.

"Smell it."

"Nineteen, I—"

"Smell. It." Her voice didn't waver.

Thirteen reached an unsure hand out and carefully lifted the flower to her nose. She closed her eyes and breathed deeply, holding in the breath for several long seconds before letting out a slow exhale. Without opening her eyes, she repeated the process three more times. The rest of the applicants waited silently for her reaction.

"Well?" Seven sat up in his bed. "You gonna stand there doing breathing exercises all night, or are you gonna say something?"

Thirteen walked over to him without answering and held out the flower.

Seven took it cautiously and sniffed it the way one might sniff a sock to see if it was dirty. Frederick saw the expression of distrust melt from the stocky boy's face. He saw the flicker in his eyes now as well. The hint of a memory. A promise to be whole.

"Alright, fine," Seven sighed. "Let's go."

They crept down the halls, retracing their steps from the previous night. One led the way, but the path was burned into Frederick's mind, and he was certain it was in Nineteen's as well. The trip didn't take as long as it had the night before. They still moved with the same caution they had previously, but they shed the uncertainty. There were no obstacles, no patrolling security guards, nor wandering scientists. In just a few short minutes, they reached the entrance. Frederick's heart pounded with excitement as he stood in the hallway. One turned and gave them a silent nod and pushed open the door.

"Where are we?" Nineteen asked in a small voice.

"What do you mean?" Seven hissed. "I thought you'd been here before!"

Frederick blinked in confusion. Before him stood a room similar to the one they had been in previously—with one marked difference.

It was overgrown. Before, it had been neat and organized, with rows of perfectly arranged plants lining the walls with scientific precision. Now, the space felt more like a jungle than a room. Bushes spilled out over the pots they grew in, some with roots poking through cracks in the bottom. Flowers grew together and formed natural bouquets. The saplings that had lined one of the walls now stood several feet high, some of their leaves nearly brushing the ceiling. As a result of the room's increased plant life, the smell was significantly stronger than the last time they had entered. Frederick breathed deeply and again felt the itch in his brain.

The discomfort of almost remembering.

The general setup was identical. The flowers were back near the closet door; the shrubs were on the opposite wall, etc. If Frederick hadn't known any better, he would have thought he had entered the same room, just several months in the future.

"It's almost the same," One said. "The plants are just bigger. Like, a lot bigger."

"So we went into the wrong room?" Thirteen turned and was about to walk back through the door they had come through.

"No." Nineteen shook her head. "It isn't almost the same; it's exactly the same. This is the room. I'm certain of it."

"So, what, they replaced all the plants with bigger ones?" Seven asked. "Why?"

An idea forced its way into Frederick's head. He walked over to the row of flowers and immediately found exactly what he was looking for.

There was a small gap in the row.

One of the flowers was missing.

"They would've replaced the whole row," Frederick said quietly.

"What?" Seven's tone was growing increasingly frustrated.

"It's the same room," Frederick said, "and the same plants."

"How is that possible?" One asked, though Frederick could tell he knew it was true.

"I have no idea. But look," he said, pointing to the gap in the row of flowers.

They stood in stunned silence. Slowly, they walked around, inspecting the plants. Seven and Thirteen moved about the room in the same amazed fashion One, Nineteen, and Frederick all had when they had first entered. Nineteen moved about with a careful precision. After several minutes, she looked at Frederick and One and nodded.

"I agree. It's the same room. Same plants."

"How is that possible?" Frederick asked. He was surprised to hear a hint of panic in his own voice. Whatever was happening felt distinctly unnatural, and he was trying not to let that bother him as much as it did.

Nineteen shook her head in disbelief.

"It's not. It's just not," she said, her voice trailing off to almost a whisper.

"We can worry about it later," One said, setting his jaw and making his way to the door that led to the accounting office. "We came here for something. And it wasn't this."

Frederick felt a similar resolve grow within. A small part of him became aware that it wasn't actually a growing of resolve, it was a revealing of resolve.

He hadn't been without the determination since he had first felt whatever it was emanating from that door. It had been covered loosely, or perhaps half-heartedly brushed beneath the rug, but nothing more than that. He was only half a step behind One as he pushed through the door.

The office was in a near-identical state of disarray to when they had entered it previously. However, Frederick saw telltale signs of fresh use. A new pile of papers here, a missing pile there, as well as several new pieces of trash strewn across the room. There was also a mug of coffee on the desk nearest to them. Frederick stared at it—something about it caught his attention, but his brain was lagging behind.

Finally, it clicked. The mug was steaming.

"One!" The word had barely left Frederick's mouth before one of the other doors leading into the office opened. A tall man in a sweater vest entered, whistling some vaguely familiar tune in a distracted manner. His nose was buried deep in a stack of papers, so much so that he didn't notice them at first.

Time stood still.

One, Frederick, Seven, Thirteen, and Nineteen all froze, barely daring to breathe. The man glanced up from his papers, and the whistle slowly died on his lips as he saw the five teenagers standing awkwardly in his office. He opened his mouth to speak, but the question died on his lips.

Instead, he reached for a telephone sitting on the desk closest to him.

One leapt into action. He barreled past the man, sending him, the telephone, and his stack of papers flying. The man tumbled to the ground with a cry of surprise. One didn't hesitate, running directly at what he had come for.

He didn't try the handle. Frederick hadn't expected him to. Instead, One threw his shoulder into the wooden door. There was a loud crunch as it burst open. One tumbled through the opening, and Frederick lost him in the darkness of the room beyond.

When the man saw One's destination, he let out another cry, this time in panic. He rushed over to the nearest desk and ripped the phone off the receiver. Frederick grabbed the arms of his two nearest friends, Thirteen and Nineteen, and dragged them through the gaping doorway. Seven growled in annoyance and followed, ripping the power cord out of the man's phone as he did so.

Frederick turned and shut the door behind them as best he could, plunging the room into a near-perfect darkness. He could hear the man scrambling around in the office outside. Then the noise faded, and Frederick heard his words rumbling into the telephone, though Frederick couldn't make out what he was saying.

"One?" Frederick called cautiously into the darkness.

"I'm here," he answered. "Can't find the light switch. Don't suppose any of you have a flashlight or cell phone?"

"Where would we get either of those?" Seven ground his teeth together. "They didn't let us bring our phones in, and I doubt any of us smuggled a flashlight into the rehab facility 'just in case.'"

"So you're telling me we can't even see what we're gonna get kicked out for?" Thirteen said.

Frederick barely heard her. The same feeling he had experienced from the door the first time he had seen it was once again pounding inside of him, though now it was ten times stronger. His hands shook with the intensity of it.

He walked farther into the darkness of the room, moving as quickly as he dared, his hands stretched out in front of him. With every step, the unidentifiable feeling within him grew. At this rate, it would consume him, but he didn't care.

His outstretched hands ran onto something—a smooth surface. At first, he assumed it was the back wall of the room, but there was a coolness to the touch that gave him pause.

"Glass," he whispered.

"What?" Nineteen called, her voice filled with anxiety. "Twenty, did you find something?"

"Yeah," he answered, only half paying attention. "I think there's a glass wall back here—maybe some kind of window."

Frederick felt someone move up next to him in the darkness and knew instinctively it was One.

"Where are we?"

"I have no clue."

Frederick detected the slightest of colors in the darkness. At first, he wrote it off as a trick played by his eyes. Perhaps a result of staring into the darkness for too long. But it slowly grew clearer, so much so that Frederick was certain it was no trick. Soon, there were two glowing red orbs floating in the darkness before him. His breath caught.

"From the storage room," he heard One breathe.

The two orbs floated on the other side of the glass, no more than twenty feet away. They began slowly approaching Frederick and One, swaying back and forth as they moved. In a matter of seconds, the orbs were merely feet from the glass, and Frederick knew what he was going to see moments before he saw it.

The reflection of the glow off the glass was just enough to illuminate what had approached them. Frederick could make out two eyes, and a vicious jaw full of teeth.

Something in him began screaming, something primal that he had only experienced in his most terrible of nightmares—and once, in a storage room. He stumbled away from the glass and back toward the door, scrambling wildly to get out of the room and away from the monster he had just seen.

When he reached the door, he found Seven holding it shut. There was someone else banging on the door trying to get in, and Seven had been doing all he could to keep them out. Frederick shoved his friend out of the way and barreled through.

He burst back into the office, knocking two security guards to the ground. Frederick was only vaguely aware of their shouts of protest and of his friends following him as he ran out of the office, through the greenhouse, and into the hallway.

Frederick didn't think as he ran. His legs pumped with a desperate power, and the hallway passed him in a blur. His mind went nearly entirely blank. There was nothing echoing inside his head except a voice screaming for him to get away. There were no thoughts of the repercussions of their actions that night. No thought of expulsion, of punishments, of having to tell his family he had actually been testing quite well until he had decided to start sneaking out. Gone too was the urge to fight, which had previously consumed him.

There was only escape.

Frederick's toe caught on something, and it sent him sprawling. He hit the ground hard, barely managing to brace for the impact. His head whipped sideways, cracking against the floor. His vision swam, and tiny pinpricks of light appeared. A groan escaped his lips as he rolled over on his back and sat up groggily.

Seven rounded the corner a few seconds later at a breakneck pace.

"Not the time to be resting, Two-Oh!" he said. Without slowing down, Seven stooped to grab Frederick by the arm and yanked him to his feet and into a run. The rest of the group rounded the corner at that moment, with One bringing up the rear. The sounds of shouting and pounding footsteps followed behind him.

"Nice of you to wait up for us!" Thirteen shouted as she caught up to Seven and Frederick.

The spill had done something of a reset for Frederick's brain. The feeling of terror at what he had seen in that dark room still lurked somewhere in his chest, but it wasn't so overwhelming that he couldn't think of anything else. He matched Seven's pace, though he had to fight the urge to sprint ahead as he had before.

"What are we doing?" Nineteen asked, her voice caught.

"Running away," Seven said. "I thought that was pretty obvious!"

"But why?" Tears were running down her face. "We'll only get in more trouble!"

"There's a chance they didn't see our faces," One said calmly. "If they catch us, we are for sure getting kicked out. This gives us a chance." He grimaced. "Even if it's a tiny one."

That ended the conversation. The sound of their breathing and feet slapping the ground filled the hallways. The voices behind them were beginning to fade. They were nearing the common room, and Frederick began to let himself hope they would reach it without being caught.

The hallway ended abruptly ahead of them. It formed a sort of T intersection. All they had to do was take the right turn at that intersection and the next left and they would be back. Frederick slowed in anticipation of making the turn.

Suddenly, a security guard ran around the corner. He skidded to a halt at the sight of Frederick and his companions. The guard was a massive man, close to seven feet tall, with bulging muscles barely contained by a too-small uniform.

He lunged at Frederick, trying to grab him by the shoulders. Frederick yelped and dropped into a slide, letting his momentum carry him between the giant's legs. The guard grunted and swiped down at Frederick. His fingers grazed his collar but found no purchase. The guard paused for a moment, clearly unsure whether to pursue Frederick or turn his attention to the rest of the group. Seven took advantage of the man's hesitation. He threw himself at him, knocking them both to the ground. It would've been a nearly impossible maneuver if the guard hadn't already been off balance from swiping at Frederick, not to mention being completely caught off guard by the gambit.

Seven rolled to his feet and was running again before Frederick had popped up from his slide. One, Thirteen, and Nineteen leapt over the fallen man without hesitating. Frederick got to his feet and turned down the hall to his right, only to see three more massive security guards charging at them.

Turning, he sprinted down the other hallway for all he was worth. His friends followed his lead. They followed closely as he bolted away from the guards. He started taking turns at random, with no plan other than to try to lose their pursuers. Once they had accomplished that, they could try to come up with something more concrete.

The hallways became shorter, with more turns available than before. They branched out like a maze, and he chose his route completely at random. They managed to gain some distance, and Frederick heard the footsteps chasing them slowly fade until they disappeared. He ran for almost another minute, making sure they had lost their pursuers.

Rounding another corner, he was stopped dead in his tracks.

Seven cursed loudly as he had to lunge to the side to avoid barreling into Frederick's back.

"What's your problem, man?" he spat in annoyance.

Frederick wasn't listening. He stared transfixed at the door before him. Seven finally caught sight of it, and his jaw dropped. Frederick became vaguely aware that the rest of his friends had gathered around him and were studying the door as well.

It was a massive, metal, circular door, like you would see in a bank vault. It was large enough that three of them could've walked through it shoulder to shoulder with no trouble.

"Why the hell is there a vault in the middle of a random hallway?" Thirteen questioned, her voice sounding to Frederick like it was miles away. He felt the same feeling as before.

A desire to enter. A *need*.

It was incredibly similar to seeing the door in the office, but at the same time, entirely different. Where before it had been an anger, a rage, a desire to fight, now it was a necessity. He felt like he had been walking through the desert his entire life and behind this door was the only cup of water left in the whole world.

And he would do anything to get it.

He felt his legs carrying him toward the door on their own accord. He, of course, did not object. His hand reached out and touched the cool metal. His fingertips rested lightly on the door, and he pushed ever so softly, half expecting it to swing open.

It did not.

Firm hands gripped his arms, and he was pulled from his trance. Slowly, his mind returned to reality, and he could hear his friends again.

"This is a really bad time for you to go completely mental, Two-Oh!" Seven hissed, hauling Frederick away from the door. A part of Frederick wanted to fight against his friend, to shove him to the ground and study the door, find a way in. Thankfully, that part of him was small enough that Frederick was able to squash it.

He let himself be dragged away.

Ripping his eyes from the door, Frederick found One standing in the same semi-trance that Frederick had been in. It took both Thirteen and Nineteen to drag One far enough away from the door that he regained his senses. Frederick once again heard pounding feet in the distance. The security guards were catching up to them again.

Thirteen took the lead, waiting to make sure One and Frederick were following before taking off down the hall. Frederick followed closely, trying to think of anything other than what he had just experienced. He bit his cheek hard anytime the door popped into his mind, nearly drawing blood. Staring at the back of Thirteen's head, he tried to focus only on keeping up. He knew that if his mind wandered back down the hall, it would only be a matter of time before his body followed, whether he liked it or not.

In a feat that was no less than extraordinary, Thirteen got them back to the common room in less than five minutes. Frederick had assumed there would be guards posted outside the door to catch them on their return. After all, where else would they go? But by some massive stroke of luck, the door was left unattended.

They slipped into the room as quickly and as quietly as they could. Frederick almost assumed that the guards would be waiting inside the common room so that they could corner the troublemaking applicants, cutting off all escape. But the common room was empty too.

"We'll talk tomorrow," One said simply and hurried to his room without any further comment.

Frederick, Seven, Thirteen, and Nineteen did the same. Frederick once again half expected an ambush upon entry into their room, but none came. They trudged to their beds, exhausted, not even bothering to turn on the lights. Frederick half walked, half felt his way to his mattress. He collapsed onto it, the exhaustion finally catching up to him and overwhelming all the other things coursing through his veins. There was a chorus of mumbled goodnights, and Frederick pulled the cover up to his chin.

Sleep didn't come.

Anxiety began to build inside Frederick. It didn't overpower his exhaustion; it worked with it. He was too tired to try to talk himself down, too tired to be an optimist, too tired to do anything but take every punch his anxiety threw on the chin and hope the bell would ring before he was knocked out. His chest tightened, and his heart pounded. He felt the sweat soaking through his clothes and into the bed sheets. A pressure built behind his eyes, and he felt like his head might burst. Tears were squeezing their way out of his clenched eyelids. He turned to face away from his now-sleeping companions. If a sob forced its way out of him, he wanted to do everything he could to not disturb his friends.

Frederick tried to focus on nothing but breathing—a nearly impossible task, but the only thing he knew to do.

In. Hold. Out.

In. Hold. Out.

Frederick felt himself calm down. The effect was almost immediate, like a switch had been flipped inside his head. He was now just a normal teenage boy who was exhausted, without a care in the world beyond that. Frederick was startled, pleased, and more than a little disconcerted. He hadn't experienced anything so sudden since his interview.

Frederick breathed in deeply, now registering what should've been so obvious. There was a strong smell filling his nostrils, coming from beside his bed. His heart began pounding again.

He strained to see his nightstand in the dark, but there was simply not enough light in the room. He placed his hand over the small reading light attached to the side of his bed to keep it from waking his friends and flipped it on. The light illuminated the nightstand. All the air rushed out of Frederick's lungs.

On the nightstand was a small black pot, and inside was Frederick's flower.

Frederick's mind whirred as it tried to understand what his eyes saw. He debated waking up his roommates but decided against it. It had been a very long night, and they needed to rest for the third test. Besides, he saw little good it would bring besides causing them to worry further. This was a burden he would have to carry alone.

He stared at the flower in its small black pot until sleep blessedly took him.

Chapter 9

Frederick woke coughing. He sat up, trying desperately to fill his lungs. Unfortunately, this only made him cough harder, and soon his entire body shook from the effort. It felt like he would never breathe again.

His chest ached as he continued hacking. He looked around the room, desperate for someone to assist him. When he looked to his companions' beds, he found he couldn't see more than a few feet in front of him. Frederick realized with terror that the entire room was filled with smoke. It swirled wildly, blown by a strong wind, which had a wildly disorienting effect on him. He reached for a glass of water he had left on his bedside table the night before and poured its contents onto an extra shirt by his bed, then tied the shirt like a bandana over his mouth and nose. This eased the coughing to a tolerable level, and Frederick moved in the general direction of Seven's bed.

Seven sat there coughing as violently as Frederick had been. Frederick assumed the only reason he hadn't heard it was because hearing anything over the sounds of his own hacking had been almost impossible. He found another shirt and wet it in the same way, holding it over the other boy's mouth until his coughing subsided.

"Fire!" Frederick shouted, his voice muffled by the wet fabric he held over his mouth.

"No sh—" Seven's response was cut short by another bout of coughing. Seven waved him away as he struggled to control his wheezing. The stocky boy pointed frantically in the direction of Nineteen's bed, and Frederick nodded, moving toward it while Seven headed toward Thirteen's.

Nineteen already had a shirt over her mouth when Frederick reached her. She sat holding her knees close to her chest; he could see her shaking, even through the gloom of the smoke.

"We have to go! Now!" he shouted.

The small girl shook her head before burying it in her knees. Frederick grabbed her and began dragging her to the door. There was a time and place for comforting a frightened friend, and the middle of a fire didn't seem to be it. Nineteen soon began to walk under her own power, and they pushed through the swirling smoke together. When they reached the door, Thirteen and Seven were waiting for them.

"What the hell is happening?" Thirteen yelled. "Why does it feel like there's a tornado in here?"

"No clue!" Frederick shouted back. "You know where the fire is?"

"No, but we need to get out of here. Now! If we don't hurry, we're toast."

She gestured to the door, and Frederick now saw it was blocked by a large beam that had fallen through the ceiling. It was sitting at an angle, crossing the door diagonally, with one end on the ground and the other still in the ceiling. The door to the room opened inward, so there was no way they would be able to get out without moving it. Frederick eyed it uncertainly.

"If we move that, is the whole ceiling gonna cave in?"

"Do I look like an architect to you?" Seven shouted in frustration. "Maybe it will, maybe it won't! What I do know is if we don't move it, we are incredibly dead. So unless you have a better idea . . ."

The stocky boy began yanking on the beam with all his might. Frederick and the girls hurried to join him. They all pulled frantically to no avail. They even tried coordinating their heaves, with Seven counting down from three. Frederick could tell they were generating more force, but they were obviously making no progress.

"Stop! We need to think about this," he shouted. "Brute force obviously isn't going to work."

"Oh yeah, great!" Thirteen chimed in. "Let's all just sit around and put our thinking caps on! Maybe I'll make some tea. Would you like cookies with that?"

Frederick flinched—not at the sharpness of her words but at the panic that radiated from them. She had a point: there wasn't time to fully assess the situation, but that didn't mean he was wrong. They needed to try something else. If they couldn't find a way to move the beam, they were all dead, and he was *not* letting that happen. Nobody was dying on his watch. Time slowed as Frederick closed his eyes and focused on finding a solution. Mere moments later, they snapped open, and he grabbed Seven by the arm, dragging him toward the nearest bed.

"What the hell are you doing?"

"Just help me!" Frederick yelled, and Seven followed reluctantly.

They reached the bed, where Frederick grabbed onto the thick board that ran the length of it. He began pulling on it, trying to rip it free. Realization dawned on Seven's face, and he joined, pulling with all of his might. The board gave way with a loud crunching sound, but luckily, it was still mostly intact. Frederick rushed back to the door and wedged the board in between the door-frame and the beam, using it as a lever.

He squeezed between the wall and the board, and Seven joined him. The boys pushed, groaning with effort, but the beam still refused to budge, though Frederick could've sworn it moved a couple of centimeters. Thirteen grabbed Nineteen, and they worked their way between the board and the wall as well. The four of them pushed with all of their might. There was a loud scraping noise as the beam moved ever so slightly.

"It's working! Just keep going!" Frederick yelled.

Then the beam stopped. No matter how much they pushed, it refused to move. The others collapsed to the ground one by one, exhausted by the effort they'd expended, until Frederick was the only one left behind the board.

"We need to find another way out!" Nineteen shouted, her voice shrill with fear.

"There is no other way!" Frederick screamed, then whispered to himself, "There is no other way out."

He shook with uncontrollable rage. After all this, he was going to die in a fire? He had finally been given hope, a way to get better. And friends! He had friends, people who understood what he went through. People who didn't look at him like he was broken or made of glass.

"No!"

An angry scream ripped from somewhere deep in Frederick's stomach. He could feel it in every cell of his body. Years of pent-up frustration and anger were released in one defiant screech.

He wouldn't die. Not here. Not now.

And neither would his friends.

Frederick pushed with a strength that simply should not have been possible, and the beam gave way. It crashed to the ground, narrowly missing his friends, who now stood staring at him with slack faces.

"Move!" Frederick bellowed at them.

Seven was the first to reach the now-unobstructed door. He tried the handle.

Nothing. It turned, but the door didn't open when he pulled on it. He gripped the handle and threw himself backward to no avail.

"It's stuck!" he shouted at them. "Twenty, get over here!"

Frederick joined him at the door and began pulling on the handle as well. It was difficult to generate much power, with both boys having to position themselves so they could each get a grip. After a few tries, they found a method of orienting themselves that was somewhat effective.

As they continued to pull, Frederick could feel the door moving fractionally each time they yanked at it. Finally, it gave way to their efforts. The boys tumbled backward, landing awkwardly, sprawled on top of one another. The girls helped them up, and all four darted through the opening. Seven slammed the door shut behind them.

The thing that most disturbed Frederick was the stillness of the room. This space was also filled with smoke but totally devoid of the odd airflow their bedroom had exhibited. Besides the thick haze, the room seemed fairly normal. There were no signs of fire or general disarray. He scanned around for any signs of life and found none.

"We gotta check the other rooms!" Thirteen shouted. They nodded, and each bolted for a room. Frederick pushed open a door and found the room on the other side to be totally empty. He checked quickly under the covers but found nothing. There was no sign of any of the other applicants. He hurried back out and met up with the others.

"Anything?" he asked.

"Not a damn thing!" Seven shouted back. Thirteen and Nineteen both shook their heads.

"It's like they all vanished!" Nineteen's small voice was barely discernible through the shirt she held over her face.

"Maybe they already got out! Either way, that's what we need to do. Nothing we can do for anyone else if we choke to death on this smoke," Thirteen said.

They made their way over to the main door. As they walked, Frederick felt something tightening in his stomach. Something he hadn't felt since he had arrived at Kinth, except for when he'd had his night terror. He felt his hands start to shake, and his breathing became labored. He tried to convince himself that it was because of the smoke, but he knew it had nothing to do with that. He was going to have a panic attack, and it was going to happen soon.

The air began to catch in his throat. It felt thick, like trying to inhale molasses. He stumbled, and Seven tried to catch him, though his grip was weak—he was unable to do more than slow Frederick's fall.

Frederick dropped to the floor, and a sound like roaring waters filled his ears. He felt like he was standing beneath a massive waterfall, slowly being crushed beneath its fury. He curled up into a ball and began screaming. These weren't screams for help. He was simply screaming. The desperate shouts tore at his throat, and he tasted blood as his screams grew ragged. Hands grasped at his shoulders, and he batted them away viciously.

Gone were all thoughts about escaping the room.

Gone were all notions of saving the others.

All that was left was the primal fear that now consumed him. He couldn't remember where he was. Where he was going. What he was doing. It all faded away before the immensity of his fear. There was an extreme pain in his chest; tears ran down his face as he clutched at it, trying with all his might to simply take another breath.

Frederick lay with his eyes squeezed shut for what felt like an eternity. The pain in his chest had become almost unbearable. He felt himself slipping deeper and deeper into the pain and into the darkness. He didn't care what happened next, as long as this was over. Anything was better than the world he found himself in. Each breath became more difficult to take. He gulped hopelessly at the air, praying for just a little bit of oxygen to satisfy his starving lungs.

None came.

He knew in that moment, he was absolutely certain, it would never come. But still, he tried because there was nothing else he could do. He struggled and struggled until finally, mercifully, he felt himself losing consciousness.

Frederick awoke with a start. His eyes darted around his room as he tried to locate the exits.

The fire. I have to get out! I have to get everyone out!

"Chill out, Two-Oh. We're fine. No fires here," Seven said flatly.

Frederick felt his head clear and his panic fade. He was lying in a bed located in what appeared to be some kind of hospital room. There were three other beds in the room, each occupied by one of his friends.

"Is everyone okay?" Frederick croaked. His throat felt as if it was filled with sand.

"Everyone is fine. Rest of the applicants are too. Someone had to drag us out. Once you went down, the rest of us kind of lost it too," Seven said, his voice morose as he stared straight up at the ceiling above his bed. "Drink some water. You sound like death," he continued, still refusing to meet Frederick's eyes.

Frederick turned to a small table by his bed and found a cup next to a large pitcher of water. He poured some into the cup and gulped at it greedily. The remnants of smoke were washed away.

Looking around the room, he saw that Thirteen was still sleeping. Her breathing was steady, and her slumber seemed to be a deep one. When he looked at Nineteen's bed, he was startled to find her eyes wide open. The small girl was staring at the ceiling as well, unblinking.

"Hey Nineteen, you okay?" he asked.

There was no response.

"She was awake before me," Seven said in the same flat tone as before. "Hasn't said a word. Think something might've snapped."

Frederick shot Seven a sharp glare. If the other boy noticed it, he gave no indication.

"What about you? Are you okay? You seem extremely . . . not."

Seven scoffed loudly before tearing his eyes from the ceiling and looking Frederick square in his pupils. Seven's eyes were red and puffy—he had clearly been crying. Frederick felt a chill run down his spine.

"What's going on? What happened? I thought everyone was okay?" Frederick's pulse began a panicked rhythm.

"Everyone else is okay. We are screwed though. Totally and entirely."

"What are you talking abo—"

"Look, I'll tell you when Thirteen is awake," Seven said, cutting him off.

Seven turned his eyes back to the ceiling, clearly indicating that the conversation was over, at least for now.

Frederick sighed and stared at the ceiling himself, doing his best to remember anything that had happened after he collapsed. It was pointless. Whatever had happened, whoever had saved them, it was all lost to him.

He instead turned his focus to the moments before his collapse. He had experienced panic attacks before, of course, but this was an entirely different beast. The oddest thing was that the attack was totally unrelated to the fire. He had been taking that in stride, as much as one could take such a thing in stride. In fact, he had almost felt good at points. But something had changed, and he had no clue what it was. That scared him more than any fire ever could.

Frederick continued thinking for the better part of an hour before Thirteen groaned loudly and sat up, putting a hand to her head.

"I really didn't think dying would give me such a nasty headache," she muttered.

"You aren't dead yet," Frederick said, smiling in spite of himself. "In fact, none of us are."

"What happened?" she asked as she poured herself a cup of water.

"I have no clue. Seven knows something but wouldn't tell me until you woke up. Guess he didn't want to tell it twice."

"I don't want to tell it once," Seven said.

Thirteen noticed Nineteen's state and looked sharply at Frederick. He shrugged and shook his head.

"Hey, Nineteen, you okay?" Thirteen said, standing unsteadily from her bed and walking over to Nineteen's. She reached for the smaller girl's hand and held it. Nineteen immediately burst into tears, throwing her arms around Thirteen and sobbing into her shirt.

"I can't go back!" Her words, though muffled by tears and Thirteen, made Frederick's stomach turn.

Nineteen cried for several minutes as Thirteen whispered comforting words to her. Once she calmed down, Thirteen crawled into bed beside her and put an arm around the still-trembling girl.

"How bad was the damage to the building?" Thirteen asked, turning to the boys.

"Oh, the building is just fine. Just some very minor smoke damage," Seven said, shaking his head in anger.

"Do we know if they're delaying the third test?" Thirteen continued. "Surely they can't expect us to go from almost dying to a physical test in the same day, right?"

"I wouldn't worry about prepping for the third test, Jinx," Seven said, his voice still unsteady.

"Will you just tell them already?" shouted Nineteen. Seven, Thirteen, and Frederick all jumped at her sudden outburst. "I know you're angry, but you don't need to take it out on them!"

Seven lifted a weary hand to his face and rubbed his eyes. "You're right, Nineteen. I'm sorry."

The girl said nothing, just nodded for him to continue. With a heavy sigh, Seven did so.

"We don't need to worry about the third test because we already took it."

Frederick and Thirteen looked at him in confusion, and then it dawned on them.

"The fire?"

"Yep."

Frederick was unsure if he wanted to laugh or cry.

"As you might imagine, our performance was less than impressive."

"How are we scored?" Frederick asked, the panic he felt now bleeding into his voice.

"It was timed to see how fast we could get out. Somehow, they isolated each room and tested us in groups of four."

"We aren't disqualified," Seven said, answering the question before Frederick could ask it. "Although we might as well be. We all defaulted to the time cap, which was two hours."

"Two hours?" Frederick spluttered.

"Do you know how the rest of the groups did? Did any of them finish before the two hours were up?" Thirteen asked, panic rising in her voice.

"As a matter of fact, I do. Every one of them finished before the two-hour deadline. In fact, I believe the worst time was just over an hour."

They sat in a stunned silence as the words fell heavily upon the floor.

"So—"

"Yes. Every single applicant picked up at least an hour on us."

Silent tears began sliding down Nineteen's face, and Thirteen's mouth hung open in disbelief.

"How could we possibly make up an hour of time on one test?" Frederick was nearly shouting.

"It's technically possible," Seven answered evenly. "Arthur explained it all to me. The thing is, it's possible for one of us to do it, maybe two. But there's no way we could all do it."

"What do you mean?"

"What I mean, Two-Oh, is that the four of us are in dead last. By a lot. I'm sure one or two of the others will bomb this last test, and that might open the door for a couple of us to sneak in. But there simply aren't enough reachable slots for us all to make it—it's mathematically impossible."

A stunned silence forced its way between them, pushing them away from one another.

"What the hell is this place?" Frederick's outburst surprised even himself. He stood quickly from his bed and paced the length of the room like a caged animal. "They can't just play with us like this! A fire? Are you kidding me? What kind of test is that? We could've died! Even if there was no fire! Smoke inhalation has killed plenty of people!"

"We take measures to ensure such things do not occur, Twenty. I can assure you of that."

Frederick froze in his tracks, slowly turning to the door. Dr. Gray stood there, his hulking frame nearly filling the entire doorway. He leaned against it casually, a smile peeking out from behind his gray beard.

"You were never in any real danger, we made sure of that. But, we needed it to feel as real as possible. You understand, I'm sure."

"I most certainly do not understand," Seven said, a dangerous level of disrespect emanating from his voice.

"Well, it is my job to understand. Not yours." The smile remained on the doctor's face, but there was now a dangerous look in his eyes. It was gone in a flash, replaced with a much friendlier one.

"I won't keep you long. I'm told Arthur explained your current situation to Seven, who I assume has relayed all pertinent information?" He looked at Seven and waited for his nod of confirmation. "Very good. I am simply here to ensure none of you give up. You all showed such promise, and I would hate for one bad test to ruin that."

Frederick bit his tongue to keep from making a snide remark. Wasn't it this man's fault that their fate was being decided by one bad test? Didn't he have the power to shape the process however he wanted? Frederick closed his eyes and did his best to swallow the anger he was feeling toward the doctor. When he opened his eyes he found Dr. Gray staring at him, his smile broader now. The expression caught him off guard. He was taken aback by the mirth painted on the doctor's face. It had an extremely unsettling effect. The man winked at Frederick and turned to go, but paused before he was all the way out the door.

"One more thing," he called over his shoulder. "If I get the sense that any of you are failing on purpose to give your friends a better chance to pass, I will be forced to send all four of you home immediately. I'm sure none of you would have such disregard for what we are doing here, but I want to make myself very clear."

Frederick flinched at the words. He noticed Thirteen wince as well.

"I will not have the integrity of my test compromised. Is that understood?"

"Yes, sir." Frederick was ashamed at the way his voice cracked as he answered.

"Good. Take care and rest up. Tomorrow is a very big day."

The doctor turned to leave, then paused again. "Oh, I almost forgot. Let's not take any more nighttime expeditions, shall we? Not a word to each other or anyone else about it, hm? You forget about it, and I will too." The doctor's smile was amicable, but there was a hardness in his eyes.

Frederick's stomach plummeted. Of course they would know who had snuck out. This was one of the most powerful corporations in the world, and they'd thought they would be able to wander around, breaking down doors, without being found out? Frederick flushed with embarrassment—he felt like a child.

"Why not kick us out?" he asked bitterly.

"The testing is what's most important." Dr. Gray replied with a tone that assured Frederick he would not be discussing it further.

"How are we supposed to forget about it?" Frederick whispered, his eyes drifting to the floor.

"I can't imagine you will," the doctor replied. "But you'll have to try."

Frederick listened to the sound of the doctor's shoes squeaking against the tiled floor as he walked away. He exchanged glances with the others. Nineteen met his eyes, and Frederick was surprised to find resolve.

"This doesn't change anything. We have to find a way to stay," she whispered with a surprising ferocity. "I'm not leaving this place, and I'm not leaving any of you."

The helpless feeling that had overcome Frederick melted away at Nineteen's words. He clenched his jaw in determination.

Having been checked by some nurses and given the all-clear, the four applicants strode down the halls. Arthur had stopped by and was leading them back to the common room. The receptionist's mood was surprisingly somber, the walk devoid of his usual stream of upbeat chatter. Frederick appreciated the silence but couldn't shake the feeling that this was a funeral procession.

As they entered the common room, which still contained faint scents of smoke, all eyes turned to them, the remaining applicants watching their entry. Some tried to hide the delight on their faces, most did not. Frederick even heard a few snickers make their way around the room. People love to see people above them toppled, and Frederick and his friends had given their fellow applicants just that. Arthur took his leave without a farewell, walking briskly out of the room.

Frederick searched the room and spotted One sitting at a table with Eight and a couple other applicants whose numbers he couldn't recall. Both One and Eight seemed fairly distraught in their own right. Eight stared down at the table, a look of pain plastered onto his narrow face. One stared straight at them. Frederick was shocked to see tears welling up in the blond boy's eyes. He stood quickly and walked over to them, brushing roughly at his eyes as he walked over.

"You guys okay?" One asked lamely.

"Oh, we are just dandy, Uno. We won't be here for more than twenty-four more hours, but we are just downright peachy," Seven said sarcastically. One winced visibly at the retort.

Thirteen punched the stocky boy in the arm, though he barely reacted to the blow. "Shut it, Seven," she said before turning to One. "We're fine. It sucks, but we are fine. How did you guys fair?"

"Pretty terrible, actually," One said, scratching his head in embarrassment. "Eight and I had panic attacks too. Our roommates had to drag us out. If they had known it was the third test, I imagine they would've just left us. Of course, I would've preferred that. I hate that Eight and I have an advantage over you four even though we did just as bad."

Frederick and the others stared at One, dumbfounded. He'd had a panic attack? The applicant who had made Arthur and four other fully grown men look so foolish the day before? The same One who had tricked the rest of the applicants with ease? That person had needed to be dragged out like the rest of them? They stood in silence for a moment, processing.

"Nothing for it now," Thirteen said suddenly. "No point in dwelling on the past."

The girl strode confidently past One, making exaggerated faces at those who still dared to stare at her. "I'm not sure about the rest of you, but I need a shower."

Frederick closed his eyes and let the water wash away the memory of the events of the day. He let his mind go blank, focusing only on the warmth the water provided. His brain eventually began working again. There were problems that needed to be solved after all. He needed to find a way to fail the test but make it look convincing. He didn't deserve to stay here. The third test had proven that. He had lain on the ground and cried while his friends needed his help. He was certain that the panic attacks they had experienced had been triggered by his own. Who wouldn't have a panic attack at the sight of a friend collapsing in agony in the middle of a catastrophe?

No. They would not be punished for what he did to them.

The issue was once again that he had no idea what to expect from the test. How could he prepare for a total wild card? After several more minutes of thought, he eventually resigned himself to simply playing it by ear. He would do his best to help his friends, and if nothing else, he would make sure he failed in order to get out of their way. Frederick stepped out of the shower feeling a little bit lighter, basking in the comfort of accepting his fate.

Frederick toweled his hair dry as he walked into his bedroom. He moved lightly, expecting the others to be fast asleep already. Instead, he was greeted by a peculiar sight. The four mattresses of the room had been dragged to the floor and arranged into a square. One, Seven, Eight, Thirteen, and Nineteen sat cross-legged, looking at Frederick expectantly. One gestured for Frederick to join the makeshift boardroom.

"Take a seat, Twenty. We've got things to discuss."

Chapter 10

Frederick made his way over to his mattress and sat down heavily on it. The shower he had taken had done much to rejuvenate him, but his legs still felt like they had lead in them.

He looked around the circle of his friends. His eyes settled on Eight, who flashed him a smile far too wide for their current predicament. Frederick was surprised to see the small boy. He liked Eight, and he had assumed the boy would be a part of their group ever since the second test, but he had thought it would take more time. Seeing him now, though, it was obvious he should be there. Frederick felt a slight pang of regret that they hadn't trusted him to come on their excursions into Kinth. They should've brought him in sooner. Now they were all in the same boat, and Frederick couldn't imagine Eight not being there.

"About time," Seven said. "I thought you had fallen asleep and gotten sucked down the drain."

"Sorry." Frederick rolled his eyes. "I didn't mean to leave the committee waiting."

"Just don't let it happen again," Seven responded primly.

"So what are we talking about?" Frederick asked, though he was fairly certain he already knew.

"We are talking about how to stay," One said.

"Oh, well if that's all," Thirteen scoffed, "I'm sure we can straighten this out in no time."

"We told Eight everything we found out about Kinth," One said, ignoring her. "Maybe we should've consulted you, but I didn't think you would protest."

"Of course not." Frederick nodded to Eight. "You are as much a part of this group as any of us now."

"Thanks, boss!" Eight beamed. "Bummed to miss out on the trips, though. Sounds like you saw some really cool stuff!"

"Of course he doesn't mention the nightmare beyond comprehension and the being chased through the halls," Seven mumbled.

"That's the best part!" Eight said. "Well, the running through the halls part, not the nightmare."

"I feel like we're maybe losing the thread here," One said, sounding a bit annoyed. "Eight is with us now—that's what matters. What we need to do is formulate a plan."

"There's no way to make a plan," Frederick said, shaking his head in frustration. "We just don't have enough information."

"We could get more," One said.

"Um." Nineteen spoke so softly, Frederick could barely hear her. "Sorry, but we can't go wandering off again. Dr. Gray knows it was us who snuck out. He let us get away with it for some reason. A part of me thinks he almost wanted us to sneak out when we did." She shook her head. "But one thing is certain—he doesn't want us to anymore. I think if we step one foot out of line from here on out, we're gone."

"That certainly seemed to be the message when he told us not to do it again," Seven said sarcastically. "'You forget about it, and I will too,' right?"

"So no more recon." Eight released a sigh heavy with disappointment.

"No more recon," One said begrudgingly.

"So what do we do then?" Frederick asked, fighting a rising feeling of help-lessness.

There was an extended silence as they each considered his words. Frederick wracked his brain helplessly in search of answers.

"There's one option." Frederick was surprised by the calm in his own voice. His friends stared at him—he could see the desperation in their eyes. A hope beyond hope that he'd found a solution. "Arthur and Dr. Gray have made it pretty clear that it's not possible for all of us to pass. The math is just work-ing against us." He paused for a moment, not wanting to continue but finally forcing himself to do so. "So maybe we pick a couple of us to pass, and the rest maybe don't do our best."

"No!" One and Seven almost shouted in perfect unison. Frederick was tak-en aback by the anger in their faces. One's eyes were hard, and Seven's face had gone bright red; the stocky boy had bolted to his feet, his fists balled. He took a step toward Frederick and crouched down until they were face-to-face.

"No one is going to leave so that I can stay." His voice was barely contained, straining at the edges. "I'm not letting you take a dive for me, and you aren't gonna let me take a dive for you, are you? Yeah, I didn't think so. No one is gonna leave so I can stay." Seven returned to his seat and finished in a whisper. "No one else is gonna get hurt because of me."

"Besides," Thirteen said, her eyes flicking to Seven in confusion at his out-burst, "Dr. Gray made it clear that if one of us did that, we would all get the boot."

"What other options do we have?" Frederick asked, his voice rising in frus-tration. "The numbers are obvious—"

"Screw your numbers!" One burst out. "We are all passing. Not one of us is getting left behind! We are all going to get better, and we are all gonna get some damn answers."

A stunned silence filled the room. The blond boy took several deep breaths to calm himself. "At this point, it's clear—we have one option, and one option only." He looked each of them in the eyes in turn. "We have to be perfect. Not good, not great, perfect. We do so well on this final test that Dr. Gray has to keep us. We give them no choice but to keep us."

Frederick felt his heart swell as One spoke. He knew what One was suggesting was impossible, but he couldn't help but believe him.

"Easy for you to say—you're some kind of freak demigod., Seven muttered.

One shot him a look that could've melted steel. "I will do everything within the realm of possibility to make sure we all pass. I will drag each of you over the finish line if I have to. I will be passing, and you will be with me. Do you understand?"

Seven tried to shrug off the comments, but One held his gaze, refusing to look away until Seven sighed and nodded. Frederick could see the belief beginning to seep into the stocky boy's eyes.

"Anyone else have any objections?" One looked around the room once more, eyebrows raised in challenge. No objections came. "Good." He nodded with finality.

Frederick could feel a swelling of belief among his friends. They were feeling the same irrational trust in One that he was. He knew it wasn't possible for them all to stay, but he also knew with absolute certainty that when the chips were down and the smoke had cleared, they would all be standing together, still here.

"Well, if there's nothing else . . ." Seven yawned loudly.

"Well," Nineteen raised her hand, "actually, if it's not too much trouble . . ." Her sentence trailed off as she mumbled something that Frederick couldn't make out.

"Go ahead, Nineteen." Thirteen gave the small girl's shoulder an encouraging pat. "Let's hear it."

Nineteen nodded and cleared her throat, then took a steadying breath.

"I know we are going to do everything we can to stay. And maybe we will be able to all stay. If it's possible, I'm sure we will make it happen. It's just— I don't—

I couldn't—" She shook her head in frustration before continuing. "There is a chance we don't make it past this test, and if we don't make it past this test, there's a chance we never see one another again, and the thought of that makes me sick." She spoke in a torrent, as if afraid that slowing down would let the words get stuck in her throat. "I can't beat the thought of living the rest of my life and not knowing where any of you came from, what your stories are, any of that. Who knows what will happen to us after this, and I don't want this to just be another blip on the radar for me. You all have really come to mean something to me, and you're the first people in my life who I've really been able to be fully myself and fully myself with. I just want to know a little bit just in case the worst happens. You know, something to treat this a bit like making a normal friendship, not making a friendship in whatever this place is." She looked at the ground sheepishly. "I'm sorry One, really I am—I want to believe 100 percent that everything will be perfectly okay, but in my experience, things rarely work out. So I was thinking maybe tonight we could share a little bit about ourselves? Just in case?"

Nineteen screwed her eyes shut so she wouldn't have to meet anyone else's. One stood slowly and walked over to the small girl, placing a comforting hand on her shoulder. When he spoke, his voice remained quiet.

"That's a great idea, Nineteen," One said and flashed her a smile that almost brightened the room. "I think anyone who is comfortable should tell us more about themselves." He looked around the room at each of them, holding their gaze for a few seconds before moving on. "I can't speak for all of you, but I'd be honored to know a little more about each of you. Even Seven."

The stocky boy made an obscene gesture in One's general direction.

"I'm in," Frederick said. He still believed they would make it, but he wanted to know more about his friends regardless.

"Me too," Eight added.

"Plus, I think knowing who each of us are outside of these walls will help us remember why we're doing any of this and who we're doing it for," said One.

"Keeping connections loose made sense at the beginning, but now I think we've got to pull together. So share whatever you're comfortable with sharing." He gave Seven a playful push.

Seven mumbled something incoherent in the way of assent. Everyone seemed to be on board—all except Thirteen. The girl sat perfectly still on her mattress, as if she hoped that her lack of movement would keep the others from realizing she hadn't answered. Nineteen scooted to the edge of her bed and put a hand on the other girl's knee.

"You don't have to tell us anything you don't want to. But we'd love to hear it."

Thirteen squeezed her eyes shut and spoke in a quick nervous voice.

"I want to tell you all, and I will. But I need you to make a promise: you won't treat me any differently after you know." Her eyes popped open, and she looked around the room, desperate. "And you can't think of me differently either! I'm still the same person," she rushed to add.

"Geez how many people did you murder?" Seven snorted.

"You got it, Thirteen," One said. The group ignored Seven entirely. "Do you want to start?"

"Ugh." Thirteen sighed. "I guess it's best to just get it over with."

She shifted about on her mattress, trying unsuccessfully to find a comfortable position. She gave up after a few seconds and turned tentatively to the group.

"My name is Jane Edmonds. I'm not sure if any of you wanted to know that, but there it is. I guess we are probably past the whole 'not using names to avoid getting too attached' thing. I certainly feel attached, at least to most of you," She glared at Seven, who grinned widely. Thirteen rolled her eyes and looked away. "Although I think I want you all to keep calling me Thirteen. It's how you know me, and anything else feels weird."

The rest of the group nodded. Frederick had been thinking this himself. He wanted to know their names because it would feel wrong never to know. Still, he would always know them by the numbers they had been given. The naming system they had been assigned to keep from growing too close was now part of the glue that held them together.

"You're insane if you thought I would even consider calling you *Jane*," Seven said in a disgusted voice.

Thirteen leaned over and punched him hard in the arm, though she was smiling as she did. "I always hated my name anyway. It never felt like it fit. When I was really little, I told my parents I wanted a new name and they could just refer to me as 'Daughter' until I thought of a better one."

Frederick chuckled softly. "How'd they respond to that?"

"They locked me in my room for a month," she said casually.

He sat stunned, trying to formulate words.

"Don't worry about it." Thirteen waved away his attempted apology. "My parents are what the common people refer to as 'pretentious monsters.' They only adopted me because they wanted to get in on those sweet, sweet, tax breaks. I guess they wanted an heir to their massive fortune as well."

"Their what now?" Seven said, eyes wide.

"They probably care about me on some level," Thirteen said, ignoring Seven. "Though I'm not sure they've ever shown it. They ignored me whenever they had the chance." She shrugged, and a mischievous smile tugged at the edge of her lips. "So I made sure they didn't get the chance to ignore me."

There was a knowing chuckle from the audience.

"I got into just about any trouble I could. Ran away, stole stuff from the house and pawned it off. I once set the guest house on fire. That was an accident, though—I never tried to do anything that could hurt anybody. I got in so much trouble at school that they pulled me out. I had a ton of tutors. They were nice. A lot of them tried to help me. They saw things my parents ignored, that I needed help. The only issue was, as soon as they said anything to my parents, they'd get fired."

Thirteen paused for a moment and adopted a far-off look. "I tried so hard to get my parents' attention that they assumed everything I did was only to get attention. They didn't believe anything about me was legitimate." Tears welled up in her eyes, and a ferocious look came over her face. "I started having panic attacks every day, and they thought I just wanted them to look at me. I once collapsed at the dinner table because my throat had totally closed up. You know what my mom said? She said, 'Jane, you are an embarrassment and a terrible actor.'"

Frederick balled his fists as rage flowed throughout him. "How could they do that to you? How could they just leave you all alone?" he said through clenched teeth.

"Because they're terrible people." She shrugged. "To be fair, they did take me to the hospital after that. Though they still insisted that I was faking. The only reason they took me was because they thought they could maybe get some meds that would mellow me out or whatever. I had to stay in the hospital for a week or so. Turns out a panic attack that bad can do a number on you. Especially when people ignore you for the better part of an hour. It ended up being for the best, though. My doctor was super helpful. He listened to me and actually believed what I said, which is still something I'm trying to wrap my head around. He recommended a therapist to me. I tried that for a while, but it didn't do much. They basically told me I was royally screwed and to try Kinth. They told my parents about it, and naturally, they were ecstatic because they saw a chance to get rid of me, so they took it." Thirteen flopped back on her bed and stared at the ceiling with both hands behind her head. "Thank God they did," she whispered.

"Amen," Seven said. The stocky boy reached over and patted Thirteen's outstretched elbow awkwardly. The girl didn't acknowledge the gesture, but Frederick could see a half smile form on her face.

"So that's that. Any questions?"

"So when you say massive fortune . . ." Seven asked.

"My parents are worth just north of a billion dollars."

"Billion? Like with a B?" Eight said in astonishment.

Seven tried to say something as well, but no words came out. Instead, he stared at the girl with his mouth hanging open.

"Wow, you know your letters! I'm impressed, Eight. Good to see the practice is paying off."

Eight was so amazed he didn't even register the dig.

"This is what I was talking about," Thirteen said in frustration. "People get so different when they know about it. Every time I made a friend at school, they would be super weird when they found out. That or they would try to get free stuff from me. I really didn't mind that one as much. It always pissed my parents off, which was nice."

"How did you do it?" Frederick asked. "How did you survive on your own?"

"Not sure I would call it surviving." Thirteen scoffed. "It certainly didn't feel like it. I wasn't keeping my head above water. I was on the ocean floor with a lung full of salt water. But then . . ." She gestured vaguely to the room around her. "And here we are."

"I don't know what pushes me more, the idea of getting better or just staying the hell away from my parents. I just can't go back." The last words came out as a whisper. Nineteen scooted over as close as she could to Thirteen and laid her head on her shoulder. Thirteen rested her head on top of the other girl's and sniffled loudly.

They all sat in silence and absorbed the words.

"I think that's as much as I want to talk about for now," Thirteen said after an extended moment.

"Thanks for sharing, Thirteen," One said in a comforting voice, he flashed her another brilliant smile, and she responded with a smile of her own, though hers was significantly more reserved.

"So who wants to go next?" One asked.

"Why don't you go, One?" Frederick called from his spot. "I'm sure we'd all love to know how a legend is born."

One scoffed at the comment. "I'd rather go later if it's all the same. I'm much more interested in hearing one of your stories." He paused and scanned the room once more, eyes resting on a huddled mass that was doing its best to pretend it was asleep. "Seven? How 'bout you?"

"How did I know it would be me?" Seven grumbled.

"You don't have to if you don't want to," One reminded him.

"No, no—it's fine, it's fine." He paused and added softly, "Just don't expect any rainbows and sunshine."

"We aren't here for rainbows and sunshine," Thirteen said. "We're here for you, whatever that entails."

Seven nodded silently and seemed to gather his thoughts. Taking a deep breath, he began.

"My name is William Wetts, although everyone just calls me Will."

Thirteen coughed loudly.

"Willy Wetts? Like, Wetts comma Willy?"

"No. Like Will Wetts."

"Yeah, you're right, that's much better," Thirteen muttered. "Certainly much better than Jane."

"What happened to being here for me whatever that entails?"

"I'm sorry but how could I have known what it would entail is your real name being wet willy?"

"I grew up poor," Seven continued, ignoring Thirteen. "Not like poor, poor. But poor. My parents both worked multiple jobs, and even then, we lived in a tiny trailer." Seven shrugged. "It wasn't so bad, though. My parents adopted two other kids about the same time they adopted me. A boy and a girl. We were all about the same age and got along real well. Right off the bat actually. We always felt more like friends than siblings." He flushed a bit at this. "Maybe that's cheesy or whatever, but it's true. We did everything together. There's not much room in a trailer, so we didn't have any alone time, but that didn't bother us at all. In fact, we preferred it that way. 'Least I did. My anxiety was always worst when I was alone. Joey and Hannah, those are my siblings, always helped manage it. They always seemed to know the right thing to say or the right thing to do. They could even tell when it was so bad they needed to get one of our parents."

He shook his head. "I don't know how they did it. I mean, we were just kids, and they helped me more than any doctor ever did. So yeah. It wasn't a particularly easy life, but I was happy. I really was. At least as happy as I could be with all the anxiety. I mean, you guys know how it is. One second you're laughing and playing in the yard, and the next you're hyperventilating on the ground."

There were several nods of understanding and a murmur or two.

"One day, when I was about twelve, my mom was home from work. We didn't get many days with her all to ourselves, and whenever we did, she made sure to spend every second with us that she could. We were all playing at a park nearby. It was a perfect day. Everybody was laughing and screaming and everything. We were playing tag, and it just happened."

He took a deep breath. "I had a panic attack. A really bad one. I couldn't breathe, could barely move. My mom was there in an instant. She helped me up and got me to the car. She didn't know how bad it was at first, just thought I needed to calm down a bit, so she decided to take me home and leave Joey and Hannah at the park. It was such a nice day, and they really wanted to stay. It wasn't until we got home that she realized I was in much worse shape than she thought. It felt like there was an elephant sitting on my chest. It was the most pain I had ever been in, and I was so sure I was gonna die. I mean just absolutely positive that it was over for me." Seven paused and took several more deep breaths, as if assuring himself it wasn't happening again.

"She rushed me to the ER. It was scary. I mean, really scary." He shrugged. "And then I was fine. The elephant finally left, and I could breathe again like nothing had ever happened. The doctor wanted me to stay for an hour to make sure everything was all good and then said I could leave."

"Sounds like a lot," One said.

"It sucked, but that's how it goes," Seven said. "Until an ambulance showed up with both my siblings in it."

Tears began to run down the large boy's face, and he made no effort to stem their flow. His voice cracked as he spoke. "Joey was okay—he was just riding along. Hannah wasn't, though. I guess after we left, she had been playing on the monkey bars. She fell and hurt her back real bad. I don't even know how she managed to do so much damage falling only a few feet. Must've just landed awkwardly. Anyway, once Joey realized how bad it was, he ran all the way back to the trailer to get Mom. It was over a mile, and he never stopped sprinting. When he got home and found it was empty, he sprinted all the way back, screaming for help the whole way. He got back to the park, and there was an old couple walking by. He ran up to them basically yelling incoherently, but they got the idea and called an ambulance. He went back and sat with Hannah until the paramedics got there. They loaded her up into the ambulance and ended up at the same ER we were at."

Tears continued to run down Seven's face unchecked. Nineteen got up and sat beside him, quietly rubbing his back. "She didn't die." He sniffed loudly, regaining some composure. "Her back was screwed up, though. The doctors said if they had gotten her in earlier, they could've done more, but she had lain in the dirt at that damn park for over an hour. She was paralyzed from the waist down."

Everyone listened in silence.

"My mom blamed herself for not taking them with us back to the house. Joey blamed himself for not finding anyone sooner. Imagine that. A twelve-year-old kid sprinting three miles by himself without stopping and blaming himself for not doing more." Seven let out a heavy sigh. "But I know it was my fault."

"It wasn't your fault," Thirteen said, her voice soft but firm.

"How the hell not?" Seven almost yelled the words as he jumped to his feet. "If I hadn't been such a freaking burden, she would be walking right now because we would've been there and got her to the hospital in time to save her! We weren't there because of me. It's not just my fault—I'm dead weight. Because I couldn't keep it together, I took away the only person that could help her! And for what? No reason at all! I was scared of my own shadow, and it paralyzed my sister."

"Seven!" One stood up and walked over to the stocky boy, who had begun to hyperventilate. He grabbed him firmly by the shoulders and forced him to make eye contact. "It's not your fault you had a panic attack. You didn't do anything wrong. Something terrible happened, but in no way is it your fault." Seven just shook his head and tried to pull away, but One held on tight, not letting him. The stocky boy's breathing eventually began to slow, and he seemed to be calming down. He stood for several more minutes, taking deep breaths but otherwise not moving. Eventually, he opened his eyes again and nodded to One, who let go of his shoulders. Seven walked back to his mattress and sat down heavily.

"Next few years were awful for all of us. No one could forgive themselves for what happened. Hannah did everything she could to make sure we knew she didn't blame us, but it didn't matter. My anxiety got even worse after that. I was having panic attacks bad enough to go to the ER once a week. I never told anyone, though—I didn't want a repeat of what happened last time. Mom found me passed out a few times and yelled at me for not coming to her. Scared the crap out of her.

"Eventually, I started trying to run away. Money was tight with medical bills for Hannah and me, and Mom had to quit her jobs to take care of her, so that was even less money coming in. They were getting help from the government but not enough to actually help. I figured one less mouth to feed, especially one who made this problem in the first place and was adding another set of medical bills . . . It was a fairly reasonable solution. Every time I ran away, they managed to track me down though. I know it broke my parents. They loved me. They really did. And it was killing them to see me trying to get away, but it was the right thing to do. Eventually, they had to give up. They sent me away to some special care facility. A little over a year or so later, they sent me here."

"That sounds awful," Nineteen whispered. The small girl was trembling, her head buried in her knees. Seven had adopted a similar position and couldn't meet their eyes.

"It was," Seven said simply, his voice muffled. "But I'm here now. Maybe once I'm better, I can go back and help my family instead of being a burden. Lighten the load instead of being it or whatever."

Frederick opened his mouth to say something but couldn't find the words. Perhaps there simply were none. He realized with a start that there were tears on his face. What do you say to someone who has been through something like that? Frederick had never experienced anything remotely close. Who was he to say it would all be okay?

"Sorry guys, I don't think I can talk about any of this anymore," Seven said. "Can someone else go?"

"Of course," Thirteen said, and leaned over to pat him awkwardly on the shoulder. She stayed for a moment, clearly wanting to say something but clearly unsure of how to comfort the stocky boy. She opened her mouth several times, but nothing came out.

"Thirteen, I'm fine," Seven said, forcing a smirk. "Though you sitting there opening and closing your mouth like a fish is making me feel better."

Thirteen looked like she couldn't decide whether to laugh or punch Seven. She decided on both, which Seven seemed to think was a fair arrangement. He smiled and rubbed his arm ruefully.

"Let's get continue with the autobiographies," he said. "I, for one, would love to hear the story behind the infamous Two-Oh."

"I think that's a great idea," One said. "You up for it, Twenty?"

Frederick stared at the ceiling for another breath or two, then sat up reluctantly. "I can if you want. There's not much to tell."

"Well that certainly explains your total lack of personality," Seven said flatly.

He was struck simultaneously by five different pillows. Frederick smiled. If a joke or two was all it took to raise Seven's spirits again, he would happily take it.

"Only joking, my boy," Seven said in a terrible British accent as he began using the pillows that had been thrown at him to construct a small fort. "Carry on!"

Frederick took a deep breath and began. "Well, first things first, I guess. My name is Frederick."

"I would make fun of that, but the name does all the work itself," Seven said from inside his fort.

"That's certainly something coming from Wet Willy," Frederick said.

"Fair enough." Seven waved for him to continue.

"It was always just me and my parents, as far back as I can remember. I didn't do the whole school thing for long. It was all just a bit too much for me. My parents homeschooled me, which was fine but had its drawbacks. I didn't really get out much, so without school, I didn't really have friends . . . ever?" Frederick cleared his throat uncomfortably, searching for the next words.

Nineteen caught his eye and nodded encouragingly.

"My attacks weren't usually that bad, but they happened multiple times a day. Well, not bad by our standards, I guess. They were enough to keep me from doing pretty much anything. I had a couple big ones that landed me in the hospital. They were pretty spread out, though." Frederick's throat felt like it was filling with sand. "Until they weren't. The bad ones started happening more often. They went from once a year, to once a month, to weekly, to almost daily. I was never very good at communicating how bad it was, so my mom came up with a system. Every morning she would ask how I was on a scale from one to ten, with one being totally normal and ten being scared I might die."

"You ever get a one?" Eight asked earnestly.

Frederick shook his head.

"Yeah, me neither," the small boy said softly.

"Anyway." Frederick cleared his throat. It felt like more and more things were trying to clog it. "It really wore on my parents. That was always the worst part. They never complained, not once. I wished they would. They could yell at me for being a burden or tell me I was ruining their lives. Anything like that would've worked. They at least deserved the right to blame me, I think."

Frederick's eyes began to well with tears, and his throat tightened even more.

"I could see it weigh on them every time I had an attack or couldn't get out of bed. I saw them crack just a little bit. They were like stained glass windows, and everything I did threw a rock at them." He wiped his eyes roughly. "Anyway. I ended up in the hospital and got accepted to Kinth the day I got home."

"What was different about that attack?" One asked softly. "You said you had been in the hospital a bunch of times," he continued when Frederick didn't answer. "What was different about that time?"

"It wasn't a panic attack." Frederick said softly, not daring to meet his eyes.

"Then what . . ." Eight started, but Thirteen cut him off with a gentle shake of the head.

One rose wordlessly and walked to Frederick, pulling him roughly to his feet.

Frederick opened his mouth to speak but was cut off as One embraced him. Frederick tried to speak again but couldn't. Instead, he simply buried his head in the other boy's shoulder and let himself cry. One by one, the rest of the group rose and joined in the hug until they stood in a circle, holding each other tightly.

They remained like that for several minutes, no one speaking. Frederick cried. He wasn't embarrassed to in front of his friends. They exuded a comfort that he wouldn't have been able to put into words. Their presence was enough to let him know that he could feel whatever he needed to feel and however he needed to feel it. He took another minute, letting himself take it all in without trying to quell any of it. All the sadness, anger, frustration, and futility. He let it all wash over him. Then he sniffled a few times and did his best to regain some composure.

"So, uh . . ." His voice was hoarse. "How do you end a group hug?"

They laughed softly, and all let go at the same time.

"Thanks you guys." Frederick smiled at them.

"Of course, Twenty." One returned the smile. "We are always here for you." He turned to the rest of them. "How about we take a second before sharing any more?"

"Thank goodness. I have to pee more than anyone has ever had to pee in the history of the universe," Eight said over his shoulder as he ran to the bathroom.

Chapter 11

Five minutes later, they had returned to their various seats on the mattresses.

"Eight?" One said. "You want next?"

"Hey, sure thing, boss! I'll tell you whatever you want to know," the small boy babbled. "Can we play cards, though? Helps my brain work when my hands aren't looking for something to do."

Wordlessly, One pulled a deck of cards from his pocket and began shuffling them, nodding for Eight to continue.

"Well, to be honest with you, there isn't much to tell." Eight collected his cards as One dealt them and began arranging them. "My name is Octavian."

Seven opened his mouth, eyes wide, a snarky comment already working its way out, but Thirteen silenced him with a sharp elbow to the ribs. If Eight noticed, he showed no signs of it.

"I was adopted by a family that already had six other kids. I was the youngest, the smallest, and the newest, so I got looked over. I had to work a little bit harder for them to hear me, you know? I had to distinguish myself somehow." Eight shrugged matter-of-factly. "I couldn't control how long I'd been around, but I could control how much they heard me. I just figured I could be the loudest."

"That adds up," Seven said in his own matter-of-fact tone. He wasn't trying to be mean, simply stating the obvious.

"I felt like I had to fight tooth and nail for them to see me, you know what I'm saying? It came pretty natural to me, I won't lie. It's always been easier to be loud than quiet Am I right, boss?" Eight elbowed Seven in the ribs and ducked to avoid his retaliatory swipe before continuing. "I ran away a few times a year. That always got their attention. I kinda liked it. I'd live on the street for a few days. Would have to find my own food and all that. It was fun, sorta like vacation!"

"Vacation?"

"Yeah! Except I learned way more stuff."

"What kind of stuff?" Frederick asked somewhat hesitantly.

"Oh you know, a little bit of this and a little bit of that." Eight shrugged and smiled mischievously. "It was always pretty fun—until I started having panic attacks. Almost dying doesn't really feel like vacation. I don't remember when I started freaking out all the time with the anxiety stuff. I was kind of like you." He nodded to Thirteen. "They thought I was just pretending to be worse off than I was for attention. I even wondered if I was sometimes. Then I started not being able to breathe, and I didn't have to wonder anymore." Eight thew a couple cards on the ground in front of One, who dealt him replacement cards. Eight was the only one keeping up the pretense of playing, but that did little to deter him.

"It was pretty bad. I didn't like it. I wanted them to see me, but I didn't want it to be 'cause I was broken. I wanted it to be because I was funny or could juggle or something—I don't know." For a moment, the small boy stopped pretending to play cards. "I wanted it to be because of who I was. It never felt like that was who I was. It was like something crawled inside my brain and started pulling the strings and there was nothing I could do about it. You know what I'm saying?"

Frederick nodded. He did know. Though he had never felt exactly that way, he had experienced that feeling of disconnect with who he was as a person and his anxiety.

"Anyway, my folks probably waited too long before they sent me off. It wasn't their fault." Eight shrugged again. "They were doing their best. They were just stretched too thin. I never felt like I could blame them for trying to do too much, you know? Just sucks I was the one who paid for it."

Seven patted him awkwardly on the shoulder.

"There's not much more to it than that," Eight continued. "I know it's not some big sob story or anything. It was hard, for sure. But, hey, I made it out, and I'm here now. I don't like thinking about how sad I was." He screwed up his nose as if he had smelled something especially pungent. "Sadness just feels gross."

Frederick had to cough to cover up a laugh. It was such a simple approach to life: Sadness is uncomfortable, so we don't talk about it. Frederick couldn't help but envy Eight just the smallest of amounts. He wished he had the ability not to dwell on the darkness he had lived through.

"So that's it, I guess," Eight said awkwardly. "I'm sorry I don't have some big sad ending. I know how much you love your teary group hugs."

"Do you want a teary group hug?" One asked in amusement.

"Absolutely not," Eight said. "There's only one thing I want."

"What's that?"

"The pot!" Eight showed his cards triumphantly.

Frederick chuckled as Eight pantomimed pulling a pile of chips toward him.

"I knew I could distract you guys with my story. Ate it right up while I robbed you blind." Eight shook his head solemnly. "You really should be more careful. You guys would get scammed out of your mind, eh?"

"What are you gonna scam from us, Eight?" Seven rolled his eyes. "It's not like we have any money."

"Lesson one, boss. There's always something to steal."

Eight pulled an object from his pocket and held it up.

"Is that my toothbrush?" Seven asked in disbelief, snatching it away from the small boy. "Why is it wet?"

"Nineteen?" One asked. "Would you like to share before this gets out of hand?" He gestured at Seven, who was trying to comprehend the theft of his toothbrush.

Nineteen nodded nervously. "My name is Toni," she began in a rush, seeming desperate to quash the fight before it began. "I don't have a last name because I never stayed with a family long enough to take their name, and I only really have memories of one family." Nineteen's eyes were glued to the floor, as if there were a teleprompter embedded there.

"They used to complain about how much I talked. Funny, right? Me, talking too much. I was just so curious. I wanted to know how everything worked. Why was the sky blue? How do birds fly? Why do I look different from the other kids? My 'mom' didn't appreciate the questions. She said she adopted me because she needed the extra money, not to play twenty questions. I couldn't help it, though. I had to ask. I had to know." Nineteen adopted a far-off look. "After about six months, she dropped me off in the middle of the closest city. Right before she drove away, she rolled down the window and said, 'Maybe this'll teach you to keep your mouth shut.'"

Frederick's mouth dropped in shock.

"She just abandoned you?" Thirteen asked, rage filling her voice. "How old were you?"

"Seven."

Frederick could hear Thirteen's teeth grinding. He didn't blame her. His stomach burned with anger as well.

"I guess she thought someone would find me and I'd get passed off to another family." Nineteen shrugged. "To be fair, that is exactly what happened. It took three days, but it happened."

"You were on your own for three days? When you were seven?" Seven asked, dumbfounded. "How did you survive?"

"Kind of like you said earlier, I'm not sure you can really call it surviving." Her voice was soft. "I had a pretty bad panic attack right after she dropped me off. I just lay down in an alley and waited for it to pass. I was kind of catatonic, I guess. All I remember is the cold. It started snowing at some point. They found me curled up, barely breathing. It's a miracle I didn't lose anything to frostbite."

"It's a miracle you're alive," Frederick said in awe.

"That too, I guess." Nineteen shrugged. "I spent a few weeks in the hospital before they found me a new home. I was there for about a month before they said they couldn't take care of me. They at least didn't drop me off in the middle of a snowstorm. Although it was tough not to feel abandoned. After that, it was all pretty much the same story over and over again. New place for a few months, some reason they couldn't keep me, new family, new problem. Rinse, repeat. Eventually, someone decided to send me to Kinth."

"I'm so sorry." Thirteen placed a hand on the smaller girl's back. "That must've been horrible."

"I don't know. I mean, it was terrible, but it was also all I knew. I don't think I really understood how bad it was until I got to Kinth. Until . . ." Her eyes filled with tears. "Until I met all of you. I didn't know what I was missing until I had it." Nineteen's face grew hard with determination. "But now that I have it, I'm not giving it up." She looked each of them square in the eyes. "Not now. Not ever."

Her words hung in the air for a moment before One spoke. "You won't have to. None of us will."

Nineteen wiped her face, and Thirteen gave her a hug.

"That's all there really is to it," Nineteen said. "Even if there was more, I don't think I'd want to talk about it. That was a different life. A life I don't ever want to think about again. I was a different person then. It honestly almost feels like someone else's memories. Is that weird?"

Frederick gave her a warm smile. "Not at all."

"It's a little weird," Seven said quietly.

Thirteen threw her shoe at him. He tried to dodge it, unsuccessfully.

Nineteen did her best to keep from laughing, but her efforts were in vain. Soon, her whole body shook.

Seven rubbed his shoulder where the shoe had struck him. "Why is it always funny when I get hurt?"

"Because you have the dumbest thoughts and don't have the good sense to keep them in your head." Thirteen shook a finger at him. "Apologize!"

"Sorry, Nineteen. Didn't mean anything by it."

Nineteen walked over to Seven, her face still alight with humor. "Don't worry about it." She gave him a tight hug. "I like your stupid thoughts."

Seven seemed caught off guard by the sudden hug. He looked as though he half expected someone to hit him with something as soon as he let his guard down. But Nineteen squeezed him even tighter, and the suspicion melted from his face. The corners of his mouth tugged upward into a smile, and he patted the small girl awkwardly but affectionately on the back. Nineteen gave a final squeeze and returned to her mattress.

"Alright, One," she said. "Let's hear it."

"Not tonight." One shook his head.

"Why not?" Nineteen asked, looking somewhat hurt.

Thirteen and Seven let out simultaneous massive yawns.

"That's why." One laughed. "We're all exhausted. It's late, and my story isn't a short one. I'll share eventually, just not tonight. Promise."

Frederick wanted to protest, but his lids were growing heavier by the second. It had been a long night after a long day in the midst of an impossibly long week. He needed to sleep—they all did.

"Fine," Nineteen said and yawned herself. "But I'm holding you to that promise. We aren't leaving this place until we've heard your story."

"Sounds good." One smiled and grabbed Eight by the shoulder, pulling him out of the room. "I'm glad I know more about you all. You might be the first real friends I've had, and I'm not about to let any of you down. See you all in the morning."

Chapter 12

Frederick awoke the next morning feeling refreshed. The previous night had been emotionally exhausting but also very necessary. He was feeling hopeful in a way he knew he had no right to be. It was still early according to the clock by his bed, and the rest of his companions were still sleeping as far as he could tell. He exited the room as quietly as he could and made his way to the bathroom. His step was light, and his mood matched it—he almost felt like singing in the shower.

Frederick made his way from the bathroom to the common room. A few other applicants had risen early as well. He spotted One sitting at a table, playing a card game on his own. He glanced up and smiled at Frederick as he pulled up a chair.

"Someone is awfully chipper, especially considering today is the biggest day of their life and they seem to be facing insurmountable odds," One said with a grin.

Frederick smiled back at him and shrugged.

"I feel that," One said, collecting the cards and dealing Frederick in. "There's something to be said for accepting your fate."

Frederick looked up sharply, and One met his eyes with an intense stare.

"I think we might be the same, Twenty. I really do."

"I'm not like you," Frederick answered. "I wish I were, but I'm just not. I certainly can't run up trees and flip over people."

"I'm not so sure about that." One chuckled as he placed a few chips on the table between them. "I think you could do it, no problem. You just need a little practice."

Frederick shook his head dismissively and placed a few chips of his own into the pot.

"They sat in silence, playing their pretend game of cards. The others joined them one by one. First Nineteen, who sat down wordlessly and carefully organized the cards One dealt her. Then came Thirteen; she yawned a hello to the group and plopped down into the chair between Frederick and Nineteen. Last was Seven, and he shuffled sleepily up to the table and immediately stubbed his toe. He muttered a string of especially creative curses and sat down on the other side of Frederick. They chatted for a few minutes until their small talk faded back to silence as they all tried not to think about what was coming next.

Arthur strode into the room and greeted them warmly, seeming to have recovered his previous sunny disposition. "Hello everyone! I'm glad to see all of you up and about and ready to get going. We will begin shortly, but I'd like to say a few words if you would be so kind as to indulge me." He smiled and made eye contact with every applicant before continuing. Frederick found it to be a sweet gesture, though slightly off-putting.

"I want each of you to know how much I have genuinely enjoyed our time together. Whether it's been a splendidly long time"—he gestured to One—"or a painfully short time." He waved a hand at Frederick. "Either way, I will miss all of you who are unable to remain. Please, take good care of yourselves, and do not lose heart." Frederick thought Arthur's eyes lingered on him a moment longer than anyone else when he said this, but he couldn't be certain.

"Now," Arthur continued as he wiped tears from his eyes, "I will explain the fourth and final test. It is simple. It will be the same format as the first test, except you will not have a written portion. You will all pass through ten rooms, with a twenty-minute timer on each door. The faster you finish, the better, obviously. It is all very straightforward."

"Unlike the rest of this bullsh—" Seven muttered, and Arthur shot him a look that was both disapproving and fond.

"Any questions? No? Well, follow me and good luck."

The room that Arthur led them to was not far. It was a shallow room but extremely wide. It felt more like an additional hallway than a separate room. There were twenty doors, each with a number above it.

"Please step up to your corresponding door, but do not enter until I say so ."

Frederick and his friends exchanged encouraging nods and stepped up to their respective doors. They stood there for what felt like an eternity, waiting for Arthur's signal. The receptionist looked fairly distressed himself. Frederick could see that he didn't want to start this test. The sooner it started, the sooner some of them would have to leave.

The sooner Frederick would have to leave.

He squared his shoulders and took a deep breath, once more steeling his resolve. He would survive; he had spent his whole life surviving. If even one of his friends could make it in at his expense, that would make everything that came after worth it.

He would miss them, though.

"Begin."

It took everything in Frederick to keep from collapsing as the door clicked shut behind him, and he immediately struggled to breathe. He placed a shaking hand on the wall next to him to steady himself.

Gone were all thoughts of sacrificing himself for his friends. He felt like he had been hit in the stomach with a sledge hammer. He doubled over, gasping for air. Sweat was pouring down his face and into his eyes. It felt like it was a hundred degrees in the tiny room he now stood in.

He had to get out. Whatever it took. He would get out and withdraw from consideration so someone else could still have his spot. It didn't matter what happened after—if he didn't get out, he was going to die. He turned and tugged on the door he had come through to no avail.

"Let me out! I don't want to pass. Just let me go! Please!"

He shouted for several minutes but was met with no response. Eventually, Frederick gave up and turned to the other door in the room. It had a small screen on it with a math equation on the front. It wasn't an overly complicated equation, and Frederick felt like he normally might've been able to solve it. At this particular moment, however, he stood no chance. The numbers swam across his vision. Just breathing was occupying his full attention. He stared dumbly at the screen until finally the twenty-minute timer expired and the door slid open. He stumbled forward, seeking some kind of reprieve.

It took everything in Frederick to keep from bursting into tears. He found the air in this room to be just as hot and stale as in the previous one. He wasted no time in stumbling to the door and staring at the screen.

If Jack has one apple and Janice has two apples and tomorrow they half half as many ables as Jim who has a fork as mini as Jasper how many staples does Jasper have?

Frederick stared blankly at the words, trying to decipher them. He wiped sweat from his eyes as he tried to focus on each individual letter, but the letters danced the same way the numbers had on the last door. He clenched his jaw and tried to make sense of the gibberish but soon gave up. He didn't have the capacity for this, and perhaps it would be prudent to save what little mental energy was not devoted to breathing for problems he might actually be able to solve.

Minutes that might as well have been days passed by, uncaring for Frederick's state of mind. He tried to keep his mind blank, but he couldn't help wondering how long it would take for him to die of dehydration at the rate he was sweating. He felt the dry portions of his shirt fading away as more and more sweat poured from him. He eventually stopped bothering to wipe it out of his eyes.

Frederick had little hope that the next room would be any better than the one he'd left behind. Somehow, it was worse. It felt like there was no oxygen left in the air. The room was tiny. He banged his head on the ceiling as he stepped in. He didn't even bother looking at the screen as he limped through. Propping himself up against the door, he whimpered and waited for the twenty minutes to pass.

This was how Frederick handled the rest of the rooms. He would have cried if he were able, but there was no liquid in his body to be used for such things. He entered each room, dragged himself to the door, and simply passed the minutes in agony. Every inch of him screamed in pain as he prayed for the end to come, whatever that may be.

Frederick took ragged breaths as he leaned against the tenth and final door. His hair was matted to his forehead, and he banged his head softly on the door over and over again, begging it to open and release him. At last, his wish was granted.

The door opened suddenly, and he spilled out of the last room. He had a vague sense of someone else tumbling out beside him. He lay with his face on the floor as cold air rushed over his body. He began sobbing with relief, tears cascading down his face. Someone grabbed Frederick and gently turned him over, cradling his head and whispering comforting words. He could hear that they were crying too. Opening his eyes, he saw the tears running down Seven's face.

"It's okay, Two-Oh," he said between sobs. "It's okay, buddy. It's okay."

Nineteen hurried forward with a bottle of water, holding it up to Frederick's shaking lips. He gulped at it greedily.

As Thirteen pulled the bottle away, Frederick found he could finally breathe again. His lungs opened up and filled with air. The relief he tasted in that moment was the sweetest thing Frederick had ever known. He looked to his side and saw that several doorways down, One lay sobbing on the ground as well. Nineteen was cradling his head in the same way Seven was Frederick's, trying to get him to drink some water.

Frederick stared at One, wondering if he looked that bad. He certainly felt every bit as bad as One looked. The blond boy's hair stuck to his forehead, his eyes were large and puffy, and lines ran down his face from all the tears he had cried. Frederick forced himself to sit up, taking deep breaths.

"When did you guys finish?" he gasped to Seven.

"I finished fifteen minutes before you. Thirteen and Nineteen were right behind me," Seven said, his voice cracking.

"We were the last five to finish," Nineteen whispered. She looked better than Frederick felt but only slightly. She was clearly fighting back tears as she spoke. "The next worst time was Eight, and he finished ten minutes before Seven."

Frederick wanted to scream. Everything he had endured since he arrived—the tests, the fires, the terrors—all of it was worthless now. They had needed a miracle for just one of them to make it, and they had failed miserably. All his plans of being a hero, of sacrificing himself for his friends, and what had he done? Curled up like a child and cried until it was over. He tucked his head in his arms, hiding his face so the others couldn't see the shame in his eyes. The pain of failure radiated throughout his body. Now they would never get better, and perhaps even worse, they would never have answers about the true nature of Kinth.

"Applicants One, Seven, Eight, Thirteen, Nineteen, and Twenty, please follow me. The rest of the applicants, please follow Peter to the common room and await further instruction."

Frederick looked up and saw Arthur standing over him. A man he had never seen before led the twelve other applicants out of the room.

Twelve?

"They're taking twelve instead of ten, and we still couldn't make it. Pathetic," Seven spat. His eyes were filled with self-loathing.

"Oh, Seven, none of you are pathetic," Arthur said, fighting back tears. "I'm so sorry it has to be this way. Please, follow me."

He walked solemnly out of the room, and they stood to follow. Frederick felt shaky as he got to his feet. Seven offered an arm for support, but Frederick shook his head. He wanted to finish this on his own power. Seven instead went and offered his assistance to One, who took it gladly, slinging an arm around the stocky boy and hobbling out of the room after Arthur.

Frederick's shoes squeaked loudly as he followed his friends down the halls after Arthur. He let his eyes fall on each one of them. Their time together had been terribly short, but Frederick would miss them dearly. It had felt like years, not days. He even felt a strong connection to Eight, whom he barely knew. The small boy walked with his head drooped, letting tears fall from his face and splash on the floor. No one spoke as they made their way down the hall. The silence was oppressive—it ate away at Frederick's mind. This was all that waited for him, a lifetime full of panic and silence.

He jumped slightly as someone slipped their hand into his. He found Nineteen walking next to him, firmly holding his hand. In her other hand, she held Thirteen's. Thirteen reached for Seven's hand, and he took it silently, still supporting One. Frederick smiled in spite of himself, tears running down his face once more. He reached out and took Eight's hand. The small boy looked up at him through his tears and began crying even harder.

Arthur led them through one final door, and Frederick was shocked to find that they were in Dr. Gray's office. He scanned the room quickly. The doctor wasn't present, but the room was nearly identical to when he had last been here. There were the same bookshelves, the overstuffed chair, and the large globe. Although he could've sworn the bottle of whiskey on the table had been a bit more full.

They walked in as a group, and Arthur instructed them to stand in a line facing the desk. Arthur himself went and stood beside the desk. The small man folded his arms and began tapping his foot anxiously.

They didn't have to wait long for Dr. Gray to burst through the door. He was a ball of energy as he flitted throughout the room. Despite the doctor's rather large stature, Frederick was reminded of a hummingbird.

"So this is them, Arthur? The ones who failed the final test? Marvelous, marvelous," the doctor said as he made his way behind his desk. He sat down, but his energy remained as he rubbed his hands together. "I've never seen a group of applicants score so poorly on the final test. Marvelous, marvelous."

"Gee, thanks," Seven said, his voice dripping with sarcasm.

Frederick felt a multitude of emotions. He didn't know how to feel about the man who sat before them. Dr. Gray had put them all through so much strife, but he had also given them hope. Of course, he had eventually snuffed out that hope. But Frederick didn't think they could blame him for that. How was it his fault that they'd fallen short? They could search for someone to blame all they wanted, but the simple truth was it was no one's fault but their own. Frederick pushed his complicated concoction of emotions away and let his curiosity take the lead.

"Why is that marvelous?" Frederick asked.

The doctor's eyes met his, and Frederick wasn't surprised to find that same ferocious hunger he had seen before. What did surprise him was how much more intense it was this time. His eyes were not filled *with* the hunger. They had *become* the hunger. Frederick could see it oozing from the man; he was overflowing.

"Because it means you are exactly what we are looking for."

Chapter 13

The silence that followed might've lasted forever if not for Thirteen's outburst.

"What the hell does that mean? You just told us we had the worst scores you've ever seen."

"Yes, Thirteen, but sometimes failures are far more telling than successes," Dr. Gray said, giving each of them a long, meaningful look.

"What the hell does that mean?" Thirteen repeated.

He barked a laugh and stood quickly, slapping Arthur on the back.

"Ha! I like this one, Arthur. Lots of spirit in this group. You were right to speak so highly of them."

The receptionist winced and adjusted his glasses, smiling fondly at the applicants. "They are a good bunch, sir."

"Please, for the love of everything sweet and holy, will one of you *please* tell us what's going on?" Seven threw his hands in the air in exasperation.

"Perhaps you should put them out of their misery, sir?" Arthur asked. "I imagine you are giving them a fair amount of whiplash at the moment."

"Yes, yes, alright, alright. Go deal with the other applicants. I'll give this group the whole spiel."

Arthur walked briskly out of the room, flashing an encouraging smile over his shoulder at the six of them as he left.

Dr. Gray paced frantically behind his desk, pausing every few seconds as if to address them but then shaking his head and resuming his hectic gait without a word.

"Hey, boss, how about before we're your age, eh?" Eight called.

"Hm, yes, that would be best. Although you won't have to worry about being my age if none of this works."

Frederick exchanged uncomfortable glances with his companions.

"Only joking, of course," Dr. Gray said, flashing them an unconvincing smile.

The doctor stopped pacing abruptly, and the smile melted from his face.

"Well, no, I'm not joking. Not even remotely in fact." The doctor raised a weary hand to his glasses and removed them, rubbing his eyes. His shoulders slumped, and he leaned against the desk for support. The sudden change in his energy levels startled Frederick. "You need to know the truth. But that is no easy thing. For you to know the truth, you must believe the truth. If I can't make you believe what I'm about to tell you, then what's the point of any of this?" Dr. Gray shook his head in frustration. Then, setting his jaw, he took a deep breath and replaced his glasses. Frederick saw a familiar look return to his eyes as he appraised them.

"Perhaps I should just show you." A smile crept across the doctor's face that sent shivers down Frederick's spine. Out of the corner of his eye, he saw Nineteen shudder and heard Eight swallow nervously.

"Well, what are you waiting for?" One called, already moving toward the door. "I'm done waiting."

Frederick and his friends struggled to keep up with the long strides of Dr. Gray. His wild energy had returned, much to Seven's chagrin. One seemed to be having no trouble, however. He walked briskly, easily matching the step of the taller man.

"I'll try to explain as much as I can as we walk. You are going to have questions, and I will answer as many as I can, but none of that will be helpful until you see. Do you understand?"

"No," Frederick answered honestly, and he heard a few others mumble as well.

"Well, I hope to soon change that." Frederick could feel the smile in the doctor's voice.

"First of all, let's establish the obvious: none of you belong here. I don't mean *here*." Dr. Gray gestured dismissively to the walls around them. "I mean *here*." He gestured much more broadly. Frederick shared a confused glance with Nineteen, who just shrugged.

"I know you all feel it. I read your applications; I interviewed all of you. Whether you said it explicitly or not, you communicated that you don't belong and never have. I imagine that has driven many of you in the testing—you felt a vague sense of belonging for the first time in your life, and you grasped at it desperately. Perhaps it wasn't even a true sense of belonging, just a whisper of what you could potentially find here. And I think you will find it." Dr. Gray glanced back at them. "You just won't find it here."

"Where will we find it?" Nineteen whispered, her eyes glued to the floor as they walked.

"Kinth."

"But you said we wouldn't find it here," Seven interjected in annoyance.

"My boy, this is not Kinth. Not really. This place is a shadow of a shadow of the real Kinth. We simply use its name because we have found there is a pull to it. Some part of you remembers it; no matter how long you've been away, you could never forget your home. The strongest of you will inevitably search it out." The doctor led them around a corner, and Frederick felt every bit of oxygen leave his body. "And you all have."

Before them was the massive bank-vault-like door they had seen two nights prior. Frederick almost sobbed at the sight of it. That same pull was emanating from it, beckoning him and his friends to come closer. He turned to One, who was smiling slightly, a look of triumph on his face.

Doctor Gray pulled out a card and held it up to a scanner on the wall. Frederick heard several locks sliding behind the heavy door before it slowly swung open. Dr Gray stepped through, beckoning for them to follow.

Frederick was transfixed by the Door. But not the one they had just walked through.

No, this was an open door standing in the middle of the room. It was a fairly small room and was entirely empty except for the doorway and several fully armed guards. Dr. Gray nodded at the guards and gestured to the hall they had just come from. The guards moved from their positions beside the doorway, though they clearly were uncomfortable with leaving their post. As they stepped into the hallway, the massive vault-like door swung shut behind them, sealing Dr. Gray and all the applicants inside.

Frederick barely noticed any of it. He couldn't take his eyes off the other door. He walked around the back of it and found nothing on the other side. Looking back through, there was nothing peculiar—he just saw his friends, gaping at the spectacle before them. It didn't seem like they could see him from their vantage point.

"This makes no sense. What is this?" Frederick whispered as he walked back to the front of the Door.

"This is Kinth," the doctor replied simply. "The real Kinth."

Frederick circled around to join his friends and looked through the doorway once more, expecting it to have changed. He expected to simply see the other side of the room. Surely, this was just another one of Dr. Gray's tricks.

Deep down, Frederick knew that wasn't true. This was the realest thing he had ever experienced.

Through the doorway, he could see an open field ringed by trees. It was late evening, and stars had begun to glisten in the sky. Short grass swayed lazily in the wind, and the trees surrounding the clearing moved to match their rhythm. A small stream cut its way through the field, weaving back and forth as it deftly dodged large rocks and the occasional bush. Frederick could hear the water chattering excitedly as it ran over stones lying idly in its bed.

Frederick felt a pulling sensation somewhere deep inside of him. He didn't notice it at first, but it grew until he could no longer ignore it. It felt like someone had tied a rope around his waist and was dragging him toward the Door, slowly but surely.

He felt himself take a step forward. Then another.

"Ahem! Sorry, Twenty, but you can't go through yet." Frederick could barely hear the doctor's panicked voice. "Twenty! It's not safe! You aren't ready—your body can't handle it yet!"

Frederick continued to walk toward the Door, ignoring the doctor's protests.

He knew there was a good reason he shouldn't bolt through the Door that very second. He just couldn't possibly fathom what it was.

As he stepped closer, he could smell the fresh air spilling through. He closed his eyes and breathed it in, relishing its sweetness. He was so close now. Just a couple more steps . . .

Someone rested a firm hand on Frederick's shoulder, gently pulling him away from the Door. Frederick turned and was surprised to find One guiding him back to the rest of the group.

"Not yet," he whispered. Frederick could see the strain in the boy's face. He was fighting with all he had against the same pull.

"Ah, yes, very good." The relief in Dr. Gray's voice was obvious.

Frederick studied his friends' faces as One led him back to join them. He saw the same strain in their eyes as well. It was taking every ounce of strength and self-control they possessed not to sprint through the open doorway. Seven was sweating, his lips drawn in a thin line. He looked at Frederick and forced a smile.

Dr. Gray looked at the six applicants and furrowed his brow, then held the same card he had used earlier up to the scanner on the wall beside the door.

"Perhaps I have made a slight miscalculation. Will you all please follow me?"

The door clicked open, and the applicants followed reluctantly. As they left the room, the guards filed back in, reassuming their positions throughout the room.

Dr. Gray led them to a nearby door and gestured for them to enter. This was a small observation room—one-way glass allowed them to look into the room they had just been in without being seen by its occupants. There was a table in the center of the room with six chairs sitting around it.

"Please sit. I prefer to stand anyway," Dr. Gray said.

Frederick and his friends sat down uncomfortably. It was awkward having the doctor pacing the tiny room around them.

"I apologize if that was too much for any of you. I tend to forget just how shocking it can be. The doctor cleared his throat. "Now, where to begin . . ."

"How about explaining the doorway standing in the middle of the room that somehow leads to a field in the middle of nowhere?" Seven suggested somewhat earnestly.

The doctor laughed softly, nodded, and clasped his hands behind his back, turning to face them.

"Well as I said before, that's Kinth—the real Kinth. We simply stole the name to pay homage. Though it ended up serving a different purpose, as it seems you all are drawn to the name subconsciously."

"You all?" Thirteen asked.

"Yes, those who were born in Kinth."

Silence filled the room as the doctor's words hung in the air. He said it so casually, as if it were the most obvious thing in the world.

"Surely you all realized it when you saw the Door?" The doctor scratched his head in confusion. "You could feel the pull, I assume? All the others have. In fact, I'm quite certain I saw it on your faces."

Frederick felt the realization spreading through his entire body. Of course. The reason the pull had been so strong—it was belonging. He had felt at home for the first time in his life. It was such a foreign sensation that he hadn't been able to identify it at first. Frederick was surprised at how easy it was for him to accept this as the truth. It was absurd, impossible, and a million other things. Still, it felt right. It explained so much. He found himself hoping with all that he was that it was true.

"Holy crap," Seven said, his voice filled with awe. "It's true, isn't it?"

Dr. Gray nodded solemnly.

Frederick looked around the room to gauge his friends' reactions and found them nodding their heads. There was surprise written plainly on their faces, but there wasn't disbelief. In fact, One was smiling, as if he had been expecting nothing less.

"But what is it?" Thirteen asked. "What is Kinth? The real Kinth, I mean."

"Frankly, we aren't sure," Dr. Gray said. He was pacing again, his hands still clasped behind his back. "A different world? A different dimension? We have many theories but no way to prove any of them."

"A different world? What, like Narnia?" Seven asked incredulously.

"Nothing quite so mystical." Dr. Gray chuckled. "Though perhaps that is not a bad way to think about it. Years ago, the people of Kinth developed technology that could open a door to another place. Where would that door lead? They had no idea, but they opened it anyway."

Dr. Gray walked up to the glass and stared at the Door and the field beyond it.

"But why? Why open the Door? Surely that could've been dangerous?" Nineteen asked.

The doctor turned and regarded her with a wild stare. Frederick could tell Nineteen was fighting to not wilt beneath the intensity of his gaze.

"Why did Neil Armstrong go to the moon? The need to explore is a powerful thing, my dear. At least, that's how it started for them. They had combed every inch of their planet, and it had lost its mystery. So they looked elsewhere to fill the void."

"What do you mean, that's how it started?" Thirteen asked. "What changed?"

Dr. Gray looked solemnly to the Door. "A sickness broke out as they were nearing the end of the development of the Door technology. It ravaged their planet. Millions of people were dying every day, and they had no hope of a cure. No way to slow it down." He removed his glasses and sighed.

"Like the plague here," Frederick said softly.

The doctor nodded grimly. "Very much like that."

"You mean . . ." Frederick trailed off as realization dawned on him.

"That's right. The Door became their last hope. They thought perhaps they would find something on the other side. Something that would help them. At the very least, a place they could send those who were not yet sick to avoid catching the plague. Instead, they found us. It wasn't long before their plague became ours."

Dr. Gray paused to allow the applicants to ask questions, but he was met only with stunned silence, so he continued. "It wasn't long before the fate of those still living in Kinth was assured. There was a tiny percentage of the population that was immune, mostly children. They sent them through the Door for us to care for and retreated back to try to fight the disease. We did the same, studying the blood of the immune children in search of a cure. We found one eventually, just in time for us to avoid being wiped out. It was too late for Kinth, however."

Dr. Gray turned to them with tears in his eyes. "An entire civilization, an entire planet! Wiped out in less than one year by a single virus." He wiped his eyes roughly and cleared his throat. "The immune children from Kinth were mixed in with the other orphans the plague had created. They blended in easily. There were plenty of parents who had lost children and could support them."

"That's us," One said firmly. "We are those children."

"Some of them, yes." The doctor nodded. "There was a side effect we did not anticipate. The children's bodies knew they were no longer in their natural home. The air is different here; Kinth has something we don't. The children knew subconsciously they weren't home, and it had a devastating effect. Their bodies responded to this information by producing a near-constant state of anxiety. They felt threatened at all times, a constant state of fight-or-flight. That, coupled with the trauma of their loved ones dying, was the perfect breeding ground for crippling levels of anxiety."

"So the reason I've always felt like an outsider. Like I didn't belong..." Frederick paused.

"Is because you don't. Not here, anyway."

There was a moment of silence as all six children tried to swallow the implications of what the man was telling them.

"So what's the point of Kinth?" Thirteen shook her head in frustration. "This building, not that place."

"We were created to try to find a cure," Dr. Gray said. "Once we accomplished that, our focus shifted."

"Shifted to what?"

"Finding the children from Kinth."

Frederick shook his head in confusion. "Why did you want to find them? Or us, I guess. And is it really that difficult to track us down? Surely there was some kind of record of where the immune children were sent."

A pained look spread across the doctor's face as he began pacing once more. Frederick shifted uncomfortably. The doctor's energy was infectious.

"We wanted you all to live as normal a life as possible. We destroyed all records of where you had gone so no one would be able to try to use your past against you. We thought we were doing you a favor." Another heavy sigh. "Maybe we were. We just didn't consider we might need your help again."

"Need our help for what?" Thirteen interjected.

The pained look on the doctor's face deepened briefly. "We can discuss that later. There's much for you to digest before we get there."

The applicants sat quietly as the ominous tone of the doctor's words settled around them like dust.

"So that's what all this has been about?" Frederick asked, breaking the silence. "The applications and tests, all of it—it was just to determine if we were from Kinth?"

"Not exactly," Dr. Gray answered. "By the time you had been in this building for ten minutes, we knew you were from Kinth."

"How?" Frederick asked.

"I imagine the online applications let you whittle it down pretty good," One replied before Dr. Gray had the chance. "Then I would guess it had something to do with those goggles you had us try on."

"Very astute, One," Dr. Gray said as he smiled at him. "We use the online applications, which have been carefully crafted, to weed you out. There are many commonalities in how the anxiety presents itself in Kinthian children. We use those to cut down the numbers to a manageable size. At that point, we invite the applicants here so we can determine if they are Kinthian or not. As for the goggles, there's a physical difference between your eyes and the eyes of children from our neck of the woods. You are able to discern a light that we cannot, and the part of your eye that allows you to do so is visible if you look close enough. So we check that as soon as you get here so we don't have anyone go through the interview that doesn't need to. As you are aware, it can be quite . . . strenuous."

Seven snorted loudly and rolled his eyes, prompting an uncomfortable smile from Dr. Gray.

"Once we had determined you were from Kinth, we had to test how strong your reactions would be," he continued.

"Our reactions to . . ." Seven coaxed.

"The air," Frederick said.

"Precisely." Dr. Gray smiled broadly, the now-familiar wild glint returning to his eyes.

"What do you mean, the air?" Seven asked with a confused look.

"Think about it," Frederick continued. "In our interviews, when we were freaking out, what calmed us down?"

"He blasted that damn AC in our face."

"Exactly," Frederick said, and he saw the realization starting to spread across the other faces in the room.

"And in the first test, the AC was blasting again," Thirteen said. "Remember how cold it was in those hallways?"

"Same with the second test," One said, eyes growing wide. "I thought they were just trying to make the trees seem more real by simulating wind."

"And in the third test, the smoke was swirling like crazy in our room but was totally still in the common area. That's when we collapsed," Nineteen said, adopting a thoughtful expression.

"Is that why it got so hot and stuffy in the last test?" Eight asked.

Dr. Gray stood quietly, apparently not wanting to interrupt the group's flow of thought.

Nineteen stood and began pacing on the opposite side of the table from the doctor. "So the tests were never about how well we performed. It was all about the difference between our performances between the tests," she said as she continued pacing.

Dr. Gray's eyes were burning more wildly than Frederick had ever seen them.

"You were looking for good scores on the first two tests, the tests with the air pumped in. And bad scores on the last two, the tests without the air."

"Indeed," Dr. Gray responded. "Every child from Kinth responds differently to exposure the air. For some, it simply has a mild calming effect. For others, the results are more . . . extreme."

"So the reason we could do all those things, figure out the problems, run so fast—all that was because you were doping us with Kinth air?" Frederick asked.

"Well, doping is a rather crude way of putting it, but yes. And that was only a little bit of air. A mere fraction of what you will experience if you are fully exposed to Kinth." The doctor cleared his throat and adjusted his glasses. "But again, I'm getting ahead of myself. You'll have to build a tolerance to it."

"How long will that take?" One asked, impatience dancing behind his eyes.

"It varies from person to person. Hopefully no more than two weeks. If it's more than that . . ." The doctor trailed off and stared through the doorway once more. "Well let's just hope it's not more than that."

"What if it's longer than that?" Seven asked slowly.

"Oh probably nothing, I imagine we have a few months at least."

"What if it takes months?" he pressed.

"We, along with everyone on our planet, dies," the doctor said. Then he smiled and walked toward the door, pulling it open and calling over his shoulder. "Let's hope it doesn't come to that."

Chapter 14

Frederick and the others followed Dr. Gray back through the twisting corridors. As they walked, Frederick was struck by the mood of the group. Despite the doctor's ominous and characteristically vague comments, they smiled and whispered excitedly as they walked. A smile spread across Frederick's own face. They were finally getting answers, whatever those may be.

"We are moving you to a different sleeping area," Dr. Gray said over his shoulder. "Now that you have been let in on our secret, we think it's probably best to keep you separated from the other applicants. Also, we told them you were sent home, so it might raise some questions if you were still hanging around."

"Other applicants? You mean they're still here?" Frederick asked.

"Well, of course," Dr. Gray said, regarding him with a confused expression. "They might not be exactly what we were looking for, but we can still help them. Our knowledge of their true nature is invaluable in their treatment. Others could potentially help them, but not to the degree we can." Dr. Gray paused and scratched his beard thoughtfully, then continued. "It also creates a natural cover for us. This way, we don't have to fake good results to get potential applicants. We simply do the work well and wait."

Dr. Gray stopped abruptly at a door that had been propped open.

"These are your new quarters and, unfortunately, where I leave you. I'm sure you have many questions. I assure you, I have many answers. Still, I think perhaps you should ponder the things I have told you. Arthur will be around to collect you when it's time. Until then, relax, unwind, play games. Whatever you need to do to be ready for what lies ahead. If you need anything, just give Arthur a shout. He always seems to be lurking around here." The doctor winked at them awkwardly and departed without another word.

As he walked away, Frederick saw One whisper something quickly to Eight. The small boy erupted into a wide smile and sprinted after Dr. Gray.

"Hey, boss! Wait up!"

"I'm sorry, Eight, I simply do not have time–"

The doctor cut off as the boy tripped and catapulted through the air. Eight let out a sharp yelp as he landed heavily on his shoulder, rolling several times before finally coming to a stop at the doctor's feet. Eight moaned softly, cradling the shoulder that had received the brunt of the impact.

"My boy, what on earth are you doing?" Dr. Gray shouted as he scrambled to help the small boy up. "Are you alright?"

Eight yelped once again as the doctor inadvertently jostled his injured shoulder while attempting to get him to his feet. Dr. Gray recoiled slightly, clearly afraid he would worsen the injury. Eight reached out and grabbed onto the doctor's white lab coat with his good arm and awkwardly pulled himself to his feet.

"Not much of a doctor, eh, boss?" Despite the tears of pain in his eyes, there was still a good-natured tone to the boy's voice.

"I'm afraid I'm not that kind of doctor," Dr. Gray said. His relief that Eight appeared to be fine was evident in his voice. "Are you alright?" he asked once again.

Eight massaged his shoulder and swung it in circles, testing its movement. There was still a look of discomfort on his face, but there didn't seem to be any major damage done.

"Should be alright, boss. I'm a master faller."

Dr. Gray raised an eyebrow at the boy, who turned and began walking back toward the others.

"Eight, what were you going to ask me?" Dr. Gray called to him.

"Oh, don't worry about it, boss. I've forgotten already."

The man gave him a puzzled look before shaking his head and walking briskly down the hall.

"What was that all about?" Frederick asked Eight as he rejoined the group.

"Ask him." Eight beamed and nodded to One.

There was a hint of a mischievous grin tugging at the corners of One's mouth, but he shook his head dismissively.

"You're planning something, aren't you?" Thirteen whispered excitedly.

"Not now. I'll fill you all in later," One said as he walked through the open door to which Dr. Gray had led them. "Let's check out the new room, eh?"

Thirteen sighed in frustration before following him in, the rest of the group trailing behind.

Frederick and his friends found themselves in a common area that was significantly smaller than the one in their previous quarters. There was a single round table standing in the middle of the room with six chairs spread evenly around it. Frederick was surprised to find no other furniture in the room. The walls were bare except for a few simple abstract paintings spaced out on the walls. Connected to the common area were six doors, and each door had an applicant's number stamped on its face.

"Wow. Really pulled out all the stops this time," Seven said sarcastically.

Thirteen snorted in agreement and walked to investigate her room. The rest of the applicants drifted toward their respective doors. Frederick walked to the door bearing the large *20* and gently pushed it open.

He whistled softly as he surveyed the bedroom. It was about the same size as the common room, with a floor covered in lush carpet that Frederick felt he might sink into if he wasn't careful. There was a large mahogany desk in the corner with an ornate lamp perched atop it. Next to the desk was a minifridge, though it was large enough that Frederick figured it barely qualified as mini. Inside, he found bottles of water, sports drinks, fruit, chips, and a variety of other snacks and beverages. On the wall opposite of the entrance was a door that led to the bathroom. Frederick stepped through the door and whistled again. A large vanity mirror hung above a beautifully carved sink. In the corner of the room was a jacuzzi bathtub with a large shower next to it. The bathroom was bigger than Frederick's own bedroom back home. He shook his head in disbelief and walked back out and into the common area once more.

One was already seated at the table, shuffling a well-worn deck of cards that he had seemingly produced out of thin air. He had carefully constructed a tower of poker chips for each of the other applicants. Frederick sat down next to him, and the rest of the group joined them one at a time. Seven was the last to arrive. One began dealing the cards as the stocky boy sat in the remaining vacant seat. He had apparently already raided the fridge in his room, as he carried a bag of chips, a candy bar, and a vast array of beverages.

"I take it back, they did go all out," Seven said through a mouthful of chips.

"You can say that again. Although I'm just glad for the change in scenery. Not sure I could've handled one more day in the other rooms," Thirteen said as she snatched the bag of chips from Seven's hands. He opened his mouth to object but was cut off by Nineteen.

"The rooms are nice, I just . . ." She paused, apparently searching for the right words. "I just don't know how I feel about us all sleeping in separate rooms."

"It'll be nice to not worry about Seven's snoring." Thirteen snorted, then grew more serious. "Still, it is gonna feel weird."

One stopped dealing the cards and looked around the room, apparently deep in thought.

"I know you guys don't have any rules or anything, but shouldn't I at least have the same number of cards as the rest of you?" Eight asked in confusion.

"Game is off for now, Eight," One said as he gathered up the cards. "Seven, a hand?"

One stood and gestured for the others to do the same. As soon as they had, he flipped the table on its side. Frederick yelped in surprise and jumped back to avoid being smacked. Seven looked confused but asked no questions as he helped One roll the table to the corner of the room and hastily stack the chairs around it.

"So, uh . . . are we just going to sit on the ground?" Frederick asked as Seven and One finished rearranging the furniture.

"Not exactly." One smiled at him, then walked into his own room. Frederick heard a fair amount of rustling around before One emerged, dragging his mattress behind him.

"I think there should be enough room for all our mattresses. Besides, I've always wanted to hear the legendary snoring of Seven."

Nineteen laughed and ran to her room. The tiny girl cut a comical figure as she returned with her mattress, which threatened to swallow her as she dragged it into the room. Frederick smiled and hurried to retrieve his own. Eight and Thirteen were quick to follow, but Seven grumbled loudly, though he did it in the end.

They arranged the mattresses in a vague circular formation, leaving a gap in the middle in which they could play cards. It was awkward stooping to retrieve the cards from the ground, but Frederick couldn't deny that this felt right. He had no desire to face the night alone, especially with what he assumed would be very difficult days ahead of them.

They played cards in silence for a time, and Frederick could almost hear the gears turning in their brains. The information they had been given that day was not something that processed quickly, and Frederick knew there was a measure of internal processing that needed to be done before they could even speak of it with one another. Dr. Gray's words bounced around his head, echoing so loudly he could barely hear anything else. He paid little attention to the game of cards, though he appreciated the familiar rhythms the game offered. Having something to occupy his hands often helped his brain work.

He was unsure how to feel. Or rather, he was unsure what to feel most strongly, as he was being bombarded by a variety of emotions. First, there was his anger at being lied to for so long. Then there was his relief at knowing why he was the way he was. He had always felt broken but had never known why. Now that he knew, perhaps that gave him a better hope for a solution.

And, of course, there was his sadness. He always knew he had lost everything somewhere along the way, but he had just never known exactly what it was. Now he had an idea of what had been taken from him, and a part of him felt that loss as if for the first time. Still, it wasn't the multitude of emotions stirring in Frederick that shocked him. No, the thing that most shocked Frederick was the emotion that churned most powerfully within him: excitement.

It burned so intensely that he could feel the warmth throughout his entire body. He was nearly shaking with anticipation, and he had to cross his legs to keep them from bouncing with the thrill of what was to come. He had a purpose, and that dwarfed every other thought in his head. His whole life, he had felt useless. Not only that, he had been a liability.

He had needed constant monitoring. He had needed to be dragged from doctor to doctor. He had been a weight on his parents since the day he had arrived. They had loved that weight; they had never complained, and he suspected they wouldn't trade a single second of it. Frederick was surprised to feel a flicker of resentment at that. They didn't allow themselves to be frustrated with him. They deserved at least that, didn't they? But none of that mattered now. Now, he was needed. He had no idea what he was needed for, but the details mattered very little to him at the moment. He closed his eyes briefly and relished the long-sought sensation of serving a purpose.

"You taking a nap, Two-Oh?" Seven broke the longstanding silence.

Frederick opened his eyes and was met by a devilish grin.

"I was thinking about it, Seven. Nothing wears me out like kicking your ass repeatedly."

Seven's smile grew even wider. "Oh yeah? Well what do you think about this?" Seven said, triumphantly throwing down his cards face-up, a look of satisfaction on his face.

One wrinkled his nose and gave Seven a look of confusion.

"Seven, that's nothing. That's perhaps the worst collection of cards I have ever seen in my life."

"Do you even know how to play this game? Have you completely forgotten the rules?" Thirteen chimed in.

"I mean, honestly, we've been playing this game for months!" Nineteen said, shaking her head.

The look of indignation on Seven's face caused the room to erupt with laughter. Frederick rolled back onto his mattress, clasping his stomach as he shook with mirth. The rest of the group collapsed in similar hysterics. Tears were pouring down Thirteen's face as she struggled to speak, with little success. One and Eight were leaning against one another for support, struggling mightily to snatch a breath between their bouts of laughter. Even Nineteen couldn't help herself. She held a hand to her mouth and shook with silent laughter as tears poured down her face.

Seven was the only exception to the uproarious laughter that filled the room. He shook his head, rolled his eyes in annoyance, and used the distraction of the laughter to scoop up the chips in the pot. He also snagged a few chips from his neighbors' stacks. He sniffed haughtily and refused to look at his laughing friends, doing everything in his power to keep from laughing himself.

The laughter subsided eventually, and they returned to the game. They played for a few more minutes before yawns began to permeate the room. Frederick's eyelids grew heavy, and he saw that his friends were also struggling to stay awake.

"Well, the sooner we go to sleep, the sooner Thirteen can wake us up with her snoring," Seven said, rubbing his eyes sleepily.

Thirteen's presumably scathing reply was cut off by a yawn of monstrous proportions. She made a dismissive gesture and curled up on her mattress without another word. The others were quick to follow. They turned off the lights, whispered goodnights, and quickly fell asleep.

Chapter 15

Frederick was awoken not by the snores of his companions, but by a gentle yet urgent shake of his shoulder. He bolted up, panic rising in his stomach. He found One crouching next to him with a single finger held silently to his lips. Frederick's panic subsided as the other boy gestured for him to relax.

"Everything's fine—follow me," One whispered.

Frederick obeyed, trying to rub the sleep from his eyes as they adjusted to the darkness of the common room. He glanced at a small digital clock on the wall and saw that it was nearly 3 a.m. He cursed softly as he tripped over someone else's mattress but was relieved to find the mattress empty. In fact, as he looked around the room, he was surprised to find all of the mattresses empty. His relief turned to confusion.

"One, where is everybody?" Frederick whispered as loudly as he dared. He was unsure why the silence was necessary if there was no one sleeping in the room at the moment, but One's body language indicated that a certain level of stealth was required.

One responded by holding up a finger to his lips once more. The blond boy turned toward his room and beckoned for Frederick to follow. Frederick did so, keeping an eye peeled for any signs of the rest of their group.

One led him through the bedroom and into the bathroom. Light spilled out from the cracks around the door, providing the only illumination in the dark room. He opened the door quietly, and Frederick had to hold his hand up to his eyes to keep from being blinded by the sudden onslaught of light.

He blinked away stars as his eyes adjusted to the brightness of the room. Once they were fully adjusted, he was pleased, and further confused, to find the rest of his friends seated throughout the bathroom. Most of them were seated on the tile floor, though Seven had filled up the jacuzzi and sat on its edge with his legs submerged to his knees in the warm water.

"Uh . . . hey, everybody," Frederick said with an awkward wave. "Is this an intervention?"

"Not quite," One chuckled.

"Pop a squat, Two-Oh," Seven said, patting the space next to him.

"I think I'll just stick to the floor."

"Suit yourself," the boy huffed.

Frederick took his seat on the tile next to Thirteen, who was still clearly fighting off sleep.

"So is anyone gonna tell me what's going on?" he asked.

"Oh, we have no idea," Thirteen mumbled, then pointed to One. "He just shakes us awake and whisks us away to his bathroom one by one. Not a word of explanation."

All eyes turned expectantly to One, who had remained standing.

"I just think we have some things to discuss privately," he said with a shrug, but there was an intensity to his posture. He was anything but relaxed.

"Privately?" Nineteen asked.

"I figure they're probably monitoring our rooms." One shrugged again. "They might be monitoring the bathrooms too, but there's a chance they aren't. I'm pretty sure it's illegal. This just felt like it might be a way to talk without being overheard."

"Why are we worried about being overheard?" Seven asked.

"Well I just wanted to run something by you all without worrying about them crashing the party before it begins." One paused, waiting for more questions, but he was met with nothing but expectant looks.

"I want to go through. Tonight," he said simply.

"Go through . . ." Seven began.

"The Door."

"Tonight?"

"Tonight."

Thirteen whistled softly.

"But why? What's the rush?" Nineteen asked quietly. "I want to go through. I really do. But do we need to do it in secret? They told us we would go through eventually."

"That's true, they did say that. And maybe they will, maybe they won't." One stood in the middle of all of them now. He turned to each of them as he spoke, his movements became more and more frantic with each word. "They've lied to us the whole time we've been here. At every single turn. Even before we got here, they were lying to us! I don't blame them for that—they had to do what they had to do. But I can't risk them using that justification down the road to keep us out."

"I agree." Frederick surprised himself by speaking. He had always stuck close to the rules, but these were extreme circumstances. "I have to know what it feels like on the other side. We all felt the pull, right?" He paused and watched as each of his friends nodded. "There's something about that place, and I'm gonna see what it is. I have to."

One nodded at him appreciatively, then turned back to the others. "I'm obviously not going to make any of you come. If you want to stay here, you can. But I want you to think about something: what if they change their minds and say we aren't allowed to go? What if this is our only chance to go through? And you spend the rest of your life with only the description of what it felt like on the other side of that door? We are so much more than we ever thought. Are you really okay with taking the risk of never being that?"

The silence that followed his question weighed heavily on all those in the room.

"Screw that," Seven said softly.

Most of the group nodded. Nineteen, however, shook her head in frustration.

"Look, this is all fine. I'll go with you because I want to know too. But why are we acting like we can even do this? The Door is functionally in a bank vault filled with armed guards. We would need a key card to even get in, and once we do that, we'd have to get past like ten full-grown men who just so happen to have assault rifles!"

One smiled at her and nodded his head in acknowledgment. "Fair points, Nineteen. Regarding the armed guards, I'm not too worried about them. Apparently, we are valuable, so I can't imagine they will do anything to hurt us. All we have to do is surprise them and push through. We should be close enough to the Door to utilize some of that air."

"And what about the key card?" Nineteen asked, the frustration still clear in her voice.

"Oh, we've taken care of that," One said nonchalantly. "Eight?"

The small boy smiled and tossed something across the room to One, who caught it deftly and held it up for the others to see.

It was Dr. Gray's key card.

"But . . . how?" Thirteen asked in bewilderment.

Seven immediately burst into laughter. He laughed so hard, Frederick feared he would fall into the jacuzzi. "You picked his pocket, didn't you? That whole bit when you fell in the hallway was totally an act! Once he helped you up, you swiped it from him!"

Eight shrugged and tried to play it off, but he was absolutely beaming. "Hey, no big deal, you know?"

"That's what you two were whispering about then? Right before?" Frederick asked.

"It was surprisingly easy to convince him to steal something from the head of a massive corporation," One said with a shrug.

"You were planning this from the moment Dr. Gray showed us the Door, weren't you?" Frederick asked, shaking his head in amazement.

"As soon as I felt whatever was coming from the Door, I knew I would be going back as soon as I possibly could. I was just keeping an eye open for any opportunities to do so." One was smiling, but his eyes were hard with determination. "So, what do you guys think?"

Nineteen sighed heavily and set her jaw. "I'm in."

The rest of the group stood and nodded.

"So when do we go?" Thirteen asked.

"As soon as Seven has dried off his feet," One replied.

They crept through the darkened halls, walking lightly on the balls of their feet. One had insisted they carry their shoes to avoid them squeaking on the linoleum floors. They picked their way carefully through the halls, doing all they could to remain as silent as possible. They didn't encounter anyone, which was relatively unsurprising given the early hour. Still, Frederick had been worried that there would be security guards roaming the halls. It wasn't a long walk, and as they neared the entrance to the room that contained the Door, Frederick's stomach tightened with anxiety. One silently motioned for them to stop as he crouched against the wall at an intersection in the hallway.

"Change of plans," One whispered. "I'm going ahead to try to lure some of them away like I did in the second test. I'll circle back and join you guys inside."

"When you say 'change of plans,' do you mean that you're just letting us in on what your actual plan was the whole time?" Thirteen whispered.

One gave her a sly wink by way of reply and took off down the hallway before any of them could protest. He scanned the card, and Frederick could once again hear the locks behind the solid metal door slide out of place. The door swung open, and a shaft of light illuminated One standing brazenly in the hallway.

"Hello, boys!" he called jovially.

"What are you doing here? You aren't allowed out of your quarters unsupervised," a gruff voice called from within the room.

"Better come supervise me then!" One bolted down the hallway, away from where Frederick and the others sat.

There were shouts from the room before several guards sprinted after One. Frederick waited a few heartbeats before sneaking toward the door, the others following closely behind him. Suddenly, the massive door began to swing shut. One still had the key, so once the door shut they would be locked out. Frederick cursed and sprinted forward. He and his companions piled through the door, falling on top of one another in their haste.

"Well, that was close," Seven said as he stood and brushed himself off.

"Don't move!"

Frederick turned to find a single guard remaining in the room. He looked younger than the others, no older than twenty or so. He shakily pulled a taser from his belt and pointed it at Frederick. "D-don't move!" the guard repeated. "You can't be here!"

At that moment, Frederick felt the air from Kinth envelop him. It crashed into him like a tidal wave. He had to resist being knocked back a step, but he stood firm and leaned into the feeling. Breathing deeply, he relished the feeling of power it gave him.

"Sorry about this," he said apologetically. Then he sprinted at the man, bowling him over on his way to the Door. Frederick winced at the heavy thud as the man hit the ground. The guard cried out in protest once more, but Frederick and the others had already rushed through the Door.

Frederick made it thirty feet from the Door before the landscape around him stopped him dead in his tracks. He heard the others skid to a halt behind him as they stopped to marvel as well.

It was nighttime, but the night was clear, and the stars and moon provided more than enough light for them to easily see the spectacle. They stood in the same clearing they had seen through the Door several hours before. The same open field ringed with trees. The same stream. The same grass, boulders, rocks. All of it was the same, but at the same time, it wasn't.

Before, it had been like looking at a picture of a dream destination. That perfect vacation spot that you doubt you'll ever see. But now, now they were there. It surrounded them and filled every pore of their bodies. It seeped into every cell of their beings. Frederick felt tears welling in his eyes from the sheer majesty of the place. He had seen the trees and the grass before, but now he could hear them rustling in the wind. He had seen the stream from afar, but now he could hear the water chattering over the rocks and feel the coolness radiating from the chill waters. He tossed his shoes to the side. It would be a crime to walk this place and not feel the grass and soil between your toes. Frederick once again breathed in deeply and realized with a shock that his number had dropped all the way to 0 for the first time in his life. The tears that had been welling now poured from his face. He smiled through them and laughed at how simply fantastic it was.

"I feel *incredible!*" Seven shouted, sprinting past Frederick deeper into the clearing.

Thirteen whooped loudly and tore off after him, her stride only broken by the occasional leap or cartwheel.

Nineteen walked up and stood next to Frederick, her face also wet with tears.

"This is the best I've ever felt," she said. "I think it's the best I could ever feel." She smiled at Frederick, then sprinted off in the direction of the other two. Eight bolted past him straight to the nearest tree, clambering up it quicker than should've been possible and clung to a branch near the top. He leaned out dangerously over the ground, like a sailor perched on familiar rigging.

"I can see my house from here!" he shouted down, smiling goofily at the others below him.

Frederick rolled his eyes, but the smile never left his face. His ears perked up as he heard footsteps behind him. He turned to see One walking toward him with hands in his pockets, a smile splitting his face in two. There was a distinct look of "I told you so" shining in his eyes.

"That was quick," Frederick said, his eyebrows raised in surprise.

"It made it easier that they were weighed down by all that gear. They didn't seem too swift of foot anyway."

Frederick shot a glance back at the Door.

"Don't worry about it," One said, sensing the question before he asked it. "I don't think they'll follow us through. The guard who stayed behind tried to stop me—grabbed onto me and held on for dear life. Once I got through, though, he let go of me like I was on fire." He shrugged. "I think we should be good for a little while at least."

The two boys stood in silence. Frederick was still mildly worried about guards storming through and dragging them back, but it wasn't difficult to push the thought from his mind.

"I think I could get used to this," One said simply as he turned in a slow circle, taking in the entire scene. Without another word, he sprinted toward Thirteen and Seven, who had started a game of tag in the middle of the clearing. They chased one another back and forth, shouting playful curses as they played.

Frederick's limbs began shaking, begging to be used, to test their limits. He happily relented, dashing toward the stream at a breakneck pace. As he neared the water, he felt no desire to stop, so he bounded over it. It was a jump he never would've been able to manage on the other side of the Door, but here, it was like stepping over a crack in the sidewalk. He landed on the other side and ran onward without breaking stride. Frederick ran until he reached the edge of the clearing, and as the trees approached him, he increased his pace.

He ran directly at the trunk of a large one that had no branches near the ground. As he reached it, he leaped and let his momentum shift upward, taking three full steps up the trunk as he did so. Frederick smiled at the ease with which he recreated One's move from the second test. However, instead of pushing backward away from the trunk as One had, he pushed upward with one last final burst of energy. He flew, barely reaching the lowest of the branches. Grabbing it tightly, he easily pulled himself into a sitting position atop the branch.

Frederick looked at the ground below, now a good twenty feet away. He clambered a bit higher into the tree, trying to get a better vantage point. Through a break in the leaves, he could see his friends. They all appeared to have joined in on the game of tag. The wind carried their laughter to him, and he smiled in contentment. The view from the tree was incredible, but Frederick's limbs once more began to ache for movement. There was simply too much to do for him to remain in one place for more than a minute or so. Frederick jumped from the lowest branch, falling a significant distance before landing lightly on his feet. He took off back toward the stream, this time at a controlled jog instead of his previous reckless sprint.

Frederick splashed into the stream and relished the cold water that rose to his knees. The water was so clear, he could see the rocks lining the bed of the stream perfectly. He stooped and picked up several of the large, smooth stones. They were vibrant colors: deep reds, sky blues, forest greens, yellows, and purples. It looked as if the stream contained an underwater rainbow. The colors were so full, Frederick felt hypnotized by them. He felt he could spend the rest of his life studying this stream bed and never grow bored.

"Well lookie here. We've traveled to a new planet where we are superhumans, and all our dear Twenty cares to do is look at the pretty rocks!" Seven laughed.

"To be fair, they are some very, very, pretty rocks," Thirteen chimed, jumping into the water beside Frederick and scooping up a handful.

"They look like flowers," Nineteen said as she carefully picked one up in each hand and admired them.

"Come here, you stupid goldfish!" Frederick turned to see Eight splashing wildly in the stream a short ways down from them. The boy was apparently trying to catch a fish, with little luck. He pounced back and forth as the creature avoided him easily. Frederick laughed at the small boy's enthusiastic, possibly naïve attempts to capture it.

"Well, it's not exactly Moby Dick, but that doesn't make it any less interesting," One said to Frederick out of the side of his mouth as he waded to join them in the water.

"Oh, give it up, Eight! You don't have a snowball's chance in—"Seven cut off mid-sentence as Eight turned toward the group with a fish held triumphantly in both hands. He beamed directly at the other boy.

"You were saying, boss?"

The whole group, including Seven, burst into disbelieving laughter. Eight held the fish high for a few more seconds to make sure everyone had fully taken in the spectacle before he released it back into the water. The group applauded wildly, chanting Eight's name as the small boy walked back to join them. Eight bowed to them in a grand, exaggerated sort of way, thanking each of them individually for coming. The thank-you to Seven was especially long and smug, as Frederick had suspected it would be. To his credit, Seven handled it graciously, playing along until Eight had had his fill of the bit.

Frederick walked out of the water and flopped onto the ground, staring up at the night sky. Though they had been on the other side of the door for some time, there was still no sign of a rising sun in either direction. The night seemed to be reaching its darkest hours, which allowed the celestial bodies to show off fully. Frederick put an arm under his head and stared in awe at the pinpricks of light that peppered the foreign sky above him. He barely noticed his friends as they joined him one by one. They lay in silence for several minutes, simply taking it all in.

Frederick jumped as Thirteen broke the silence.

"I don't recognize any of these." Her quiet voice was filled with awe. "I mean, of course I don't. It's a different sky—a different universe, probably. I just can't wrap my head around it. I used to spend every night staring through this stupid telescope with my dad. He made me memorize all the major constellations and their stories. I hated it at first, but he broke me down. Eventually, I loved it more than anything." She paused in thought for a moment before continuing, "I guess those were never my stars."

No one replied as they let her words sink in.

"I believed it before," Seven said. "All the Kinth stuff, I mean. I really did. At least, part of me did. It all made sense and just felt right. You know? But there was a small part of me that wasn't convinced. Somewhere inside of me, I was expecting the curtain to be pulled back. For Ashton Kutcher to jump out of a trashcan or something, I don't know."

"Who is Ashton Kutcher?" Eight asked.

"Not important," Frederick said, not wanting Seven to get derailed.

The boy waited a few seconds, then continued. "As soon as I saw the stars, that part of me died. And I'm glad it's gone."

"I think I always knew," One said, his voice quieter than usual. "I always felt so out of place. I never understood it. God, I'm so sick of it. So sick of always feeling so . . ." He trailed off, sighing in frustration as he tried to find the right word. "I don't know, just wrong, I guess."

Frederick glanced at him and was shocked to see the ferocity in his face.

"I can't do it anymore. Not ever again," One whispered. Frederick was unsure if any of the others even heard him.

"I have a question," Seven said tentatively, "but I need you all to promise not to laugh."

"That's asking an awful lot," Thirteen mumbled.

Frederick shot her a glance, then waved for Seven to continue.

"Does this make us aliens?"

Frederick smiled to himself and thought he could sense a few of the others smiling as well. Thirteen broke into a rather suspicious coughing fit, but no one laughed.

"Technically, yes. Though I'm not sure how I feel about that," Nineteen answered.

"Well, technically no, actually," Frederick said. "On the other side we are, but not here. I guess it means we grew up aliens. Lord knows I always felt like one."

"I always said you looked like one too," Nineteen said, almost to herself.

Frederick sat up and gave the girl a look of faux indignation. "How dare you?" he sputtered in an overly dramatic voice.

"How dare you indeed, Nineteen! How could you say that about our dear Twenty?" Seven said, also sitting up and regarding the girl with a harsh stare. "Is it his fault his eyes are so large and inhuman? Or that his hair sticks up so that it looks like antennae? Or that his skin is such a sickly green? Can we really hold any of that against our poor friend?"

One, Eight, and Thirteen keeled over in fits of laughter. Seven winked at Frederick, and they both joined in, laughing loudly. It acted as an echo chamber. The harder he saw the others laugh, the harder Frederick found himself laughing. Before long, he was gasping for air between his hysterical fits. Nineteen alone remained in control, one hand held up to cover her mouth. Every time it seemed the group was about to compose themselves, another one of them would begin all over again, causing them all to return to their hysteria. Frederick dropped down to the ground once more, relishing the ache in his side from the laughing. It had been a long time since he had laughed that hard, a very long time.

Over the noise, Frederick heard Nineteen say something. He couldn't make out the actual words, but he detected an urgency in her tone that cut off his laughter.

"What?"

"I said to shut up! I hear something," she hissed. Frederick could hear fear radiating from her voice.

"Guys! Shut it!" he whispered harshly as he gestured to get their attention, then raised a finger to his lips. The rest of the group immediately grew silent.

What's wrong? One mouthed to Frederick who simply shrugged and pointed to Nineteen.

In turn, Nineteen pointed to the other side of the stream, then pointed to her ears.

One crouched and stalked toward the water. Frederick joined him, straining to hear any sounds over the running water. There was something else that Frederick couldn't quite make out above the sound of the water. He closed his eyes.

Several seconds later, he snapped them open. He knew exactly what the sound was.

It was growling. And it was getting closer.

Frederick couldn't see anything in the darkness, but he could sense something stalking toward them. The horrible growl continued, growing in volume. Frederick didn't have to think hard to remember where he had heard that sound before.

"The storage room," Eight whispered frantically. "it's the same noise from that cage!"

"Shut up!" One hissed at the small boy. Frederick could see he was staring into the dark, straining to catch a glimpse of their stalker. "Twenty, Seven, with me. Eight and Nineteen, stand behind us—Thirteen, you behind them. I don't want anything sneaking up behind us."

The boy's voice was quiet but firm. Frederick and the others were quick to follow his orders. Eight whimpered from behind him as the growling continued to grow louder.

"Here's the plan," One said loudly. The thing clearly knew where they were, so there was little point in whispering anymore. "Seven, Twenty, and I are gonna take care of this thing, and we are all gonna run for the Door. We have no idea what we are dealing with, so maybe it's best to retreat and get some more answers after all. Nobody runs for it until I say so. Got it?"

Frederick muttered a confirmation along with the others and focused his attention fully on the darkness before them. The growling grew so loud that he was certain the mystery beast couldn't be more than a few feet away.

His suspicions were soon confirmed.

Frederick had to fight to keep from screaming as a pair of blood-red eyes appeared mere feet in front of him. They were identical to the ones he had seen on the other side of the glass in the small room in Kinth, although now there was nothing separating him from them. The fear he had felt then returned in full force—it took everything in him to stand his ground.

Now that he knew where to look, he could just make out the creature's body. It looked vaguely like a massive wolf, though the general shape wasn't quite right. There was a strange formlessness about the thing, almost like it wasn't quite solid. On all fours, the beast was as tall as Frederick's chest, and Frederick's mouth went dry at the sight. He jumped as One released a blood-curdling screech and threw himself at the monster. The beast screeched in reply and leapt at the boy. They clashed midair with a force that should've shattered bones. One, however, seemed unfazed. He wrapped his arms around the monster's neck, pulled it to the ground, and struggled to choke it out.

"A little help, guys?" he shouted at Frederick and Seven, struggling now just to keep his grip as the monster strained for his throat, which was just out of reach of its snapping jaws.

Frederick and Seven sprang into action, recovering surprisingly quickly from their shock. Both boys leapt at the monster, Seven diving at its lower body in an attempt to neutralize its movement, while Frederick went for the snapping maw. He would've certainly been bitten had the monster not been so focused on One's throat. Frederick got the jaws under his arm and clamped down as hard as he could. The monster began to writhe wildly, trying to throw the boys off.

"Thirteen, take them! Go!" One shouted.

"I'm not leaving you!" the girl yelled back.

"Yes you are!" One's tone sent a chill through Frederick, and Thirteen wordlessly grabbed Nineteen and Eight and hauled them back toward the Door. Frederick was forced to turn his full attention to the jaws.

"What now?" Seven shouted. "I can't hold this much longer!"

"Neither can I!" The jaws were slipping from his grasp.

The boys waited for a response, but none came from One.

"One?" Frederick yelled.

"I'm thinking!" he shouted back.

"We don't have time for—" Seven was cut off as the monster bucked and threw the large boy in the air. He landed heavily on his back, gasping for air. The monster used its newfound leverage to throw Frederick into the air as well. He landed next to Seven in a similar fashion, unable to regain his breath. One yelled and rolled away from the monster, narrowly dodging the razor-sharp teeth.

He came up in a crouch between Seven and Frederick, who scrambled to their feet. The monster began circling the boys, its hellish growl returning once more.

"You think the others made it?" One asked, his voice a mixture of fear and excitement.

"Surely by now," Frederick replied. His muscles burned, but he still felt good, like he could go all night.

"Good. Then we don't need to waste any more time. This thing will kill us if we drag this fight out. We need to end this now if we want to have any chance of surviving."

"And how exactly do you propose we do that?" Seven hissed out of the side of his mouth.

"Simple. Grab something hard and hit it in the head until it stops moving," One said as he picked up a rock. Frederick smiled at the casual nature of the words. He shook his head ruefully and scooped up two large rocks of his own, handing one of them to Seven.

"What a stupid way to die," Seven muttered as he took the rock from Frederick.

"I can think of worse," One said simply and threw himself forward.

The monster wasn't caught off guard a second time. It leaped forward and sank its teeth deep into One's shoulder. The boy shouted in pain and anger and swung his rock at the monster's head, scoring a solid blow. The monster stumbled backward, shaking its head.

One collapsed to the ground, holding his bleeding shoulder. Frederick rushed forward, trying to take advantage of the opening he had created. The monster came to its senses as he neared, and it snapped at Frederick's throat. Frederick raised his arm instinctively to block the attack and felt white-hot pain shoot up his arm. He screamed in agony and began swinging his rock wildly at the monster's head. He landed several solid blows, and blood began to pour from the places Frederick had struck. As he reared back to deliver what he hoped would be the finishing blow, the rock slipped from his hand, soaring through the air and landing with a soft thud several feet away. The rock had become so soaked with the creature's blood, it was like trying to hold on to a bar of soap. The shock of losing his only weapon threw Frederick off balance. The monster took advantage of the opening and used its superior weight to throw Frederick to the ground, jaws still clamped down on his arm. Blood flowed freely over both boy and beast, drenching them. Frederick's head became light from blood loss, and he struggled to remain conscious. Seven roared and threw himself on the monster's back, pounding its head, punctuating each blow with a curse.

"Die. You. Overgrown. Mutt."

The monster shuddered and released Frederick's arm, trying to stumble away. But the damage had been done, and it didn't get far. Frederick's eyes slowly closed as Seven continued to pound away with his rock.

PART TWO

Chapter 16

The pain pounding in Frederick's head was rivaled only by the pain throbbing in his arm. He groaned, refusing to open his eyes for a few more precious moments.

"We simply must stop meeting like this."

Frederick pried his eyes open and was met with the sight of Dr. Gray sitting in a chair near the foot of Frederick's bed. He sat up groggily, squinting against the harsh LED lighting of the room as he tried to take in his surroundings. It was a small, hospital-like room, complete with a heartbeat monitor, curtains for privacy, the whole deal. The floors, walls, and ceiling all bore the exact same shade of off-white.

There were no windows, which Frederick found more disconcerting than he cared to admit. The curtains around his bed were pulled back at the moment, allowing him to survey the rest of the room. There were five empty beds spread evenly throughout, all neatly made.

"The others . . ." Frederick started.

"All perfectly fine. Well, mostly fine. All in better shape than you, if that's any consolation. You apparently had the strongest reaction."

"The strongest reaction to what? Being mauled by a wolf?" Frederick asked.

"No, not quite. And One's injuries from the Bristle were worse than yours, but he's been out and about for a full day now."

"Bristle?" Frederick asked.

"Yes, that's what we call those creatures. Or rather what the Kinthians called them. I am curious as to what the origin of the name was. Alas, that is a secret I fear died with them."

The doctor's eyes adopted a far-off look. Frederick tried to determine if the sadness was for the lives lost or all the answers that disappeared with them.

"So what then?" Frederick prompted.

"Hm?" Dr. Gray's eyes snapped back into focus.

"You said I had the strongest reaction to . . ."

"Ah, yes of course." The doctor straightened in his chair, clearing his throat loudly. "Well, I thought you'd have guessed by now. You had a reaction to the air of Kinth. You remember me saying your body wasn't ready to handle it, hm?"

"Oh, right." Frederick shook his head, embarrassed for not having connected the pieces sooner.

"This is what happens when you have a strong reaction," Dr. Gray continued. "It's similar to when people crash after spikes of adrenaline. Your body could operate at a higher level than ever before, even in the tests. It wasn't ready for the strain, so you've spent the last three days recovering."

"Three days?" He couldn't quite believe it.

"Frankly, you should be happy you didn't tear any muscles or do any permanent damage. It's almost a good thing you ran into the Bristle when you did. If you had stayed much longer, the damage might have been irreparable."

"Dr. Gray!"

"Hm?"

"Did you say three days?" Frederick asked, frustration creeping into his voice at the man's absent-mindedness.

"Ah, yes, I did. You've been unconscious for three days. Everyone else was out for about twenty-four hours. Except for One, of course—he was out for two full days," the doctor said casually.

"Didn't you say we were on a tight schedule? Like, 'die if we take too long' kind of schedule? Why are you being so chill about this?" Frederick felt his number climbing rapidly. His pulse quickened, and his breaths dashed to and fro from his lips.

"Twenty! Twenty! Calm down. It's alright. We've been acclimating your body to the air. Also, the sudden shock of just barreling through the Door was actually quite beneficial in this case." He cleared his throat uncomfortably. "I never would've encouraged you all to do so, as it was extremely dangerous, but this might've been the best way to start your training."

Frederick stared at Dr. Gray in disbelief.

"You wanted us to sneak through," Frederick said, shaking his head in amazement. The realization hit him like a freight train. "That's why it was all so easy. You knew that Eight took your key card, and you let us get through the Door."

"Well, I wouldn't say that," the doctor said with a small grin. "I didn't want you to go, per se, but I certainly wasn't going to kill myself stopping you."

Frederick stared at the aging man, unsure of what to feel. Eventually, he just laughed and shook his head. It was exhausting trying to figure out the hundreds of emotions swirling around inside him these days. Part of him had to simply laugh at the absurdity of the man. This man who seemed to care so much but at the same time be so incredibly reckless.

"If you are feeling up to it, Twenty, I've got some explanations for you," Dr. Gray's voice cut through Frederick's thoughts. "I suppose further explanations is a more accurate way of framing it."

"Shouldn't we wait until everyone is here? It seems like it would be easier to do it just once." Frederick glanced once more at the other beds in the room. Somehow, he felt the absence they carried had grown since the conversation had started.

"Ah, yes, well I already told them, you see," Dr. Gray said, seeming mildly uncomfortable. "We were not entirely certain when you would wake up, and the sooner they had all the information, the better."

Frederick knew he shouldn't feel left out by this. Of course it made perfect sense that they had already told the others. He just hated learning anything without them sitting next to him.

"Of course," he said simply, feeling rather silly for assuming they would have halted everything for him.

"I'm sure you have a plethora of questions, and I'll try to answer them all. If you don't mind, though, I'll just give you what I see as pertinent, and you can ask questions to fill in the gaps. Is that acceptable?"

Frederick nodded and waited for the doctor to continue.

"Well, first things first, I suppose. I'm going to tell you why we need you, and I hope you'll forgive me for not beating around the bush." Dr. Gray paused, his mouth working as he searched for his next words. Frederick could see pain in his eyes. "Frederick, we need you to close the Door. Permanently."

Frederick balked at the doctor, who sat uncomfortably, trying to gauge his reaction.

"You want us to close the Door? Forever? You just showed us this place. This wonderful place where I get to finally feel at home. And you want to take that away forever? Not only that, you want *me* to do it for you?"

Dr. Gray sighed and stood, placing one hand in a pocket while the other journeyed through his tangle of hair. He began pacing back and forth.

"I don't want this, Frederick. In fact, I hate it almost as much as you do. We are cutting ourselves off from literally an entire world of knowledge. The Kinthians may be gone, but there is still so much we could learn from them. The advancements we could make in technology and medicine alone would change everything about our lives."

The doctor stopped pacing and looked Frederick squarely in the eyes.

Frederick was startled by how pained he truly looked. "But we have to. There is no other way. It will destroy us, all of us, and there's nothing we can do to stop it."

"What do you mean?" Frederick asked.

"It's going to happen again, Twenty," the doctor said in an exhausted voice.

"What is?" His stomach clenched.

"The virus from Kinth has mutated, and if we don't close the Door, we are going to have another plague on our hands. This time, we might not find a cure, and even if we do, it might be too late." The doctor closed his eyes and took a deep breath. "If we don't act, I fear we will suffer the same fate as Kinth."

"How do you know this?" Frederick asked. He felt a numbness spreading throughout his body. He was going to lose everything again.

"Bristles, like the one you encountered, have been wandering up to the Door. They have been more aggressive than any we previously encountered. We've been doing tests on them for several months now, and we've seen the virus slowly mutate. Eventually, it will mutate to the point that our cure will no longer be effective."

"How long do we have until then?" Frederick heard himself ask.

"We have no idea," the doctor replied. "Not really, anyway. We suspect it will be a few more months, but that's mostly guesswork. We don't have anything resembling a functional timeline."

Frederick's stomach dropped. "So it's a ticking time bomb, and we can't see the countdown."

"Precisely." The doctor nodded.

"Can't we just barricade the Door or something? Surely there's a way to do this without cutting ties forever," Frederick said with little conviction.

"Twenty," the doctor began, with a balance of annoyance and patience in his voice, "on some level, you are going to just have to believe me. We have looked at this from every angle, and this is the only way. Yes, we could barricade the

Door so the bristles couldn't get through. But what if a mosquito that is carrying some of their blood gets through a tiny crack? What if the virus mutates to the point that it becomes airborne? No matter the precautions we take, there is always a chance of the virus finding its way through. Is it really worth risking our entire species to leave it open?"

Frederick looked down, his face flushing. He was ashamed that there was a part of him that wanted to take that risk.

"I know this is difficult to hear, Frederick," the doctor said. Frederick started at the use of his real name—it felt like it had been years since anyone had called him that. "But we won't abandon you; we can help you when you get back. It will be better than it was before, I promise you that. We are experts in this, and we've stockpiled plenty of air from Kinth. You will not be totally cut off. You will not be alone."

Frederick tried to force himself to believe the words. He tried to connect with the sincerity that resonated in Dr. Gray's voice. Despite his best efforts, though, he couldn't accept it, not fully. There was a part of him that whispered that he should've expected this. The other shoe was always going to drop. Frederick was never going to be happy, and he was a fool to have thought otherwise.

With a shaky breath, he pushed the thought away. There would be time for all that, but this was not it.

"Why us?" Frederick tried not to sound like a whiny child. "Why do we have to do it? I get that the air makes us stronger, but surely there are people who would still be better equipped?"

"I'm not sure about that, Frederick." Dr. Gray shook his head. "Even if it were true, there is one major issue. The Bristles. Only someone born in Kinth can see them. Their bodies reflect a specific kind of light that doesn't exist here. People from this world never developed the ability to see it because they never needed to. Since you were born in Kinth, you have that ability—the physical makeup of your eye allows you to see them."

"Arthur told us about that," Frederick said "That's what you were checking for with the goggles when we first got here."

"Indeed." Dr. Gray nodded solemnly. "It's as sure a sign as any that someone is from Kinth."

Frederick closed his eyes and leaned back into his bed. His head had started spinning, and he felt he would be sick if he didn't lie down.

"We could send in soldiers, but they wouldn't be able to see the Bristles. They'd be wiped out eventually. Besides, for some reason, our weapons don't work there."

"What?" Frederick's eyes popped back open. "We won't even have guns?"

"I'm afraid not. Despite our best efforts, we can't manage to make any guns work in Kinth. We have no clue why—they simply won't fire."

"So you want me and my friends, a bunch of high schoolers, to go to a different world, fight off a bunch of disease-ridden, invisible super-wolves, then close the gateway between our two worlds like it's no big deal?"

"Well, technically the Bristles aren't invisible to you."

Frederick laughed in disbelief and closed his eyes once more.

"I understand the lunacy of this, Frederick, I really do. Please understand, I would not do this if there was another option. Just—just think about it. I'll be back tonight for your answer."

"My answer?" Frederick asked without opening his eyes.

"Well, of course," Dr. Gray said. "I cannot and will not force anyone to risk their lives. No matter how high the need. This is your choice, though I think we both know what your answer will be."

Frederick didn't respond, his eyes still shut. A few quiet footsteps and the squeaking of the door hinges announced Dr. Gray's departure.

Frederick sat in silence as he pondered the implications of all that he had been told. He had expected there to be risk in whatever he was needed for. He had expected the stakes to be high. Still, there was a difference between knowing of risk in an abstract way and knowing in a very concrete way. That concrete weighed heavily on him as he sat in his bed.

A sudden knock at the door caused Frederick to jump.

"Um, come in?" he said hesitantly.

The door swung open to reveal a smiling Arthur. The bespectacled man bounced into the room, the relief painted across his face mixing with his smile.

"Hello, Twenty! It's so very lovely to see you! You had us very worried there for a bit," Arthur said as he walked up to the foot of Frederick's bed. "Although, I should've expected the air would hit you hardest after what you showed us in the tests!"

Arthur's hands were as restless as ever. He was attempting to occupy them with a pen at the moment, performing several very complex spins between, around, over, and under his fingers. It took no small amount of effort for Frederick to focus on the man's words and not his pen aerobics.

"You look much better! Though I expected you would want to wash away some of the last few days before seeing your parents again," Arthur said, his eyes scrunching together slightly.

Frederick opened his mouth to speak, but the words got stuck somewhere in his throat. The more he tried to say something, the more words got clogged. He shook his head in confusion, mouth still hanging open.

Arthur's eyes went wide.

"He didn't tell you?" His eyes shifted from confusion to anger. The look was odd on the usually jovial man. Frederick shook his head dumbly, still not able to force words out of his mouth.

"That man!" Arthur gripped his pen so tightly, his knuckles cracked. "For such a brilliant mind, you'd think it could hold more than one or two things at a time. I told him . . ."

"My parents are coming?" Frederick interrupted Arthur's tirade.

Arthur's expression softened, and his face flushed with embarrassment.

"Ah, well, actually, they're already here." Arthur gestured for Frederick to stand. "I'm sorry. Here I am ranting about Dr. Gray, and I'm being just as thoughtless. Taking up even more of your time with my childish fits. I can tell them you will be with them in, say, twenty minutes? That'll give you some time to shower and perhaps process a bit?" Arthur smiled warmly at Frederick, and it had a comforting effect.

"Thanks, Arthur. That would be great."

Frederick stood from the bed and reached out in a half panic to keep himself from falling as his legs wobbled beneath him.

"Woah, there!" Arthur said, appearing at Frederick's side to help steady him.

"I guess this is what happens when you don't use your legs for three days after being attacked by a monster and overdosing on magical air," Frederick said dryly. Arthur snorted as he assisted Frederick to a bathroom in the corner of the room.

"I suppose this will also give you a chance to reclaim your sea legs," Arthur chirped as he handed Frederick a towel and a fresh change of clothes. "I'll be back in twenty minutes to collect you. If you need more time, just let me know."

Frederick nodded in response and closed the door before Arthur could flash him a reassuring smile.

After he had undressed, Frederick stared at the large bandage on his left arm that was covering the Bristle bite. He had been given no instructions on whether or not to remove it. After a brief moment of deliberation, he decided to. Surely Arthur would've mentioned if he was supposed to keep it on.

Frederick took the bandage off carefully, dreading both the pain of fabric pulling on his wound as well as the sight of the wound itself. As he unwound the bandage, Frederick was astounded to find no oozing scabs nor feel any sharp pain. Where he had expected to find the recent marks of his altercation, he found only several small scars. They were tiny and hardly noticeable if you weren't looking for them. He ran his other hand over the pale marks and shook his head in disbelief. The scars looked months old at least, perhaps years. Frederick shoved the confusion to the back of his mind, making a mental note to ask Arthur if his injury had been as bad as he had first thought.

Stepping into the shower, he closed his eyes as the warm water peppered his body. Before Kinth, he had often used showers as a way to clear his head. If he was having an especially high-number day, he would lock himself in the bathroom and not emerge until he found the world to be a manageable place again. There was something about the warmth the water provided, the sound of it all, the isolation. Frederick had discovered that showers served as a kind of sanctuary for him. He had always been slightly embarrassed by the thought, but he thought it unwise to turn his nose up at any effective remedy considering how few he had found in his life. Frederick's mind wandered from those nights spent spiraling to his parents. He wasn't sure what he should be feeling at seeing them again. Obviously, he was excited to see them—he loved them more than anything and had missed them dearly. On the other hand, it would be difficult. How could he communicate all that had happened to him since he had arrived at Kinth? It felt like he had lived an entire life since he'd last seen them. He was certainly a different person now than he had been then. When he had left, he had been terrified of his own shadow, and now he attacked monsters in the night with nothing but a rock.

Frederick was jarred from his ruminations by a loud knock on the bathroom door.

"Your twenty minutes are up! Should I tell your parents you need more time?" Arthur called.

Had it really already been twenty minutes?

"No! I'll be right out!" Frederick answered. He finished showering, toweled off, and threw on the fresh clothes Arthur had provided. He emerged from the bathroom feeling refreshed, though more than a little nervous. Arthur led him through a series of hallways to a small empty waiting room that felt vaguely like a therapist's office. There was a couch and two sitting chairs with a small coffee table between them. The room was warmly lit and smelled faintly of cinnamon.

"I'll go grab you parents from the waiting room. Should only take a second." The small man turned to leave but paused at the door. "Hey, Twenty. I know I probably don't need to tell you this, but I'm afraid you can't tell your parents the truth. At least, not the whole truth. They can't know anything about the specifics of the testing or anything the doctor has told you in the last couple days." There was a regretful look in Arthur's eyes as he spoke. He clearly didn't enjoy having to tell Frederick this. "It's all covered in the NDA you signed your first day. I know that it will be difficult, but we can't let word of this get out. I hope you understand."

Frederick nodded curtly. The truth was, he hadn't been planning on telling his parents any of that anyway. He had no desire to put a burden of that magnitude on them. He had weighed them down his whole life, and he wasn't going to leap at the opportunity to do so again.

He took a seat in one of the chairs and twiddled his thumbs as he waited for Arthur and his parents. True to his word, Arthur returned shortly, with Henry and Emily following close behind.

"Freddy!" Frederick's mother threw her arms around him and squeezed for all she was worth. "How are you? Are they feeding you enough? You look great!"

"Hey, Mom," Frederick gasped. "I'm doing well—they're feeding me plenty. I feel great too."

"Emily?" Frederick's father said in a sweet voice.

"Yes?" she responded, without releasing Frederick.

"You are murdering our son," he said in the same sweet voice.

She shot him a sharp glare but released Frederick reluctantly.

"Hey, bud, I was gonna ask you a question or two, but I figure I'll give you a minute for your ribs to recover." Frederick's father hugged him warmly, giving his shoulder an affectionate squeeze as he pulled away. "It's good to see you."

"It's so good to see you both," Frederick choked, and he was shocked to find that he was fighting back tears.

"Oh, Freddy." Emily hugged him again.

"Is everything okay, Frederick?" Henry asked, a look of concern flashing across his face.

Frederick fought to compose himself. He took a large breath and gave them what he hoped was a convincing smile.

"Everything is fine. It's just been a long week, and I really missed you both," Frederick said.

"Long in a bad way or long in a long way?" his father asked.

"More the second one than the first, although it's certainly been both. But it's all good. I knew this wouldn't be easy. It'll all be worth it in the end." His parents nodded firmly, but Frederick could see by their faces that their resolve had been tested over the past week.

"How's your number?" Frederick's mother asked. There was concern in her voice that she managed to hide from her face.

"It's actually been really low ever since my first day here. Right now? Around a 1, I'd say." It felt nice to not have to lie to his parents about this. They probably would've been able to tell if he had anyway. His parents had an uncanny ability to tell where his number was most of the time. He wondered if Arthur or Dr. Gray had pumped Kinth air into the room to keep him from breaking down in front of them. Either way, he felt great—far better than he'd anticipated.

"Freddy, that's great! I could tell you were doing well. I just didn't realize how well!"

"So they really are as good as everyone says?" his father asked.

"Better, I'd say. It's not at all what I thought it would be, but that's maybe a good thing," Frederick said. "I've also made some really good friends already! I can't wait for you to meet them. Dad, you'll love Seven."

"I'll like seven of your friends? What about the rest?" Frederick's father raised an eyebrow at this.

"No, his name is Seven."

"Your friend's name is Seven?"

"Oh, uh, yeah. That's not his real name, I guess. We all have numbers. Mine is Twenty."

"You go by numbers?" Frederick's mother said uncertainly, and his father's other eyebrow jumped to join its partner. "That's odd . . ."

"Yeah, it's just kind of a fun thing we do. Like nicknames or whatever," Frederick said awkwardly.

"Oh, yes. That does sound very fun." Henry's voice dripped with sarcasm, though it still bore its good-natured tone.

"Henry!"

Frederick's father received a light slap on the arm as payment for his comment. He rubbed his arm and winked at Frederick, smiling ruefully.

"Well, regardless of their numerical values, I cannot wait to meet them."

"Tell us everything, Freddy." His mother sat down on the couch and patted the seat next to her. Frederick sat beside her, and his father took one of the chairs across from the couch.

"No detail is too minute, my boy," Frederick's father said as he leaned in close and adopted a more serious tone. "But first, I have to know something: you have to tell me the truth, Frederick. I know they might want you to be tight-lipped about this kind of stuff, but I must know."

Frederick began sweating, completely caught off guard by the sudden shift in his father's demeanor.

"Have they been feeding you enough pancakes?"

"Henry, enough about the pancakes!"

"My love, how can we talk with any depth until we have addressed the syrup-laden elephant in the room?"

Frederick laughed at the faux look of betrayal on his father's face. His mother simply rolled her eyes and turned back to Frederick.

"Ignore your father. Let's hear it, Freddy."

"Well I actually can't tell you anything specific about treatments and all that." Frederick felt a sharp pang in his chest at the hurt look his parents tried to cover up. "I'm sorry—really, I am! I would tell you if I could. It's just they made me sign that NDA on the first day, and they reminded me of it just now, and I don't want to get either of you in troub—"

"Honey! Honey!" his mother interrupted. "You have nothing to apologize for! We completely understand." She gave him a warm smile. "We're just worried about you. Is there anything you can tell us? Maybe you could talk about your new friends! I'd love to hear more about them."

Frederick's father smiled and offered an encouraging nod.

Frederick sighed in relief. He'd been afraid his parents would be frustrated at the mysteriousness of it all. They probably were, but at least they seemed to understand that he would tell them everything he could.

A part of Frederick was burning to tell his parents everything, every last detail about who he was, what he could do, the obstacles before him and behind him. He wanted to tell them so maybe they would see it wasn't all his fault. His life of uphill clawing was a result of something none of them could control. Frederick silently berated himself for the thought. His parents didn't blame him for any of it and never had. He was projecting, and he knew it.

"You still with us, bud?" Frederick's father asked. Frederick blinked and realized he had been zoned out. His parents were looking at him expectantly.

"Sorry about that. Just pretty tired from this week," Frederick said, blushing.

"Your friends?" his mother prompted.

"Right, they're great! I really think you'll love all of them." Frederick described the rest of the group as best he could without revealing any information about Kinth or what they had been through in the last week. It was difficult but not impossible—he just had to be careful with his words.

He talked for several minutes, pausing multiple times to allow his parents to laugh at his friends' antics. Frederick felt a weight lift. Before, there had been concern in the general way in which they held themselves. It was slight, but he had learned to spot it easily over the years they had spent worrying for him. Now, however, as he told them about their fake games of cards, Seven and Thirteen's constant banter, Eight's antics, and so much more, he saw that a fear they had been holding was slowly melting away. They hadn't sent him away to sit in a room by himself while doctors muttered to themselves and scribbled notes. He had found something all three of them had been hoping he would one day find: friends who understood him.

They talked for about an hour more before a knock at the door interrupted them. The door opened to reveal Arthur's sunny disposition.

"Hello, all. I'm very sorry to tell you this, but I'm afraid time's up." The sunny smile shifted to an apologetic one.

"Will they be able to visit again soon?" Frederick asked, panic spiking at the thought of not seeing his parents again before he went through the Door. He paused at the thought.

When had he decided he was going through?

It hadn't been a conscious decision, but sure enough, the resolve was there.

"I'm so sorry, Frederick, but I'm not sure. That is all decided by Dr. Gray, and I have no idea what his thoughts are. I can discuss it with him later and let all three of you know once I have an answer."

Frederick nodded and tried to paste a smile to his face. He stood and turned to his parents, who had similarly strained expressions.

"I'm so proud of you, dear," his mother said and hugged him tightly. When she pulled away, there were tears in her eyes that she made no effort to brush away.

His father stepped up and hugged him as well.

"Love you, kiddo," he said fondly. As he pulled away, he stuck his hand out for Frederick to shake. Frederick gave him a confused look before grasping his hand and shaking it firmly.

"Hug *and* a handshake, Dad? Seems like overkill to me."

"Just covering my bases," he said slyly, then retreated, putting a comforting arm around Frederick's mother.

"I love you, Freddy. Keep up the good work!"

"Bye! Love you both!" Frederick said, holding up his hand in farewell.

He watched as Arthur led his parents down the hallway and out of sight. Frederick fought back tears and tried not to think about the fact that he might never see them again. Instead, he turned his attention to the item his father had slipped into his hand when he had shaken it.

He opened his fist to reveal a tiny plastic bag filled to the brim with small disks. Frederick laughed aloud and removed one of the miniature pancakes from the bag and threw it in his mouth, relishing the taste.

Chapter 17

There was a spring in Frederick's step as he followed Arthur through the twisting halls and back toward his friends. Despite the emotional weight that had been piled upon him in the last few hours, he was excited to see them again. He would need their help in bearing the pressure of what they had been tasked with, and who better to share that load?

"Twenty!"

The word assaulted Frederick's ears from several different sources as he stepped through the door into the common room. It seemed that the room had been converted back to its original state. The mattresses were gone from the floor, and the table and chairs had reclaimed their position in the center. His friends sprang from their chairs—they had of course been in the middle of a game of "cards."

The cards were thrown into a careless pile as his friends rushed over to greet him. Seven and Thirteen hit first, barreling into him and hugging him tightly as they forced him to the floor. Next came Eight, who took a few running steps before sliding across the floor and clinging to Frederick's leg. One and Nineteen followed quickly, though at a slightly more rational pace. Once they reached the dog pile, however, they joined in enthusiastically, leaping on top of the others. Frederick gasped at the added weight and tried to focus on breathing, though it became increasingly difficult as both the weight of his friends and his laughter increased. His friends were laughing too, which only caused him to laugh harder, which only caused them to laugh harder, and so on. It was an endless, breathless cycle.

"Come now!" Arthur said in as stern a tone as he could muster. "Surely your roughhousing can wait until he's had time to recover. Twenty woke up from a semi-coma two hours ago!"

"Sounds like he should be good and rested to me!" Seven gasped from his position under One. Arthur cracked a smile despite his best efforts.

After several seconds, all parties were able to compose themselves, and one by one, they extracted themselves from the pile. Seven stood last and held a hand down to Frederick, who accepted it gratefully. The stocky boy pulled Frederick up roughly and slapped him on the shoulder.

"It's good to see you, Two-Oh. You really had them going there for a bit. I told them you were just a heavy sleeper, but no one listened to old Seven, did they?" he said lightly, returning to his seat at the table.

"I wasn't worried until you started saying he'd be okay," Thirteen snorted. "Your ability to be wrong is truly awe-inspiring. If you had told me he was dying, I wouldn't have spent a second worrying about him."

Seven opened his mouth to retort but was cut off by Arthur.

"I'm headed out now. Let me know if you all need anything. Twenty, let me know when you have an answer for Dr. Gray."

"Will do," Frederick said simply.

Arthur paused in the doorway for a moment, and Frederick thought he could detect a slight look of disappointment on his face, though it was rapidly replaced with a sunny smile. Then the man waved and walked out the door, whistling as he went.

"You haven't given them an answer?" One asked, a look of confusion creeping across his face.

"I haven't had a real chance to think about it. I woke up two hours ago and have been talking to my parents this whole time. When would I have made up my mind?"

"You've made up your mind," One said in a matter-of-fact tone. "I saw it the moment you walked in this room. You're in this for the long haul, just like the rest of us."

Frederick sat looking at the resolved faces of his friends. They smiled in support, and he felt a fierce determination rising inside of him.

"Might as well tell him now," Thirteen said dryly. "That poor man is stretched thin enough as it is. No sense in making him take another trip over here just for your one-word answer."

Frederick smiled broadly and jumped up from the table, bolting down the hallway.

"Arthur!" The man was just about to turn the corner.

"Yes, Twenty?"

"Tell him I said yes."

Arthur smiled, eyes twinkling behind his large spectacles. "Will do."

Back in the room, Frederick reclaimed his seat at the table and picked up the cards that One had dealt him.

"How were your parents?" Nineteen asked him as he sorted through the cards.

Frederick paused for a moment before replying. "Pretty good. Felt weird to not be able to tell them everything. They're worried of course, but that's to be expected."

"Probably not nearly worried enough," Seven mumbled. One shot him a glare, and Seven shrugged and buried his nose in his cards.

"What have you guys been up to while I was, uh, sleeping?" Frederick asked, desperate to change the subject. He needed a little more distance from the encounter before he could talk about seeing his parents.

"We all got to see our parents, or grandparents, or whoever," One said. "As soon as we woke up, they had them ready. Same as you."

"Those of us who wanted to anyway." Thirteen snorted.

Frederick looked around the room and saw that she wasn't the only one who hadn't had anyone to meet with. He thought about asking who had spoken with family and who hadn't, but he decided against it so as not to stir up any unwelcome emotions in his friends.

"So, besides that . . ." Frederick prompted.

"You're looking at it," Eight said, sounding annoyed. "I'm starting to get pretty sick of this. Any chance we learn a real game?"

"Absolutely not," One chirped back at him, then turned to Frederick. "Just in case they didn't mention it to you, we start training tomorrow. I'm not sure if they were waiting for all of us to be ready or if they just wanted to give us time to rest up. Either way, tomorrow it is."

Frederick felt a shiver of excitement at that. He had spent three days in a bed and, conscious or not, he was ready to push himself again.

"Did they tell you guys what it would be like? The training, I mean?"

"Not a word," Thirteen sighed. "I'm just hoping it's slightly less intense than the tests."

"I'm not sure why it would be any less intense now," Nineteen shrugged. "They've seen what we can handle. We fought a Bristle and won. I imagine the intensity won't drop much from here on out."

Seven and Thirteen groaned in perfect harmony.

Frederick studied One, who remained silent. He sat in his chair with a look of raw excitement on his face. His leg bounced slightly as if it were itching to get going. Any remaining doubt was banished from Frederick at the sight of it.

"So you guys bailed on the joint sleeping arrangement? Too much snoring?" Frederick asked. He was tired and didn't want to worry about the tests either at the moment.

"Not exactly," Seven said, nodding to the corner of the room. Frederick turned and was delighted to see all six mattresses stacked neatly against the wall. "We thought about putting the table in one of the rooms, but the routine of moving all the stuff around is pretty nice. Also, those rooms feel weird. What on earth would any of us need a desk for? We aren't exactly writing the next great American novel here, are we?"

Frederick rolled his eyes but shared the sentiment. The rooms were too nice, too pampered. It felt wrong to live like they were vacationing. Those luxuries could make them grow complacent, and they couldn't afford such things.

They played for two or three more hours. The conversation was light and easy, and Frederick could sense the silent agreement they had come to: *It starts for real tomorrow. Let's take this time to laugh while we still can.*

The time passed quickly, and Frederick felt immensely better as the others started to yawn. He himself gave a massive yawn and stretched, trying to blink the tiredness away.

"Why are you yawning?" Thirteen elbowed him as she walked past. "You've been asleep for almost a week."

"Apparently," Frederick answered in a sarcastic tone, "there is a difference between being knocked unconscious and taking a long nap. One of them is more restful. I'll let you guess which one."

"It all seems the same to me." She shrugged.

One and Seven began moving the table and chairs to the side to make room for the mattresses. Meanwhile, the rest of the group retreated to their respective bathrooms to get ready for bed.

Frederick brushed his teeth in a hurry. He had been apart from the others for long enough. He was going to spend as much time as possible with them going forward. If that was detrimental to his dental health, then so be it.

They trickled from their rooms one by one, flopping down on the mattresses in the way one does when running on fumes. Once they were all settled, they whispered goodnights, and One turned off the lights. Frederick sat in the darkness for a few minutes, surprised to find that his exhaustion had fled. He stared at the dark ceiling, replaying the day's events. Thoughts swirled at a breakneck pace, and try as he might, Frederick just couldn't quite keep up with them. Every time he felt like he was about to grasp closure, peace would scamper a few more inches away, just out of reach. But he had spent much of his life chasing peace—all of it, in fact. Since the day he was born, he had searched for it, and now, finally, he felt it was possible to find. And he had people who would help him get there.

Chapter 18

Frederick was ripped from his peaceful slumber by a figure bursting through the door.

"Good morning!" Arthur said in a cheery voice. He paused in bewilderment at the sight of all of them still sleeping. "Why are you still asleep? It's almost six in the morning!"

"Six?" A howl of outrage came from underneath Seven's pillow, a makeshift barricade against the light that now filled the room. "This is torture! Cruelty! It's disgusting!"

"Somehow, I think you'll survive. Though I know how difficult it can be to break a sleep schedule for such a delicate flower as yourself." Arthur was forced to duck as Seven's pillow flew through the air, narrowly missing his head. The bespectacled man straightened with an ornery grin. "I'll give you all fifteen minutes if you'd like a shower and have a quick breakfast, but that's all I can give you. We've got work to do."

Frederick emerged from the shower feeling alert and refreshed. He grabbed a banana and a bottle of orange juice from his refrigerator and joined his compatriots in the common room. They were all working their way through some makeshift breakfast or another. Seven and Thirteen both still fought against sleep. They stood with eyes barely open, swaying on their feet as they ate.

"You guys okay?" Eight asked between bites of apple. "I've never seen a dead person before, but I imagine they look a lot like you do right now."

Seven ignored the small boy completely, and Thirteen turned to him, but as she opened her mouth, presumably to berate him, all that emerged was a massive yawn. She waved dismissively and sat on a nearby chair. Right then, Arthur burst through the door once again.

"You are all ready to go? Delightful! No time to waste!" He set off down the hall without another word. Thirteen groaned and rose from her chair.

"I'm gonna kill him."

They followed Arthur down the hallways at a brisk walk. Frederick had half been expecting him to sprint away from them, similar to how he had during the second test, so he was grateful for the reduced pace.

"So what do you have in store for us there, Arty?" Seven asked in a chipper voice. The boy seemed to be in significantly better spirits now that he had food in his stomach and was on the move.

"Well, Seven, I think it's probably best to wait until we reach the training room."

"Will Dr. Gray be there?" One asked.

"He will be observing but will not be present in the room. He claims he can be a distraction if he interacts with you directly too frequently."

One snorted but otherwise didn't respond.

Their conversation was cut short as they reached their destination. Arthur pulled out a card very similar to the one Eight had stolen from Dr. Gray. He held it up to a sensor on the wall, and the door before them slid open easily.

The room was a large rectangle. It contained no windows, and there was only one other door, located against the far wall. As Frederick entered, he felt a rush of power surge through his body. It was the increasingly familiar touch of Kinthian air. Closing his eyes, he took a deep breath.

"That's the stuff," Eight said, smiling as he filled his lungs as well.

"This is about 80 percent saturation," Arthur said. "We normally would start you off at a much lower level, but your little, ahem, excursion, shall we call it, escalated your training timeline significantly. We hope to have you at full saturation by the end of the week."

"What the hell . . ." Thirteen trailed off as they inspected the room further.

Between them and the far wall was a large pit. Frederick inched closer and saw that it dropped about twenty feet, and the bottom was filled with hundreds of foam cubes. The pit ran from one wall to the other, leaving no room to walk around it.

The oddities did not stop at the pit, however. Several thick chains dangled from the ceiling down over it. They were spaced out evenly and swayed gently from the air pouring into the room. There were also several thin poles that rose from the pit up until they were even with the floor. Each pole was approximately six feet away from the next closest one, and each was slightly smaller around than a balled fist.

"Tell me what I'm looking at, Arthur," One said as he walked the edge of the pit.

"This is your first training session. You must get from this side of the room to that one." He pointed over the pit. "Once across, you may proceed through the door. On the other side, you will find refreshments."

"Refreshments?" Thirteen and Seven asked in unison.

"What's the point of this?" One asked before Arthur could answer.

"We are working on several different things here. Primarily, we want you to get used to your physical limits as well as your problem-solving skills while submerged in the Kinthian air. Essentially, we want you to find your limits and push them. Don't be afraid to try something and fail. There is a ladder on this side of the pit to allow you back up if you try a method and it doesn't work out. This is just like any other muscle—the more you use it and understand it, the more useful it will be to you."

"A muscle we didn't know we had," Frederick said.

"Precisely!" Arthur chirped. "Any questions?"

"How much can we work together?" Nineteen asked nervously. She was clearly not looking forward to the training.

"Excellent question! You may assist one another in planning but may not physically assist one another in any way. This means no throwing, boosting, pushing, pulling, etc."

"I thought this would be a team exercise," Frederick said, frowning.

"Teamwork comes in many varieties," Arthur said with a twinkle in his eye. "If there is nothing else, I'll see you all on the other side!" He began to depart but paused halfway through the door and turned back to them with an embarrassed look.

"I almost forgot! As soon as one of you uses a specific method to get across the pit, no other person may use that same method. Good luck!"

With that, Arthur was gone.

"Well, that could get annoying," Frederick muttered to himself.

One was prowling the edge, inspecting all aspects of the challenge. He placed his foot lightly on the nearest pole, then gradually put more and more pressure onto it until he was standing on it with his full weight.

"Well, at least we know they'll hold us up," he said, more to himself than anyone else. "That's one way across."

"How far across you think that is?" Seven said as he joined One at the edge of the pit.

"Just over forty feet," Nineteen said, holding a hand to her mouth in concentration.

"Forty feet? Isn't the Olympic long jump record like thirty feet?" Thirteen chimed in. "No way we are jumping across—how are we supposed to find six different ways?"

One smirked but didn't respond.

"Well, I say we start with the obvious ones," Nineteen said. "The poles and the chains are clearly meant to be used. That's two ways right there. It won't be easy by any means, but if they are wanting us to work on pushing ourselves, that's as good a place as any to start."

"So who do we send across?" One said, turning to them. "We have to make sure that we're utilizing our strengths."

"Do we want to send anyone across yet?" Frederick asked. "Maybe we should figure out our six ways across, and then we can play to our strengths?"

"Not a bad idea," One said.

"I think we should send a couple people across as soon as possible," Nineteen said. "There's no rule about us coming back if we get to the other side, and there might be some advantages to having a fresh view of the pit."

"I like that idea." One nodded firmly. "So who wants to give it a go? Eight or Nineteen for the poles, I would think. You two have the smallest feet, which should help with standing on those things."

Frederick studied the poles once again. They were just wide enough to stand on, though not comfortably. The main issue with the pole route was the way in which they were spaced. There was just enough distance that even the most long legged of them wouldn't be able to step from pole to pole. They would need to jump. Nineteen was studying the poles as well and seemed to reach the same conclusion.

"I have as good of balance as anyone, but I'm not sure it's possible to jump and land on one of those things without falling," she said, eyeing the pit warily. "And I'm not too keen on taking a fall down there. I know it's probably a mental block, but . . ."

The small girl was interrupted as Thirteen shoved her over the edge of the pit. Nineteen let out a startled yelp as she fell into the foam below.

The rest of the group turned to Thirteen and eyed her with a mixture of shock and bewilderment. The girl shrugged in response.

"She said herself it was a mental block. We can't be worried about falling as we're doing this. Plus, somebody had to be the first one to fall." She shrugged again. "I just figured two birds with one stone."

At that moment, Nineteen hauled herself up over the ledge from the ladder. Her face was red, and she looked furious. She walked up to Thirteen and pointed an outraged finger at her face. Frederick was shocked. He had never seen anything like this from Nineteen. Her mouth worked silently as she tried to find the words with which to berate Thirteen.

"Thank you," she finally said, though she sounded annoyed.

"Don't mention it!" Thirteen said cheerily, throwing her arm around the smaller girl. "You ready to take on these poles or what?

Nineteen toed the top of the first pole gingerly, trying to ascertain the general feel of it. After a few seconds, she stepped onto the pole, putting her full weight on it. She wobbled briefly during the transfer but quickly stabilized, spreading her arms wide for balance. She stood completely motionless atop that pole as she eyed the next one. Frederick was shocked by the level of control Nineteen displayed. She moved with an almost inhuman grace. Every motion contained pinpoint precision. With little warning, Nineteen leaped from the first pole to the second. For a moment, Frederick thought she had stuck the landing, but her foot slipped at the last second, and she plunged into the foam pit once more.

"That's okay, Nineteen! You got this!" Thirteen called before helping Nineteen up over the edge. The rest of the group joined in with loud encouragement. Seven even began chanting her name.

"Would you all mind shutting up for a moment? I need to focus." Nineteen's face was a mask of frustrated determination. Clearly, the gauntlet had been thrown down, and she was keen to answer. She wasted no time stepping out onto the first pole once again. The transition was much smoother this time, and she barely paused before leaping to the next pole. This time, she stuck the landing. She wavered a bit but steadied quickly.

"I think I'm starting to get the hang of this," she muttered.

Nineteen made it to the fifth pole on her second attempt before once more falling into the foam. Frederick winced as she slipped and fell without a word.

No one said anything as the girl hauled herself back up the ledge. She didn't even break her stride as she began her third attempt.

"See you on the other side," she called over her shoulder as she stepped out.

This time, Nineteen stuck the landing on the second pole perfectly. Not a hair was out of place as she stood motionless on her new perch.

From there, it was simple. She picked her way steadily across the chasm, pausing only to assess the simplest path forward. It took her less than a minute to reach the other side.

The group erupted in applause as she touched down. Seven once again began chanting, and this time everyone joined in. Nineteen blushed and performed an overdramatic curtsy for their benefit.

"So who is going to join me?"

"How about you, Two-Oh?" Seven elbowed Frederick. "I think those chains got your name on them."

"Why me?" Frederick said, surprised that he'd been nominated. "I mean, I'll do it, but I'm not sure I'm the best option."

"I think Seven's right," One chimed in. "You're going to have to swing from one chain to another. That requires a decent amount of athleticism that you've already displayed. Also, you've got a better reach than most of us, which should be a big advantage."

"Not to mention you weigh all of fifty pounds soaking wet," Seven said, shaking his head. "It won't take you any effort to hold yourself up."

"Fair enough." Frederick shrugged and approached the first chain. He reached out and grabbed it, pulling his feet up off the ground. As he did so, he swung gently out over the pit and back again, stepping onto solid ground and nodding to himself. The chains were the perfect size for his purposes—not so small he wouldn't have anything to grip, not so big that he would have trouble getting his hands around them.

"What happens if I fall and get impaled by one of those poles?" Frederick asked, half-jokingly.

"I wouldn't worry about that, boss," Eight said. "The more you worry about it, the more likely it is to happen."

"Well, now I'm sure he's ecstatic to go," Seven said, slapping Frederick on the back.

Frederick smiled at the comments. He knew that he should be legitimately worried. This was dangerous, even with the Kinthian air. But ever since he set foot in the room, his muscles had been screaming at him, begging him to use them, to try something new, to push them further and further. He would happily oblige.

Frederick pulled himself up onto the first chain, scaling about halfway up before beginning to shift his weight back and forth. It was difficult going at first, but soon the chain began to move easily. Similar to the poles, the chains were spaced out just far enough that to reach the next chain, he would have to leap from his current one. Frederick swung back and forth a few more times to get a feel for the timing of his jump. A thrill was building in his stomach. A voice inside him screamed that he had tested enough—it was time to do.

Frederick agreed. He took a deep breath and threw himself into open air.

The jump was timed nearly to perfection on his first try, which Frederick supposed he should've found surprising. The chains slid through his hands briefly, but he quickly found his grip. Momentum carried him forward, preventing him from having to create the force himself as he had with the first chain. This allowed Frederick to leap quickly to the next, and then the next and the next. Soon he was swinging from chain to chain with remarkable ease. In mere seconds, he had made his way across the pit and landed lightly next to Nineteen.

"Um. Nice one," she said, her face a mask of wonder.

"What the hell was that?" Seven shouted from the other side of the pit. "You didn't tell us you were raised in the circus!"

The rest of the group burst into applause as they had for Nineteen. However, there was a look of astonishment on all of their faces that he hadn't seen before.

"Not too difficult when you barely weigh fifty pounds," Frederick called as he shrugged his shoulders nonchalantly.

"What do you see? Any other ways across?" One yelled.

Frederick took in the pit from his new vantage point. There was little new information to report except that he could now see the ladder that Nineteen had already used multiple times. It was more accurate to say that there were several handholds cut into the wall. While it functioned like a ladder, there would be no way to repurpose it for their needs.

"Nothing yet! Give us a few minutes."

Frederick and Nineteen walked to either end of the pit, inspecting every inch they could.

"Hey, Twenty, come look at this!" Nineteen called, waving for him to join her without looking over her shoulder. The girl was staring closely at the wall.

"What have you got?" he asked as he stepped up beside her.

"Well, maybe nothing, but maybe . . ." She trailed off as she stepped to the side and gestured for him to take her place. "Look close at the wall. Notice anything?"

Frederick placed his face where she had been. "Looks like it's rougher on this side than on the other wall. There's a lot more texture, I think."

Nineteen nodded as if her suspicions had been confirmed. "What else?"

"Well," Frederick continued, "it also looks like the walls bow in a little bit."

"Exactly." Nineteen nodded again, more firmly this time. "Almost like they were wanting to add a little grip."

Frederick smiled at her. "You think they want us to try to run along the wall?"

"I do."

He turned and gave the wall another look. "You know, I think you're right."

"You two gonna let us in on your little secret or what?" Seven called from the other side.

"They've added some grip to this wall, and it curves in a bit. We think you could probably run along it if you got enough of a head start." Frederick yelled.

One walked over to the wall and inspected it. He seemed to be talking quietly to himself as he switched between regarding the wall and the pit.

"I think you two might be onto something."

A conversation followed amongst those still on the other side of the pit that Frederick couldn't quite make out, presumably about who would be selected to attempt running along the wall.

Eventually, they decided on Thirteen.

She looked slightly nervous as she slowly backed away from the pit, creating distance to build momentum. Once her back was against the wall, she took several deep breaths and closed her eyes for a moment.

"Whenever you're ready." Seven yawned as he sat at the edge of the pit, dangling his legs over.

Thirteen smirked and made a rude gesture in the boy's general direction as she took off at a dead sprint. The edge of the pit neared, and Thirteen took off in a mighty leap. She hit the wall hard and managed only a few steps before she toppled into the pit. When it was all said and done, she had managed to make it about 60 percent of the way across. A loud curse escaped her mouth as she sullenly waded back through the foam cubes. As Frederick watched her weave between the poles, he was struck with a sudden inspiration.

"Nineteen." He turned to her. "Do you think we can use the same object in different ways?"

She looked back at him thoughtfully, and then her eyes went wide. "Arthur said we couldn't use the same method twice, but he didn't say anything about using the same object more than once!"

"Exactly! Maybe if we had someone use the poles in a different way, it could work?"

"Like if they climbed from the middle of the poles? Kind of like you did on the chains?"

"Exactly!" Frederick said excitedly. He turned his attention to the group on the other side of the pit.

"Hey! We've got another one for you to try!"

"Let's hear it!" One called back.

"Arthur said we couldn't use the same method, but he didn't say we couldn't use the same object in a different way. What if someone slid halfway down the pole and climbed that way? Then, once you got here, you could just climb up the last pole and pull yourself up over the edge."

"That's brilliant!" One shouted back. "I can't believe I didn't think of that." He turned to Seven and gave him a look. "You ready to give something a try, or do you have more trash talking to do?"

"Why not both?" Seven smiled viciously. The stocky boy cracked his neck and stepped up to the edge of the pit. Thirteen had just returned from her trudge through foam and begun walking back to her position against the far wall.

"Race you to the other side, Jinx!" Seven said as he grabbed the first pole and slid halfway down it.

The girl cursed loudly at the use of the nickname and sprinted toward the pit once again, channeling her anger at the comment into her efforts as she flew toward the wall. This time, her jump was much more controlled, her transition from air to wall much cleaner, and as a result, she was able to take several more steps than she had on her previous attempt. She ran out of momentum a few feet from the ledge of the pit. She leaped forward, hands grasping desperately at air. Her fingers brushed safety before she fell into the pit once more. She again cursed loudly as she did her best to sprint back through the foam.

Seven was making his way from pole to pole at a steady pace. Each time he made it to a new pole, he would scurry up a few feet to regain the altitude he had lost.

He reached the last pole just as Thirteen got to the far wall once again.

"Give it up, Jinx! You're toast!" Seven called over his shoulder.

"I told you to never call me that!" Thirteen shouted back, her voice filled with anger. She ran toward the wall with more speed than any of her previous attempts. This time, however, she did not jump when she reached the edge of the pit. Instead, she simply shifted her sprint from the ground to the wall. Frederick gasped audibly at the sight of the girl running full speed nearly sideways, the full forty feet. With one final effort, Thirteen pushed off the wall and sailed through the air, landing a full five feet past the edge of the pit.

Seven pulled himself up over the ledge, a massive smile plastered across his face.

"I knew that would get you across. All you needed was a little rage, eh, Jinx?"

Thirteen's eyes were fiery as she walked over to Seven.

"Woah, easy, I was just trying to motivate—" Seven's voice cut off as Thirteen reached him and shoved him into the pit. He yelped in surprise as he windmilled his arms to retain his balance but to no avail. He managed an impressive string of curses before hitting the foam. Frederick and Nineteen did their best to hold back laughter as Thirteen turned to them.

"He had that coming," she said.

"Absolutely," Frederick and Nineteen said in unison.

The customary applause rang out in the room once Thirteen had concluded chastising Seven, though whether it was for her feat or for pushing him into the pit, no one could have said.

Seven, to his credit, took it well. He trudged through the foam, up the ladder, and back across the poles, then pulled himself up over the ledge and walked up to Thirteen.

"Good form," he said, extending his hand.

"Thank you. I've spent many a night picturing how I would shove you into a pit." She took the offered hand, shaking it firmly.

"Well, now that that's settled. Any more ideas?" One called. "How are we gonna get Eight across?"

"Isn't it your turn to come with some ideas?" Frederick called back.

"If you want less responsibility, stop coming up with good ideas!" One shrugged.

All six of them went to work on their respective sides, searching for the next avenue across. They searched for the better part of an hour with no success.

"I'm not sure how optimistic I am about this," Thirteen said in an exasperated tone as she sat down on the edge of the pit, her legs dangling over the edge. "We can't find one more way across, let alone two."

"Don't worry about that," One said. "I'll take care of it. Let's just get Eight across and then see what's what."

Another hour of looking yielded no tangible results. Frederick flopped down on the ground in frustration. "This is infuriating. Surely there are more ways across."

"You don't think they would give us four total options, do you? See how long it takes us to give up?" Nineteen asked as she joined Frederick.

"I don't think so," he said, shaking his head. "It doesn't seem like they would want to encourage us to give up."

Frederick continued to stare blankly at the ceiling. "Sure are a lot of sprinklers in here," he said, more to himself than anything.

"Yeah," Nineteen snorted. "What are there, ten of them? That seems like overkill."

Frederick sat up and studied the sprinklers more closely. There were indeed ten of them. They ran in a jagged line from one end of the pit to the other. The first sprinkler head was located at the anchor point of the first chain.

"Very much overkill." He scratched his head. "You don't think Eight could swing across them, do you?"

"Probably not," Nineteen said. "There's no way a sprinkler could hold any-one's weight, even Eight's."

"Maybe they're fake." Frederick stared at the sprinklers, certain the answer lay with them. "We could at least have Eight test it out. Worst-case scenario, we flood the room, and they let us out."

"Worth a shot." Nineteen shrugged.

"Hey, Eight!" Frederick called across the pit. "Climb that chain and check out the sprinkler. We think they might be fake."

The small boy scurried up the chain—he had clearly grown restless with their search and was desperate to be doing anything else. He arrived at the sprinkler and pulled hard. Frederick winced as he did so, expecting a deluge of water to greet them. Instead, the sprinkler held firm. Eight pulled harder and harder until he finally shrugged his shoulders and grabbed on with both hands, swinging back and forth wildly.

"Think you were right, boss!" he called happily. The boy swung from sprin-kler to sprinkler. It was probably the least physically demanding of any of the methods they had employed so far. They made ideal handholds, and it took him almost no time at all to reach the other side.

He landed lightly next to Frederick.

"Good call, boss! I got the easy one too." As he spoke, the small boy threw himself backward into the pit.

The group looked over the edge in confusion as he fell. Eight disappeared into the foam for a moment and resurfaced quickly, trudging back to the ladder.

"What the hell was that?" Seven shouted at the retreating figure.

"It looked like fun! Besides, you all got to do it!"

"What are we going to do with that boy?" Thirteen shook her head.

Eight made his way back across the sprinklers even faster than he had the first time.

"Just our fearless leader left," Seven called to One. "Any ideas?"

"Just one." He had backed up against the wall in a similar fashion to how Thirteen had.

"You can't do the wall run, One. Thirteen already—" Frederick stopped short as One sprinted forward, not toward the wall but to the very center of the pit. He gained speed at a frightening rate. Just before he reached the edge of the pit, he threw himself into an impossibly powerful leap. Frederick gaped as One flew through the air, arms flailing as he tried to control his trajectory. The blond boy landed beside him with a thud, tucking into a roll to absorb the shock from his landing. He popped to his feet and began brushing off his clothes.

"Well that wasn't so bad, now was it?"

Chapter 19

Frederick sat with his friends as they all ate the lunch that had been waiting for them on the other side of the door. It was a light meal, just a few sandwiches, some fruit, and several bottles of water for each of them. They ate in silence, either too hungry for conversation or still processing what they had just witnessed. Arthur sat with them, though he hadn't spoken beyond a few words of congratulations. It was unclear whether or not he had even watched their training. Arthur had mentioned that Dr. Gray would be observing the session but gave no indication as to whether he had witnessed it or not.

"Well." Arthur finally broke the silence. "How do you all feel?"

"One or two more sandwiches and I should be good to go again anytime," Eight said.

"Well, I'm glad to hear that. You have about"—Arthur paused, checking his wristwatch—"oh, I'd say another five minutes before your next training session."

Seven looked up sharply at the man, his mouth still full of sandwich. "We have another training session today?"

"Why, of course!" Arthur wrinkled his eyes in confusion. "You didn't think you would have a single session a day did you? Football teams practice twice a day, and our objectives are far more important than theirs."

Frederick didn't blame Seven for his surprise. In fact, he had been expecting just the one session for the day as well, though he hadn't consciously thought about it. Still, it made sense—they had much to learn and little time to do so.

"What's next then, Arthur?" Thirteen asked around a mouthful.

"Your next training exercise will be similar to the second test with a few critical changes. I'm afraid there will be no need for your heroics this time, One," Arthur said, smiling at the boy. "You may have to fight against your instincts a bit."

"Not sure I like the sound of that, Arthur." One scratched his chin. "Though I'm all for identifying and eliminating weaknesses."

"I'm not convinced you know what a weakness is, One," Thirteen said, rolling her eyes. "Except maybe your teeth being too white or your hair being too perfect. Perhaps you're so gifted at everything that it gets boring? Now that I think about it, you have plenty of weaknesses."

This time it was One's turn to roll his eyes, though Frederick could tell he enjoyed the praise. "I've got plenty of weaknesses, Thirteen. I imagine you will become increasingly familiar with them over the next few weeks."

"Whatever you say, Mr. Kent."

"If you two are quite done," Arthur interrupted, "it is time to proceed to the next training location."

Frederick hurried to finish his sandwich, then grabbed an apple to eat as they walked. Thirteen was stuffing her pockets with as much food as she could carry. Arthur cleared his throat loudly and gave her a reprimanding stare. The girl sighed and replaced most of the food, then gestured sarcastically for the man to lead the way.

As they walked, Frederick had an odd sensation of déjà vu. Admittedly, nearly every hallway they had walked down in the last week had looked essentially identical. Still, Frederick felt as if they actually had walked down these exact halls before. His eyes fell to the floor. He watched carefully, afraid that if he blinked, he might miss what he was looking for. And then, just as they were turning a corner, he saw it: a faint, dark smudge on the floor. It was close enough to the wall that it would have been easy to miss if he hadn't been looking for it.

"You said this is similar to the second test, Arthur?" Frederick asked.

"Yes, indeed."

"Is there any chance it's going to take place in the same room?"

Arthur smiled at Frederick over his shoulder, not breaking stride. "I would say there is a very good chance."

They stood in the same waiting room they had before the second test, waiting patiently for Arthur to explain the next training session. The man was currently speaking into a small walkie-talkie. He seemed to be put out by whatever the person on the other side was saying.

"Is it possible to be nostalgic for a place I've only been to once?" Frederick asked no one in particular as he scanned the room. Memories that felt like a lifetime ago bombarded him.

"Maybe if it's been more than four days," Thirteen scoffed.

"What if your entire world has been turned inside out since then?" Nineteen asked.

"Fair enough."

"Sorry about that," Arthur said, turning back to them. "There's been a bit of a delay on Dr. Gray's end, so we can't start just yet. Shouldn't be more than a few minutes. In the meantime, I'll explain this exercise to you."

Arthur pulled out a pen and began fidgeting with it as he talked.

"As previously stated, this will be very similar to the second test. You will enter the room, and a countdown will start. This time, however, you will have fifteen minutes. You may do as you wish in those fifteen minutes, but your objective is this: find the best hiding place you possibly can. You will notice I explicitly said 'hiding place.'" Arthur paused and gave One a look. "This time, I only have to see you for you to be considered caught. Once your fifteen minutes are up, you are forbidden from moving from whatever spot you find yourself in until you are found or until time runs out."

"I see what you mean about fighting against instincts, Arthur," One said in a flat tone. "It's a bit passive for my taste."

"There will be times on the other side of the Door where running simply is not an option," Arthur responded. "You must be able to hide and hide well. After the fifteen minutes are up, I will enter the room and another timer will start, which will be an hour long. If I find any of you before the hour is up, you will all be considered caught, and we will start over. We will continue until you are able to last the full hour. Is all of that clear?"

"So we're playing hide and seek?" Eight said excitedly. "I'm so good at hide and seek."

"Aren't we at a disadvantage here?" Thirteen asked. "You've had time to comb the area already. Last time, we had five minutes to find the first hiding place that wasn't garbage. You had a full twenty minutes to find any potential spots."

"That won't be an issue, I assure you," Arthur said with a sly smile.

"Can we help one another this time?" Nineteen asked. She seemed embarrassed to ask again, but apparently her desire for aid outweighed her shame.

"By all means! In fact, I strongly encourage it. This is even more of a team exercise than the last one."

"Any pointers beyond that?" Frederick asked hopefully.

"Don't be afraid to get creative, whatever that may entail." Arthur winked at them.

A voice garbled from his walkie-talkie, and Arthur held up a finger toward the children. After a quick back-and-forth, he walked over to the door and opened it.

"They are ready for you. Good luck!"

Frederick stepped through the door, already racking his brain for potential places to hide that they had overlooked their last time in the room. He was so focused on that thought that he was the last to notice.

"Well, that's unexpected," Thirteen said, and let out a low whistle.

Before them was presumably the same room they had taken the second test in. However, it bore little resemblance. There were still trees and grass, but the faux landscape had changed completely. Where before there had been a large clearing, now the entire room appeared to be filled with the synthetic trees. There was also now a large stream cutting its way through. Frederick gaped at the stark changes.

"How . . ." He trailed off.

"They are a multi-billion-dollar organization—it's not that hard to figure out, Twenty," One said. "Don't get distracted. We've only got fifteen minutes. Let's start looking. Split up. Find as many potential spots as you can. Don't hide, though. When the fifteen minutes are almost up, let's meet back by the door."

"We aren't even trying this round, then?" Thirteen asked.

"Why wouldn't we try?" Eight asked.

"Because we are going to lose regardless," Nineteen said. "At this point, Arthur will have an hour to find one of the five spots we found in fifteen minutes. We don't want to accidentally waste any good spots. Better to just use this round as reconnaissance and give ourselves a better chance for next round."

"Exactly." One nodded and moved off on his own without another word.

Frederick strode through the trees, keeping his eyes peeled for anything resembling a hiding spot. He found several mediocre spots: a hollow tree trunk, a treetop with particularly thick foliage, and a rather robust bush. But none of them were remotely good enough for his purposes. He would have to think outside the box to survive an hour. He had seen Arthur at work, and the man was no joke. It had been borderline frightening to watch him searching during the second test. It was easy to forget that the small man was so physically gifted. He would be able to scour every inch of this room in thirty minutes. The odds of him finding at least one of them seemed almost certain.

As Frederick searched for his spot, he stopped at the edge of the stream. It was surprisingly large, though to be fair, Frederick had little experience with indoor water masses. Perhaps this was an average size. The water was extremely clear, and he could easily see the bottom. It looked to him like if he were to wade in the water, it would rise to about his waist.

His eyes came to rest on an oddity several feet upstream. The water ran faster there, which removed a significant amount of the visibility he had previously enjoyed. The water flowed in a peculiar way—it swirled unnaturally as it ran through this particular stretch. Frederick hurried up and down the bank, searching for any other occurrences of this phenomenon. He found some other places where the water swirled in the same odd fashion, but it wasn't nearly as prevalent. Frederick returned to the original spot and studied it closely for several more minutes, an idea beginning to form.

"Twenty!"

With a start, Frederick realized his fifteen minutes were probably up. Odd. He had been expecting an air horn or something of the like to indicate when the allotted time had elapsed. There were no clocks in this room as there had been last time, so there was no other way for them to gauge how much time they had remaining other than their internal clocks. Frederick trudged back through the trees toward the door, where he found the rest of his group waiting. Arthur stood before them with his arms crossed, a look of confusion on his face.

"Did I not explain the rules clearly enough?" he asked.

"No, you were crystal clear," Seven said. "We are just very very bad at hiding. We will do better this time, we promise." The stocky boy smiled sweetly, and Arthur rolled his eyes.

"Well I suppose that means I win. You have fifteen more minutes. I expect a better performance this time around." Arthur raised an eyebrow at them, then spun on his heel and walked back into the waiting room, the door sliding shut behind him.

"Let's go. Eight, you're up first," One said as soon as the door had clicked into place. "Show us what you got."

Eight bolted away, and they dashed after him. He led them to a corner of the room where the outdoor façade began to break down. The walls had some vines on them so as not to completely ruin the ambiance of the place, but it was easy to see the metal behind them. Eight leapt at the vines and began climbing them. He scaled the wall easily, hand over hand until it was difficult to see him. This corner of the ceiling was particularly shadowy, and even now, Frederick had to focus to keep track of the boy. Eventually, he reached the ceiling, and Frederick lost sight of him entirely.

"How's this?" Eight's voice floated down to them.

"Well we can't see you, so it isn't bad, but what if he decides to climb the vines?" One called up.

"They go all the way up the wall and around the entire room, so he would have to randomly choose to climb this exact spot to find me. There's even a little nook up here too that I'm smooshed into. No way he could see me unless he was right on top of me."

"Excellent." One nodded appreciatively. "Good luck, Eight. See you in an hour."

"You got it, boss!" Eight's disembodied voice answered.

"Thirteen, you're next."

The girl nodded and began walking briskly through the trees, talking over her shoulder as she did. "I couldn't stop thinking about how crazy it was that they completely changed the entire room. Especially on the scale they did. It looks just about perfect. But I figure there's no way it's flawless. So I looked for somewhere someone messed up." Thirteen stopped at an inconspicuous-looking tree, smiling triumphantly. "And eventually, I found it."

"What are we looking at?" Seven asked.

"A flaw." She walked to the base of the tree trunk and reached down, forcing her hand between the tree and the grass. "Whoever laid the new sod down messed up here. It's not a huge mistake and a totally understandable one to make." Thirteen grunted with exertion as she yanked hard on the edge of the turf to which she was clinging. There was a noise like Velcro being pulled apart, and a section of turf about four feet across pulled free. Thirteen gestured for the others to look where the turf had previously lain. There was a small hole, just large enough for a person to fit into. The girl winked at them and climbed in, pulling the turf back over her like a blanket. Frederick was astonished at how natural it looked once the grass was replaced. There were no signs of disturbance.

"You got air in there?" One asked.

"Think so. I can feel a little something coming through."

"Good." He nodded again.

"Hope you aren't claustrophobic," Seven called as they began walking away.

A muffled noise came from Thirteen's hiding spot that Frederick couldn't quite make out, which he assumed was for the best.

"Nineteen?" One said.

The small girl nodded and moved quickly through the trees. After only a dozen or so yards, she approached a large tree with a hole in the trunk at about waist level. She wordlessly climbed in.

"Nineteen isn't this a little obvious . . ." One trailed off as the girl disappeared.

"What the—" Seven started in confusion.

"It's hollow all the way up." Nineteen's voice echoed eerily from the opening. "There's a natural ledge about six feet up that I can sit on. I doubt anyone would be able to see me unless they climbed up here."

Frederick walked up to the tree and inspected the hole, sticking his head inside. It was difficult to angle his body so that he could see, and even when he did, there wasn't enough light for him to make out anything above his head. As far as he could tell, there was nothing there.

He stepped back and looked at One, nodding.

"That'll do, Nineteen. See you soon." One turned to Seven. "Would you like to pretend you found a good hiding spot, or shall we proceed to Twenty's spot?"

Seven smiled sheepishly. "Hiding's never been my strong suit."

"Not a problem." One gestured to Frederick to lead the way. "I'm sure Twenty has a brilliant spot for both of us."

"I have to find three different spots?" Frederick asked. "I'm not even sure I have a single spot. You couldn't find a place?"

"Well, my plan was just to observe all your spots and join whoever had a spot multiple people could fit in. All the spots so far have been extremely single-person focused, so I'm hoping you come through for me."

"Seems a bit lazy," Seven muttered. "At least I tried to find a spot."

"Lazy or not, it's the best plan. It's best to minimize the number of hiding spots if possible. Since we lose if even one of us is found, it makes more sense to give Arthur as few options as possible."

Frederick nodded in understanding. "Makes sense. Just not sure why all the pressure is on me to find the spot."

"Oh, stop grumbling and take us to your spot already," Seven said.

Frederick rolled his eyes and jogged toward the stream. They reached the flowing water, and he gestured at it. "Notice anything?"

"How long do you think I can hold my breath, Two-Oh? I'm not a freaking dolphin," Seven said skeptically.

"We're running out of time, Twenty. Best to just get on with it. I gotta say, I have no idea where you are going with this."

"Hopefully somewhere," Frederick said, more to himself than anyone else, and leaped into the water.

He gasped as the icy flow rose to his chest—it was slightly deeper than he had anticipated. He waded to where the water swirled in its slightly unnatural way. On the other bank was a large boulder that was almost entirely submerged. The top just barely poked above the water, and Frederick grabbed onto it for support.

"Here goes nothing," he whispered, and plunged beneath the icy water. He kept his eyes open and was rewarded with a surprisingly clear image before him. As he had hoped, there was a gap between the bank and the boulder just wide enough for him to squeeze through. He said a silent prayer and forced his way through.

Frederick breathed in fresh air as his head broke above the water in the small underwater cavern he had managed to force his way into. He could feel the water swirling around his legs, alternating pushing him farther into the small cavern and pulling him back out into the main part of the stream. There was just enough room for Frederick to get his shoulders out of the water without hitting his head on the ceiling. He was pleasantly surprised to find that the area was bigger than he had expected. By his estimations, it was just enough room for One, Seven, and himself. It wouldn't be comfortable by any means, but it was certainly viable. Frederick took a deep breath and ducked back under the water.

The trip out was even easier than the entry. He popped out of the water once more and was met by confused stares from One and Seven.

"Are you a dolphin?" Seven asked, scratching his head in confusion.

"Not quite. There's an underwater cavern with an air pocket on the other side of this boulder. I thought that might be what was causing the weird water-flow here. Should be enough room for all three of us."

"You guessed that from the weird waterflow?" Seven asked, sounding bewildered.

Frederick just shrugged. "Something had to be causing it."

One chuckled and jumped into the water beside Frederick. "Let's go, Seven. Time's almost up, and if Arthur sees us standing chest-deep in the water right here, I think it might waste Twenty's brilliance."

One by one, they forced their way into the cavern. The three boys crouched in the cool water with a couple feet of space between them. It wasn't at all comfortable, but it seemed to be an effective hiding place.

"How worried should we be about running out of air? The entrance is totally underwater, so no oxygen is coming in from there," Seven said nervously.

Frederick nodded to a thin beam of light working its way through the ground above them. It provided the only illumination in the room.

"I imagine there's air coming through there," Frederick said. "Though there might be some irony to us running out of oxygen and dying in here."

"Only if they never found us," Seven said, grim humor mixing with the anxiety on his face. "I do love a good training session turned entombment."

One snorted softly. "Maybe we should not talk for a bit? I imagine sound doesn't travel too well to the outside, but I'd rather not take any chances." Quietly, he added, "Also I'd like to avoid having to smell your breath for the next hour."

Time passed slowly in their new underwater home. It was an oddly disorienting feeling. There was no sound beyond that of their own breathing, which echoed in the small chamber. Frederick's body from the neck down grew used to the water's temperature, and he soon stopped shivering. He closed his eyes, waited for the sixty minutes to be up, and tried not to think about the sound of their breathing bouncing off the walls or the aching in his back.

Before long, Frederick had totally lost track of time. For all he knew, it could've been ten minutes or ten hours since they entered. Frederick studied his companions in the dim light. One's eyes were open, though he was clearly somewhere else mentally. He looked to be trying to solve some problem, occasionally muttering to himself. Seven was breathing steadily with his eyes closed.

There's no way he's asleep, Frederick thought, but he wasn't entirely convinced. If anyone could fall asleep while hiding in an underwater cavern, it would be Seven.

The semi-silence was finally broken by a shout that Frederick could just faintly make out.

"Well done, all! That's one hour. Come on out now." Arthur's voice found its way to their ears.

"Thank goodness." Frederick sighed in relief and began moving toward the exit.

One blinked back into awareness and began moving as well.

"Not yet," Seven whispered, keeping his eyes closed.

"What do you mean?" Frederick asked in confusion. "I can't stay in here much longer. It isn't exactly my ideal hangout spot."

"It hasn't been an hour."

"How do you know?" One asked, but he moved back to his original position as he did so.

"I've been counting. It's only been about fifty minutes."

"You've been counting," Frederick said flatly.

"Yes," Seven replied, his eyes still shut. "And I gotta say, it's wildly difficult to continue doing so with you jabbering away at me."

Frederick exchanged a look with One, who simply shrugged and settled back down.

"Guess an extra ten minutes won't hurt," Frederick said and followed suit.

"Probably should wait a little bit more than that. There's no guarantee my count is exactly right, and there's no reason to take the chance," Seven said. "Now please, shut the hell up."

They sat in silence as the seconds dragged by. Frederick began counting in his head as well, since there seemed to be little else to do. He was nearly to nine hundred when Seven opened his eyes.

"Alright, let's go. I just peed in here, and I don't want to reabsorb that."

One guffawed, then ducked under the water and pushed his way past the boulder.

Frederick cursed softly and followed, trying not to think about the tainted water he was now surrounded by. He splashed awkwardly to shore and flopped down on the grass next to One, waiting for feeling to return to his numbed limbs. Seven stumbled out of the water and crashed to the ground next to Frederick.

"That was terrible."

Frederick just nodded in agreement.

"Oh, it wasn't that bad," One said cheerily. "And besides, you had the counting to keep you occupied!"

Seven shot One a glare and threw a pebble at him. Of course, the blond boy caught it and flicked it into the stream nonchalantly.

"Come on," One said, standing. "Let's see if Arthur found the others."

He began a brisk walk back toward the waiting room.

Arthur was standing by the door, waiting for them. None of the others were anywhere to be seen. He smiled as they approached.

"Go for a swim boys?" Arthur asked, shaking his head. "I seemed to have underestimated you this time around. I must say that I'm impressed. Success on your second attempt is very good indeed."

"None of the others came when you called earlier?" One asked.

"Not a single one. I really thought that would work at least one time. I guess none of you trust me as much as I hoped." Arthur adopted a faux look of hurt.

"You had me fooled," Frederick said honestly. "One too. We would've been toast if not for Seven."

Seven yawned and stretched in an exaggerated kind of way. "It does get tiresome carrying the weight of the entire group solely on my back. If anyone else feels like they could start contributing, please do."

Frederick rolled his eyes, and One simply ignored the comment.

"One, would you mind gathering up the rest of the group?" Arthur asked. "They obviously won't come if I call them, and I suspect that you know where they all are."

"Sure thing." He set off through the trees, returning shortly with Eight, Thirteen, and Nineteen in tow. One was shaking his head, and it appeared that Eight and Nineteen were suppressing laughter.

"I cannot believe you fell asleep. I truly cannot fathom that. You were underground!" One said.

"I wasn't asleep!" Thirteen said, her face flushed.

"I had to shake you! I said your name five times, and nothing happened. I thought you had run out of air and died."

"Oh, don't be so dramatic." Thirteen rolled her eyes. "I told you I had air in there."

"You fell asleep?" Seven laughed. "That's some effective training, Jinx. Now we know you can defeat the great evil lord of daytime drowsiness!"

Thirteen merely sighed and shook her head, uncharacteristically turning down the opportunity to start a fight. Frederick raised an eyebrow and exchanged a glance with Seven, who looked equally perplexed.

"Why are you guys wet?" Eight asked, interrupting the silent exchange.

"Ol' Two-Oh was just trying to freeze us to death. Or maybe drown us. Maybe both? I honestly couldn't tell," Seven said, quickly recovering from his confusion. Eight nodded solemnly, as if that answered his question perfectly.

Arthur cleared his throat. "I think that is probably quite enough for the day, don't you?"

Chapter 20

Frederick had headed directly to the bathroom upon returning to their rooms, desperate to banish the chill he had acquired while hiding in the stream. The shower was supposed to be a quick one—Frederick was exhausted and needed a nap badly. However, he found his mind drifting and decided he needed to let it wander a bit before he would be able to sleep. The familiar rhythm of the water pounding into his back had a hypnotizing effect on him, and he let his mind replay the events of the day before eventually going blank.

Frederick was shocked back into awareness by his head lolling forward. He shook it to recover his wits and quickly turned off the shower.

How long had he stayed like that?

Wrapping a towel around his waist, he walked back into his bedroom and checked the clock on the large mahogany desk.

"An hour?" Frederick gasped to himself. How had he managed to waste that much time just staring at the wall? He did have to admit he was emotionally and physically exhausted. He was just about at his limit, and he knew it.

Frederick dried himself and put on a clean pair of clothes that had been laid out on his desk. He smelled moth balls as he pulled the shirt over his head. It was a strangely nostalgic smell and somehow made him even more tired, though he hadn't thought that possible. Frederick turned to collapse into his bed and found an empty frame with no mattress. A groan escaped his lips as he placed a hand to his forehead. Of course. His mattress was out in the common area with the rest of the mattresses. Retrieving it would be easy in theory, but Frederick wasn't sure he had the required mental energy to talk to anyone else. He doubted he would be able to escape the room without a jab from Seven about his hour-long shower.

Scanning the room for any alternative, he was delighted to find a thin foam mattress topper sitting on the floor beside his bed. He surmised that it must have fallen off when he had initially removed the mattress from its frame. He laid it out on the floor and grabbed a thin spare blanket and pillow from his closet, then curled up on the topper. It wasn't the most comfortable experience of his life, but it beat sleeping on the floor by a long shot. Barely a minute passed before Frederick fell into a deep sleep.

He awoke disoriented in the way one can only be when taking a nap that borders on comatose.

What time is it? Where am I? Why am I on the floor?

The questions drifted through Frederick's mind as he groggily sat up and tried to rub the sleep from his eyes. The answers followed at a leisurely pace.

Once he had regained the majority of his senses, Frederick stood and stretched. He checked the clock on his desk and was surprised to find he had only been asleep for an hour or so. He had worried it might be three or four in the morning, but the clock only read six thirty. He stretched once more, then walked out the door into the common room.

The table was still in the middle of the room, and the mattresses were still neatly stacked in their holding place. One, Seven, Eight, Thirteen, and Nineteen were all seated around the table, playing cards. The group was so absorbed in their game, they didn't notice his entry. Frederick studied the cards more closely and was surprised to find they were not playing their usual game of fake poker. All the cards had been laid out face-up on the table, seemingly at random. They were organized into five rows that were ten cards deep each. The remaining two cards were face-down.

It appeared that only Nineteen and Thirteen were playing the strange game at the moment. They sat on opposite sides of the round table, a face-down card sitting directly in front of each of them. They studied the face-up cards intently, faces screwed up in concentration. The rest of the group studied the cards as well, though in a much more casual way. Their expressions and postures identified them as spectators, not competitors.

Frederick could see no indication as to the objective of the game. There were no chips on the table, and no betting of any kind seemed to be taking place, which he found surprising. In fact, Frederick doubted he would've been able to identify it as a game at all if not for the competitive look on Thirteen's face.

"I'll get you this time, you little twerp," Thirteen growled at the smaller girl, eyes never leaving the upturned cards.

Nineteen didn't respond, apparently too focused on the cards before her to even hear the comment.

"Five of hearts!" Eight shouted.

Frederick jumped at the sudden noise, turning to the boy for an explanation. However, he was distracted by a burst of movement from the two girls. Eight's call had apparently been the starting pistol for this race, and they both began swiping at cards frantically. Frederick tried to identify the pattern of the cards they lunged for, but they were collecting them so quickly he could barely make out which ones they were grabbing. Thirteen cursed loudly as Nineteen snatched a card that Thirteen had been reaching for. Apparently, it was the last card they had been going for, though there were still many left on the table. The girls sat back and began counting the cards they had collected.

"What's the new game?" Frederick asked, taking an open seat beside One. "Did Eight finally convince you all to learn something?"

"Not sure it has a name yet. Nineteen thought it up while you were sleeping," One answered without looking at Frederick. He was watching the girls count their cards.

"Eight," Nineteen said happily, not paying attention to One or Frederick.

"Five," Thirteen said in frustration. "She cheat, Eight?"

"Looked all good to me, boss!"

"Oh don't look so smug, small fry," Thirteen spat at Nineteen, who was clearly pleased with herself. "There's still a lot of game left."

The girls placed their newly collected cards face-down in front of them, in a separate pile from the single cards. Then they turned back to study the face-up cards remaining on the table.

"So how does it work?" Frederick whispered to One. He didn't want to interrupt the focus of the competitors, especially as Thirteen appeared to be in a particularly foul mood.

"It's a two-player game," One whispered back. "Just the two sitting across the table, playing each other." He nodded to Thirteen and Nineteen. "And a ref." He nodded to Eight.

"The ref calls out a random specific card, and the players race for that card. Once they get that card, they move on to the next card in the suit. You can't grab a card until the card before it has been grabbed, savvy?"

Frederick nodded in understanding.

"So you can't grab the queen of spades until the jack of spades has been picked up."

"Exactly. You pick up the cards in order as fast as you can until all the cards of that suit have been picked up. It wraps around, so when an ace is picked up, you pick up the two next, and so on. Once a suit is gone, the round ends."

"So there are four rounds, and whoever has the most total cards at the end of the four rounds wins?" Frederick guessed.

"Yep, you get minus two points for every card you take out of turn or just a wrong card you grab in general."

"What's with the face-down card?" Frederick asked. The game made sense to him for the most part otherwise.

"Ah, yes, that is my one contribution," One said with a smirk. "Each player gets one card dealt face-down to them before the rest of the cards are laid out, and they only get to look at their own face-down card. It throws a bit of a wrench in the whole thing. Let's say you have the eight of hearts, and the seven of hearts just got picked up. Your opponent is scouring the table for the eight, and you're already onto the nine. Just another way to keep you on your toes."

"Nine of clubs!" Eight shouted, and the girls burst into motion once again.

Now that he knew what to look for, Frederick was able to follow the game a bit more closely. He was even able to identify a card or two before they were snatched from the table. This time, Thirteen was able to grab the last card from underneath Nineteen's hand. She smiled triumphantly but offered no trash talk as she counted through her cards.

"Seven."

"Six."

Thirteen's smile shifted back to a look of concentration, and she added her new cards to the growing stack in front of her. Nineteen's face was impassive as she did the same. The score was now 14-12 in favor of Nineteen.

"They get less and less time between each round," One whispered to Frederick. "Fewer and fewer cards to study. Also, it adds to the drama a bit, which never hurts."

"Seems like a pretty high-energy game," Frederick said, running his hands through his hair as he studied the table now as well. There were only two suits remaining, and the table was beginning to look bare. The large rectangle of cards now bore many gaps.

"That's the point," One said, glancing at Frederick. "This isn't really a game. It's training disguised as a game. We wanted something we could work on in our own time. If we're gonna be saving the world, it seems like there isn't much time to waste."

"Doesn't seem like a card game could help much," Frederick said skeptically.

"Maybe not." One shrugged. "I'm not so sure, though. This takes reaction time, speed, observation, strategy, memory, and probably a handful of other things. All things we're gonna need, right? Seems like there's a chance it could be helpful before it's all said and done."

One had a point—maybe the game really could help. Either way, it was better than just sitting around.

"Ace of spades!" Eight shouted, and they were off again. This round was significantly shorter than the others, presumably because there were fewer cards to distract the competitors.

"Seven," Thirteen called.

"Five," Nineteen responded.

Thirteen flipped over her face-down card, the three of spades, and added it to her pile. "Saw you looking for this one," she said with a smile. "All tied up, and now I know what you got under there. Worked out pretty well for me, eh?"

Frederick glanced at the board—it was easy to see what Thirteen meant. With only one suit left, it wasn't difficult to identify the missing card. The queen of diamonds was the only card missing from the table. They had grabbed thirty-eight cards from the table, nineteen each, and Nineteen's advantage of her face-down card was now gone.

"I know we only just started playing this game an hour ago, but this is the most exciting match I've ever seen," Seven whispered.

"Are you sure you've got nineteen cards?" Nineteen asked skeptically. "Your pile looks shorter than mine."

"Seriously, Nineteen? You think I can't count that high?"

"No, I just think you might be cheating."

Thirteen barked a laugh and looked down, quickly counting her cards so that they could see them.

"See, nineteen total. You're right, I would cheat if I needed to, but I don't need to to take you down."

"Big talk for someone on a three-game losing streak," Seven mumbled.

"Whenever you're ready, Eight," Nineteen said without looking at the boy. She and Thirteen were staring at one another intently.

"Fun twist for the last round," One said to Frederick. "Since they know the suit, they aren't allowed to study the board. They have to hold eye contact until Eight calls a card."

Right on cue, Eight shouted the final card. "Two of diamonds!"

The girls attacked the cards with a ferocity they had not yet exhibited. Their hands flew through the air as they strived to beat their opponent to the cards. From what Frederick could tell it was neck and neck, though it was difficult to know with the speed at which the girls were moving. Suddenly, Thirteen paused, a look of confusion covering her face. She looked about frantically as Nineteen scooped up the final cards. Thirteen managed to recover and snag the ace, but the damage was already done.

"What the—" Thirteen shook her head, the same look of confusion spread across her face. "Where's the ten?"

"Oh, you mean this?" Nineteen smiled wickedly as she turned her card over for all to see. Sure enough, it wasn't the queen of diamonds they had anticipated but the ten.

"But I checked before! The queen was missing!" Nineteen's face shifted to an impassive expression as realization dawned on Thirteen's face. "You switched them! You didn't think I miscounted, you just wanted to distract me. You dirty cheat!"

Nineteen shrugged as she counted her cards. "Nothing in the rulebook against it."

Seven burst into laughter, pointing at the red-faced Thirteen. "You got so hung up on the missing ten, you let her snag the next three cards! She got you good, Jinx!"

Thirteen huffed in such annoyance that it appeared she was unable to formulate a response.

"Seven, which puts me at a total of twenty-six, I believe."

"Five," Thirteen managed to force between her clenched teeth.

"Which I believe gives you a total of twenty-four," Nineteen said as she extended her hand across the table. "Good game."

Thirteen's look of anger fractured slightly, and Frederick was convinced he could see humor somewhere deep in her eyes. "Good game." She shook the offered hand.

"Who dares challenge the master next?" Seven said in an overly dramatic voice. The stocky boy was trading seats with Eight, apparently assuming the position of referee for whoever decided to take on Nineteen. All eyes turned to Frederick.

"What, me? I learned this game about thirty seconds ago," Frederick said, holding his hands up defensively. "I'd like to watch a few more rounds before I jump into the ring."

"We all learned this game within the last hour, you idiot," Seven said, still talking in the dramatic voice. He sounded like an announcer at a boxing match.

"Everyone else has already played," One said. "You'll lose the first match, but that's fine. You pick it up faster if you just play."

Frederick gave in begrudgingly, taking the seat that Thirteen had just vacated.

"In the blue corner we have the one, the only, Two-Zerooooooooo!" Seven kept up his announcing routine as he collected the cards and began shuffling them before dealing. "And in the *red corner*—"

He was cut off as Thirteen punched him hard in the arm.

"That feels like more than enough, don't you think?"

Seven offered only an annoyed grumble in reply, but he didn't use the voice again.

Frederick tore his attention from his distracting companions and studied the face-up cards before him. He had never been particularly good at memory games, but neither had he been particularly bad. As was most often the case with Frederick, he had simply been.

As he stared at the table before him, Frederick was struck by how, despite the general simplicity of the game, he had no earthly idea how to strategize for it. There was no way he would be able to memorize the location of each and every card. Even with the assistance of the Kinthian air that was now being constantly pumped into their rooms, there was simply no way he could memorize the random locations of fifty individual cards. He decided to just pick a suit and learn it as best as he could. Frederick chose hearts at random and studied each one carefully. After several seconds, he closed his eyes and quickly tested himself, mentally pointing out where each card was located. Unfortunately for him, that was the exact moment that Seven called the card.

"Six of spades!" he shouted, still with a trace of the announcing voice, though not enough to earn any more than a stern glare from Thirteen.

Nineteen had grabbed three cards before Frederick had even registered what Seven had said. He managed to push aside his panic and snag a few himself before it was all said and done. Nineteen grabbed the last card, the five, and they began counting. It didn't take long for Frederick to count all three of his cards.

"Nine," Nineteen said sheepishly. She gave Frederick an apologetic look.

"Um, three." He couldn't help but laugh at his dismal performance.

"Um, Twenty?" Nineteen said. "I think your card might be a spade."

Frederick flushed and checked his facedown card for the first time. Sure enough, it was the three of spades. He flipped it over in frustration, and the humor was quickly replaced with embarrassment. One let out a low whistle.

"You sure you understand the rules there, Two-oh?" Seven said, shaking his head slowly. "That is a truly awful round, even for a first try."

"Yea, boss, maybe we should go back to fake poker," Eight added.

"Don't listen to them, Twenty!" Thirteen cut in. "That was a valiant first effort. Inspiring, even! I bet this kind of game is almost impossible for a blind man like yourself."

"Oh, come on, you guys, none of you were much better!" Nineteen said reproachfully as the three continued to laugh at Frederick's expense. "I certainly wouldn't be so high and mighty with a collective record of 0-10."

That tempered the laughter a bit but wasn't enough to quell it entirely.

Nineteen shot Frederick another apologetic look, which he shrugged away good naturedly.

"Don't go easy on me because of them," he said to the small girl across from him. "Give me everything you got."

She winced but nodded.

It was a massacre.

Frederick traded seats with Seven, eager to get out of the game. Hopefully, by observing the others play, he would be able to pick it up faster. He studied Nineteen intently as she played the next several games against a variety of opponents. They were playing a winner-stays format, and no one could manage to topple her. There were several close games, but in those, Frederick got the distinct feeling that Nineteen was never worried. He concluded that she was keeping the games close when she sensed her opponent was about to give up for good. His hypothesis was confirmed when Seven tried to quit, stating that he "wouldn't win in this or any lifetime." Nineteen talked him into one more game, which she narrowly won. Seven was frustrated by the loss but motivated by the narrow margin.

Frederick smiled to himself—the girl was kind enough to throw the games so they wouldn't lose hope but competitive enough that she would never let them win. Strangely, One declined to play for the time being. He offered no reason as to why he withheld, and the others didn't ask—they were eager to get as many games as they could. Frederick himself played a few more games, none of them were remotely close; in fact, he barely improved on his previous score. But these games weren't about winning, they were about reconnaissance. Frederick was using the games to piece together Nineteen's strategy.

They were halfway through another game. Nineteen was of course trouncing him again. Frederick smiled. He assumed she had seen the determination in his eyes and knew he had no intention of giving up anytime soon and thus didn't need to pull any punches. When they finished the second round, Frederick had only accumulated nine cards to Nineteen's sixteen. They announced their scores, and Nineteen turned back to the cards. Frederick returned to his studies of Nineteen. They sat for several seconds, and just before Seven called the new card, Frederick finally saw it.

Nineteen wasn't focusing on the cards.

Not individually, anyway. He had assumed she had been focusing on each card and committing them to memory. However, he noticed that her eyes had almost glazed over. She wasn't looking at the cards but at the table as a whole.

"Three of hearts!" Seven called, but Frederick didn't even look at the cards as Nineteen began snatching them. As she worked, Frederick saw that her eyes were unfocused—they didn't move as she went from card to card. It looked like she was in a trance.

So that's the trick eh? Study the whole, not the individual, and let instincts take over.

"Just move if you aren't even gonna try, Twenty," Thirteen said in annoyance. "Stop wasting our time."

The girl stood to take his seat but paused as One spoke.

"Let him have one more go," One smiled. "I think it might get interesting if we give him a clean slate."

"Whatever." Seven rolled his eyes but gathered the cards, foregoing the final round and starting over. The stocky boy shuffled and dealt with a clear air of boredom. Frederick received his single card and glanced at it quickly. It was the king of clubs. Nineteen checked her card and looked at the board, adopting the stare that Frederick now knew to be the key.

Here goes nothing, I guess.

Frederick let his eyes lose their focus slightly—just enough that he could see the entire table at once but not so much that he couldn't make out what the specific cards were. He sat there, attempting to imprint the cards as a whole into his mind. It was difficult to do, as he wasn't used to thinking in that way. Still, he could feel an image forming in his mind.

"Three of diamonds." Seven yawned, barely watching the cards.

Frederick was delighted to find that he could easily locate the three of diamonds without having to scour the board. It was in the second row, three cards down. He reached for it gleefully but paused as he grasped open air. Nineteen had just barely managed to get to it before him. He decided to skip the four of diamonds and move straight to the five. He grabbed it as soon as he saw Nineteen grab the four in his peripherals, and then he was on to the next card.

"Seven."

"Six."

A silence fell over the spectators.

"What was that?" Seven sat slack-jawed in his chair.

"Told you it would be interesting." One looked almost downright gleeful at this point.

Even though Frederick had lost the round, it had been significantly closer than any he had participated in up to that point—not only in total number of cards but in how close he had been to each individual card. Most of the cards he had lost, he had been mere milliseconds behind Nineteen.

Frederick didn't have time to dwell on their reactions. He had to figure out how Nineteen managed to get to the cards before him. He felt he was physically faster—the physical tests they had done so far seemed to support that notion. Now that he could see the cards in his head, he felt he should be able to beat her, but still, she managed to stay ahead of him.

"Nine of clubs!" Seven called, his previous energy returning.

This time, Frederick managed to tie Nineteen with six cards apiece. She turned over her card to reveal the king of clubs. It was now 13-12 in favor of Nineteen. She smiled at Frederick, but there was little humor in her expression. There was a fire burning in her eyes that he hadn't seen before. She said nothing, but the message was clear. *Game on.*

"Ace of clubs!"

Frederick's hands felt as if they were everywhere at once. He knew for certain he was moving faster than Nineteen at this point, but still they reached every card almost simultaneously.

He snagged the last card and looked down triumphantly. He had seven cards in his hand. Since his face-down card was a club, that meant Nineteen only had five. He would have a one-card lead going into the final round.

"That's a penalty on Two-Oh, grabbing a card out of order," Seven said.

"What?" Frederick turned to Seven in disbelief. "What're you talking about?"

"You grabbed the queen before the jack."

Frederick looked at the cards in his hand and groaned. He had gotten distracted and forgotten that his card was the king of clubs, not the jack. When the ten had been picked up, he had immediately grabbed the queen. The oversight would be extremely costly.

"So, I take that card from you," Seven said, reaching over and snatching the card. "As well as two more as a penalty." He took two more cards from Frederick's pile.

"Five," Nineteen said without any emotion.

"Four? I guess?" Frederick shook his head in frustration. He'd gone from a one-card lead to having a two-card deficit. It was now 18-16. He would need to get eight of the remaining thirteen cards to beat Nineteen. A tie seemed to be off the table too, since he was down by two cards with an odd number remaining.

He pushed away his frustration and tried to still his mind. Lifting his eyes, he met Nineteen's gaze.

I'm faster than her. How is she beating me? Frederick gritted his teeth in concentration. Nineteen stared back at him, though it seemed like she was staring through him rather than at him. The girl was entirely relaxed.

His eyes went wide.

She's not thinking about it at all. It's all instinct. That's how she's beating me there. She knows where the cards are and trusts herself to grab them without pausing to think.

"Six of spades!" Seven's words had barely reached his ears before Frederick was moving. He didn't pause to think about where the cards were before reaching for them, simply letting his hands go to where they knew they were.

It was over in a matter of breaths. Frederick looked down to see a small stack of cards in his hands. He counted them quickly.

"Ten," he said in disbelief. The entire room turned to Seven, who sat dumbfounded, staring at Frederick. If he had collected all the cards in the right order, he would win 26-21.

"Well?" Eight asked impatiently. Seven blinked away his amazement and turned to the others, shrugging.

"I didn't see him cheat, but how the hell would I know? He was a freaking blur."

"He didn't cheat," Nineteen said, her face a mixture of frustration and appreciation. "It was all in the right order." She held her hand out across the table to Frederick.

"Good game."

Chapter 21

They played the new card game, which Eight proudly dubbed "Swipe," for the rest of the evening. They took only one short break to eat, scarfing down their meals quickly so they could return to the game. Frederick was surprised by how addicting the game was for all of them. The others had seemed inspired by his defeat of Nineteen and had attacked the competition with a new intensity.

Frederick managed to win a few more games in a row before he was toppled from his throne. They had taken note of how he had studied Nineteen and had begun studying him in turn. After only three more games, Thirteen was able to defeat him. It was an incredibly close game, only separated by a couple cards. Frederick sighed, half in frustration, half in relief as he surrendered his seat. The game was mentally and physically stressful, and he was glad for the reprieve.

They played late into the night, with only One and Seven failing to win a single round, the former due to lack of participation and the latter due to lack of success. Seven was growing more and more frustrated with every passing round. He ground his teeth as he studied the cards to no avail. Yawns spread across the room, and Thirteen began to gather up the cards.

"What're you doing?" Seven asked indignantly. "I'm almost there! Just one more game!"

"That's what you said half an hour ago." Thirteen rolled her eyes. "We'll play more tomorrow. Maybe then you can end your abysmal streak."

Seven mumbled something unintelligible but moved to gather the chairs and stack them in the corner, apparently conceding.

The chairs and table were moved to the side of the room, and the mattresses were dragged into their position in the center. The group retreated to their respective rooms to prepare for bed, then trickled back out and dropped onto their mattresses.

Frederick felt remarkably untired. His earlier nap seemed to have done its job a little too well. He worried that sleep would not come easily to him. One of the drawbacks of sleeping in a room with five other people was that he would be self-conscious anytime he readjusted, fearing his movement would rouse them from their slumbers. As Frederick stared at the ceiling fretting, the others chatted softly. One by one, the conversations fizzled until all that was left was silence. As the breathing of his friends evened out into the cadence of sleep, he felt the familiar feeling of loneliness wash over him. He wasn't alone; in his head, he knew he wasn't alone. He had five friends less than an arm's length away, but still he couldn't kick the sensation of utter isolation. The feeling had come on so quickly, so unexpectedly that it nearly took his breath away. Panic rose in his chest.

What if it never goes away? What if no matter what happens I'll always be alone? How can anyone live like this? How can anyone—

A thunderous snore tore through the silence of the room. Frederick felt himself laughing before he even registered what had happened. He tried to stifle it, and he heard one or two others in the room do the same. Apparently, they weren't all asleep after all. And in that moment, the feeling of isolation had been dispelled, vanished without a trace. That single ridiculous snore from his ridiculous friend had finally allowed his body to understand what his brain already knew. He wasn't alone. He wouldn't ever be alone again.

Arthur roused them the next morning around six thirty, though Frederick had been drifting somewhere between sleeping and waking for most of the night. It hadn't been an overly restful experience. The stress of the last several days weighed heavily on his shoulders, and from the way his friends carried themselves, he suspected it burdened them as well.

"Back at it!" Arthur called cheerfully. "One good day of training deserves another!"

A puzzled look crossed his face as the group began to rise wordlessly and move to get ready. He had clearly been expecting something from them, whether it be banter or insults. The silence obviously concerned the man. But, to his credit, he didn't push them, allowing them to get ready in silence.

The group's mood seemed to be improving marginally as they followed Arthur down the halls. They were still devoid of their typical back-and-forth, but there was talking at least. The curiosity of what was to come was enough to draw them from the dark places in their minds.

"What do you have for us today, Arthur?" One asked.

"Perhaps you would prefer to have a look," the man replied, scanning his keycard and leading them through a door.

Before them was the same room they had trained in the previous morning—or Frederick assumed it was the same room. The general dimensions were the same, and the foam pit was there, but beyond that, it was vastly different. The chains hanging over the pit were gone, as were the poles that had risen up out of the foam. Instead, there were several small, spinning platforms hanging from ropes from the ceiling. Most were stationary, but more than one appeared to be swinging back and forth above the pit. There also appeared to be a giant pane of plexiglass starting from ground level and extending almost to the ceiling about halfway across the pit. Frederick suspected there were several other oddities that would be revealed upon further inspection.

"Welcome to day two of training!" Arthur said. "As you can see, this is much the same concept from yesterday but with new obstacles. You will find these obstacles to be slightly more difficult than the last, I think. This will be the format for the rest of the week for both your morning and afternoon training: similar tasks that will be tweaked to push you to further your limits. Every morning, you will do a different obstacle course; every afternoon, you will work on hiding in new surroundings. The afternoon's environmental changes will not be drastic, but you will be given less time to hide and be required to hide for a longer period of time. At the end of the week, you will have one final test that will be much more difficult than anything you've encountered thus far. We will use your performance in that test to determine if you are ready for the other side of the Door."

"And if we aren't ready?" Nineteen asked.

"You will be. Of that I have no doubt."

It took them twice as long to get through the obstacle course as it had the first time. There was also a significantly higher number of falls into the foam pit. It was doubly frustrating and doubly exhausting.

This carried into their afternoon training session. It took them fully four tries to manage to evade Arthur. By the end, they were all drained both physically and mentally. They dragged their exhausted bodies back to their rooms and collapsed onto their mattresses. No showers, no brushing of teeth—they were far too tired for that.

"Anyone wanna play Swipe?" Eight said, face-down into his pillow.

His question was met with a chorus of groans. Even the mighty One seemed to be running on fumes.

"I'm making an executive decision. No games, no stories. Just sleep."

Thirteen voiced her assent with a single melodious snore.

The next day was easier, though not by much. They were met with another obstacle course, which they managed to conquer faster than they had the previous day, though still not as quickly as their first. The afternoon training, on the other hand, looked to be headed for disaster. In three tries, they had found no viable hiding spots. Their fourth try had been mere minutes from success when an ill-timed sneeze from Eight had given them away. The boy redeemed himself the next round, however, when he discovered a hollow boulder large enough for all six of them to hide in.

The group walked wearily back to their rooms, though this time they were able to make it to the showers before collapsing. Frederick rinsed off quickly, knowing that if he dawdled, there was a very real chance that he would fall asleep underneath the deluge. He emerged from his room and found that his companions had had much the same idea. They were all sitting on their mattresses, except One, who was presumably still in the shower.

"Screw this," Seven groaned.

"Amen," Thirteen added.

"I can feel every muscle in my body burning," Eight said in awe. "How are my ears sore?"

Nineteen tried to say something, but only a groan escaped her lips.

Frederick walked over to his mattress and, with no small effort, picked it up and began moving it to the corner of the room.

"What the hell do you think you're doing, Two-Oh?" Seven called. "No one wants to play that stupid card game."

Frederick laughed in spite of the pain coursing through his body. "You think One is going to let us sit around two nights in a row?"

"Fat chance of that," Thirteen said, cursing to herself as she stood and gathered her own mattress. Eight and Nineteen followed their example, working slowly but surely.

"You lot have fun," Seven said, rolling over. "There's not a snowball's chance of me getting out of bed."

"Well, perhaps I'll help you." Seven jumped at One's voice. The blond boy stood over him with a towel slung behind his neck. His hair was still wet from the shower, and he showed no signs of fatigue.

"Oh, lay off, One. I'm exhaust—"

One reached down and lifted the mattress from under him, effortlessly throwing the stocky boy to the floor. "Now that wasn't so bad, was it?" he said cheerily as he placed Seven's mattress in the corner and rolled the table out into the middle of the room. "Who's up first?"

This was the routine for the next several days. Train, train some more, shower, play Swipe, sleep. It was difficult, but Frederick could see the benefits almost immediately. Despite the difficulty of the training increasing, they were spending less and less time in both the obstacle courses and the hiding sessions, not to mention they were less sore every day. Frederick could feel his muscles growing.

Perhaps the most noticeable improvements, though, were in the games of Swipe. They played at a speed which Frederick would've sworn impossible just a few short days ago. Entire games passed in a minute or two at most. Rounds took little more than a couple heartbeats.

They improved as spectators too. Where before they had struggled to even identify if the cards had been collected in the correct order, they now could tell if someone reached for a card a fraction of a second too early. Despite all of this, there was a single fact that showed them with absolute certainty that they had progressed dramatically.

One began to play with them.

He had apparently been waiting until they were nearing his level, deeming it useless to participate before they had reached a certain skill. It wouldn't help anyone for One to destroy them round after round. He had simply been too good and incapable of going easy on them.

Now he played.

He still always won, and the games were rarely close, but Frederick thought someone might give him a run for his money before long. That became the goal: not to beat each other but to improve enough as a unit to defeat One.

"Someone has to take that dude down," Seven said in frustration as One excused himself to go to the bathroom after once again trouncing his opponent. Seven threw down a handful of cards in disgust. "I can't die in another dimension knowing he never lost a game."

"You aren't going to die," Nineteen said sharply.

"That's neither here nor there . . ." Seven trailed off. "Do I still not have a nickname for you?"

"You do not," Nineteen said simply.

"Prime?" he suggested. "Because it's a prime number?"

"So is thirteen," Thirteen said.

"Argh!" Seven shouted and threw his hands in the air. "Well what the hell has anything to do with the number nineteen?"

Nineteen shrugged.

"Ugh, I'll think of something," Seven said. "Regardless, the point remains, we have to beat him."

"How?" Frederick asked. "He's faster than us. Has better instincts. Better memory."

"Better hair, better teeth," Thirteen added.

"Better smelling, taller, blonder," Eight chimed in.

"Enough! We are all aware of his never-ending qualities," Seven said. "I mean, holy hell, if he isn't the most likable person I've ever met. Still! We have to beat him. Just once."

"I have an idea," Nineteen said, her face impassive.

Thirteen smiled broadly. "That's your 'let's cheat' face. I'd know it anywhere. What's the plan?"

"Hold on, are we sure we want to resort to cheating?" Seven said. All eyes turned to the boy, whose face split into a wide smile. "Only joking, of course. Tell us what you got, 'insert nickname here.'"

"Did you just say 'insert nickname here?'" Thirteen asked.

"I did."

"Okay."

They huddled closely as Nineteen shared her plan.

One emerged from the bathroom a short time later to find a determined group sitting tight-lipped around the table.

"Talkative bunch, aren't you?" he said sarcastically.

His comment was met with only stares.

One looked at Frederick, who sat in one of the seats reserved for competitors. "What? Giving me the silent treatment just because I've been winning? Imagine how upset you all would've been if I had started playing a few days ago."

Still no response. A wicked smile spread across One's face.

"It's about time you all got serious."

There was a quiet tension in the room as the two boys studied the table before them. Nineteen sat perfectly still, giving the competitors slightly more time than usual to prepare. Seven cleared his throat uncomfortably a couple times. The silence apparently lasted too long for his body to handle. Nineteen knocked quickly on the table, three times. One shot her a confused glance. Frederick remained motionless, one hand resting palm down on the edge of the table, the other held to his forehead in concentration.

"Five of hearts!" Thirteen shouted.

"Jack of spades!" Eight yelled.

"Four of diamonds!" Nineteen called.

One seemed mildly confused by the shouting but recovered quickly. The fraction of a second cost him, though. He scrambled to catch up to Frederick and even managed to get the last two cards. Even still, the damage was done.

"Seven," Frederick said.

"Five," One responded, an even bigger smile cutting his face. "So it's like that, is it?"

No reply. One turned his card over. "And look at that. Already lost my leg up."

Twelve eyes returned wordlessly to the table. Nineteen rapped the table with her knuckles a single time. Seven sneezed loudly.

Frederick sat biting the fingernails of one hand nervously, with the other hand face up on the table.

"Queen of spades!"

"Eight of clubs!"

"King of hearts!"

Once again, Frederick got the jump on One, though the margin was much slimmer this time around. Their hands were a blur as they removed all the hearts from the table in just a few heartbeats.

"Six," Frederick said.

"Seven." One's face maintained its wolfish grin. "You're gonna have to do better than that. Pretty soon, I'll know the suit before she calls too."

Frederick took a deep breath. It didn't matter: One knew they were cheating. They hadn't had time to approach it subtly, and he doubted subtlety would've been any more effective anyway.

Frederick rested both hands on the table as if to steady them.

Knock. Knock. Knock. Knock.

Cough. Cough. Cough.

"Ace of clubs!"

"Three of spades!"

"Eight of spades!"

"Six," Frederick called a short time later.

"Seven," One smirked.

The game was tied, with a single round to go. The room vibrated with anticipation as the two boys turned to look at each other. The look in One's eyes was almost enough for Frederick to lose his nerve.

Fire. Intensity. Hunger. Call it what you want, it was practically bleeding from him.

Frederick gritted his teeth and returned the stare, feeling something burning in his own gaze. He placed both hands on his face in an effort to focus.

Knock.

Hiccup. Hiccup. Hiccup. Hiccup.

"Ace of clubs!"

"Three of clubs!"

"Ace of clubs!"

Frederick didn't think. He didn't need to. He barely had an advantage at this point, but that didn't matter. He had realized something right before his friends had started their final round of shouting. They had chosen him to face One because he was the only person who could compete with his speed, but he wasn't as fast as One.

He was faster.

It was over in a blink, and Frederick already knew before he looked down to count his cards.

"Seven," he said, allowing himself a small smile.

One stared at him, dumbfounded. His disbelief quickly turned to respect as he dropped his cards in front of him. "Five."

The room erupted into cheers.

Seven tackled Frederick out of his chair and pinned him to the ground. Thirteen leapt on him as well, and Eight was there in a flash. Even Nineteen jumped on top of them, whooping hysterically.

One walked over to the dogpile and crouched beside it. He reached down and shook Frederick's hand, or rather shook it as much as he could while it was pinned beneath the mass of bodies.

"Good game."

"You too," Frederick gasped.

"You aren't done yet though," One said. "Get off him! We're going again."

One figured out exactly how they were cheating halfway through the next game.

"So if I'm not mistaken," he said as he counted his cards, "Nineteen's knocks are distractions. The suit is determined by however many random noises Seven makes. Once for hearts, twice for diamonds, thrice for spades, and four times for clubs, I believe."

Seven rolled his eyes, which was confirmation enough.

"Eight and Thirteen are obviously also distractions," the blond boy continued. "And finally, our dear Twenty. He determines the specific card by how many fingers he has on the table. Palm down and it's a lower card, and palm up means face card. That all sound about right?"

"Well these last two rounds aren't gonna be much fun, are they?" Seven muttered.

Frederick kept the game fairly close, all things considered. He ended up losing 28-22, which was still better than any of them had done before they had decided to cheat. He shook One's hand and felt an odd sensation in his stomach. It was a combination of disappointment and thankfulness. He was disappointed because he knew he could never be like the boy sitting across from him and thankful because that boy would do everything he could to protect every person in the room.

They played Swipe for another hour or so, and One relinquished his spot in the game so they could all get some work in. Eight and Nineteen were playing one another now, with Seven acting as referee.

One leaned over and whispered to Frederick. "That was impressive."

"It was basically all Nineteen," Frederick whispered back. "She came up with and explained the whole idea in the time it took you to pee."

"That's not what I'm talking about." He looked thoughtful. "Although that is impressive. We need to make sure to use her brain whenever we can if we are going to succeed." He shook his head and dropped his voice even more. "I'm talking about you, Twenty. You can be stronger than any of us. The only reason I ever beat you is I trust myself. You are faster than I'll ever be." One pulled away a little bit, smiling. "I can tell you know it's true. You believed in the last round of the first game. If you thought like that all the time, well . . ." One let out a soft whistle.

Frederick just shrugged and tried to hide his reddened face by turning back to watch the game.

"We are gonna need you, Twenty." One turned back to the game as well. "Best start believing."

Later, Frederick lay on his mattress, staring at the ceiling, thinking about what One had said to him. He wanted to believe—he wanted it with everything he was. But he had a lifetime's worth of evidence screaming at him that he was dead weight, that when the chips were down and everyone looked to him, he would let every single one of them down.

Chapter 22

Frederick woke to someone shaking him roughly.

"You okay, boss?"

He forced his eyelids open to find Eight's smiling face about three inches away from his own. It was obvious the boy had not yet brushed his teeth this morning.

"Just peachy," Frederick mumbled. "Could use some space though."

"Sure thing, boss." Eight jumped back to give him room.

"Where is everyone?" Frederick asked, rubbing sleep from his eyes.

"They are all getting ready," Eight said, bouncing from one foot to the other. "Arthur woke us up about fifteen minutes ago. Said we got that big test thing or whatever today."

Frederick stood and stretched slowly, groaning as several of his joints popped. He had been so emotionally exhausted the night before that he had forgotten about the final test entirely.

"You slept right through it. Seemed like it hurt Arthur's feelings a bit. They said to give you ten more minutes of sleep, then try to wake you up again. I've been shaking you like a tambourine for a solid five minutes and nothing. You hit your head in the night or something?"

"Not as far as I know," Frederick said. "I'm gonna go get ready." He turned to leave, then paused. "Oh, and Eight?"

"Yeah, boss?"

"Brush your teeth. Twice"

Frederick got ready as quickly as he could manage, then returned to the common room, where he found his friends waiting with Arthur, who was tapping his foot and staring at his watch.

"You picked a hell of a day to sleep in," Seven said to Frederick.

"Sorry, Arthur. Not sure what happened, but I was really out of it."

Arthur looked at Frederick with a strained severity. It was clear he knew he should reprimand Frederick but didn't quite have it in him.

"Oh, it's alright Twenty. Just don't make a habit of it, yes?"

"You got it," Frederick said.

"Well, let's get to it. We're already running behind." Without another word, Arthur turned and strode briskly down the hall.

"What's this big test, Arthur?" Thirteen asked as they walked.

"You should know by now I can't get into specifics, Thirteen. Suffice it to say it will be in the same vein as your training up to this point with a slight . . ." The man paused and adjusted his oversized spectacles. ". . . raising of the stakes, shall we say?"

"Don't like the sound of that," Seven muttered.

Frederick studied Arthur as they walked. The receptionist was even more energetic than usual. His hands continuously pulled objects out of his pockets, fiddled with them for a few moments, then returned them. He was also sweating more than a short walk would justify.

"What's got our beloved receptionist so worried, I wonder?" One whispered.

"I'm not sure," Frederick whispered back. "Makes me nervous though."

"Yeah." One seemed to barely be paying attention to Frederick at this point—his eyes were alight with excitement. "Nervous." The blond boy turned and winked at him.

Well at least one of us feels ready.

Arthur led them on the now-familiar path to the room that had contained the obstacle courses they had done over the last week.

"This is where I leave you. Same rules as always. Get across as quickly as you can. Only one person can use each method to cross the pit." Arthur paused and cleared his throat. The sweat was practically pouring down his face. "Good luck."

His standard cheery tone was gone. A knot formed in Fredrick's stomach as the man walked away without another word. Three words began rattling around in Frederick's mind.

He is terrified.

The room was identical to the first time they had entered it, or at least it appeared so at first glance. There were the chains hanging from the ceiling spaced out evenly, as well as the several poles rising from the pit.

Seven scoffed loudly. "Well this is a bit of a letdown," he said. "They made it seem like this was gonna be some big thing and then gave us not only a course we've already had but one that we crushed."

"It's not the same course," Nineteen said softly. She stood at the edge of the pit, and there was something in her voice that caused them all to pause. Frederick walked up beside the small girl and looked over the edge of the pit, though he knew what he would see before he did.

"That does seem to raise the stakes a bit," One said as he joined them.

The foam pit was no longer a foam pit. It was just a pit.

Where once there had been several feet of foam cushioning, now there was only concrete. Not only that, but the pit appeared to be about twice as deep as it had been before. What had been a twenty-foot fall into foam was now a forty-foot plunge onto concrete.

"What, are they trying to kill us?" Eight asked, his face growing pale.

"There's more," Thirteen's voice shook. She stood inspecting the chain nearest to the edge of the pit. "There's no grip on these. They must've oiled them or something."

Frederick inspected the chain himself and ran his hands over its length. Sure enough, as he pulled his hand away, he could feel a slick substance between his fingers.

"Poles are for sure smaller," Seven called. "Looks like they have some goo on them too."

"The bow in the wall is gone. Straight as a string," Thirteen said with her face pressed up against the wall, looking down its length. "Least they didn't goo it far as I can tell."

"It's not the same course," Nineteen repeated in a small voice.

"Not remotely," One said. Frederick couldn't see the boy's face, but he knew from experience what he would see if he could.

"What do they expect us to do?" Eight asked. "Grow wings?"

"They expect us to do it the exact same way as before," One said. "They just want us to know our limits. And it looks like we are gonna be pushing them."

"You're excited, aren't you? How are you excited?" Nineteen asked in a frustrated voice. "We could die!"

"We aren't gonna die," One said.

"We might die," Frederick said, eyeing the drop.

"We will not die," One said firmly. "Not now. Not on the other side of the Door. It isn't going to happen."

The intensity of the boy's voice left little room for debate.

"Let's just calm down and analyze this as much as we can," Nineteen said, speaking to herself more than anyone else.

"I'm telling you, there is no analyzing to do." Now it was One's turn to shake his head in frustration. "This isn't about finding a clever solution or working together or anything like that. Sometimes you just have to trust in your strength.

So trust it!" He almost shouted the last sentence. "The only way we die is if we doubt. If you can't trust yourself when all that's on the line is a broken bone or two, how are you gonna do it when all of our lives are on the line? Get your crap together, and let's go!"

This time, he did shout the final words. Frederick felt something bubble up inside of him: a fire that One was stoking with every word. Soon, it was burning so intensely it almost hurt. The feeling was so foreign that Frederick almost didn't recognize it at first.

He was starting to believe.

He looked around at his friends and could see that they were starting to as well. So far, the only thing they had been able to trust was One. He had proven himself time and time again. Now it was their turn.

Frederick strode over to the nearest chain and grabbed it. He tested it, pulling himself up so that he was holding up his entire weight. He could feel his grip grow stronger than he had anticipated, stronger than he would have thought possible. Even still, he could tell he was barely holding on. No amount of strength could counteract whatever substance they had put on the chains, not entirely at least.

Despite One's words, it seemed he would have to think slightly outside the box. He had enough strength to keep from sliding off the chain when simply holding on, but he doubted he would be able to withstand the extra force when jumping from chain to chain. This wasn't an issue of strength—it was an issue of physics.

Frederick let himself slide back to the ground but kept his hold on the end of the chain. He turned his attention to the individual links. They appeared to be just big enough for him to fit a couple fingers through. Sure enough, he was able to slip two of his fingers through a link. He closed his eyes and sighed, then turned back to look at the rest of the group.

Frederick gave them a small smile and shrugged.

"You've got to be joking," Nineteen said flatly.

"Hope you all still like me with a broken leg," Frederick responded.

"Bold of you to assume you'll only break a leg," Thirteen said.

"Or that we like you now," Seven added.

Frederick snorted and pulled himself up onto the chain.

He clung to it, about halfway up its length, wishing he had stayed home. The issue with the maneuver he was about to try was not simply that he would have to catch and hold the entirety of his weight with two fingers, it was also that he would have to accurately throw himself at the next chain. If he was off by more than a few centimeters, he would fall to the ground below. He looked down and felt his stomach fall to the distant floor. The height he'd gained from climbing the chain made the drop seem even more intimidating. He would be lucky to escape with only a broken bone or two if he fell from this height. Frederick began swinging back and forth, slowly building his momentum as well as his nerve. He realized as he swung that he wouldn't have time to think about the jump. He was losing his grip, and if he stalled, he would ensure a fall. He cursed loudly and threw himself forward as the chain reached its apex.

Frederick's life didn't flash before his eyes. Nor did time slow. He hurtled through the air, the only thing between him and disaster a single chain link. He managed to get his middle and index finger in about a third of the way up the chain; his aim had been for somewhere in the middle to allow for over or undershooting his mark.

Frederick grunted in pain as his full weight yanked on his fingers. Four gasps of shock sounded from the edge of the pit, accompanied by one unimpressed sniff. His momentum caused the chain to swing wildly, and it took every bit of strength to keep his hold on it. He waited for the chain to stop swinging, then scrambled up to his previous height.

Eight and Nineteen watched through gaps in their fingers, half turned away. Seven and Thirteen gaped at him with looks of utter disbelief. One stood studying his fingernails, yawning softly. Frederick laughed and cursed at the boy before turning his attention back to the chains.

He managed to move from chain to chain with similar amounts of success. It wasn't easy, and more than once, his hands slipped free a second too early, nearly causing him to undershoot his mark. Each time, though, he managed to hold on and hoist himself back up the necessary height. He was just starting to feel somewhat comfortable with the whole thing.

Frederick had been so focused on retaining his grip that he hadn't realized a chain had been removed until it was time for him to jump. He had nearly reached the other side of the pit, and up to this point the chains had been spaced out evenly, each jump had been almost identical. But now as he swung, he saw that the distance to the next one was twice as far as his previous jumps. His hands began to slip, and he knew he had no time to think.

Frederick swung his weight forward with all the force he could muster and flung himself toward the final chain. He flew through the air, arms windmilling wildly in a futile effort to maintain as much height as possible. His focus was on the bottom link in the chain, the only link he had a chance at reaching. He stretched his arm as far as he could, straining for the extra inch that could make all the difference. His two fingers managed to find their way into the link, and his body jerked wildly as they found purchase. A terrible pain shot from Frederick's finger, up to his arm. He yelped and almost let go of the chain reflexively.

The extra distance he had been forced to cover had affected his grip, causing his fingers to awkwardly sit on top of one another and injuring his middle finger. Frederick had never dislocated anything before, but he suspected that was exactly what had just happened. The finger was now useless. He heard shouting from behind but was too focused on the pain and the prospect of falling to make out the words. His full weight now rested on his index finger as he clung to the bottom link of the last chain. Frederick gritted his teeth against the pain and began to swing his weight back and forth. There wasn't time for him to climb up the final chain—his finger wouldn't hold for that long. He would need to jump as soon as he could. With a final shout of defiance, Frederick threw himself through the air toward the safety of the other side of the pit. He floated toward his destination, and for a moment, he was unsure where he would land. Then, blessedly, his feet hit the ground on the other side of the pit. His toes clipped the edge, and he awkwardly tumbled to the ground clutching his hand close to his body.

"Two-Oh! You okay?"

"Ow," Frederick responded weakly.

"Good enough for me!" Seven called over.

Frederick gathered the courage to look down at his finger, which still throbbed in pain. It was bent at an awkward angle, and his stomach turned at the sight. He averted his gaze and waited for his head to clear. The fact that his finger was still attached provided some solace, but the pain was still excruciating.

"Any of you know how to pop a finger back into place?" Frederick said, trying to keep his voice from breaking.

"I do!" Seven called.

"Anyone else?"

No reply came from the other side of the pit.

"All of you just get over here as quick as you can so Dr. Gray can yell at me for getting hurt again."

Seven immediately walked toward the edge of the pit and stooped, grabbed the top of one of the poles, letting his body hang below it. He swung from pole to pole with apparent ease. The tops of the poles provided a better grip, and Frederick suspected that their reduced size was actually a benefit for this method of crossing. The stocky boy crossed the pit in almost no time at all, easily pulling himself up over the ledge. Without a word, he walked up to Frederick and grabbed his injured hand, turning so that Frederick's arm was now braced in the other boy's armpit.

"Wait wait wai—"

Frederick's protests were cut short as Seven popped his finger back into place. There was an intense flash of pain, but it quickly subsided. Frederick looked down at his finger and was surprised to find it now looked fairly normal—besides the significant swelling.

"Gonna need a splint, I imagine," Seven said.

"How do you know how to do that?"

"Me, Joey, and Hannah hurt ourselves all the time." He shrugged. "After a few trips to the ER, I started to pick a thing or two up. Did some research on my own and all that. It's really not that hard."

Seven motioned for Frederick to look back toward the pit. Eight was struggling up the chain in an effort to get to the sprinkler heads, as he had before. Once he reached the top, he immediately began swinging from sprinkler to sprinkler. A few had been removed in the same manner that Frederick's chain had been, but the small boy seemed undeterred by this.

"Betcha I can do this without breaking anything, boss!" he shouted as he swung his way across. Eight landed lightly by the two larger boys, a smile plastered across his face. He held up all ten fingers and wiggled them in Frederick's face.

"Lookie there! All still in place! What do you think of that?"

Frederick ignored him and turned just in time to see Thirteen sprinting toward the wall. She leapt and ran along it. After a few steps, she pushed off the wall and sailed through the air, landing on the very edge of the pit. She stood there, trying to fully gain her balance for a moment, arms spinning wildly. She shouted in alarm as she slowly began to tip backward, her efforts to stabilize herself unsuccessful. Seven leaped forward and grabbed her arm to haul her to safety.

"Bit of a klutz, eh there, Jinx?" he said with a grin.

Thirteen blushed and punched him in the arm. Seven wisely did not push his luck and instead joined the others in observing One and Nineteen.

"Whenever you're ready!" Thirteen called. "I'm ready for a sandwich and . . ." Thirteen trailed off as she looked more closely at the pair.

Neither One nor Nineteen responded. Nineteen's entire body shook, and she had sunk down to her knees, pulling them closely to her chest. One crouched beside her, whispering. Frederick strained his ears but was unable to make out anything. After a few moments, One stood and reached a hand down to Nineteen. She accepted it wordlessly and let herself be pulled to her feet. One grabbed her firmly by the shoulders and locked eyes with her. He said no more, apparently already having said everything he thought necessary. He simply nodded to her.

She returned the nod and Frederick was surprised by how confident it was. Nineteen's body language had undergone a complete transformation in a matter of seconds. Gone was the terrified girl who had shaken like a leaf. There was now a look of determination on her face that Frederick could easily make out despite the distance. She took a single deep breath and sprinted across the tops of the poles. Frederick gasped as he watched her. The bottoms of her shoes seemed to merely skim the poles as she ran. It was over in a flash. She stood among them, breathing heavily, though Frederick suspected it was more from the rush of what she had done than the exertion.

"Well, that looked easy," Thirteen said, a note of disbelief in her tone. "Hey, One—you gonna join us or what?"

The words had barely left her mouth before he had landed beside her.

"Of course they didn't make yours any harder," Seven said sullenly. "There should've been attack drones or something you had to get through."

"Maybe they just knew that I already knew to push my limits," One shrugged. "Or maybe they knew drones wouldn't have made a difference."

The comment inspired an eye roll from the stocky boy.

"Um. Can we leave now?" Frederick asked, holding up his injured finger.

"By all means, lead the way." Thirteen gestured grandly. "I wouldn't want you to have to wait for a Band-Aid!"

"I dislocated my finger," Frederick said flatly.

"It's not dislocated anymore, is it?"

Frederick sighed and moved to the door, the others following closely behind him.

Arthur was waiting for them. The relief was clear on the small man's face, and he looked exhausted as he greeted them. Frederick could see where he had sweated all the way through his shirt.

"Oh, thank goodness," Arthur gasped, his smile returning.

"Didn't have much faith in us, eh, boss?" Eight said.

"Frankly, that's offensive," Thirteen chirped.

Nineteen shook her head in disappointment. "I expected more from you, Arthur."

"After everything we've been through?" Seven chided.

Arthur's face grew red as he tried to find a response.

"Oh I didn't . . . I mean, of course I knew . . . I was just—"

"Oh, ignore them, Arthur," One said. "They're just giving you a hard time."

The relieved smile returned to Arthur's face. "Oh, yes, of course. Very good!"

"Hey, not to be a broken record—" Frederick started.

"Yeah, yeah, yeah, we know," Seven interrupted him. "You got any Band-Aids, Arthur?"

"Ah, yes." Arthur walked over and inspected Frederick's finger, which had continued to swell. "It'll be hard to know for sure until the swelling goes down, but it looks like you did a marvelous job resetting this, Seven."

"Why, thank you, Arthur. While I certainly didn't need any confirmation of how incredibly good I am, it's still nice to hear the words," Seven said, adopting a look of superiority.

Arthur produced a splint from somewhere on his person and placed Frederick's finger in it. Once the splint was in place, Arthur handed him two pills.

"For the pain and swelling. You'll need to get some ice on that eventually." Arthur grimaced. "Unfortunately, you'll have to power through the next test. We simply don't have time for you to wait for it to heal completely."

"That's okay, Arthur," Seven said cheerily. "Our Two-Oh is a real trooper. Ain't that right?"

Frederick smiled in spite of himself. "That I am."

"Fantastic!" Arthur said. "Well, no time to waste."

He turned and walked out the door.

"Oh, like right now, right now," Thirteen said.

"Right now, right now," Arthur's voice called from the hallway.

"We didn't even get a sandwich this time," Thirteen grumbled as one by one, they filed out after the receptionist.

Chapter 23

They followed Arthur to the waiting room outside where their previous hiding tests had taken place. With each step, the man's demeanor grew more and more distressed. Sweat poured down his face, and his hands moved with a distinctly unsettling freneticism.

"I didn't think it was possible for him to be even more nervous than he was before," One whispered to Frederick.

"Yet here we are," Frederick whispered back.

"How you holding up, Arthur?" Frederick jumped as One loudly asked the question.

Arthur looked over his shoulder and made an underwhelming attempt at a smile. "Well, to be frank, One, I've been much better."

"Anything you care to share?"

The man chewed on his lip.

"Let me guess, you can't tell us any specifics," Thirteen cut in, then continued in a remarkably accurate impression of Arthur's voice: "We are also testing your ability to react to the unexpected."

Arthur's smile widened in spite of himself, and while his anxiety didn't disappear, it did wane slightly. "Quite right. Unfortunately, all I can tell you is that the stakes will once again be higher this time around."

"Oh, fantastic. Let me guess, you'll be chasing us with chainsaws this time," Eight said, his voice dripping with sarcasm.

"Do not take this lightly." The smile melted from Arthur's face, and the hardness of his voice caused Frederick's stomach to flip.

Arthur adjusted his glasses and cleared his throat uncomfortably.

"Good luck. And I hope to see you all soon."

The door to the testing area slid open, and the applicants stepped through.

"You worry too much, Arthur," One called as he walked through the door.

It closed before the receptionist could offer a reply.

"I half expected it to be the same as the first time," One said as he scanned their surroundings. As with all the previous times they had entered this room, they were met with a totally unique setup. Trees, bushes, boulders, and grass filled the enclosure. There was also a large pond that spread out before them in the middle of the room, taking up approximately a quarter of the enclosure. Frederick turned to a clock placed above the door through which they had entered. It was counting down from thirty minutes.

"Looks like there's nothing especially difficult about the new terrain," he said aloud. "And we actually have even more time to hide than usual. Which means—"

"The raising of the stakes will have something to do with how they are seeking," Nineteen finished his thought.

"I don't think it'll be Arthur this time," One said. "He didn't look like he was in any condition to be searching."

Thirteen nodded. "It'll be something to make hiding more difficult while also punishing us for failure."

"What could it be?" Nineteen muttered to herself.

"Maybe some kind of dog?" Thirteen suggested. "They'll whip it up into a frenzy and release it in here. It could have our scent. Makes it more difficult to hide and also raises the stakes."

"Makes sense." Frederick nodded. "They'll probably have some way of controlling it in case things get out of hand. A shock collar or something like that."

One raised an eyebrow at both of them but didn't weigh in.

"Regardless," Nineteen said. "We need to hide—and hide well. Shall we split up?"

"Let's do it," One nodded. "Meet at the edge of the pond in fifteen minutes. We can compare hiding spots and see if we can put multiple people in the same ones like we've been doing."

Fifteen minutes later, Frederick returned to find One leaning against a boulder at the edge of the pond. The boy was coated head to toe in dirt and mud. He was breathing heavily, and he gave Frederick a rueful smile as he approached. Seven and Thirteen emerged from the trees simultaneously with Nineteen and Eight, joining the rest of the group just a few seconds later.

"What the hell have you been doing?" Seven asked One. "You look like you were in a cave-in."

"We'll get to that. First up, let's hear your spots. We don't have time to check each of them, so just be honest. How good and how many people could hide there."

"I got nothing," Frederick answered, his eyes dropping in embarrassment.

"Same," Seven and Thirteen said in unison.

"I found a big tree covered in some thorns that're pretty thick," Nineteen said. "We could maybe fit a couple people in there. It won't hide us well, but it'll make getting to us difficult."

"How good of a spot do you think it is? One to ten?" One asked.

Nineteen bit her lip, looking to the ceiling briefly in thought.

"A four, maybe?"

One shook his head.

"Alright, Eight. We need some help here."

"I gotcha, boss." The boy beamed. "I found some more vines to climb. I found an area up there with three or four spots, I bet."

"Which one is it? Three or four?"

Eight screwed his face up in thought. "I think it's four, boss. So long as it's neither of you." He nodded at One and Seven. "It would be a bit cramped for you guys."

One smiled broadly. "Excellent work, Eight." He turned to Seven. "I found a spot for us."

"Oh, lovely," Seven said. "I was hoping to get some nice quality one-on-One time today."

One rolled his eyes and turned to the boulder, bracing his shoulder against it and pushing. It rolled slowly to the side, revealing a hole that looked to be just big enough for both boys to fit.

"There was a bit of a depression there already. I just had to expand it a bit," One said, gesturing to his muddy clothes.

"So what are you, like part mole?" Thirteen asked.

One merely shrugged in response and hopped in the hole. Seven eyed the space warily.

"Not sure how I feel about pits. Are we sure there isn't room in the rafters for me?"

"You're with me, Seven," One said firmly. "I might need some backup, and you make the most sense."

The stocky boy exhaled sharply out of his nose and climbed down reluctantly.

"Wanna get that for us, Twenty?" One asked, nodding to the boulder.

"Please don't crush me," Seven added.

"Not sure I can do anything about that," Frederick muttered as he placed his shoulder against the boulder and pushed. It was lighter than he expected and rolled easily back into place.

"See you on the other side." One's muffled voice made its way up from the ground.

"Good luck," Frederick called and turned to Eight. "Lead the way."

Eight sprinted into the trees, making his way to the corner of the room where vines crisscrossed their way up the wall. Without pausing, the small boy leaped at them, pulling himself up hand over hand. In just a few short seconds, he reached the ceiling and his hiding spot within.

"There's room for one more with me"—his disembodied voice floated down—"and another spot for the other two about fifteen feet to the right."

"Thirteen, you go with Eight," Frederick said as he moved the appropriate distance and began to scale the vines.

"Roger," she said and climbed after Eight.

"Nineteen, you're with me." The smaller girl followed Frederick up the wall wordlessly.

It took a little bit of searching, but Frederick soon found the hiding spot the other boy had referenced. It was a small nook just below the ceiling, a result of rafters that ran throughout the room. Upon closer inspection, Frederick found that the rafters held large lights that lit the room in a way that gave off the impression of natural light. The rafters ran just below the ceiling into a space cut out of the wall. The space was just big enough for the two of them to squeeze in.

Nineteen scrambled in after Frederick.

"I don't like how split up we are," came a whisper from Frederick's elbow.

"I don't either," he whispered back. "But I'm not sure we have many options here."

"I know. Still."

Frederick nodded without answering. Several seconds passed in silence before Nineteen spoke again. "It's a shame we can't see the door. Being able to see what's seeking would be a huge advantage. Not to mention we could know how much time is left on the clock."

Frederick nodded—he had been thinking the same thing. From their vantage point, the door was hidden entirely. They weren't particularly close to being able to see it either.

"We need to be able to see it. We're too in the dark," Frederick said, more to himself than to Nineteen.

"It doesn't matter now. It's too late for us to do anything about it."

Frederick eyed the rafters thoughtfully.

"What are you thinking?" Nineteen asked.

"How much weight do you think those could hold?" Frederick asked without looking away.

"They could probably hold your weight," Nineteen said, understanding spreading across her face. "And the lights would make it impossible for anything below to see you while allowing you a perfect view. All you have to do is not make too much noise."

"Exactly."

"I don't love it." Nineteen shook her head then sighed. "But it's probably our best option, and I can tell by that look on your face that there's no stopping you either way."

Frederick gave an apologetic smile, to which she sighed.

"It's fine. Just—just be careful, okay?"

"Always." Frederick tried to do his best impersonation of One's reassuring smile.

"He uses his eyes more when he does that," Nineteen said dismissively. "Besides, your own faces work just fine. Just get out there."

Frederick snorted and pulled himself up on top of the rafters.

The metal creaked beneath the new weight as he climbed fully atop the rafter. His heart paused for several breaths as he waited for it to crumble and send him tumbling to the ground.

It held.

Frederick exhaled and fixed his eyes ahead of him. The rafter cut through the middle of the room, extending out almost directly over the pond before reaching the far wall.

"Maybe I can manage to fall into the water once this thing breaks," Frederick muttered to himself as he began scooting forward on his stomach. He moved as quickly as he could justify. The clock was still not visible, but Frederick was certain it had to be close to zero by now. Every few feet, he would reach a new section of metal, and it would protest his presence loudly. Each time, Frederick's heart leapt into his throat and his stomach plummeted.

Each time, the rafter held.

Soon, his progress was rewarded with a view of the clock. As it came into view, he saw that his assumption had been correct—less than thirty seconds left. Frederick increased his pace, trying to get as far along the rafter as possible before the timer ran out. He managed to get to almost exactly the middle of the room. Glancing down, he saw that he wasn't quite over the water. In fact, he was almost directly above One and Seven's rock.

Frederick's thoughts were interrupted by a loud chime, and his eyes snapped to the door, waiting for it to open.

But it didn't.

Instead, the ground split in front of the door. A trapdoor that had been hidden beneath the grass opened, and a cage slowly rose from it. The thing was huge, easily twenty feet across and every inch as high. Frederick strained to see its contents. There was something inside. He could detect movement but couldn't make out what it was. The longer he stared, the more the thing took shape. Soon, Frederick realized it wasn't one creature in the cage, but two.

Frederick's heart skipped several more beats.

Are those bears? He wasn't overly familiar with bears, but whatever the things were, they seemed to be the right color and size.

Frederick nearly toppled from the rafters as two terrible howls filled the room, followed by a sound like concrete being ground together.

Bristles?

He blinked in disbelief, unable to fathom the sight before him. He had expected Dr. Gray to do something extreme.

But not this.

Every joint in his body locked up. No matter how hard Frederick tried, he couldn't make them move. His breathing grew shallow, and he felt his throat start to close up. He began to slip into darkness. Somewhere in the corners of his mind, Frederick knew he was about to have a panic attack. He would be paralyzed and would topple from his perch. He would fall, and that would be the end.

His weight began to slowly shift sideways.

Then the air rushed in.

Frederick felt everything inside him unlock. He had control again. The breaths came easily, and he could move freely. His fear was replaced with something else. Something he hadn't expected to find.

White-hot anger.

How dare they? How dare Dr. Gray unleash these monsters on him and his friends for a *test?* Frederick shoved the thought viciously from his mind. He would deal with that anger eventually, but first he had to win.

The Bristles moved slowly, methodically. It surprised Frederick. Once he had identified the creatures, he had expected them to scour the room in a frenzy, tearing apart anything in their path. Instead, they moved with great care. The murderous intent was still heavy in the air, but it was calculated and patient, and that shook Frederick more than anything else.

He watched as the two beasts made their way toward the center of the room, heads hung low, swinging slowly back and forth. With a start, Frederick realized what was happening. They were tracking their scent. Sure enough, they made their way steadily toward the boulder under which One and Seven hid.

The metal behind Frederick creaked, freezing him once more. He turned slowly toward the noise. Not three feet behind him was Nineteen, inching toward him. Their eyes met, and she gave Frederick a small awkward wave.

What are you doing? Frederick mouthed.

Nineteen wormed her way up beside him and spoke so softly he could barely hear her.

"I had to know what was going on. I couldn't stand just sitting there. Once I heard what was in the room, I knew I had to get out here to help you." She looked away from Frederick, down toward the Bristles. "They're gonna find One and Seven, aren't they?"

"Yes," Frederick whispered. "Eventually, at least. We just have to hope the clock runs out before then."

"Runs out?" Nineteen gave him a puzzled look. "You didn't see?"

Frederick turned quickly to the clock above the door and had to swallow a shout of frustration.

The timer had been replaced with an infinity symbol.

"It's not about if they find us," Nineteen whispered. "It's about when."

"There's no way," Frederick said to himself, but he knew what Nineteen said was true.

"What do we do?" Nineteen asked, turning her attention back to the Bristles. They had reached the boulder and were circling it slowly.

"They probably won't find One and Seven yet," Frederick said. "They'll follow our scent to the wall, then . . ." He shrugged. "Who knows? Maybe they'll try to climb the vines, mayb—"

Frederick was interrupted by two bloodcurdling howls.

Both Bristles stood by the boulder with their heads thrown back, baying wildly. Their howls turned to growls, and they began tearing at the ground around the boulder. Clumps of grass and dirt flew through the air as the beasts dug furiously.

Muffled cursing came from below the boulder, just barely audible over the growling.

"What do we do?" Nineteen asked again, significantly more panicked this time. "They'll dig them out in no time!"

"Hey!" Frederick shouted down at the Bristles, unable to come up with a better plan. "Hey, you ugly mutts!"

Nineteen joined in, but the Bristles carried on digging, unfazed. They were on the scent, and nothing was going to distract them from their prey.

The cursing below the boulder grew clearer as more and more dirt was dug up.

"Get out of there!" Frederick screamed. "Run!"

"Working on it!" Seven shouted back.

Suddenly the boulder flew from its position in the ground toward the two Bristles. The beasts yelped in surprise and jumped backward. One and Seven scrambled from their uncovered hiding spot and turned to run. The Bristles recovered quickly, however, one leaping to cut off the boy's escape. One and Seven stood back to back, a Bristle on either side of them.

"They're going to have to fight," Nineteen whispered.

"I have to help!" Frederick said.

"How can you help? It'll be too late by the time you climb back to the rafter and down the wall."

"I know!" Frederick clenched his teeth.

The Bristles circled the boys slowly, occasionally snapping at them. "We'll be okay!" One called out without looking up. "You all stay put. We can handle ourselves."

"But—"

"I said to stay where you are!"

Frederick and Nineteen flinched at the anger in his voice.

"We have to initiate the attack, take them by surprise," One said to Seven in an even tone that Frederick could just make out. "Ready?"

One threw himself at the Bristle in front of him, not waiting for the other boy's answer. Seven didn't hesitate, attacking his own Bristle.

Four bodies crashed together in a mixture of screams and howls. Both Seven and One managed to land solid blows without being bitten. Seven grappled with his Bristle, wrapping his arms around its neck and slipping behind it, out of reach of its razor-sharp teeth. One alternated punching and kicking his Bristle. Every time the beast regained its feet, One would throw a flurry of blows, mixing in just enough feints to keep his opponent off balance. He was making it look remarkably easy as he moved with his signature casual air.

"They're winning," Frederick said in disbelief, searching for relief but finding none.

As he spoke, Seven's Bristle twisted violently, creating an opening. Seven cursed and twisted as well, putting his back to the Bristle while still holding on to its neck. He shouted in his effort and threw his weight forward, sending the Bristle sailing over his shoulder. The creature landed heavily on the ground several feet away, crawling to its feet.

"Come on!" Seven shouted. "Is that all you've got? Hellhound my big toe— I've met more vicious kittens than you!"

The Bristle snarled at the boy and prepared to pounce.

"I said come on! I don't have all day!" Seven shouted with a wild look.

The Bristle sprang, and Seven crouched, preparing to repel it. But it sailed over his head, directly onto One's back. One shouted in surprise and stumbled forward under the weight. As he fell, his head smacked hard against the boulder. The blond boy slumped beneath the Bristle, motionless.

Seven reacted instantly, turning and throwing himself at the Bristle before it could sink its teeth into One. The maneuver created just enough force to toss the Bristle off of him. It skidded to a stop next to its companion. Seven grabbed the now-unconscious One and dragged him backward, placing himself between the Bristles and his unconscious friend.

"Hey, guys!" Seven yelled. "I know One said stay put, but I could really use a hand!"

"Just buy some time!" Frederick shouted down. "I'll be down as fast as I can."

"He doesn't have time," Nineteen said frantically. "We need to help him now!"

"How?" Frederick fought against the panic rising in his chest.

"Hold on to me!"

"What?"

"Just do it!" Nineteen shouted, and Frederick grabbed hold of her quickly. As soon as he had a grip, she leaned out over the rafters and began pulling at one of the large light fixtures hanging below them. Realization flooded through Frederick.

"You're a genius!"

"We'll see," Nineteen growled, her hands working furiously to loosen the light. Frederick glanced down at Seven. The Bristles hadn't attacked him yet. They seemed to be aware of their advantage and were in no hurry.

"Seven, you have to make them come about five feet closer to you!" Frederick shouted.

"I think they're planning on getting a lot closer than that!" the boy yelled, but he slowly backed up. The Bristles followed, inching closer and closer.

"Nineteen?" Frederick asked.

"Not yet," she answered through gritted teeth.

"Nineteen?"

"Not yet!"

"Nineteen!"

The girl yelled and yanked on the light one last time with all her strength. The fixture ripped free and plummeted to the earth below. The Bristle nearest to Seven looked up just in time for the hunk of glass and metal to crash into its face.

There was a horrible sound of metal and bone cracking as the Bristle fell to the ground, incapacitated.

"Holy . . ." Seven said as he glanced up. "Thanks!"

A howl ripped through the air as the remaining Bristle attacked him ferociously, undeterred by the aerial attack that had felled its counterpart. Seven had let his guard down, and the intensity of the attack threw the stocky boy onto his back. The Bristle snapped repeatedly, teeth inches from his throat. Seven used his legs as much as he could to keep his distance, kicking at the Bristle's body and face in an attempt to create any kind of separation.

"Helphelphelphelp!" Seven shouted.

"There are no more lights over them!" Nineteen shouted at Frederick. "What do we do?"

Frederick moved without thinking. He rolled off the rafter into open air.

Nineteen let out a choked shout of surprise as Frederick flew toward the earth. Air whistled past his ears, ruffling his hair as he sped toward the ground.

Frederick shouted as he fell, twisting his body so that his heels were aimed at the Bristle's head.

Seven kicked out one last time and rolled back instinctively, throwing his arms over his head.

Frederick hit the Bristle with a force that rattled every bone in his body. He felt a crunching beneath his feet as if he had just stepped on a particularly dry stick. Bones snapped loudly, and Frederick prayed they weren't his. He landed in a roll in an attempt to absorb some of the force of the fall, but pain still shot throughout his body.

Frederick lay in the mud and groaned loudly. He was alive.

He summoned all his strength and rolled over to look at Seven.

"You okay?" The words had difficulty making their way out of Frederick's throat.

"What the hell is wrong with you?" Seven responded, his voice a mixture of amazement and disbelief.

"I'm addicted to saving your sorry skin."

Seven snorted and climbed to his feet, hurrying to check on One. As Seven reached him, a groan escaped from the prone boy's lips.

"I take it that since I'm still alive, you guys took care of the Bristles," One said, sitting up slowly and placing a hand on his head.

"Two-Oh took care of them alright. Just about took care of himself in the process," Seven said.

At that moment, Eight, Thirteen, and Nineteen burst from the trees.

"Are you okay?" Nineteen rushed to Frederick.

"I'm good. Bristles are surprisingly absorbent."

Thirteen raised an eyebrow. "What?"

"I'll explain later," Frederick said. "Let's get out of here."

As expected, they found Arthur in the waiting room. His face was a perfect picture of relief as he split into a smile that was exhausted but warm. To Frederick's surprise, Dr. Gray was also there. He wore a broad smile as well, though it carried very little of Arthur's warmth.

"Well do—"

"Spectacular!" Dr. Gray cut off Arthur's congratulations. "Truly spectacular. Now if you all will follow me, it's time for a briefing."

"A briefing for what?" Thirteen asked.

"Your first mission, of course!" Dr. Gray gave them a wide smile. "Tomorrow, you are going through the Door."

Chapter 24

Dr. Gray led them to a conference room not far away. It was a small room with a single long table and eight chairs running along either side of it. The only other thing of note in the room was a small monitor mounted in the wall.

"Please take a seat," Dr. Gray said.

There was a cacophony of creaking chairs as they did so. Frederick was pleasantly surprised to find that Arthur would be joining them. He took a chair near Dr. Gray and began drumming his fingers silently on the table.

"So what's the deal?" Seven asked. "You said *first* mission. I thought there was only one mission."

"Technically, there is only a single mission," Dr. Gray replied. "Think of this as more of a test run. We want to see how your bodies react to being fully submerged in the Kinthian air. By now, you should be adjusted, but it never hurts to be certain."

"That being said," Arthur chimed in, "this is still very important. In fact, it could be vital to your main objective on the other side of the Door."

"How?" Eight asked.

"That will all become clear as we explain the details of both missions."

Dr. Gray paused for a moment, allowing the group one last chance to weigh in before he began.

"Before I explain tomorrow's endeavor, I must explain your objective as a whole more specifically. You know you must close the Door. Now I will tell you how you will do that, so please do pay attention. I'd really rather not have to go over this twice. I do hate redundancy."

Not as much as you claim, Frederick thought, but held his tongue.

"That being said, please do interject if you have any questions. We can leave no room for loose ends." Dr. Gray raised his eyebrows at them, and they nodded their understanding.

"Very good." The doctor cleared his throat. "The method you will employ to close the Door is actually dreadfully simple."

"Simple?" Thirteen said. "I wasn't exactly expecting the closing of an interdimensional door to be *simple.*"

"And yet it is." Dr. Gray walked over to the monitor. "The Kinthians were not afraid of someone trying to close the Door—why would they be? In fact, they went to great lengths to make sure that any person, in theory, could close it."

"In case they found something on the other side," Nineteen said. "Something bad."

"Precisely." Dr. Gray nodded. "Thankfully for us, they took these precautions. If they had held their cards a little closer to their chests, we might not have any hope of survival."

"So how do we close it?" Seven asked.

"You flip a switch."

They stared at the doctor dumbfounded.

"We flip a switch?" Frederick asked in disbelief. "All this? The training, the tests, secrets. All of that, and the big mission is to flip a switch?"

"Indeed." Dr. Gray smiled at him.

"That's a tad on the anticlimactic side."

"So it is. But I'm not entirely sure what you were expecting. A journey to the top of a volcano to cast some jewelry into lava?"

Frederick wasn't sure what he had expected. He honestly hadn't thought about it. Now that he did give it some thought, it all made sense. The Kinthians had potentially been playing with fire, and they knew it. They would want a way to extinguish the fire if they needed to. The only issue was that they had become the flame.

"This is what it will look like." Dr. Gray snapped several times at Arthur, who picked up a remote from the table and flicked the monitor on. Sure enough, on the screen was a picture of what appeared to be a large light switch. There was little of note about the device—just some numbers running along it.

"We retrieved this photo from a computer on one of our rather unsuccessful attempts into Kinth."

"You already tried going in?" Frederick asked.

"Of course." Dr. Gray gave him a puzzled look. "You didn't think we would send in a handful of high schoolers before trying some other methods, did you?"

Frederick flushed. Again, he hadn't given it much thought, but of course there would be others who had gone before them.

"In fact, you aren't even the first group of high schoolers," Dr. Gray said softly.

A silence filled the room to the brim.

Nineteen was the only one who seemed able to break it. "What happened to them?"

"They went through the Door, and we never heard from them again," Dr. Gray said, turning to look at them. "I cannot stress to you how real the danger you will be facing is." There was a tremble in his voice.

"We know the risks," One said. "And we're ready."

"I think you just might be right." Dr. Gray nodded and turned back to the monitor.

"This switch is located about a three-day hike from the Door. You will need to find the building, find the switch, flip it, and return. There will be a delay between when you flip the switch and when the Door closes. This should give you enough time to make it back through to this side."

"Should?" Seven asked.

"Yes. Unfortunately, there is no way for us to be certain how much time will pass before the Door closes. We haven't been able to ascertain that information in any of our previous missions. I'm afraid this is just another risk you must take."

"We might get trapped there?" Nineteen asked, her voice growing very small.

"I find the possibility highly unlikely." Dr. Gray ran a hand through his unkempt hair. "Though I'd be lying to you if I said it was impossible."

"So how do we find this place and the switch inside of it?" Frederick asked, eager to get back to the issue at hand. He didn't want to spend any time dwelling on something they couldn't help.

"That's where tomorrow's mission comes in. We found documents describing the location of the lab containing the switch in one of our later missions. What we need from you tomorrow is to travel to a library."

"Why the hell do we need to go to a library?" Seven asked.

"Blueprints," One said.

Dr. Gray nodded. "Inside the library, you will find a blueprint of the lab that will tell you the exact location of the switch and any additional information you might need. Upon retrieval of the blueprint, you will return so we can formulate a more specific plan before sending you back through. Does that make sense?"

"Why come back?" One asked. His voice was even, but Frederick could tell there was something lurking beneath the surface. "Wouldn't it make sense for us to just keep going? Every extra step we take on the other side exposes us to Bristles, not to mention we are on a bit of a time crunch. Seems like it would be safer to just continue from there."

"We considered this." Dr. Gray nodded. "There is certainly some validity to what you are saying. However, we want to provide you with as much assistance as we can, and we need you to return to fully do so. Also, as previously stated, we need to determine what effects a second full submersion into the Kinthian air will have on each of you. We have been increasing your exposure steadily and I am confident there will be no ill effects, but we cannot risk you all getting sick after a day or two. "

One pressed his lips into a thin line but did not object.

"Luckily for you all," Dr. Gray continued, "this library is not far from the Door. You'll only have to travel a couple of miles to reach it. The entire excursion should take no more than a few hours."

"That being said, do not underestimate the danger of this task," Arthur said, giving them a stern look. He was getting better at that.

"Yeah, yeah, yeah, we get it. Certain death around every corner, danger in every step, doom in every breath." Seven yawned.

"Well, I'm glad I don't have to worry about you losing your nerve," Dr. Gray chuckled.

"What else do we need to know?" One asked.

The doctor shrugged. "Nothing at the moment. We will provide you with a detailed map to the library, and it should be fairly easy to locate the blueprints once you get there. You know to be careful—there's not much else to it."

"We recommend you rest up for the remainder of the day," Arthur said. "You leave at dawn tomorrow."

Dr. Gray nodded to them and left the room abruptly.

"Bye!" Eight called at the man's back, though he seemed not to hear.

"Sorry about him," Arthur said. "Always something else to get to. It's very much a gift and a curse. Anyway, you all just let me know if any of you need anything. And really do try to get some rest."

"Will do, Arthur," One said. "See you tomorrow."

The man waved farewell and exited the room. One led the way back to their rooms.

Frederick sat with the rest of his friends around the table in the common room. Several hours had passed since their briefing, and they had spent most of the time playing Swipe, but they had decided they needed something lower intensity. Frederick had been glad for the break from the game. His finger still throbbed, and the splint proved a fairly considerable handicap. They had returned to their old game of "poker." While it didn't serve a practical purpose as Swipe did, it was an extremely effective method of decompressing. The simple motions and constant banter helped them all relax.

"So we go through tomorrow," Nineteen said, trying in vain to hide her discomfort at the thought. "How are you all feeling about it?"

"I'm terrified," Thirteen said in a matter-of-fact kind of tone. "But I've also never been so excited for something in my life. I haven't stopped thinking about that place since we left. I can't wait to taste the air again."

"Spoken like a true addict," Seven said in a cheery tone.

Thirteen rolled her eyes and turned to Frederick. "What about you, Twenty? How you feeling?"

"I can't wait to get back," Frederick heard himself saying. "Being there will be good. That feeling is better than anything I've ever felt. But I'm more excited to take a tangible step toward our final goal. Training is great and all that, but I want to just be able to point at something we've done and know it's made a difference."

"I'm excited to be able to run fast again," Eight said earnestly.

Seven nodded. "I'm with him on this one."

Frederick joined Nineteen this time in rolling her eyes.

"What about you, Uno?" Seven asked.

One smiled and shrugged. "Should be a good time."

Frederick could tell the blond boy was nearly bursting with anticipation. It had to be taking every bit of self-control One had to keep from trying to get through the Door immediately.

"I don't want to go," Nineteen said softly.

All eyes in the room turned to the girl. Her eyes were fixed on her cards, and she seemed incapable of meeting any of their gazes.

"I'm sorry. I know I shouldn't say that, but I really don't." She was stumbling over her words, they were coming out so fast. "I'm still going to go. I know I have to, and I want to help." She finally raised her eyes to meet theirs. "I just wish we didn't have to. I just want to stay here with all of you."

"We all wish that, Nineteen," Thirteen reassured her. "There's nothing wrong with feeling that way. In fact, it's brave of you to admit it. I think we should all be a little more like you." Thirteen smiled warmly at Nineteen, who dragged her eyes from her cards and managed a small smile of her own.

Frederick glanced at One. He suspected there was one person in the room who didn't share Nineteen's sentiment.

Chapter 25

Frederick had been certain he wouldn't sleep a wink, not with Kinth being only a few hours from his grasp. How could even the mere notion of sleep find its way into his mind with what the next day held? He was so filled with excitement and terror that it took everything in him to keep from shaking. With all that in mind, Frederick bid the others goodnight and lay down in his bed, expecting a grueling night of anticipation and ceiling staring.

He was asleep in mere seconds. It was a heavy sleep, as if his body knew it would need every ounce of energy it could save for the next day.

Frederick woke feeling refreshed. His companions began to wake as well as he tip-toed to the bathroom to brush his teeth. By the time he had returned, they were all awake and in various states of lucidity. One and Nineteen were chatting softly, and Eight was standing by the door, already bouncing from foot to foot. Seven and Thirteen barely qualified as awake, but they seemed to be doing their best to progress in their wakefulness. Thirteen rubbed her eyes roughly, and Seven was slapping himself in the face.

"Why can't missions to save the world start in the afternoon?" Seven mumbled.

"To be fair, this isn't to save the world. It's a pre-world-saving mission," Thirteen yawned.

The door burst open, and Arthur strode in. The arrival of the man was more than slightly disconcerting.

"Geez, boss," Eight said. "I thought you looked freaked out yesterday. That was nothing compared to your face now! I didn't believe in ghosts until I saw that look."

Sure enough, Arthur looked terrible. It appeared he had slept little, if at all. There were bags of concerning size under his eyes, and his face was contorted into a look of pain as if he had a migraine. Sweat ran freely down his brow, and he had to keep blinking as it made its way into his eyes.

"Good morning!" Arthur croaked, his voice hoarse. He tried his best to smile at them, but it only served to deepen the grimace of pain in his face. "I hope you'll excuse me. Sleep has been difficult for me to come by these last few nights."

"Too much late-night caffeine?" Eight said brightly, elbowing the man.

"Something like that." A fond smile replaced the forced, pained one.

They stood there in a somewhat awkward silence. Then Nineteen walked to Arthur and hugged him briefly, as if unsure if it was allowed.

"We'll be fine Arthur, I promise," she said.

The receptionist seemed stunned by the act, and he patted the girl awkwardly on the head and smiled down at her. "I'm sure you will, Nineteen." He wiped a single tear from his face. "I have no doubt."

Arthur led them down a series of hallways to a now familiar door. He scanned a keycard, and they listened as the thick bolts securing it from the other side began to slide out of the way, allowing the door to swing open. Dr. Gray stood waiting for them in the middle of the room beside the Door.

The Door.

The Kinthian air poured through it and enveloped them. Frederick's body sang at the sweet embrace it offered. He gazed at the Door like he would a long-lost friend. The sun was rising on the other side, illuminating the field with brilliant red light.

It was perhaps the most beautiful thing Frederick had ever seen.

He felt a tugging in his gut as his body urged him to run forward.

"Good morning," Dr. Gray greeted them. His hair seemed to be especially disheveled today, as if he had spent a few extra minutes running his hands through it.

The children offered nothing in the way of reply. Their eyes were fixed solidly on the Door.

Frederick took a step forward.

"Not yet," Arthur said softly, placing a hand on his shoulder. "We still have a few things to cover."

"Let's get this over with," Dr. Gray said in an excited tone. "You've waited quite long enough." He gestured to the wall, where six large backpacks lay in a pile. "We've packed your supplies. Each backpack contains several miscellaneous items that might come in handy in a pinch and enough rations for several days, including plenty of water. You will find each also contains a map and a compass. The map clearly marks the library as well as the building where you will close the Door."

"Why all the gear?" Thirteen asked, hefting a backpack. "I thought this was just a test run."

"It is. This is just a precaution. We don't anticipate you needing any of it, except the map and the compass, of course."

"You can never be too careful, I guess." Frederick muttered, picking up a pack for himself. It was heavier than he had expected.

"My thoughts exactly," Dr. Gray nodded. "You will return immediately upon completion of your mission at the library. Is that clear?"

They nodded in unison.

"Good. Arthur, is there anything else?"

"Good luck," the receptionist said quietly. His eyes shone as he looked each of them in the eyes.

"Good luck, indeed. We will see you upon your return."

Frederick closed his eyes and let the morning sun bathe him in warmth as he stood in the field just a few feet away from the Door. It was the same field they had been in when they had first snuck through, but they had never seen it in daylight. Colors burst from every direction. Flowers grew thick throughout the field, varying in size and color. The whole area looked like a painter's palette. The colors wove and almost seeped together. The sound of the wind in the leaves and the water of the stream running over rocks was almost enough to bring a tear to Frederick's eye.

"It feels so good to be back," Thirteen sighed.

"You can say that again," Seven agreed.

"This is no time to relax," One said, though there was a hint of a smile on his face. "Form up, single file. I'll take the lead. Twenty, you take the rear."

Eight saluted sarcastically. "Sir, yes, sir."

"This isn't a joke," One said firmly. "You remember what happened last time we were here? I'm not about to let one of you get eaten alive because you were too busy smelling some damn flowers to notice a monster sneak up on you."

"Sorry," Eight said sheepishly.

"Don't let your guard down. No matter what."

One led them through the field and into the trees. He walked at a quick but steady pace. There was a comfortable rhythm to their steps, but still, Frederick felt his body begging him to push its limits. He thirsted to run, to jump, to climb. He had to grit his teeth against the desire to sprint ahead of the others into the foreign trees. Despite One's warning, Frederick found his eyes wandering over the trees, taking in their beauty. He could see the rest of their group from his vantage point and could easily see he was not alone in this. Even One let his eyes peruse the beautiful scenery.

The grass was short here, and the trees were fairly sparse, which made their trek easier. Frederick had anticipated having to hack their way through overgrown forest with machetes, but this was much closer to a walk on a park trail. There were flowers here as well, painting the ground between the trees and shrubs. Frederick felt as if he would never be able to comprehend fully all the colors before him. It wasn't just the flowers, either—the trees and shrubs bore the same expanse of color. Reds, blues, whites, blacks, pinks, purples, yellows, and greens flowed from tree to flower to shrub. Even the grass bore some faint hues, as if the other plants had bled into it.

"I've never seen so many colors!" Frederick called out, unable to keep to himself any longer.

"Shhhhh!" One shushed him. "No talking until we've arrived at the library and secured it. There could be Bristles behind any one of these trees."

Frederick flushed, feeling foolish for his careless words. He knew on the same level how much danger they were currently in. Still, it was difficult to really feel in danger when surrounded by such beauty. And when feeling so incredibly good. He felt better now than he had even when they had first snuck through the Door. Before, there had been a level of shock that had kept him from fully experiencing the effects of Kinth. Now he could revel in it with no barrier. He was finally where he was supposed to be, and his body nearly burst with satisfaction.

They walked silently through the trees, drinking in the views that surrounded them. After about an hour, One began to slow their pace steadily until the trees ended abruptly. He knelt and waited for the rest of the group to catch up to him. Frederick couldn't see anything from his position in the back of the group, but he heard several of the others gasp quietly. He crept silently forward and knelt beside One, surveying the new landscape that lay before them.

What had once presumably been a thriving metropolis spread out before them. Buildings towered into the sky, their tops brushing the clouds that floated lazily by. The streets were choked with long-abandoned cars, and Frederick could see their dilapidated state even though they were still several hundred feet away. What was truly remarkable about the city was how overgrown it had become. It looked as if the forest itself was waging war against the city. Plants had sprung up from the cracks in the concrete and begun to infest what remained of the civilization. Vines crept up buildings to impossible heights, crisscrossing their way higher and higher until the buildings themselves looked like trees. Massive bushes grew seemingly out of nowhere and threatened to consume the cars stalled in the roads. Trees towered over streetlamps and even challenged some of the buildings. If this was a war between nature and city, nature was winning.

"It's beautiful," Nineteen whispered. "I expected it to be run-down but this . . . this is something else."

"Let's go," One said. "We don't have time for this." He pulled out his map and compass and began walking into the city.

The library wasn't far; they reached it in a matter of minutes. The walk was eerie. Frederick hadn't spent much time in big cities. Still, he had been to a few, and each one had overwhelmed him with sound and movement. It was disconcerting to be walking the streets and be blanketed in total silence. The plant life also had a strange muting effect. What little sound they produced was consumed by the leaves in the same way it would be swallowed by a heavy snow. Shivers ran down Frederick's spine as they made their way to the library. It was a large, ornate building with stone pillars flanking massive double doors at its entrance. The building had not been spared from the greenery that spread over the rest of the city. Vines wrapped their way around the pillars and over the face of the building. They were so thick over the doors that Frederick worried they wouldn't be able to force their way in. One padded up silently to the door and set his bag down, rummaging through it silently. The others walked up to join him, crouching beside him.

"Everyone keep watch," One murmured without looking up from his pack. "Stay alert—don't get lazy just cause we got this far."

They nodded and turned their gaze outward. One found what he was looking for—a large knife buried deep in the pack—and began sawing at the vines. He wouldn't need to cut them all down, just enough for them to get to the door and squeeze through. He worked as quickly as he could without making too much noise.

Frederick became overly aware of his breathing as he scanned the abandoned city. He did his best to quiet it, which only made him more conscious of it. He became so consumed by trying to breathe quietly that he almost missed the blur of movement at the edge of his vision. He yelped despite himself, and the entire group jumped. One turned, wielding the knife, ready to take on whatever danger befell them. Frederick pointed dumbly to where he had seen the motion. There, in the middle of the street, stood a small deer. It chewed on a particularly green patch of grass springing up between the cracks in the road.

"Are you kidding me?" Seven hissed. "I sincerely hope they packed me a change of pants, Two-Oh. If not, you are giving me yours."

"S-sorry," Frederick managed.

The rest of the group was clearly just as shaken. Nineteen in particular looked petrified. The small girl was trembling uncontrollably, and One placed a hand on her shoulder.

"Relax," he said. "We aren't the defenseless kids we were before. We don't need to be afraid of our own shadows. Be careful, but don't be afraid." He gave Frederick a severe look. Frederick turned back to keep watch, unable to meet One's eyes.

It took One several more minutes to saw his way through the vines. Even with the knife and Kinthian air to assist him, it was no small ordeal. The vines had grown thick and had woven together in many places. They were tougher than any rope would've been. Frederick heard a faint snapping behind him, then the sound of the vine One had been working on falling to the ground.

"That should do it. I'm gonna make sure it all looks safe. Don't move."

They waited anxiously as One slid inside the building.

It felt like an eternity before Frederick heard a soft rustling sound behind him, announcing the boy's return.

"It all looks good, as far as I can tell. Let's go one at a time, and don't turn around until I call your name. Keep watch until it's your turn."

He called them one by one until it was only Frederick standing watch. Frederick resisted squirming as sweat ran down his back. His breathing felt thunderous now.

"Alright, Twenty. Let's go."

With a deep breath, he gave the abandoned street one final extended look before turning and forcing his way into the gloom of the library.

Chapter 26

Frederick suppressed a cough as he stumbled into the dimly lit building. Unsurprisingly, the overgrowth had fought its way inside the library as well. Vines filled the interior, scaling the walls and running along the ceiling. The scene invoked a peculiar sensation. As long as Frederick ignored the tile beneath his feet, It felt like walking through a tree canopy.

The room was nothing extraordinary as far as overgrown libraries go. It was a large corridor running from left to right. Directly in front of them was a large receptionist's desk made of rich mahogany that had long ago been swallowed by leaves. Behind the desk was another set of wooden double doors that presumably led to the main area of the library. One made his way over to the desk and began cutting away the vines that encased the desk's drawers.

"What are you doing?" Thirteen whispered.

"There's gotta be a directory or something," One whispered back. "Something to help us find the blueprints."

He made quick work of the vines, tearing them away and pulling open the large drawers, rifling through the papers within. In the second drawer, he found a large laminated map listing the detailed locations of everything a person could hope to find in the library.

"Well that was easy," Seven said.

"Maybe for you," One said as he pulled a pair of thorns from his palm. "These vines aren't as friendly as they look."

"'Friendly 'snot the word I woulda used, boss," Eight said, eyeing the plants. "They give me the creeps.

One pulled a flashlight from his backpack and studied the map.

"Looks like the blueprint would be just through these main doors and to our left. Keep going until we hit the wall, then about halfway to the back wall. We might have to wander a bit to find the right one, but I don't think it'll take too long."

"Can I take a look?" Nineteen asked, reaching for the map without waiting for an answer.

"Be my guest," One shrugged.

Nineteen studied the laminated paper for a full minute. The silence in the room was becoming oppressive—Frederick could almost feel his shoulders begin to sag beneath the weight of it. After what felt like an eternity, Nineteen looked away from the map and sheepishly at One.

"What is it?" he asked, worry filling his voice.

"Well, I'm not positive. But I think the blueprints are behind a locked door."

"Well, that's not a huge deal," Seven said. "We can just have Eight work his magic on the lock or have Thirteen bash her head against it until it shatters."

Nineteen shook her head. "Not that kind of lock. I think it's an electronic lock."

She held the map up to One and pointed to a symbol next to the door. One studied it for a moment, then cursed. "How did I miss that?"

"That's not the issue right now," Nineteen said dismissively, still studying the map. "We need to figure out how to open that door."

Eight walked over to the desk and tried to flip on the lamp that sat atop it. He flicked the switch off and on several times, with no results.

"Looks like we don't have to worry about it, boss. There's no power in here, so the door will probably just be wide open, eh?"

"It's possible," Frederick chimed in. "But it's also possible if the power went out while it was locked it just stayed locked. And now, without power, there's no way to open it."

"So all we would need to do is get the power back on," Thirteen piped up. "There has to be a generator somewhere. Probably in the basement, assuming this place has one."

"This map only shows the first floor," Nineteen said.

"Hold on, I think I saw another map in the desk." One returned to where he had found the first map and dug through the drawer. A moment later, he walked back to them with a triumphant smile.

"Got a map of the lower floors, and something even better," he said as he held up a lanyard with a dusty nametag on the end.

"Great, now we can identify who worked the front desk," Seven said dryly.

"R. Muldoon. But I'm far more interested in their keycard." One flashed a smile.

"With this, we should be able to fire up the generators and open the door, no problem."

"So we send one group to the basement to turn on the generator and one group with the key card to the room with the schematics," Thirteen said. "Once the power is on, we open the door, grab what we need, and get the hell out of here."

"Seriously?" Seven looked at Thirteen in disbelief. "You want to split up? That's just asking for disaster. Have you never seen a movie?"

"I think I'm with Seven on this," Nineteen said. "We don't know what we're up against, and I'd rather take some extra time and have the safety in numbers."

She looked to One for confirmation. He stood rubbing his forehead, eyes closed and deep in thought. Frederick felt himself waffling back and forth between which plan he preferred. Both had their significant advantages as well as significant risks. There was no wrong answer. Or rather, there was no right answer. Frederick couldn't decide on that either.

"I don't think we have the luxury to play it safe here," One said at last, opening his eyes and squaring his shoulders. "If there's anything in here with us, every second we waste is increasing our risk of being found. We've been training, and now that we have the Kinthian air, we'll be able to handle ourselves."

Nineteen opened her mouth to respond, but the objection died on her lips. Her mouth formed a straight line, and she nodded tightly.

"Nineteen and Eight, you're with me. We'll go to the schematics room." One continued, "Twenty, you take Seven and Thirteen and get the generator going."

One handed Frederick the map of the lower floors. Frederick scanned it. "Looks like the stairs we need to take are in the same general direction as the schematics room. We can stick together until then."

"Makes it easier to group up if anything goes wrong too," Thirteen chimed in.

"*If* instead of *when* is rather optimistic of you."

Seven's comment drew a piercing glare from One. The stocky boy shrugged and put his hands up defensively. One let the glare linger for another full second before speaking.

"As soon as you get that thing going, make your way back here. If we aren't here in ten minutes, come help us look. Any questions?"

The rest of the group shook their heads.

"Good. Let's get to it."

Frederick was pleasantly surprised to find, upon further inspection, that they wouldn't need to cut away any vines to enter the next room. They had grown in such a manner that the door stood free.

"Not a word when we get in there until we've had a chance to look around. I doubt a Bristle could've made its way through the front door, but there's no telling what other entrances there are to this place. Stay close and stay sharp," One said.

Without another word, he pulled the door open as gently as he could manage. There was a soft creaking as it protested, but Frederick suspected they should count themselves lucky it wasn't louder considering it hadn't been used in over a decade.

They stepped through the door one at a time. Frederick came last and was surprised to find the room to be almost pitch-black. One had kept his flashlight out, and Frederick could just make out windows on the ceiling by its light. It was getting close to midday, and sunlight should have been pouring into the room. However, the vines had grown so thickly over the glass that almost no light could make its way through. One gestured at them to retrieve the flashlights from their own packs before they continued. Five individual beams of light winked on and began scanning the room.

Rows upon rows of shelves of books filled the room. Many of the shelves had begun to rot and were falling apart. In some places, there were gaps where the shelves had once stood, and now only piles of broken boards and moldy books occupied the spaces.

The room was arranged in such a manner that it was difficult to see much beyond the rows directly in front of them. The shelves were tall and reached far above their heads, making it impossible to see over them. Only the gaps allowed them to get a decent look at the room. It was massive—the size of a warehouse, by Frederick's best guess. Pillars dispersed intermittently throughout the room ran to the ceiling, which was covered in several paintings depicting scenes from ancient mythology. Frederick studied them for a long moment, trying to recognize any specific scenes. He blinked and was struck with the realization that of course he wouldn't recognize them. This was a different world—it would have its own myths. The thought made him feel farther from home than anything he had yet seen.

They picked their way to the left wall of the room, following One's lead and stepping carefully to avoid the various piles of wood and books. They reached the edge of the wall, and One froze, holding up a hand. An uneasiness fell over the group as they stopped in their tracks. Six hearts pounded in the silence as each of the applicants did their best to breathe as quietly as they possibly could.

One stood perfectly still, hand still raised, head cocked to the side, eyes closed in concentration. After several excruciating minutes, One gestured for them all to gather around.

"I thought I heard something. I think there might be something else in here. It could be just an old abandoned building settling, but I want to be careful." He said it so quietly, Frederick could barely make out his words, even though he was mere inches from the boy's face.

"We need to move with precision and care. No idle steps. Do everything you can to step exactly where the person in front of you does. Got it?"

Five heads nodded in the murk as One turned and began walking once more. Frederick took several deep breaths to steady himself before following.

His heart leapt into his throat at a sudden noise from directly beneath him. He froze, eyes going wide as he searched for the source.

"Calm down, boss," Eight whispered from his elbow. "It's just a squeaky board."

Frederick lifted his foot, and sure enough, the same low moan came from the floor.

He shook his head and pushed away his embarrassment. There would be time for that later. He took a deep breath to steady himself once more and continued walking.

Frederick stifled a scream as there was another noise, though this one was far louder than the last, like a tree being ripped up by its roots. He felt himself go weightless as the floor collapsed beneath him, and he hurtled into the darkness below.

Time didn't slow for Frederick as he fell. He didn't see his life flash before his eyes, nor was there some moment of clarity or enlightenment. There was only the air whistling past his ears and the scream stuck inside of his chest.

It was over in less than a second. A crash echoed through the gloom as Frederick landed on top of something that shattered beneath him. He hoped desperately that his back hadn't shattered with it.

Frederick groaned loudly as he rolled off whatever had broken his fall. His entire body ached from the impact, but nothing seemed to be seriously damaged.

"Twenty!" a frantic whisper sounded from above Frederick. Several beams of light cut through the darkness, sweeping through the hole in the floor until they located Frederick. "Are you okay?"

Frederick wiggled his fingers and his toes before standing, confirming they hadn't been broken. It took more than one try for him to find the breath to answer.

"I'd be doing a lot better if you'd stop shining those lights in my eyes," he managed to wheeze.

The lights immediately flicked away from his face, allowing him to get a view of where he had fallen.

"Well, I guess I won't need to find the stairs," he whispered, though he doubted those above could hear him. He had fallen about thirty feet into what appeared to be a large storage room, though it was difficult to be certain in the darkness. The floor was lined with boxes that were almost entirely rotted. Frederick turned to see what had broken his fall. The box and its now-unrecognizable contents had decayed to the point that they had barely been solid even before he had body slammed them.

Frederick scoured the floor for his flashlight, which had flown from his hand as he fell. He found it several feet away, between two boxes. The light was off and remained so despite him flicking the switch on and off repeatedly. He cursed softly and whispered hoarsely at the ceiling. "My flashlight is shot. Any way one of you can send one of yours down here so I can get a better look at this room?"

"Sure thing, boss!"

One of the beams of light began to tumble wildly from the ceiling. Frederick cursed again and lunged, snatching it out of the air right before it hit the ground. He had to stop himself from shouting at Eight, though from the fierce whispers coming from above, it seemed the others were properly chastising him.

Frederick combed the room with the light and saw that his suspicions had been correct. He was in the middle of a large storage area. There was nothing of note in the room other than the boxes littering the ground and the doors at either end. Frederick searched around the room until he located the map he had been carrying when he fell. After a few seconds, he found the room he was currently in.

"What's the word?" One whispered.

"It's a storage room. It's actually pretty close to the generator, only a couple of rooms away."

"I always knew you were lucky, Two-Oh," Seven said.

"So how do we get you back up here?" Thirteen asked.

"I think it might be better for you all to join me down here, actually." Frederick studied the map again. "If you can find an easy way down, it'll save us some time."

"You want me to jump into a black hole?" Seven asked incredulously.

"No, I want you to use the rope from your backpack and climb down."

Frederick could make out some huffing but nothing from Seven in way of response.

"What do you think, One?"

"I'm all for it," One answered without hesitating. "If it saves time and there's no risk, I say go for it. There's a pillar here we can use as an anchor."

There was a soft rustling as they moved to execute the plan. In a few short moments, a rope dropped down next to Frederick's head, the last few feet coiling lazily on the ground.

Thirteen was the first to clamber down the rope, her flashlight gripped between her teeth. She dropped the last few feet and landed lightly next to Frederick, scanning the room without removing the flashlight from her mouth.

"Nout to-chabby."

Frederick gave her a confused look. She removed the flashlight from her mouth, rolling her eyes dramatically as she did so. "I said, 'not too shabby.' I usually prefer a more modern look, but we can make this work."

"You sure this thing is gonna hold me?" Seven tried unsuccessfully to hide the nervousness in his voice.

"'Course it will. And if it doesn't, your head is harder than any brick I've encountered. You'll be fine," Thirteen chirped. Seven had begun his descent and blessedly was too distracted to reply. He arrived at the bottom of the rope slightly slower than Thirteen. Though, to his credit, his descent was no less sure.

"What did you say?" He turned to Thirteen, who smiled wickedly and opened her mouth to respond.

"Nothing," Frederick interrupted. "I was just telling you to be careful."

"Gee, thanks, Two-Oh. Never could've figured that out on my own."

"Good luck!" One's disembodied voice floated down. "We'll see you out front once it's done."

"Good luck to yo—" Frederick was interrupted by a horrendous and unmistakable sound.

A Bristle howl tore through the air. The horrible sound shattered the near-perfect silence so suddenly that Frederick was almost stunned. The sound clearly came from above them, from the same room One, Eight, and Nineteen still occupied.

One cursed and started whispering, though Frederick couldn't make out the words.

Frederick turned to his two companions, whose faces had gone stark white.

The rope began bouncing wildly, and in an astonishingly short time, Eight stood beside them.

"Hurry! Get one of the doors open!" he said, darting toward the door at the end of the room. The rope began swinging wildly once more, and another howl split the air.

Nineteen dropped the last ten feet to the ground, landing hard and stumbling. Frederick rushed to help her to her feet.

"They're almost on him!" she said with terror in her eyes.

Sure enough, the sounds of the Bristles were growing closer with each breath.

"One, get down here!" Frederick shouted.

"On it!"

Frederick pointed his flashlight at the ceiling and watched as One slid down the rope like a fireman down a pole. He landed with a thud and a yelp of pain. Frederick and Nineteen helped him to his feet, and even in the poor light, Frederick could see the burns on the boy's hands from the friction.

He turned and gave one last look at the hole through which they had come.

Two pairs of red eyes burned bright in the gloom.

They stared at Frederick, unblinking. They were fierce, hungry, and wild, but most disturbingly, they were calculating. Frederick could almost see the gears turning inside them, working furiously to solve the problem that now stood before them.

Another howl erupted from above, and both pairs of eyes dove through the hole.

Chapter 27

The Bristles landed with a deafening crash, each managing to break their falls on boxes in the same way that Frederick had.

"Run!" One shouted, grabbing Nineteen and Frederick by the wrist and dragging them toward the door. Frederick allowed himself to be dragged as he fought the urge to look over his shoulder at the Bristles. The risk of tripping over a box was too great for that, and besides, he didn't need to look to know what lay behind him. The sounds of the monsters regaining their feet and leaping into pursuit were clear.

Ahead, Seven, Eight, and Thirteen worked frantically to force open the heavy metal door that represented escape.

"It's stuck!" Seven shouted as he threw his shoulder into the door repeatedly to no avail. The door clanged with each impact, like a war drum sounding retreat.

Instinctively, Frederick shoved One and Nineteen to the side, throwing them between a pair of boxes. At the same time, he used the momentum of the push to launch himself in the opposite direction as both Bristles landed in the space the three of them had just occupied.

Frederick rolled to his feet and immediately began to run back the way they had come. He opened his mouth to shout in an effort to get the Bristles' attention but found very quickly it wasn't necessary. Both of the monsters had scrabbled to a halt and turned their attention to him. He sprinted away for all he was worth. Every fiber of his being screamed from the exertion, singing to be used to their fullest potential. Frederick found a gear he hadn't known he possessed.

"What are you doing?" Thirteen shouted from behind him.

"Open the door!" was all Frederick could manage. Not because he was out of breath, but because doing what he was currently doing required every shred of focus he could muster. He weaved frantically through boxes without breaking stride, leading the Bristles around the room. His pursuers ran through the obstacles, not bothering to dodge them. Debris flew through the air, creating a steady rain of decayed boxes and their contents. Despite his best efforts, Frederick could feel the Bristles gaining on him; if his friends didn't open the door soon, he was done for. He waited until he could almost feel the Bristles' breath on his neck before stopping on a dime, ducking, and changing directions completely. Both Bristles slid past as the unexpected change in direction had its desired effect. Frederick felt the snapping jaws of his pursuers graze his shirt as they flew by him on either side, crashing into another pile of boxes.

Frederick was up and running again without a second thought.

"Well?" he shouted.

"Almost!" Eight called back.

"Not good enough!"

The Bristles were right back on his trail, and Frederick once more ran away from his friends, deeper into the room. He ran for all he was worth, and still they gained on him. He was nearly back to the hole through which he had fallen when he heard a shout.

"We're in!"

Frederick didn't chance a reply, instead sprinting on, trying to gain as much speed as possible. This time, he really could feel hot breath on his neck as he ran.

Just a few more steps.

The breath burned his neck now—they were only inches away.

With a shout, Frederick threw himself as high into the air as he could, grabbing the rope that still hung down from the floor above. He swung forward and up just as the Bristles leaped for him.

He heard a yelp of surprise from under him as he swung out of reach of the two monsters, who flew several feet farther into the room with yet another massive crash. The rope carried Frederick nearly to the ceiling before swinging him back in the direction of the door. He released and hit the ground running, using the momentum of the swing and sprinting wildly for the door. The Bristles turned to follow, but Frederick's maneuver had created more than enough space. He reached the door with a full twenty feet to spare.

Lunging through the now-open doorway, he tumbled to the ground, and Seven slammed the door shut behind him. One had been waiting with a large metal bar, which he shoved through the handle, barricading it shut. Frederick stared at the door in disbelief.

"It was a pull?" He closed his eyes and took a deep breath. "All you had to do was pull?"

Seven looked at him sheepishly.

"Um, yeah." He smiled apologetically. "Although, in my defense, it was a little bit stuck."

Seven reached a hand down and helped Frederick to his feet. A smile tugged at the corner of Frederick's mouth, and it took a considerable amount of effort to keep it from spreading across his face.

"Didn't know you were a gymnast, boss! You gotta teach me some of those moves," Eight said as he bounced up and down next to Frederick.

"You should know by now, our Twenty never ceases to amaze," One said while bandaging his hands with the first aid kit from his backpack. He looked at Frederick and smiled. "Always expect the unexpected."

One's sentence was punctuated by a Bristle throwing itself into the door. The group jumped at the sound, but the door held.

"I imagine they will have some real trouble getting through that, but let's not stick around to find out." One shone his light around the room, glancing at Frederick. "Where to?"

Frederick studied the new space they found themselves in. It was more hallway than room, with several doors lining the walls on either side.

"Let me just check the map agai—" Frederick paused mid-sentence and began digging through his pockets.

"Oh, you have got to be joking." Thirteen sighed.

"I must have dropped it back in there. I'm sorry, I thought I still had it!" Frederick continued searching his pockets, though he knew he wouldn't find the map.

A Bristle slammed into the door once again. This time, the metal groaned against the force.

"It's okay," One said, his voice calm. "Just focus, Twenty. You got a good look at the map. You can remember the way to go."

Frederick closed his eyes and blocked out everything around him. His friends, the Bristles—he cast all of it aside and focused only on the map.

Almost instantaneously, lines began forming in his mind's eye. The flew across the blank canvas he had created, quickly recreating the map he had held just a few short minutes before.

"There!" Frederick pointed to one of the middle doors on the right side of the corridor. His friends didn't hesitate, pushing through the door without question. One stood by and waited until all had passed through before stepping in himself and slamming the door behind them. Thankfully, this door had a deadbolt, which One quickly engaged.

"Quick, barricade the door. That's an old lock—no telling how long it'll hold."

His sentence was followed by the sound of the Bristles breaking through the first door and gaining access to the room the applicants had just vacated.

"Now," One said flatly.

Frederick turned, sweeping his flashlight across the room. It was little more than a supply closet. Several metal shelves lined the walls, holding plastic bottles presumably filled with cleaning materials. There was a terrible grinding noise as they dragged the shelves across the floor and threw them down in front of the door. Almost instantly, a pair of bangs came as the Bristles threw themselves at the barricade.

The door didn't budge.

"That should hold them," One said, brushing off his shirt.

"A lot of good it does us," Seven said, turning in a slow circle. "We're trapped!"

Frederick turned and felt his stomach drop as he saw what Seven said was true.

"But I was sure there was a hallway in here! I was positive!" Frederick ran a disbelieving hand through his hair. "It leads right to the generator. It should be right there!"

He pointed to the barren back wall.

Thirteen stepped up next to Frederick and stifled a laugh.

"What's so funny, Jinx? You really that excited to die?" Seven said.

The girl grabbed Frederick's outstretched hand and pushed it up. Frederick ignored his confusion and looked down his arm. It was pointing directly at an air vent.

"Oh, you have got to be joking," Seven said.

"Awesome!" Eight smiled.

"Well, I guess it's pretty close to a hallway." One smirked and walked to the wall beneath the vent. "Eight, wanna give me a hand?"

"You got it, boss!"

The small boy bolted over and clambered up One's back so he could reach the vent. He pulled out his knife and made quick work of the four screws that held the vent in place. The metal grate clattered to the ground, and before any-one could protest, Eight crawled into the hole in the wall.

"Alright, everybody after him."

One positioned himself against the wall beneath the vent and began boost-ing the rest of the group up into the wall. The girls went first, making it with relative ease.

"Not a chance," Seven said, crossing his arms and resolutely shaking his head. "You are out of your damn mind if you think I'm gonna fit in there."

"There's plenty of room!" One said, beckoning Seven forward. The stocky boy set his jaw and shook his head firmly once more.

"Not gonna happen. I'll fight those hell beasts before climbing in there."

"Oh, hurry up, Seven!" Thirteen's voice echoed out from the vent. "Even your massive block head will fit in here. Once that's in, the rest is easy."

There was a low creaking sound that Frederick soon realized was Seven grinding his teeth together.

"You gonna let her talk to you that way?" Frederick asked, cocking an eyebrow.

"Shut up, Two-Oh."

Seven pushed past Frederick and walked up to One, who was doing his best to not smile.

"Oh, you can shut up too, Uno."

With One's help, Seven made it into the vent easily, though his grumbles echoed as he crawled. Frederick followed closely behind. The vent was actually more spacious than he had assumed it would be. There was plenty of room to maneuver, though not enough for him to fully turn around.

"You need help, One?" Frederick asked over his shoulder.

"Nah, I think I got it."

Frederick saw a pair of hands grab onto the edge of the vent, and soon there was a bright smile accompanying them.

"Wanna move up a bit for me?"

He mumbled an embarrassed apology and crawled forward to allow room for One to enter.

As Frederick made his way, there was little he could make out beyond the soles of Seven's shoes ahead of him. They didn't have far to go, and it wasn't long before Eight called back to them.

"I'm at the end. Just give me a second to get this grate off! Shouldn't take two seconds."

There was a soft clanging sound from ahead in the darkness.

Frederick closed his eyes and redrew the map in his head. He had made a mistake, one that hadn't been too punishing, but a mistake nonetheless. He couldn't let his friends down again. So he went over the map again and again in his mind, making sure he knew exactly how to get to the generator and how to get upstairs from there.

Frederick was pulled from his thoughts by a light sensation making its way up his arm and over his hand. For a moment, he thought it was just his imagination. Then it happened again. And again. And again. Frederick twisted his body awkwardly to try to see what was causing the sensation. Finally, he was able to position himself so that he could make out what it was. A line of spiders was crawling over him, moving in the same direction he was. Frederick just managed to stifle an instinctual shout at the sight of the arachnids.

"I see you met our new friends," One whispered from behind. Frederick could hear the smile in his voice.

"Thanks for the heads-up," Frederick answered.

"I didn't want to ruin the surprise. Plus, they seem harmless," One said, then added thoughtfully. "Maybe the weirdest thing we've seen so far, though."

Frederick looked closer at the small creatures. By his best guess, there were about fifteen of them, though it was hard to tell. They were about the size of quarters, and their bodies were a light bluish color. As they passed briefly into a shadow cast by the flashlight, Frederick realized with a start that the spiders were glowing softly. The soft blue color was not just that of the spiders—it was light being emitted from their bodies. Upon further inspection, Frederick could see that the spiders' hard bodies were almost like jewels. He focused his ears and found he could hear a soft *tink-tink-tink* as the spiders' legs made contact with the metal of the air vent.

"Hey, Seven," Frederick called ahead.

"What?" Seven replied shortly.

"Don't freak out."

"What are you—" A gasp cut the sentence short, and Seven pushed himself as far from the spiders as the vent would allow.

"I said 'don't freak out,'" Frederick smiled.

"I'm not freaking out!" Seven hissed. "I just don't like spiders. Especially not the freaky glowing kind." He took several deep breaths before whispering to himself, "I'm starting to get pretty sick of this place."

The rest of the group ahead of Seven took the spiders in stride, having been warned by his outburst. Thirteen and Nineteen seemed rather fascinated by them, though they shied away to give the creatures as much room to pass as they could.

"Woah! These are awesome!" Eight exclaimed as they reached him. He began chattering unintelligibly in excitement, and from what Frederick could tell, he was doing his best to snag one of the crawlers.

"Hey, snowman," Seven called, "how about we stay on task?"

"Already done!" Eight's response was punctuated by the sound of a grate clattering to the ground.

One by one, the applicants made their way out of the vent and into the room below. Frederick landed on his feet and stepped aside to let One descend, surveying his surroundings as he did so. It was a small, damp room with some kind of fungus coating almost every surface. It grew thick in gaudy colors along the floors, walls, and ceiling, and there were even a few patches splashed across the generator.

The machine itself sat against the back wall, covering the wall almost in its entirety. Despite the patches of fungus, the generator appeared to be in fairly good condition. It wasn't overly rusted, nor structurally damaged as far as Frederick could tell.

He realized with a start that he had gathered all this information without the aid of his flashlight. It sat uselessly in his hand pointed at the floor. He furrowed his brow in confusion.

"Why do the lights work in this room?" he asked aloud.

"They don't," Nineteen said with a slight awe in her voice. She walked to the wall and inspected the fungus more closely. Every square inch of the fungus was glowing softly, easily illuminating the entire room.

Then the smell hit.

"What the . . ." Thirteen gagged and slapped a hand over her mouth. They were assailed by a terrible stench, a smell of rot and decay. Frederick scanned the room to see if a small rodent was decomposing somewhere before he realized it was the fungus. Nineteen had disturbed it while inspecting and released the odor.

"It reeks in here! Do you think it's safe? Like, it won't kill us to breathe this stuff in, right?" Thirteen's voice was muffled behind her hand.

"The alien planet with a deadly virus that has mutated animals and caused some to become rabid killers? I'm sure this glowing mold is nothing to worry about," Seven said sarcastically, placing his arm across his face.

"Honestly, you might be right, but I doubt it matters now," Nineteen said. "If it's that deadly, we are probably already past the point of no return."

"Well, now I feel loads better. Thanks!"

"I'm sure it's fine," Nineteen said unconvincingly. "Besides, we shouldn't be here too long."

"Well, here's hoping," One said as he switched off his flashlight and shrugged. "Might as well save the batteries."

The rest of the flashlights were turned off, and soon the room was lit only by the odd light of the fungus.

One walked over to the generator and began inspecting it. "Anyone know how to work one of these?"

"Is there not just a big button labeled 'on?'" Seven asked.

"As if anything would ever be that easy," Thirteen grumbled and moved to join One, inspecting the machine.

"I've never seen a generator this big, but I'm okay with this kind of stuff. I can probably figure it out."

"Oh wow," Seven said in mock awe. "The girl mechanic? She's not like other girls."

"I will literally break your nose," Thirteen said without looking at him.

"And I'll help," Nineteen said, glaring at Seven. He raised his hands in genuine apology.

"You really think you can figure it out on your own?" One asked. "I'm garbage with this kind of stuff."

"Should be able to." Thirteen nodded. "It might take me a bit, but I think I can handle it."

One nodded and left her to work. The rest of the group settled down to rest.

Eight glanced at the door nervously. "Should we be worried about the dogs, boss? Maybe we should be a bit more quiet?"

"They'll find us sooner or later by smell," One said, shaking his head. "Probably in a minute or two. This door seems solid enough, though. I wouldn't worry too much. I'm much more concerned about how to get out of here after they've found us."

The next few minutes passed in a tense silence. Thirteen continued inspecting the generator, poking and prodding at the lightly rusted metal and brushing away any fungus that got in her way. Frederick found the closest thing resembling a clear space on the floor and tried to make himself as comfortable as possible. There was no telling how long it would take Thirteen to get the generator going, so he readily accepted the chance for a rest. He placed his backpack against the wall and leaned against it, closing his eyes and listening to the ambience.

"You really that tired, boss?"

Eight's voice pulled Frederick from his near slumber. He blinked himself fully awake and shook his head.

"Well, Eight, it hasn't been the most relaxing of days," Frederick snorted.

"I guess you're right about that," Eight replied. "It's been pretty amazing though, right?"

The tone of the small boy's voice caused Frederick to crack an eyelid. Eight was speaking almost reverently.

"It has been," Frederick agreed.

"As long as you don't mind all the almost dying," Nineteen chimed in, walking over and sitting next to Frederick.

Eight shrugged. "I've felt like I've been almost dying my whole life. It's just nice to get to experience the living part for once."

"I know exactly what you mean," Thirteen called without looking up from the generator.

"I sure could get used to it."

"Amen," One said softly. He was leaning against the door, staring off into the distance.

The group turned to Seven for his input just in time for him to release a raucous snore.

A chorus of stifled laughs filled the room as the slumbering boy earned his namesake.

"How's it coming over there, Thirteen?" Frederick called. "Need a hand?"

"If I thought any of you could be of service, I'd say yes, but I doubt that's the case," Thirteen said matter-of-factly.

"Fair enough," Frederick laughed.

"Only joking." Thirteen waved absentmindedly. "This will take a while, though, so get comfortable."

"So much for not being here long," Eight mumbled.

"Anyone fancy a game?" One pulled a deck of cards from his backpack and tossed it to Frederick.

They played Swipe for the better part of an hour. It was more subdued than their games on the other side of the Door, but Frederick found the familiar rhythms to be calming. They took turns playing, chatting idly between rounds and each managing a win or two at the least.

"Surprised we haven't heard from our Bristle friends," Frederick said offhandedly as they finished a game. One had beaten him soundly from start to finish.

"We may not have heard from them, but they're here," Eight said nonchalantly, moving to take Frederick's position across from One.

"Yeah, I guess you're right. They'll never be too far away." Frederick nodded.

"No, I mean like they're here right now. Just outside the door." Eight began setting up the cards for the next game of Swipe.

One's eyes shot to the small boy. "How do you know? I haven't heard anything."

"Couldn't tell ya, boss," Eight shrugged. "I haven't heard anything, but I'd bet tomorrow's breakfast there's at least two of them outside that door. I can just tell." He paused and looked at them. "Can't you?"

Nineteen, Frederick, and One all shook their heads. Eight raised his eyebrows in surprise.

"I just assumed you all knew. If you don't believe me, check for yourselves." Eight shrugged again. "They're waiting right outside."

One stood and walked over to the door, pulling out his knife. For a panicked moment, Frederick thought he was going to unlock the door and pull it open. Instead, he lay down on the floor and carefully placed the blade under the crack of the door, using the reflection as a mirror to try to scout the hallway outside. After a few seconds, he turned and sat against the door, eyeing Eight.

"He's right. I can't tell how many there are, but there's at least one of them out there. Not moving—just waiting in the shadows next to the door. I could barely see it, but it's there for sure."

"Why haven't they tried to get in?" Nineteen asked in a small voice.

"It's an ambush," Frederick said softly. "Breaking through didn't work last time, so they're trying to wait us out this time."

"Well, that's more than mildly disconcerting," Thirteen said, turning from the generator. "What do we do?"

One walked back and took his place by the game of swipe. "Nothing to do but cross that bridge when we get to it."

"Not the most reassuring thing." Frederick raised his eyebrows.

"There's nothing we can do about it at the moment," One said. "Once the generator is on, we'll formulate a plan."

Another hour passed before the generator roared to life. It happened suddenly, startling the occupants of the room, Thirteen included.

"Um, I did it," she said, walking over to join the rest of the group.

"Thanks for the heads-up," Frederick said, letting out a half laugh.

The lights slowly came to life, filling the room with artificial illumination to accompany the bioluminescence of the fungus.

"Is that it?" Seven rubbed his eyes and sat up. "Not too bright, are they?"

"They're just auxiliary lights," Thirteen said. "The generator doesn't have enough juice to power the main lights, so this is what we get. Still, it should be enough power to get the door open."

Eight walked over and slapped her on the back. "Nice work! I gotta say, I'm impressed."

Thirteen rolled her eyes.

"It took me two hours to turn on a generator. Let's not get carried away."

"True," Seven said thoughtfully. "It's almost like you did nothing."

"Unlike you," Thirteen replied flatly, "who actually did nothing."

"I rested myself for whatever comes next. That will be invaluable when I have to save you all again."

Frederick turned away from the bickering pair's predictable descent to insults. "So what's the plan?" he asked One.

The boy furrowed his brow and chewed his lip in concentration. "I'm not sure I have anything to brag about. A few half-baked plans but nothing foolproof."

"I got something for ya, boss," Eight cut in.

One raised an eyebrow and gestured for him to continue.

"Well, I figure we gotta get them away from the door. We could maybe fight them off, but that feels risky, and I don't much feel like getting chewed up. I was thinking maybe I could climb back through the vent and make a bunch of noise and whatnot from the other room, making them think we've doubled back. They'll run over to check it out, and you guys can make a run for it when they leave. Then I climb back through the vent and catch up to you. Easy!"

"It's not a bad plan." One nodded slowly. "I just have one problem with it."

"What's that, boss?"

"I should be the one to go through the vent. I'm faster and a better fighter than you, if it comes to that."

"You may be faster than me out there, boss"—Eight gestured vaguely toward the door—"but I'm a lot smaller than you. Moving through that vent is nothing for me. I can get there and back a heck of a lot faster than you can. I guarantee it."

"Sorry, Eight but I have to insist." Now One was shaking his head. "This is my call, and I'm saying it's me. It's too dangerous for you."

Eight's eyes blazed with anger. One had clearly offended him, though he failed to notice the slight he had caused the smaller boy. One turned to address the group as a whole.

"I'll give you some kind of signal from over there when they are in the room. Once you get the signal, make a run for it." He paused, eyebrows raised. "Any questions?"

"Nah, boss, I think I think that pretty much covers it!" Eight's voice echoed out from the vent.

One's face turned sour, and he managed to turn to the vent just in time to see Eight's sneakers disappear fully inside of it.

Frederick couldn't help but smile, and as he inspected One's face, he could see that somewhere buried in the anger was a dash of amusement.

Less than a minute later, a loud banging sound came from the vent as Eight pounded on the metal door in his room.

"Oh wow, I forgot my keys in this first room! I hope no demon dogs from the depths of hell come chase me! That sure would be terrible!"

Eight carried on like this for a full minute, banging on the door and calling out progressively more colorful insults at the Bristles. Finally, the racket faded, and a hoarse whisper called from the vent.

"No sign of them here, but it's hard to tell. Are they still with you?"

One made his way wordlessly to the door and used his knife once more to check for the Bristles. He stood again almost instantly, shaking his head in disgust.

"Still there. It doesn't even look like they flinched."

"Smell," Nineteen whispered.

"What?" Seven asked.

"They can probably smell us," she said, louder this time. "They know we didn't leave the room because they can still smell us."

Frederick shook his head in frustration. "How did we not think of that?"

"Don't dwell on it," One said, though from the look on his face, he wasn't taking his own advice. "Just focus on the problem at hand. We need to cover up our scent somehow."

"Also, we probably need to step up the distraction to get them over there," Thirteen chimed in.

"Well the smell problem is easily solved," Seven said as he wrinkled his nose.

"I swear, if you make a joke about me having BO . . ." Thirteen said, taking a threatening step toward Seven.

"As if I'd go for such low-hanging fruit at a time like this." Seven rolled his eyes.

"Well then, what's your solution?" Thirteen tapped her foot expectantly.

"Isn't it obvious?" He looked at the rest of them in genuine confusion. "We are in a room filled to the brim with fungus that smells like literal feet."

Frederick smile. "Nice thinking, Seven."

"Someone's gotta do it ." Seven shrugged.

"That's one problem down," One said. "Any ideas for the second?"

Frederick cleared his throat awkwardly and winced.

"I have an idea."

One raised his eyebrows.

"It's risky, and I'll need your help," Frederick continued slowly, "but I think it might work."

One's face split into a wild smile. "Sounds like my kind of plan."

Chapter 28

Frederick and One made their way through the vent to join Eight in the other room. It was a fairly simple plan in theory, so it hadn't taken Frederick long to explain, and One had been quick to agree. They hopped down from the vent to find Eight lounging on one of the metal bookshelves they had used to barricade the door closed.

"You guys smell awful!" He wrinkled his nose in disgust.

"You get used to it," Frederick said and handed Eight a clump of the glowing fungus.

As Eight slathered the fungus across his arms and face, Frederick relayed the plan he had concocted. Eight's face grew more and more excited with every word—he was practically glowing by the end.

"I gotta tell ya, boss, that's one of my favorite plans I ever heard."

"Let's see if it works before we start praising it," Frederick said. "Any questions?"

Both Eight and One shook their heads.

"Let's get started then."

The three boys worked in tandem, removing the bookshelves that made up the barricade and stacking them in a precarious pile next to the door until the door stood clear. Frederick took a rope from his backpack and tied it to the middle of a shelf near the base of the pile. One used his own rope and did the same to a bookshelf near the top of the pile. Frederick and One then made their ways back up into the vent, still holding the ends of the ropes. Eight bounced around on his feet and did some light stretching, his eyes shining with excitement and fear. He turned and smiled at his friends in the vent.

"Well, here goes nothing."

Eight threw open the door and stepped out into the hallway.

"Look, now I'm actually out here, and if you make me wait I'm gonna be mad, and nobody here wants that!" Eight shouted and banged on the walls. Frederick could barely see the boy from his position in the vent. He held his breath and strained his ears for any sound of movement over the shouts.

"Are you listening to me? I said—" Eight's tirade was cut short as he yelped and dove back into the room. Frederick saw a shadowy figure slide past the door in the hallway.

"It's go time, boys!" Eight said and positioned himself behind the open metal door. There was a horrible mixture of howls, growls, and claws tearing at the floor as all three Bristles barreled into the room.

The massive animals were cramped in the small space, they furiously struggled to turn, looking for their prey. Eight kicked hard at the door, sending it slamming shut and trapping the Bristles in the room with him. The monsters turned and snarled at the sudden sound.

"Now!" Frederick shouted and heaved on his rope with all his might. He heard One grunting in exertion as he did the same with his own rope. There was a sound like thunder as the shelves crashed to the ground in front of the door, once more acting as a barricade. Eight didn't pause to admire their handiwork but instead ran full speed at the wall. With a shout, the boy leaped toward the vent. Frederick grabbed both of his outstretched arms and hauled with all his might while One pulled on Frederick's legs at the same time. Frederick was yanked backward into the vent, pulling Eight fully in after him at the same time. The Bristles howled in frustration, and Frederick could hear their attempts to reach the vent as he and his two friends scrambled back to the other room.

"How'd it go?" Nineteen asked anxiously as the three dropped from the vent.

"Awesome!" Eight said earnestly. "I love being bait. What a rush!"

"It went as well as we could've hoped," Frederick said with a smile. "Eight really did do a great job."

"That he did," One nodded approvingly before growing serious. "We can't wait around though. There's a chance they could still get past that barricade, and I don't wanna be here if that happens."

One turned his expectant gaze toward Frederick. "Well? Lead the way."

Frederick tore down the halls without looking back, trusting that his friends would be able to keep pace with him. He had gone over the route to the stairs over and over in his mind in preparation for this moment, but now that it was here, he didn't give the map a second thought. He knew the correct path was somewhere in his brain, so he trusted his feet to take him where he needed to go. His only thoughts were on the rhythm of his shoes pounding against the floor. For a moment, Frederick felt like he was back in the second test, chasing Arthur down the hallways, only this time he was the one being followed.

The group sprinted through doors and around corners at a breakneck pace. Their surroundings blurred together as they ran. It wasn't long before Frederick skidded to a halt in front of a door labeled *Stairs*. One moved past Frederick, clapping him on the shoulder.

"Good work, Twenty. You seem to know this place like the back of your hand."

One reached the door and pressed his ear against it, closing his eyes in concentration.

He stayed like that for several minutes as Frederick and the others did their best to make no sound. After what felt like an eternity, One opened his eyes and nodded to them.

"Once we are up there, we need to move fast but quiet. I can't imagine those were all the Bristles in this place. Let's get to the schematics and lock the door behind us. We can reassess after that."

He didn't wait for an answer, pushing the door open and stepping into the stairwell.

The stairs doubled back and forth on themselves, obstructing any view of the levels above them.

"Why is it so much darker in here?" Seven whispered. "I can barely see!"

"Hey, look! I'm glowing!" Eight looked down in delight at his arms, which glowed softly in the dimness.

"You rubbed bioluminescent fungus all over yourself, and you're surprised you are glowing?" Thirteen scoffed. "Just a heads-up for next time you jump in some water. You might be wet when you get out." Eight carried on studying his arms, oblivious to the jab.

One stopped and gave the entire group a severe look, casting them into an embarrassed silence.

The emptiness of the stairwell caused the little sound they created to echo uncomfortably loudly. Every step and every breath was magnified ten times over as they did their best to move in silence. Frederick felt his heart jump and his stomach drop at every sound they made. Mercifully, they reached the top of the stairs without any incident, and Frederick felt his body relax for a moment before tensing again.

Don't relax now. The most dangerous bit is still to come.

One looked back and wordlessly asked a question: *Ready?*

He was answered by a collection of nods and determined looks. With a nod of his own, he eased the door open.

They emerged from the stairwell into the main room of the library. Though the lights throughout the room had come to life, the space as a whole was only slightly brighter than it had been before—the vines that had blocked out the sunlight also covered most of the light fixtures. Still, the visibility was noticeably better than when they had first entered.

One moved along the wall to their left at a speed between a brisk walk and a jog. His steps were calculated, careful to avoid the copious debris littering the floor. Frederick copied the care with which One moved and hoped the rest of his friends had the good sense to do likewise.

They walked for what felt like hours, though Frederick knew it was less than a minute. He hadn't had a chance to study the map of the first floor, so he had no reference for how far they would have to travel to reach the door. They passed several rooms with electronic locks, which One pointedly ignored. Each door had a simple scanner in the wall next to it. There was no place for the card to be inserted, so Frederick assumed that simply holding the card up to the scanner would be sufficient to gain access. With each door they passed, Frederick could feel a tightening amongst his companions. Their bodies tensed like springs, barely fighting off the urge to burst into action.

Finally, One's pace began to slow. He approached a door that looked no different from any of the others except for a single word painted across its face: *Schematics.*

One held up his hand, and the rest of the group froze as he pulled the keycard from his pocket and raised it to the scanner beside the door. The door slid open easily, and One stepped in without looking back. The rest followed, eager to escape the unsettling aura of the main room of the library.

Frederick was the last into the room. It wasn't large, perhaps a few hundred square feet at the most. The room was lined with filing cabinets that appeared to be in better shape than anything else they had encountered thus far in the library. The lack of moisture and vegetation in this particular room had made a world of difference. There were no windows, and the lights were dim enough that Frederick flicked his flashlight on to be certain he was getting a good look. The additional light confirmed no other exits. Frederick opened his mouth to ask One where they should start, but he was cut off by a low growling from behind him. He whipped around and was greeted by a pair of Bristles.

The wolflike creatures stood in the open doorway, hackles raised. Frederick's hands began to shake as he stared into the blood-red eyes of one of the monsters. He tried several times to take a deep breath to calm himself, but the air wouldn't enter his lungs. The Bristles moved toward them. In the gloom, their bodies had no form, shifting like smoke.

One stepped forward, his posture disturbingly relaxed.

"Twenty, you and Seven are taking the one on the right. Thirteen and I are taking the one on the left." He spoke as if describing what he had eaten for breakfast. "Eight, Nineteen, you stay back. If it looks like any of us are in trouble, step in and try to help however you can. Otherwise, stay out of the way."

"We can't fight them!" Frederick hissed. The beasts were inching forward in unison. "It took all of us to fight one of them last time, and it just about killed you and me!"

One turned and looked Frederick dead in the eye. "That was before." His voice was like sharpened steel; Frederick winced at the words. "You aren't the same person, and neither am I. If you keep thinking like the old you, then I don't know what the hell you are doing on this side of the door." He paused and flipped his knife idly in the air, catching it deftly in a backhand grip. "And besides, this time we have toys."

Frederick set his jaw and turned toward the approaching Bristles.

One was right. He wasn't the same. Wasn't that what all their training had been about? Proving to themselves that they could trust their abilities? He felt his finger throb slightly and looked down at it. He had removed the splint that morning, electing instead to tape it as it had healed with remarkable speed. The pain brought back images of the final test, of him flying through the air and catching himself with a single finger.

"Sorry," Frederick whispered. "It won't happen again."

One smiled widely at him. "I'm sure it won't."

Together, they charged the Bristles.

Frederick had no plan other than to throw himself at the creature and give himself over entirely to his instincts. The beasts howled and charged at the two approaching boys. Frederick was vaguely aware of Seven and Thirteen rushing to support them.

As he charged the Bristle on the right, it leaped through the air. Its teeth glinted in the flashlight's beam, seeking Frederick's throat. He dropped into a roll, swiping at the monster's legs as it flew past his head. He was rewarded with a sharp howl of pain. Unfortunately, he had not thought of where the Bristle's momentum would carry it. It crashed directly into Seven, who was caught unawares. Both boy and monster tumbled to the ground, and Seven yelped as the full weight of the Bristle came down on him.

"Seven!" Frederick shouted, leaping to assist his friend, who had both his hands around the Bristle's neck, desperately pushing upward and trying to stay out of reach of its snapping maw.

"Anytime, Two-Oh!" Seven yelped.

Frederick jumped on the Bristle's back and drove his knife deep into the creature's neck. It screeched and pulled away from Seven. Frederick clung to its back, ramming his knife into the Bristle over and over again. He held tightly as the monster tried to buck him, leaping wildly in circles and craning its neck to try and reach him. Frederick let out a desperate yell and plunged the knife deep into where he hoped its heart would be. The Bristle shuddered and fell to the ground, blood pooling around it.

"Twenty!"

Frederick spun to the voice. It was Nineteen, eyes full of horror, pointing at the other Bristle.

It had One pinned, massive paws holding the boy down. His knife lay abandoned on the ground a few feet away. Thirteen lay on the ground near One as well, a line of blood running down the side of her face. She was still conscious but appeared to be severely dazed. One shouted in anger as he caught the snapping jaws of the beast and tried to push it back away from him. Unfortunately, he couldn't generate enough power from his position to free himself. The Bristle was pushing back, its teeth mere inches from One's throat.

"Do something!"

Frederick was unsure if one of his companions had shouted at him or if the voice had come from inside his head.

The Bristle made one final mighty push toward One throat. Frederick screamed. The creature's head snapped to the side, and it collapsed to the ground beside One.

A knife protruded from its left eye.

Frederick looked down at his hand that just a moment earlier had held the same knife.

"What the . . ." Seven trailed off.

"You gotta teach me that one, boss," Eight said in disbelief.

"Nice throw," One coughed and rubbed at his throat. He stood hurriedly and knelt beside Thirteen, who was slowly sitting up. "You okay?"

"Oh, just lovely," she mumbled, getting to her feet. "What's a little concussion amongst friends?"

"Maybe we should shut the door?" Nineteen said.

Several howls ripped through the main room of the library.

"Now?"

One began looking around the room frantically.

"Where's the keycard?"

"You lost it?" Seven almost shrieked.

"I was a bit busy fighting for my life!"

"There!" Nineteen pointed to a spot farther back in the room. The keycard lay halfway underneath one of the many cabinets spread throughout the room.

One lunged for it.

Frederick instinctively ran toward the door. As he neared it, he could hear the thundering of the Bristles.

There were more. A lot more. And they were nearly to the room.

"Twenty!"

Frederick turned toward One's shout just in time to see him throwing the keycard in his direction. He flicked his wrist like he was throwing a frisbee. The card flew across the room, spinning wildly. The throw started on target but quickly curved to Frederick's right as it neared him. He dove for it and was rewarded by the feeling of cool plastic between his fingers. He hit the ground hard and rolled. Fortunately, his maneuver had placed him on the ground directly beneath the scanner. Frederick slammed the card into it and looked up in time to see a dozen Bristles charging toward him just as the door slid shut.

Chapter 29

The six sat on the floor, trying to catch their collective breath.

"Is everyone okay?" Nineteen asked and made her way around to each of them, not waiting for a response. There were a few bumps and bruises but nothing serious. Even Thirteen seemed to be fully recovered from the knock she had taken to the head.

"Well, good news and bad news," One said as he paced around the room. "We don't have to worry about Bristles coming from anywhere else."

"And we have nowhere else to go but back to the Bristles we just locked out," Frederick finished.

"Correct." One swept his flashlight across the walls and ceiling. "Doesn't look like there are any vents we can use this time either."

"Lovely," Seven grumbled. "At least we get to die with some really lovely schematics."

"Let's just find the schematics first before we give up, eh? We'll deal with getting out when we need to," One said and turned to inspect the filing cabinets. "Hopefully this means everything inside is in good shape."

He walked to the nearest cabinet and pried it open using the tip of his knife. He nodded in satisfaction and gestured for them to spread out.

"Looks like the insides are in pretty good shape. Cover as much ground as you can. We are looking for something called 'Wharton Science Schematics.' Should be the blueprint as well as some additional general information on the building. If you find it, give a shout, and I'll come confirm it's the right thing."

"Sure thing, boss," Eight said enthusiastically, throwing himself at the nearest cabinet. The others nodded and moved throughout the room.

Frederick made his way to the back and began opening cabinets in the same fashion. It took a significant amount of effort to pry them open, and more than once, his knife slipped and almost took a finger with it. Inside, Frederick found various schematics of buildings located both in the city and in the surrounding area. Each cabinet had dozens of folders, but he was able to move through them quickly, spending less than a minute on each cabinet.

Several minutes passed with more than one false alarm. The room was filled with the sound of concentrated muttering along with the scraping sound of metal being pried open. At last, Nineteen's voice cut through the noise.

"One," she said simply, waving the blond boy over without looking up from a packet she held carefully, as if it might shatter.

One moved quickly to Nineteen, taking the collection of papers from her. He glanced at them and smiled as he flipped through the pages, giving her a good-natured wink.

"Shoulda known you'd be the one who found it."

"I just got lucky," Nineteen said, though Frederick could see she enjoyed the praise.

One put the packet into his backpack, then set it on the ground, lying down and placing the backpack under his head.

"Is now really the best time for a nap?" Thirteen asked. It seemed like she was trying to sound skeptical, but Frederick got a much more hopeful vibe from the question.

"I think so. Twenty, what do you think?"

Frederick answered without thinking. "Well, we aren't in a particular rush at the moment. We have the schematics, which is all we came for. We have plenty of supplies, so we don't need to worry about those running out. The longer we wait, the better rested we are for either fight or flight, whichever method we use to get out of here. Also, the longer we wait, the higher chance the Bristles get bored and leave." He shrugged. "If that's something they do."

"See?" One folded his hands on his chest and closed his eyes. "This gives us time to rest and to think. The two things we most need to do at the moment."

"Don't have to tell me twice." Seven flopped to the ground and was snoring almost immediately.

"We should still have someone on watch," Nineteen said. "Just in case."

"I agree," One said. "Let's do it in pairs. You and Twenty take the first watch, then wake me and Eight up in an hour, and we'll switch."

"Sounds good to me, boss," Eight said with a dramatic salute from atop a row of cabinets he had turned into a makeshift bed.

One by one, the flashlights in the room switched off until only two remained. Nineteen and Twenty moved as far from their slumbering companions as they could so they could talk without disturbing them.

The two began trying to formulate a strategy but quickly realized they simply didn't have enough information to make a plan of any real worth. After that realization, they shifted to idle chit-chat and from idle chit-chat to thoughtful silence. Frederick's eyes wandered absently over the room, looking for nothing in particular. They eventually landed on a stack of boxes in the corner, not far from where he and Nineteen sat.

"How did we miss those?" Frederick said softly, nodding toward the boxes.

"I'm not sure." Nineteen was already moving toward them. "I guess they are kind of in the shadows, and our focus was certainly elsewhere."

Frederick moved to join Nineteen, helping her unstack the three boxes. They were heavier than he had anticipated. "Wonder what's in these things," he grunted, wiping sweat from his brow. "Feels like bricks."

Nineteen pulled open one of the boxes and peered inside.

"Twenty! You aren't going to believe this!"

"What?" Frederick moved to see inside.

"Books," Nineteen said flatly, holding a leather-bound tome aloft. "The boxes in the library have books in them."

Frederick rolled his eyes, opening one of the other boxes, which was also filled to the brim with books.

"You've been hanging around Seven and Thirteen too much," Frederick said.

Nineteen snorted. "I could've told you that."

She sat down cross-legged on the floor and cracked open the book she had pulled from the box. "Kinth, a history," she read aloud.

"Could be interesting," Frederick said. "Do you think 'Knitting for Beginners' will be equally compelling?" He held up his own book for her to see.

"Only one way to find out," Nineteen said without looking up.

Frederick set the book on the floor and began sifting through his box in search of anything that appeared compelling or even slightly useful.

The pair sat quietly. The only thing disturbing the silence was the occasional rustle of a page being turned or Frederick selecting a new book to flip through. Nineteen remained engaged with her first one, while Frederick was having significantly less luck. He went from self-help books to romance novels to technical grammar books. Somehow, each book he selected was even less intriguing than the last. It took Frederick nearly half an hour to work his way through all three boxes, and still he had found nothing of note. He turned to talk to Nineteen, but when he saw how engrossed she was with her book, he thought better of it. Instead, he began to gather the books he had strewn about and return them to the boxes. He finished filling the first two boxes and moved to begin refilling the third when something at the bottom of the box caught his eye. There was a collection of papers stapled together. Frederick had somehow missed it when he had first emptied the box. Even looking at it now, the stack looked more like packaging than anything interesting.

The papers were slightly brittle to the touch as Frederick retrieved them. He handled them with great care until he was convinced they weren't going to crumble away in his hands. Then, still exercising extreme care, Frederick flipped open the first page.

What we Know: The Virus.

Dr. Jacob Parke

What follows will be my best attempt to document the frighteningly little we know about the Virus. The Virus has gone by many different names, none of which I care for. I trust that you know which virus I am referring to. The virus that I am certain will be our end.

First of all, there are the obvious effects of the virus on the human body. It works with astonishing speed and ferocity. Some patients lose their lives within three days of contracting the Virus. The physical symptoms are relatively few at first, which makes identifying the moment of contraction remarkably difficult. Headache, nausea, fever, etc. From that point, the symptoms grow dramatically worse. Profuse bleeding from the ears, eyes, nose, and mouth. Vomiting, hallucinations, loss of bodily functions, among other things. Each case seems to vary.

Frederick skimmed the next few pages, which relayed in agonizing detail several specific cases, which the author of the paper seemed to deem as "noteworthy." He felt his stomach turn.

This is what we are fighting against. You can't ignore it, a firm voice whispered inside him. He closed his eyes and took a deep breath. This information could be valuable, and he couldn't let a weak stomach keep him from that. Frederick steeled himself and returned to the paper, though he skipped ahead a bit, telling himself he would return to read that portion later.

Next, I will discuss the effects the virus has had on the flora of our world. The differences are few but fascinating. There is not much change in the plants except for the rate at which they grow. By my estimates, the virus is causing the plants to grow somewhere between 5-10x faster than their natural rate. There is a small amount of evidence that indicates the virus could eventually alter the genetic makeup of the flora, but I highly doubt we will be present to witness the changes.

The section continued, speculating on different possibilities, and by Frederick's standards, there were a significant number of rabbit trails that were nearly impossible to follow. He soon gave up and flipped to the next section.

Lastly, I will discuss the effects of the virus on the fauna of our world. At first, it seemed the Virus had left the animal kingdom alone for the most part, though I suppose we missed the initial changes due to our focus on surviving ourselves. As that has begun to look less and less likely, I have taken some time to look into how it has impacted our animal counterparts. From what I can tell, the effects are slowly increasing.

The first sign I observed was an elevated hostility in many species, something akin to rabies. This seemed to worsen over time, to the point that the most loyal animal would attack its owner over nothing at all. What most fascinates me about this is that the aggression apparently differs from species to species. Although, to be clear, most suffer from the increased aggression. However, there are some species that show no signs of elevated aggression and some that even show a decrease. This is truly fascinating, and I wish I had more time to fully understand why species react in the way they do. Another symptom I have observed in some species, though not all, is a heightened level of intelligence and problem solving as well as physical ability. I ran several tests to be sure, and there was overwhelming confirmation that some animals were simply smarter than they had been before. This, I have no reasonable explanation for. A virus that has done nothing but destroy has remarkably granted the precious gift of intelligence to a select few. I want to be clear on what I mean by intelligence. I am not suggesting that animals affected in this way have become on par with humans. They have simply risen above their previous capabilities. I cannot help but speculate as to how far this could progress after we are gone.

Finally, there are the physical changes in the animals. This, I have found to be the most disturbing to me, as there is simply no explanation, no rhyme, no reason, for any of the physical changes that occur. I have seen species turn translucent, harden, change shape, change color, and a multitude of other things. Some change to the point they are barely recognizable. I wonder what these creatures will look like after we have gone. Will they continue to change? Will they morph into something we could never have imagined? Only time will tell, and I mourn that I will not be here to learn the answer.

Frederick sat back and stared at the wall, processing all he had just read. He knew the Virus had done things to the Bristles, and he had even suspected it had done things to many of the animals of Kinth. He just hadn't anticipated it would be on this scale.

"You okay?" Nineteen's voice pulled him back to reality.

"Yeah," Frederick said simply. "It's just a lot."

"What did you learn?"

Frederick spent the next several minutes relaying all the information to Nineteen. She listened, nodding occasionally but never interrupting. Frederick finished, and she sat chewing her lip.

"I wondered if it had done anything beyond the Bristles," she said. "But I didn't expect this much.

"Neither did I," Frederick replied. "It makes you wonder . . ."

"If there's even more the Virus has changed since that was written."

Frederick simply nodded, not wanting to pursue that line of thinking for the time being. He took the papers and placed them carefully inside of a random book to keep them from being bent, then placed the book inside of his backpack.

"What about yours?" Frederick turned back to Nineteen. "Anything interesting?"

"Oh, plenty interesting," Nineteen said, flipping through the pages. "Not sure if any of it is overly helpful, but I've got a lot left to go through. I'll update you on anything I find."

She paused for several moments, looking thoughtful. "It's so strange," she whispered at last.

"What is?"

"Reading a history that is mine but also isn't. I mean, this is the history of my home, but at the same time it's not at all. I've barely spent any time here, and I'm not gonna spend much more time here before it's sealed away forever." She let out a heavy sigh. "I just feel like I'm in a bit of purgatory. I have two different worlds, and I don't belong in either one."

Frederick opened his mouth to speak but found no words ready to come out. He closed his mouth and simply nodded—he knew the feeling. They sat in silence for several minutes as Nineteen's words hung in the air.

"Actually"—Frederick jumped as Nineteen spoke again suddenly.—"I don't think that's quite right." She chewed her lip as she sought her next words. Frederick dared not speak lest he ruin her train of thought. "I guess. Well, I guess it's true I don't belong in either world. None of us do, really. But we belong somewhere."

"Together." Frederick smiled.

"Goodness, it sounds so cheesy when you say it that way." Nineteen blushed but smiled. "But I guess that's exactly it, isn't it?

"Just because it's the corniest thing anyone has ever said doesn't mean it isn't true." Frederick shrugged.

"You guys are lucky that Seven and Thirteen are passed out, or else you'd be cleaning up their puke."

Frederick and Nineteen both jumped to their feet, Frederick reaching for his knife.

"Woah, easy, boss." Eight smiled in an ornery fashion from his position next to Frederick. "Didn't mean to scare you. Just thought you could use a break is all."

"How did you do that?" Frederick's heart was still pounding in his chest.

"Not too hard when you two are blabbering each other's ears off." Eight shrugged. "You gonna get some sleep or what?"

Frederick opened his mouth to say he was fine to keep going but was interrupted by a massive yawn. The events of the day had exhausted him more than he had realized.

"You were saying?" Eight raised his eyebrows sarcastically.

Frederick rolled his eyes and gave a dismissive wave. He walked back toward where the rest of the group was sleeping.

"You going?" Eight asked Nineteen.

"No, I'm alright." She pulled out her book once more. "I've got some reading to do."

"I guess we can let the boss keep sleeping then. You got any comic books in here?"

Frederick pulled out his sleeping bag and made himself as comfortable as he could. He stared at the ceiling and let the exhaustion wash over him, surrendering the fight to stay awake that he had unconsciously been fighting. He let himself be lulled to sleep by the sound of Eight's hyper whispers and the snores of Seven and Thirteen. A smile made its way across his face that remained even after he was carried off to sleep.

Chapter 30

Frederick woke to the frustrated voices of his friends.

"Well then, what are we supposed to do? There's no way they just got bored and left—we aren't that lucky. If anything, there will be more of them now!"

It was Thirteen talking.

"We have to figure some other way out."

"Well, no duh, Jinx, but that's easier said than done. Unless you've learned to walk through walls in the last half hour."

Frederick sat up just in time to see Thirteen give Seven a solid punch in the arm.

"Now look what you've done! You've woken up the sweet resting Two-Oh. Lord knows he could use the rest. Look at the bags under those eyes."

Frederick walked over and was surprised to find all his friends awake. He sat next to them and rubbed the sleep out of his eyes.

"How long have I been out?"

"Only an hour or so," Nineteen answered.

"Why didn't you wake me up when everyone else woke up?"

"Because Seven is right about the bags under your eyes." One chuckled softly. "Don't worry, you haven't missed anything. We are pretty much stumped here. It's looking like we will just have to fight our way out."

Nineteen shook her head but didn't speak, and Frederick could see the rest of the group didn't much like the idea either.

"We're sure there are no other options?" he asked. "We've exhausted every possibility?"

"There are no other possibilities," One said, a tinge of annoyance in his voice. "We've searched the room, and there are no other exits. Not even anything small enough for Eight to squeeze out, let alone Seven or me." He sighed heavily. "I know you all don't like it, and believe it or not, I don't much like it either. But I just don't see any other options."

No one offered a reply.

Frederick leaned forward and placed both hands on his forehead, screwing his eyes shut in concentration.

There had to be another way out, and he would find it.

He chewed anxiously on his lip, his frustration growing until he tasted blood. He exhaled slowly to calm himself down and opened his eyes.

He caught a bit of movement on his leg.

A small, blueish spider was making its way over his left knee. It made the journey quickly, scuttling for all it was worth. When it reached the ground, it repeated the journey over Frederick's right leg before marching off toward the cabinets to his right.

"It's the spider from the vents," Frederick said softly.

"What?" Thirteen asked.

Frederick pointed at the small creature. "Spiders like the ones from the vent."

"Oh great." Seven grimaced. "I was so hoping we'd see more of them."

"Maybe we should try to stay on topic," One said. "We need to formulate a plan of attack.

Frederick's eyes remained glued to the spider. He watched it as it neared the cabinets.

Without thinking or really knowing why, Frederick jumped to his feet and followed it.

"Not the time for collecting pets, Twenty," Thirteen called.

Frederick barely heard her. He reached the cabinet at the same time the spider did. It crawled into the small gap between the back of the cabinet and the wall. Frederick climbed on top of the cabinet, trying to catch a glimpse of where the spider had gone.

"Turn out the lights!" Frederick called urgently, an idea sprouting in his head.

"What?" Thirteen asked, as if she feared for his sanity.

"Do it!" Frederick shouted, causing his friends to jump.

One's eyes widened in understanding. He flicked off his flashlight and lunged to the light switch by the door. It clicked off, and the room was plunged into an almost perfect darkness.

Almost.

From Frederick's position on top of the cabinet, he could just make out a faint blue light moving steadily down the wall behind the cabinets. He wasn't able to see the spider itself, but the glow it emitted was just enough for him to track with the lights turned off. He followed it, awkwardly scooting down the row of cabinets, until suddenly the light disappeared. Frederick waited for a full three count, making sure the light was well and truly gone.

"All right, turn them back on."

One flipped the lights back on and made his way over to Frederick.

"Here?"

Frederick nodded, and both boys grabbed the cabinet, pulling with all their strength.

"Oh, okay, cool, so you guys have fully and totally lost your minds?" Thirteen said in a matter-of-fact voice.

"You really hate to see it," Eight said, shaking his head sadly.

"Shut up," Frederick grunted.

The cabinet groaned in protest. It was bolted to the ground, and for several seconds, it stubbornly refused to move. After a few more pulls, however, it finally gave way to the efforts of its assailants. With a loud ringing noise, the cabinet came free of the wall and tumbled to the floor. One and Frederick knelt and examined the now-revealed portion of the wall. One pointed triumphantly to a small hole where the wall met the floor. Frederick held his hand close to it and was rewarded by a cooling touch of air flow.

Frederick forced his knife into the hole and wiggled it back and forth until the hole was big enough for him to fit a couple fingers in. He worked quickly, chipping away at the wall until he could fit his whole hand into the gap. Gripping the wall tightly, he yanked hard.

Nothing happened.

Frederick gritted his teeth and placed both feet against the wall for a bit of added leverage. He took a breath to steel himself, then pulled for all he was worth.

There was a loud ripping sound, and Frederick tumbled backward to the floor.

A two-foot portion of the wall tore away, revealing an old air vent.

"What the . . ." Seven said in an awed voice.

"So much for there being no air vents for us to go through." One smiled. "They must've covered it up for some reason."

Nineteen stared in awe at the newly revealed tunnel. "You used a spider to find an escape tunnel." She turned to Frederick. "Are you a genius or just stupidly lucky?"

"A bit of both, I hope." Frederick scratched the back of his head. "I just figured he had to be going somewhere."

"And you were right." One clapped Frederick on the shoulder. "Everyone, get your stuff. Let's get the hell out of here."

There was a feeling of relief in the air as the applicants scurried to gather their belongings. None of them, sans One, had been anticipating another tangle with the Bristles. Frederick found himself relieved but not in the way he'd expected. His relief wasn't that he wouldn't have to fight the Bristles—it came from the fact that his friends would be safer this way. And while relief was the main thing he felt, he would have been lying if he didn't admit to himself that there was a small corner of him that was disappointed. He did his best to silence that part of himself and turned his attention back to prepping for their departure.

It didn't take long for the group to gather their meager belongings. Frederick slung his backpack across his shoulders and watched as Nineteen stuffed several of the books he had browsed earlier into her backpack.

"Stocking up on some light reading?" Frederick asked, walking over to her.

"I just figure there's always a chance that something in one of these books helps us," she said without meeting his eyes. "Even if they seem to be no help at all."

"Fair enough," Frederick said, grabbing an armful and placing them in his own backpack. "I guess there's no harm in taking them."

"I doubt anyone will miss them," One chimed in, though he didn't move to take any himself. "You all ready or what?

One led the way through the vent, with Frederick bringing up the rear. This vent was slightly more spacious than the last they had occupied. It slanted gently upward, and after a dozen feet or so, it turned sharply to the right. Several of the blue spiders were traversing the vent as well, and Frederick thought he could just make out a whimper from Seven every time they encountered another one.

"You doi—"

"Shuddup," Seven said, cutting off Frederick in a choked, annoyed voice. Frederick smiled to himself and carried on crawling.

The vent leveled out and began to move relatively straight.

"This should head back toward the entrance," Nineteen said hopefully. "At least, if I'm still oriented."

"I think you're right," Thirteen said. "I was getting the same impression."

"Have we always been this lucky?" Eight said. "I'm trying to remember if this is normal or not."

"Oh, just give it time," Seven huffed. "The other shoe always drops."

His statement was punctuated by a loud groaning of metal. The vent swayed slightly beneath them, then collapsed.

They tumbled sideways out from the wall and into the main room of the library. There was a thunderous crash as metal and debris fell to the ground along with the applicants. It wasn't a long fall, but it was awkward, and Frederick's breath was nearly knocked from him entirely. He turned to look back at the wall and was shocked to find that the section they had been in had essentially collapsed.

"You just had to open your stupid mouth!" Thirteen hissed and leaped to her feet.

Seven's retort was cut off by the howls of the Bristles that had been waiting outside the door to the schematics room.

Frederick didn't hesitate. He leapt up and dragged Eight and Nineteen to their feet as One did the same with Seven. They ran without another word, not daring to look back at their pursuers. Blood pounded in Frederick's veins as he sprinted, jumping over fallen bookshelves and other debris. He devoted half of his attention to watching to make sure his friends didn't stumble or fall behind and the other half to moving his legs as fast as they could possibly go.

"Just get to the exit, and we can try to barricade the door!" One shouted from beside Frederick.

The group nodded in agreement, not daring to waste breath on anything but running.

They were nearly halfway to the door when a pair of Bristles jumped out from the murk in front of them, cutting off their path to the door.

Frederick shouted in surprise and bolted to his left without slowing down. He grabbed the arm of whoever was closest to him—he thought it was Eight—and dragged them with him farther into the rows of shelves. He weaved in and out of the mazelike collection of bookshelves, aware that both his friends and the additional Bristles had followed him. Frederick slowed ever so slightly, allowing his friends to catch up with him.

"Split up?" he managed to say to One as he fell in line with him.

One shook his head coolly. "There are too many. Enough to follow all of us. Just gotta get out." His words were even, unbothered.

Frederick nodded and allowed himself to run fully. If there was nothing to do but run for it, he was going to give his friends something to chase after.

He had danced far enough into the room amongst the books that he had to think for the briefest of seconds before remembering where exactly the exit would be. As soon as he was certain of the direction he needed to go, he ran toward it. Straight toward it.

He barreled through a shelf to his right. The rotting wood exploded in a shower of splinters and paper. Nearly immediately, Frederick was bursting through another. He moved with such incredible power that he ran almost as if uninhibited. He heard cursing from his friends behind him as he cleared their path. Over and over again, he burst through whatever was unfortunate enough to stand in his way. In a matter of seconds, he burst free from the shelves directly in front of the massive double doors that led back to the receptionist's desk.

Frederick pushed through them, only now turning to check his friends. They weren't far behind; one by one, they sprinted through the door, and Frederick slammed it shut as the last of them made it through, barring it shut with a tall lamp that had been standing nearby.

"Let's go, Twenty!" One shouted from beside the door. The rest of the applicants had already made their way outside. Bristles pounded on the door as

Frederick sprinted away. The last thing he heard as he burst outside was the splintering of wood.

Frederick blinked in confusion as he stood outside. He had been expecting to see the sun blazing above him, but instead, only the moon and stars shone down at him. He had been so disoriented by the time he had spent inside that he hadn't realized it was already dark.

"No time for stargazing, bud," One said, grabbing Frederick by his upper arm.

The confusion cleared, and Frederick followed. He could see the backs of the rest of his friends sprinting through the stalled cars that choked the long-abandoned streets.

Howls tore through the night. First from behind them, then gradually from all directions. "They are everywhere!" Seven shouted in a panic.

Frederick caught a glimpse of Eight and Nineteen's faces in the moonlight and saw terror etched into them.

"What do we do?" Thirteen gasped.

"We can't run like this!" Frederick heard himself saying. "Not all the way to the Door. We have to lose them!"

"How are we gonna do that? They're right on our asses! Not to mention they're ahead of us too!" Seven said.

Thirteen shook her head. "It's only a matter of time before one cuts us off, and then we're screwed!"

"We have to hide again. Barricade a building and find a way to lose them!" Even as he said it, Frederick began looking for potential candidates.

"Screw that!" One shouted. "I'm not hiding again!" There was anger in his voice—true, deep anger that made Frederick's stomach churn.

"One, please!" Nineteen plead. "It's our only chance!"

"No!" One shouted, his eyes ablaze.

"Yes!" Frederick put all he had into the shout. Every ounce of strength, every drop of emotion, everything. "That's the plan!"

One's eyes shot to him, eyebrows raised in surprise. He set his jaw and gave a resigned nod.

Frederick ran to a convenience store he spotted not far away. There were bars on all the windows, and it was relatively spacious while still appearing to have only one entrance. He reached the front door and yanked it open, saying a silent thank you to whatever higher power allowed the door to be unlocked. His friends piled in, and he threw the door shut and locked it. The Bristles arrived a few long heartbeats later. They threw themselves at the door and the windows; glass shattered and rained down on Frederick and his friends. For one horrible moment, he thought they were going to get in. But the bars held.

"Is everyone okay?" Frederick asked shakily.

"Never been better, boss." Eight smiled, though he was trembling visibly.

"You know, I'm starting to get pretty sick of this place," Seven said. The stocky boy was lying flat on his back, his chest rising and falling rapidly.

The rest of the group remained silent, either nodding or ignoring Frederick's question entirely.

Frederick studied One. The blond boy stood with his eyes fixed on the Bristles outside. The monsters screeched and threw themselves repeatedly at the bars, trying to get at their elusive prey. A hatred boiled from One's eyes as he watched. Frederick could almost see it running down the boy's face, pooling on the ground and eating away at the floor until all that was left was a gaping hole.

Then, suddenly, One turned back and surveyed his companions. He looked at the trembling Eight, the prone Seven, the embracing Thirteen and Nineteen, and finally at Frederick. Ever so slowly, Frederick saw the hatred disintegrate from One. His eyes filled with something else entirely, a protectiveness that burned every bit as intensely as the hatred. Frederick's own fear and doubt faded at the sight.

The Bristles continued to throw themselves at the bars covering the windows. The metal groaned in protest at the onslaught. With each impact, Frederick was less and less certain that they were not in immediate danger. He glanced over at One, who was eyeing the potential intruders as well.

"Come on, back here," Nineteen said in a shaky voice. She stood with Thirteen by a door in the back of the store that Frederick had assumed was a closet but now saw was a set of stairs leading to a basement. "I want to get as far away from those things as I can."

"You all go down and look for anything that could help us," One said. "Twenty and I will stay up here and keep watch."

Seven, Eight, Thirteen, and Nineteen did so without any hesitation, clearly eager to put even a fraction more distance between them and the dozens of Bristles. As the door closed behind them, One turned to Frederick and gave him a wry smile. "How much time, you think?"

"I'd give it five minutes before they break through," Frederick answered.

"Always the optimist, Twenty. I'd say we have two minutes tops."

Even now, as he looked, Frederick could see that the bars over the windows were beginning to bend. It was only a matter of time before there would be a gap large enough for the Bristles to fit through or before the bars snapped altogether.

"So what do we do?" Frederick asked, waiting for anxiety to flood his veins. Surprisingly, he found none—only a grim determination.

"We buy as much time as we can." One shrugged. "Hope it's enough for the others to find something that will somehow save us."

"And if they don't find anything?"

One's face split into the borderline maniacal smile Frederick had come to know so well.

"We take as many of them with us as we can." He turned and surveyed the rabid beasts. "Maybe it won't make a difference in the end, but I can't help but like the idea of going down fighting."

Frederick grimaced and set his shoulders.

"Let's hope it doesn't come to that."

The first Bristle to break through almost seemed surprised to find itself on the other side of the bars it had so viciously attacked. It crashed between a gap just to the left of the door. One was on it before it could regain its composure, dispatching it with a well-placed knife thrust.

"Told you five minutes was optimistic," One called as he positioned himself where the Bristle had just broken through to deal with any others who tried to take the same route. "Wanna give our basement dwellers an update?"

Frederick ran to the door to the basement and threw it open. "We got company!" he shouted down into the murk. "You all have anything yet?"

"No!" Thirteen shouted up. "It would be awfully helpful if we had any idea of what we were looking for!"

"Besides a miracle!" Seven shouted.

"A miracle would be perfect," Frederick answered and rushed back to help One.

Another Bristle had forced its way in, and One had dealt with it in the same manner as he had the first. The two Bristles lay next to one another on the ground, their blood pooling together.

"They are gonna start coming in thick. I hope you're ready for a fight," One called without looking at Frederick.

Frederick's reply was cut off as two more Bristles burst through the bars simultaneously.

They landed on their feet with vicious teeth bared. Drool dripped from their gaping maws and gathered in small pools on the floor. Frederick crouched in a defensive stance, his knife held out in front of him.

"No time for that, Twenty!" One shouted, and threw himself at the nearer of the two Bristles. It snarled and snapped at the boy, its teeth grazing his shirt and tearing at the fabric. One danced back nimbly and threw himself forward once again. "If we play defense, we're gonna get overrun in no time!" he added as he continued to try to breach the Bristle's defenses.

Frederick cursed and charged the second Bristle without another thought. His opponent was ready for him: it reared up on its hind legs and brought both paws crashing down at Frederick's skull. He ducked into a roll at the last minute, swiping at the Bristle's leg. The thing stumbled as the blow struck true. The cut Frederick had inflicted wasn't enough to incapacitate the leg, but it was enough to make the Bristle move more gingerly.

"Don't get too distracted by the teeth!" Frederick yelled to One. "The paws are like bricks, and those claws are no joke either!" Frederick eyed the talon-like claws carefully.

One simply grunted in reply as he battered his foe relentlessly.

Frederick turned his attention back fully to his own opponent. The Bristle circled him, snapping at Frederick whenever he ventured too close. The wound on its leg was clearly bothering it because it limped visibly as it moved. Frederick began to dart back and forth as quickly as he could, trying to use his now vastly superior mobility to his advantage. He felt himself move faster and faster as he let his mind focus on one singular thing: killing the Bristle.

He became a blur of motion, testing the Bristle's defenses and pushing it to its limits. He managed to score several nonlethal hits, battering it further. The blows began to accumulate, and the Bristle stood panting heavily, blood dripping from the multiple wounds that now covered its body. Frederick saw his opening and went for it. He feinted left and lunged to the right, aiming his knife for the Bristle's left eye. His maneuver worked perfectly. The Bristle tried to dodge the feint, which opened him up perfectly for Frederick's killing blow. Frederick reared back, knife poised, all his weight behind the thrust that would end the fight. His foot hit the ground, and he pushed hard off it to generate as much power as he could.

Suddenly, he was weightless.

His foot had landed on a large shard of glass from the broken windows, and when he tried to push off, it skittered across the room, throwing Frederick completely off balance. He had put so much force into the step that he was now completely airborne. He floated, parallel to the ground for a full breath before crashing down on his side. Another shard of glass pierced his side, and he gasped in pain. The Bristle didn't waste the opening—it was on him in a heartbeat. Frederick tried to roll out of the way, but the glass in his side slowed him just enough for the Bristle to pin him.

Frederick winced as the full weight of the beast bore down on his shoulders. He tried desperately to wiggle free but was unable to move more than a couple inches. He stared helplessly upward directly into the open mouth of the Bristle. He could just make out the glowing red eyes staring down at him in triumph. It almost looked like the creature was smiling at him. He struggled wildly to get free to no avail.

"One, help!"

"Twenty!"

The Bristle's jaw snapped downward.

Frederick put all his strength into one last attempt to wriggle free. He managed to move fractionally before the Bristle's teeth hit. The movement kept the bite from Frederick's throat; instead, it sank in his shoulder. He screamed at the white-hot pain spreading across his chest as the Bristle clamped down and shook its head wildly from side to side. Frederick felt like a chew toy as the beast tore at him. He slapped at the Bristle helplessly, growing lightheaded as blood poured from the bite in his shoulder. It reared back to deliver the final blow. Frederick could barely make it out as his vision swam.

There was a guttural screech, and Frederick closed his eyes. His life didn't flash before his eyes, and he was thankful for that. There was enough pain in this moment without having to relive the years and years of fighting for breath. Instead, all he saw was a picture of his parents. They were both smiling widely, and even though they weren't looking at him directly, he knew they were smiling at him. Frederick felt a small smile of his own spread across his face.

"Sorry I didn't make it back. I love you both," he whispered, hoping the words would find their way to them somehow.

There was a bone-rattling impact above Frederick. At first, he thought it was the Bristle finishing him off, but there was no additional pain, and as far as he could tell, he was still very much alive. He forced his eyes open and found that the Bristle was no longer on top of him. It lay on the ground just a few feet away, struggling with a new foe.

"Wake up, Two-Oh!" Seven shouted from his place atop the Bristle. "I could really use some help!"

Frederick dragged himself from his stupor and groggily looked for his knife. He had lost it somewhere in the fight with the Bristle, and there was no sign of it now.

"Now, Two-Oh!" Seven's shouts grew even more panicked.

Frederick's eyes settled on a long, jagged shard of glass on the ground between his feet. He grabbed it and stumbled over to Seven and the Bristle. His shoulder and his side screamed with pain as he dragged himself to help his friend. With one last burst of effort, he plunged the glass into the roof of the Bristle's open mouth. The glass cut into Frederick's own hand as he plunged it into the Bristle. The beast shuddered horribly, and Frederick barely managed to extract his arm from its mouth before it snapped shut. The Bristle spasmed twice more, and Frederick braced himself for a continued fight, but then mercifully, the Bristle took one last ragged breath and stopped moving.

"Thanks," Frederick gasped at Seven, who was already moving to help him.

"Back atcha," Seven said, slipping under Frederick's arm to support him. "Let's get you outta here, eh?" Frederick's vision blurred, and he had to focus all his energy into surveying the room. The store was in wreckage. Shelves were thrown everywhere; glass was strewn wildly throughout the room, and the corpses of Bristles littered the ground. One stood among them, teeth and knife bared. He had to have killed five of the monsters himself, which explained why he hadn't been able to aid Frederick in his own battle. The Bristles were pouring through the windows at an increasing rate. One would clearly soon be overrun.

"One, we gotta go!" Seven shouted. "We found a way out!"

One fought on, oblivious to the calls.

"One, *now*!" Seven had dragged Frederick all the way to the stairs, and still, One had not acknowledged his pleas.

"Take Two-Oh. I'll get him," Seven said to someone. The stocky boy handed Frederick off to the person he had been talking to. It took multiple seconds for Frederick to realize it was Thirteen.

"Hi," he managed to mumble.

"You look like crap, my dude." Thirteen grimaced.

"Hi," Frederick repeated.

Frederick did his best to blink away the blurriness of his vision, with a moderate level of success. Thirteen began to lead him back down the stairs, but he shook his head and pulled against her. She looked down the stairs and out into the room in a moment of indecision before sucking on her teeth and giving in.

Seven was fighting alongside One, shouting the whole time. One ignored him, screaming at the Bristles, taunting them. He fought like a demon. He had managed to pick up the knife Frederick had dropped and now fought with two blades. He spun between Bristles, slicing at them without ever getting hit himself. Frederick was amazed at how perfect and calculated One's movements were. It was a dazzling display.

And it wouldn't be enough.

Everyone in the room knew it except One. No matter how hard he fought, no matter how perfect his movements were, eventually he would be overrun.

There was a brief lull in the fight as One dispatched of the final Bristles in the room and the ones outside struggled to get in.

"We have to go now! We have a way out" Seven screamed in One's face. One brushed the stocky boy away and prepared to fight the next wave of Bristles.

Seven's face grew bright red with rage. He grabbed at One's arm, but the blond boy shook him off. Seven stumbled back and glanced over at Thirteen and Frederick.

He shrugged at them, walked over to One, and cracked the hilt of his knife hard against the boy's skull.

One dropped like a sack of bricks, and Seven scooped him up quickly, carrying him effortlessly to the stairs.

"Time to go," he said simply as he reached Frederick and Thirteen.

The basement was filled with cleaning supplies and boxes of food long ago decayed. It was pitch-black, so they had been forced to retrieve the flashlights from their backpacks once again. With Thirteen's help, Frederick managed to stumble to the middle of the room.

"Where are the others?" he gasped, scanning the darkness for Nineteen and Eight.

"Down here, boss!" Eight's voice floated up from the floor. Frederick looked down and blinked several times before he could make out a large hole in the floor.

"Thank God for sewers," Thirteen mumbled before shouting down into the hole. "Incoming!"

The next thing Frederick knew, he was shoved into the darkness.

Frederick splashed into the water and collapsed beneath the surface. There was a gentle current that tugged him away. His feet brushed something solid, and he pushed against it in a panic. His head broke above the water, and he gasped greedily at the air.

"Twenty! Are you okay?" Nineteen's voice was nearby.

"I've been better," he groaned. The water wasn't as deep as he had first thought, though it rose nearly to his chest. As his eyes adjusted to the dark, he saw that Eight and Nineteen were just a few feet from him, struggling to keep their heads above water. They made their way to either side of him and offered what little help they could.

Three more splashes sounded in quick succession. Soon Seven popped out of the water, with One slung across his shoulders. Thirteen followed close behind and took Nineteen's place supporting Frederick.

"Let's get moving. There's no way they can fit down that hole, but we need to get Twenty somewhere we can get a good look at those wounds," Thirteen said and began trudging onward through the water.

The water was significantly cleaner than Frederick had any right to hope it would be. It was so clear that their flashlights almost allowed them to see the bottom. The gentle current also made their walk a bit easier. Frederick would take every aid he could get. They walked in silence, everyone focusing on either keeping their own head above water or someone else's. It took all of an hour before Seven halted and looked up.

"There's a manhole above us," he said. "We gotta be close to the edge of town now. I think we should at least check this one out. There's a chance we don't find a good exit for a while after this one."

The stocky boy began splashing water into One's face. "Time to wake up, Uno. I don't want to lug your ugly butt up this stupid ladder."

It took just a few short minutes to rouse the unconscious boy. A groan escaped his lips as his eyes fluttered open.

"Am I dead?"

"You are not. In spite of your best efforts, I might add," Seven said.

One stood unsteadily for a moment, leaning heavily on Seven as he tested his footing. "I guess you all found that miracle you were looking for."

"That we did," Seven said. "Now if you're all quite ready, I'd like to get somewhere where I don't have to constantly fight off getting sewage in my mouth."

"Oh, stop being so dramatic. This is just rainwater," Nineteen said. "And if you think it's hard for you—" Her words stopped abruptly as she lost her footing and slipped briefly below the water.

Seven rolled his eyes and began to climb the ladder. It took a few solid tries before he managed to dislodge the manhole cover and shove it to the side. He pulled himself out, and the rest of the group waited anxiously for his signal. Frederick could make out the stars burning in the night sky through the gap Seven had just disappeared through. A few more tense moments passed before the boy whispered down to them.

"All clear."

They hurried up the ladder, one by one. Frederick gritted his teeth against the pain in his shoulder and his side as he climbed. The water had been cool enough that it had slightly numbed the injuries, which aided in his ascent, but both still ached terribly. He emerged from the manhole to find himself near the edge of the city.

"There was a barn not far from here in the woods—we passed it on the way in. We should get to that and regroup and tend to our wounds," Nineteen said, then gave Frederick a worried look.

"I know the place." One nodded. "It should be perfect."

"You got it, Prime!" Seven said, nodding at Nineteen.

The small girl raised an eyebrow at him.

"Prime?"

"Oh, you know," Seven said. "Because nineteen is a prime number."

"So is thirteen," Thirteen said.

"And Seven," Nineteen said slowly. "Didn't we already do this?"

"Look, there are literally no other possible nicknames!" Seven hissed in frustration, throwing his hands in the air. "I've spent literal weeks trying to think of something! Anything. But there just isn't a possible nickname for nineteen! So prime is what you get!"

"You could just call me Nineteen." She shrugged.

"Absolutely not," Seven said simply, and began walking. "No matter how dire things get, I will never stoop to that."

"Hey guys," Frederick said through clenched teeth. "Maybe we can discuss this later?"

They sprinted through the abandoned city at a speed bordering on reckless. There was a fine line between moving quickly and causing enough noise to draw attention, and by Frederick's estimations, they were toeing that line. But the moon and stars were bright, and One led them well. He somehow managed to find the path with the fewest obstacles every time. The few times they did encounter potential noise-causing obstacles, he was sure to point them out so that the rest of the group could easily avoid them.

It took just a few short minutes for them to make their way out of the city and into the cover of the trees. Frederick knew he was pushing his body past even its Kinthian limits. He was running on pure adrenaline now.

Upon entering the forest, One slowed his pace, though only just. He veered off slightly to their left, away from the path they had originally followed into the city. The barn soon loomed in the night in the middle of a small clearing. One slowed gradually until he came to a stop at the edge of the trees, crouching close to the trunk of a large tree as he inspected the structure.

"How the hell did you see this thing?" Seven whispered.

"We have to be at least a quarter of a mile from the path. Even in daytime, it should've been almost impossible." Frederick shook his head in wonder.

"It's a wonder what you can see when you use your eyes." One smiled playfully but didn't look away from the barn. "Seven, you're with me," he continued. "We'll clear the building. Once we know it's safe, I'll whistle the all-clear, then you all follow. Got it?"

Seven looked reluctant to go, and Frederick could have sworn he saw the boy glance worriedly at Thirteen. However, he followed One as he took off into the barn.

Two minutes later, Frederick heard a whistle from inside the structure. He and the others hurried inside, where they found One and Seven waiting for them. They rushed to put together a makeshift camp, clearing things from one corner of the barn and sitting in a circle. Frederick leaned heavily against the wall and groaned.

"Oh, stop whining," Seven said as he approached with a first aid kit and began assessing the damage. He worked quickly and carefully, beginning with Frederick's injured shoulder. He cleaned and dressed the wound as best he could, then moved on to the wound in Frederick's side.

"Oh, hey, look at that. There's still a chunk of glass in you," Seven said in a cheery tone. Frederick wasn't sure if he wanted to laugh or punch his friend in the throat. "Honestly, it might be a good thing it stayed in there. Probably helped keep you from bleeding out." His tone grew more serious. "I have to pull it out now. It's gonna hurt like hell. You ready?"

Frederick nodded his head tightly, and Seven didn't hesitate. He yanked the glass free from Frederick's side. As Frederick gasped in pain, it took everything in him to not cry out. His vision began to go dark, and he feared he would pass out.

"Hold on, buddy," Seven said as he grabbed Frederick's shoulders to keep him from toppling over. The pain faded second by second, and Frederick's vision cleared. He looked down and found that Seven had cleaned and bandaged his second wound.

"Take a nap or something, my man," Seven said. "You look like crap."

Frederick happily obliged, leaning back and closing his eyes.

"So what next?" Thirteen asked. "How do we get back to the Door? I feel like crap right now, and Twenty's obviously in a bad way."

"I think we stay here for the night," One said. "Give you a chance to rest up completely, and it gives me time to plan a route."

"What do you mean?" Frederick asked, opening his eyes but not sitting up. "Can't we just go back the way we came?"

One pulled the map from his backpack and began studying it, ignoring Frederick's question.

"You want to keep going, don't you?" Nineteen said in a surprisingly harsh voice. One continued to study the map. "I knew this would happen! I knew you'd try to convince us to stay!" Nineteen stood abruptly and stalked over to him.

"Nineteen, calm down," One said steadily. "Let's just think about this."

"How can you even consider this?" The small girl was almost shouting. "Twenty just almost died! You almost died! We all almost died. It's too dangerous to go on."

"It's too dangerous to go back!" One snapped. "Every second we spend putting off closing the Door is another second our families are closer to a painful death. We have to keep going! We gain nothing from going back."

"Dr. Gray wants us to go back," Nineteen said through gritted teeth.

"No he doesn't."

"Of course he—"

"Nineteen, you are supposed to be the smart one. Use your brain for one second," One said in an exasperated voice. "They gave us more supplies than we ever would've needed for this mission. They gave us a damn map to where we close the Door! Now that we have the blueprint, we don't need anything else. We certainly don't need to go back so Dr. Gray can stroke his beard and tell us how fascinating we are."

One let out a heavy sigh and ran his hand through his hair.

"I'm not making any of you come with me. But we've finally got the chance to make a decision for ourselves. We don't have Arthur, or Dr. Gray, or our parents, or even our anxiety telling us what to do. For the first time in our lives, we get the final say. The only say."

"Why wouldn't they tell us this before?" Nineteen shook her head. "Why wouldn't they give us the choice?"

"Maybe it's another one of their tests," One said. "I have no idea, and I don't care. This is our choice—each of us needs to decide." He looked at them one by one, holding his gaze for several seconds before moving on. "I'm not going back, and I'm taking the blueprint with me. You can do whatever you want."

"I'm with you." The words were out of Frederick's mouth before he had even registered the thought. He realized he had been hoping for this since they had crossed through the Door. It didn't make sense for them to go back. And even more than that, he wouldn't want to even if it did make sense. It felt so right to be here. He wanted to enjoy it as much as possible before they destroyed it forever. One nodded to him, looking thankful.

"Oh, fine," Thirteen said. "I'm not sure how helpful I'll be with this concussion, but I'm in."

"Sounds like fun." Eight smiled broadly.

"Whatever," Seven mumbled. "Just don't get us killed, eh? Getting eaten by massive demon dogs ranks pretty low on ways I want to go."

"I'd like to see what tops that list," Thirteen said.

"Death by pudding."

"What?"

"Death by pudding," Seven repeated.

Nineteen clenched her hands and ground her teeth together before suddenly relaxing.

"Fine," she said meekly. "I won't fight you on this, and I'm certainly not leaving any of you. I just really don't like the idea. But if you think it's what's best, then I'm in."

One nodded. "Good, then it's settled. We aren't going back."

THE END

Acknowledgments

Thank you first and foremost to my parents and my siblings. This book would not have been possible without their relentless support, encouragement, and answering of the question, "Does Timothy have a real job yet?"

Thank you specifically to Olivia for sifting through the unedited version of this book. Your bravery knows no bounds.

Thank you to my "Beta readers," Taylor Brantley, Trinity Griffin, and of course Mom. Your belief in me and this book is perhaps the greatest gift I have ever been given.

Thank you to Abby Friesen, whose love for Kinth (and more specifically Henry) helped me finish that first draft when it felt impossible.

Thank you to Taylor Smith and Laurel Becker for telling me what I needed to hear so this book could become what it was supposed to be.

Thank you to everyone at the Fedd agency, specifically Tyler Bertola and Mariah Swift, for their endless help and willingness to answer my equally endless questions.

Thank you to my editors, Kendall Davis and Dylan Garity for their help in making my book into what I dreamed it would be.

Thank you to Callie Feyen, whose feedback made me believe this book could really be important.

Thank you to Gregory Kolsto for his work as a creative coach and for his impossible achievement of actually getting me to start this book.

Thank you to the Steering with Ursula crew. Jenna Brack, Kelly Key, and Mom again. Our little book club was every bit as nurturing as it was fun.

Thank you to everyone at Oddly Correct Coffee Bar for creating a safe environment and many lovely drinks.

And lastly, thank you to all my friends who loved and supported me along the way.